Copyright © 2025 by Aneka "Ani" Bailey

All rights reserved.

No part of this publication may be reproduced, distributed, or transmitted in any form or by any means, including photocopying, recording, or other electronic or mechanical methods, without the prior written permission of the publisher, except as permitted by U.S. copyright law. For permission requests, contact Aneka Bailey at aneka.bailey91@gmail.com.

The story, all names, characters, and incidents portrayed in this production are fictitious. No identification with actual persons (living or deceased), places, buildings, and products is intended or should be inferred.

Character Art Book Cover by Reyna Rochin

Discrete cover by Aneka Bailey

First edition 2025

Pretty Something Book Two

Pretty Petty

Aneka Bailey

Mental Health Boundaries

This book contains themes and elements that can be triggering such as: *Drug abuse and use, mention of overdose, physical assault and abuse, harassment, brief mention of sexual assault/abuse, alcohol use, anxiety, attempted murder, road rage, emotional abuse, profanity, PTSD, sexually explicit scenes, dubious consent, physical injuries, and abandonment.*

Kinks: *Breath play, choking, rough sex, spanking, cum play, water sex, barebacking (unprotected sex), begging, clothed sex, oral sex, dirty talking, slight edge play, voyeurism, public play, exhibition, wax play, praise and degradation, dubious consent, threesome (MFNB), and light bondage*

If you find any of these themes triggering, please do not force yourself to read further.
Your mental health matters.

The Mental Health Hotline at 866-903-3787

Playlist

Ebony's Playlist
Han (Stray Kids) - Volcano
RM - forever rain
JoJo - Feel Alright
Taeyeon - INVU
Sabrina Carpenter - Skin
Jordy - Close To You
SZA - Nobody Gets Me
Dayseeker - Without Me
Band's Playlist
Get Scared - Time Keeps Running
nightlife - All I Know
nightlife - No Pleasure
coldrain - Stay
All Time Low - Dirty Laundry
Karaoke Playlist
Shayne Orok - As it Was (Cover)
Shayne Orok - Middle of the Night
Ebony and Kane's Playlist
Pink Sweats - 17
Stray Kids - The View

PRETTY PETTY

Dove Cameron and Khalid – We Go Down Together
Kehlani – everything
Justine Skye – I'm Yours
BTS – Euphoria
6lack ft. J Cole – Pretty Little Fears
Snow Aelegra – I Want You Around

1

Ebony

After the chill settles over my body, rage takes over, grabbing hold of each of my limbs. It propels me forward in its hot, hate fueled fury. Red and black are intermingling in my vision as my sights lock on a laughing Ren, or should I say Eva.

I never thought I'd see them again, not so soon. But here they are, staring at me like I'm the most comical thing they have ever seen. Like a cockroach at the bottom of their shoe. My body moves in autopilot as my legs carry me quickly to my target.

So fucking sick of running, hiding.

My fist collides with their face with such force, tingles skitter up my arm. Shouts ring out as I rear back and hit them again.

Their head flings to the side viciously when I make contact. Hitting them so hard, we tumble as a mass of limbs. They swat at me, pushing at my body to retreat. Their nails dig into my arms as I pin them down and punch them again. They yelp, throwing their arms over their head to protect their face.

Not this time, bitch.

I swing again, my dress ripping as someone tugs at me.

I swat them off taking another swing, grabbing handfuls of Ren's brittle hair and slamming their head back against the freezing ground below.

"Ebony! Ebony stop!" someone shrieks.

I can't distinguish voices in the place that I'm in. Fury is clogging my ears and only letting the sensation of their flesh beneath my hands. My senses are dull. All of them but my touch. My mind moving to one single, life altering thought.

Kill. This. Bitch.

This bitch tried to hurt me. Tried to *kill* me. The only thing that will alleviate my pain is to unleash my darkness and take them down to the hell they created for me.

Hands underneath my arms hinder my next swing. I growl as I'm yanked back.

Ren stumbles, staggering to their feet, face bloody.

I kick my feet hard. The heel of my stiletto digs into their gut satisfyingly deep. They crumple back towards the ground, releasing a hiss of air as their body folds.

"Arrogant, fucker!" I shout, flailing violently, trying to use my body weight to get free. "Let me go!" I roar.

"Kane, don't just stand there! Fucking help!" Han's frantic voice booms from behind my head. The only voice I can slightly make out in my fury.

He's holding me, using all of his strength to keep me from further attacking Ren. My wild movements make him stumble with me still pinned to his chest. Sharp, dead grass at my side before he rolls us, his body weight on top of me. I feel his legs moving over mine to pin me down.

A new feeling emerges, grabbing hold of my lungs and my heart, squeezing them so tightly. My movements are more frantic as I swing my fingers towards his face, clawing and reaching with more urgency.

My chest constricts with every violent pant as I panic. My rage flees for the hills like a snarling lion cub no longer brave enough to finish what it started.

"Ebony, stop!" Han dodges my hits, but his body is still on mine. Thick legs are straddling my body as he attempts to pin me to the cold ground.

"Please, stop. Please let me go!" My voice is frantic, panicked as I screech up at the fogginess of what should be Han's face.

I can't make out his features, only the outline of his suit. Spiraling thoughts are clouding my logic further as the fogginess of panic consumes my brain, my body. Then everything that tells me that this is Han fades. I'm back in the room, with a lumpy bed that smells like vomit and sweat from the party. His hands are no longer trying to pin or protect me, but ripping at my clothes. Hot, furious hands keeping me in place. The sound of laughter takes over the shouting that was once around me. Lights flashing and music blaring. I can't see anything but that, can't hear anything but that.

Then, I feel a phantom sensation I would hope no one ever feels. My scream pierces the air as I buck my hips and kick to get him off. Jumbled chaotic words of protest falling from my lips. All ear splitting and frightening sounds.

Han staggers up quickly, I can register him, but not like before. His face frightened, eyes large as his chest rises and falls. "I didn't touch her I promise," his voice wavers as he panics.

Kane is at my side, pulling me up, but I swing, decking him in the jaw. "Ebony!" his voice is garbled, almost angry as he holds his face.

Hands are on me and I'm flailing again, fighting to get free from the fucking hands that feel like hot coals dragging across my skin. So many fucking hands, ripping and prying at my body. Surrounding me and as voices beckon me to relax. I can't. I won't.

"She's having a panic attack," Denise concludes before I feel her hot hands on me. "Hey, hey, breathe! I need you to fucking breathe, E!"

"What the fuck!?" Ren's voice sounds distant like it did that night. "No one's going to see if I'm okay!?"

They spit and it lands with a disgusting splat. Their heeled feet stagger, dragging across the cement. There's a rustling as they adjust their clothes and dust themself off.

"You're fine!" Miya snarls from a distance.

"She split my fucking lip! I'm not fine," Ren protests.

"Shut the fuck up, Ren," Zeke growls. "E, focus. We need you to focus, Chica."

My chest burns as the vision of distorted, blurry hands invades my sight. Staccato pants fall from my lips as dizziness consumes me. My panic only makes my rugged breaths worse.

"I can't breathe," I pant. "I can't fucking breathe."

Blackness tickles the edges of my blurred vision and I grab at something, someone. My lungs, my throat, my *everything* burns and constricts tighter. With each pound of my heart, my body begins to collapse in on itself, straining like frayed rope suspending a grand piano high in the air.

Everything fucking hurts.

"Back up!" Clint's voice is near me, firm and commanding. "Give her space. Someone get water. Kane, give me your jacket."

Feet are pounding against concrete as everyone, but Ren, moves into action as Clint barks orders. A distant argument happens for a split second, then silence falls over me. The blackness is rushing forward like a car entering a tunnel. A single light that only gets smaller as the darkness carries me deeper and deeper.

"E, baby, I need you to breathe," Kane's voice is in my ear, but it sounds so far away. His hands are rubbing my back roughly. "Focus on my hand."

"Keep rubbing her back slowly," Clint instructs Kane. "Come on, E. Just like when we were kids. Focus."

I try, putting all the strength I can to focus on my breathing, but I can't slow it. My mind's viciously bouncing from one thing to the next like a bouncy ball going downstairs. My tongue feels dry, heavy in my mouth as their voices get more distant. Each of my emotions dart forward, colliding before dimming. My body is going numb, my breathing more labored.

"Come on, baby," Kane's voice pleads as he puts a little more pressure on my spine then my shoulders. "Focus on me."

Ice cold water yanks me out of my dark stupor with a ragged gasp. My lungs burn from the sudden sharp, cold air that fills them. I tremble, wrapping my arms over my body as Clint's face comes into view. Kane's jacket covers my shuddering shoulders. His hand still rubs my shoulders, but with less pressure. My eyes dart around the worried faces until finally locking on a disheveled Ren. They spit out blood. Their trembling hands smooth out their suit anxiously, but there's mud and dead grass clinging to it. Then, they wipe their hand over their mouth, then glare at me.

"Crazy bitch," they snarl.

My mind clears, targeting exactly who I need to, switching tracks like a train about to crash. And mine heads straight for Ren's.

"Give me your knife," I say to Clint, my eyes still glued to Ren. Rage creeping back, lurking like the monsters I've created to keep me safe. I hold my hand out, palm up, glaring.

"You don't need to do that, E," Denise says slowly.

I push to my feet and everyone quickly shuffles to give me space. Their eyes dart between me and Ren.

"They don't need a savior." My voice is low, raspy as I attempt to step forward.

"I don't give a fuck," Denise shouts. "Don't throw your life away."

"E," it's Kane's voice. Soft, cautious. He places his hand on my shoulder and I shudder, scrambling away and snapping my head in his direction. His eyes are wide, horrified. He's never seen my panic attacks. Never witnessed the blinding rage that lays beneath my skin, pricking its way through like angry fire ants from their hives.

Then more realization settles in the nooks of my brain.

"You brought them here," I state, setting a glare on

him.

His eyebrows shoot up, hurt and confusion lancing his handsome face. He lifts his hands, palms out, shaking his head. His mouth hangs open as he attempts to speak.

"Had I known, E..." he pleads, taking quick steps towards me before he falters. "I promise I didn't know."

"They told him they didn't know you. I swear, Ebony." Miya's wide eyes find mine.

"Believe me," he pleads, reaching for me. I step back, shaking his jacket off my shoulders. My mind spins in so many different directions.

"E, breathe," Clint's voice is firm in my ear. His grip tightening on my arm as I realize my shallow, rapid breaths. "I won't let you do nothin' stupid."

Ren laughs bitterly. They sit on the ground, their arms propped up on their bent knees. Cocky, arrogant, and *safe*. They spit another wad of red goo to the pavement. Their eyes lazily drag up to mine as they smile.

"You need me," they start cockily. They shove their sleeves up with a smile, which makes their split lip glisten. They swear under their breath, then dab at the wound.

"Like hell I do," I spit looking at them. Disgust rising in my throat as I watch them laugh again.

"You do," Ren offers. "And I unfortunately need you."

"Fuck. You."

"How," Denise speaks. She shoots me a 'be cool' look before stepping forward. "How does she need you?"

"I have what you need to get the person that gave me those drugs put away for a *long* time," Ren says.

"And that is?" I ask, letting the disgust slip out in every

word.

They stare at me, spitting more blood out of their mouth, then look over at Kane.

"Don't drag me into anymore of this shit with you," he growls.

I subtly glance at him. He runs his hands through his disheveled hair and paces. Eyes to the sky as he laces his fingers at the nape of his neck. Clouds puffing out from his mouth as he breathes. Han rushes over to him, grabbing him and whispering. Kane glances at me and I divert my eyes.

Ren scoffs, rolling their eyes. "Kane and Miya didn't know I knew you. *Dated* you. So, being mad at them is only going to fuck up what you guys did. Shame."

I snort, giving them my own eye roll.

"Believe me or don't. I'm fucked either way," Ren states, pushing to their feet. They take a step towards the parking lot.

"You really expect her to trust you?" Isaac speaks up. He's been quiet up until this point. Not much for the drama, not used to the chaos that comes with crossing me, or Denise for that matter. His handsome face is angry. Fury takes over his dazzling brown eyes as he steps forward. His shoulders squared more, making him look bigger, more dominating than he actually is. "She came back to us so fucking broken because of you. Do you know the shit *we* had to do to piece her back together?" he whispers harshly, his voice breaking in the middle of his statement.

"Boo fucking hoo," Ren snorts. "She's not the only victim."

"No, she isn't, but watching your best friend become a

shell of who she used to be…" He eyes them, dragging his brown irises from their face, down to their dirty pant legs, and back up. "I wouldn't expect you to fucking know."

"Write me a fucking essay then."

"Shut the fuck up," Zeke hisses. His body shifts, growing with his agitation. "Had you've been honest with everyone, none of this shit would have happened. Should have let E have her fun beating your ass."

"So you'd rather her beat me to death?" Ren asks, feigning shock.

"Abso-fucking-lutely," he growls.

Denise puts a tentative hand on Zeke's forearm, her eyes fixed on Ren.

Denise was betrayed like me. Not because of something Ren did to her per se, but at one point she considered Ren a friend. Included them in everything we did and they happily accepted the invitations, the care, the love we poured into our union. What they did caused a ripple effect of insecurities to bubble up in Denise, too. She didn't deserve it. None of it.

"Listen, what you went through is what you went through, but you keeping shit to yourself like some bargaining chip? That's fuckin' foul and you know it," Denise says, her voice strained as she teeters between unrestrained anger and being civil.

Kane shifting takes my attention away from the tense stare off between Denise, Isaac, and Ren. He pulls his phone out of his pocket, the screen illuminating the confusion on his face. He opens his mouth to speak, but his jaw snaps shut.

"Someone better explain this to me and they better start explaining quickly," a voice demands.

Shocked eyes take us in collectively. Each of us is covered in dead grass, but Ren and I are the dirtiest. The most disheveled. Clint steps to the side as we finally give the speaker our full attention.

2

Kane

Tension makes the air thicker than it already is. My mom stands, eyes wide as they ping pong between Ebony and Ren, both covered in dirt and scratches. The panic attack that Ebony had a minute ago lingers on at the surface of her eyes as she clings to Clint. Her head bowed, avoiding my parents' shocked faces. She's still on edge. So many emotions exploded from her, catching everyone — including herself — by surprise.

"I'm waiting," my mother's voice is stern as she looks around the group.

"Ebony," Ren snickers. "You do the honors."

Ebony shoots a deathly glare at Ren and goes to take a step. Clint tenses, squeezing her, then whispers something in her ear. Her shoulders deflate, but not before giving Ren one last menacing glare, wound tight and ready to strike.

I shove my hands in my pockets, chewing at the corner of my bottom lip. My mind repeats the events and I'm immediately regretting my decision to invite Ren here. It didn't matter how satisfying it was to watch Ebony fight them. Ren is still here because of me.

"Ren and Ebony got into a fight," Miya says, stepping forward quickly.

"What? Why on Earth—"

"Ren is Ebony's ex. The one that drugged her," I say over my mother. I pick my jacket up off the ground and sling it over my arm after shaking the dead grass from it.

"I thought her ex's name was Eva?" my mother asks, looking between the two.

"I lied to her," Ren says softly.

Despite being a massive pain in the ass earlier, my parents' presence humbles them, which unsettles me. The way they switch demeanor gives me mental whiplash, much like Ebony's current emotional state. Unlike Ebony, I'm sure that's Ren's intention. I'm sure that's exactly what they did to Ebony.

"Ren," my mother's voice is soft, but firm. "You drugged her?"

"I have my reasons," Ren pleads.

Ebony lets out a bitter laugh as she looks up to the sky, then seeks comfort in Clint's shoulder. He pulls her closer, wrapping his arms protectively around her.

Denise rubs her back softly, using the movement to dust the remaining debris off of her back. She even manages to get most of it out of Ebony's locs before giving her shoulder a reassuring squeeze.

I clench my fist, my jaw working in sync with the movement. Irritation and pain intermingling in my heart as I watch. She won't let me near her. Won't let me touch her, comfort her. My eyes lock on Ren's.

"Explain why you used me?" I ask through gritted teeth.

It's Ren's turn to laugh bitterly. A sound that rattles from their chest and out into the night air. Loud, raw, and heavy.

"I didn't use you to get to her. She's easy to find," they shoot Ebony an annoyed glance. "I genuinely wanted my best friend's help."

"You lied to me and my family," I argue, jabbing my finger at them. "I asked you if you knew her. You lied. Why?"

"Because she meant absolutely nothing to me. She was a waste of space in my mind. How was I supposed to know she was on the hunt, hmm? She was never part of any of my plans, so I lied," Ren spits.

"I hope you know that you telling me I'm 'nothing' is a pathetic attempt to not shoulder the reality that you still tried to kill me," Ebony butts in with a raised eyebrow.

"You don't mean a damn thing to me," Ren hisses.

"If I didn't," Ebony starts, "we wouldn't be in this predicament now."

Ren is silent, glaring at Ebony so venomously that Isaac, Denise, Zeke, and I take a few steps between them. Clint's hands grip Ebony's shoulder.

"If I meant nothing," Ebony continues, "my help would mean nothing to you. So, Ren, try again."

"You two," my mother says softly. She steps forward, palms respectively facing Ebony and Ren as she peers at them. "I think everyone needs to separate for a moment. We can come back to this."

Ren snorts, dabbing their lip with their suit jacket and swearing under their breath. Their lip starts to gradually swell, the blood staining their teeth no matter how many times they wipe or spit. Every time they move their mouth to snarl or smile, it splits more.

"I don't ever want to see them again," Ebony says with a thick, emotional voice. She tears her eyes away and shrugs out of Clint's jacket. "Mrs. Yamada, have you seen my Gramps?"

"He's with your father, trying to convince him not to come out here to find you," my mother says softly.

Ebony eyes the event space we were in and nods her head. She looks back at my mother and gives her a soft smile before sighing, her shoulders falling subtly as her head droops. My father clears his throat, stepping into view. He slides his hands into his pockets, looking around the group before speaking.

"The Dean issued a campus wide lockdown while they investigate what happened, per the mayor's orders. You guys are to stay put."

My father's eyes scan our little group before stopping on Ebony, who leans closer into Clint. Her head bowed slightly. My mother reaches out, brushing her knuckles against Ebony's pebbled skin.

"We're going to go back and see if we can offer our services, but you guys should go inside. Take a moment to decompress," my mother adds.

No one rushes to speak. Instead, we pass around quick glances filled with questions before looking back at my parents. I nod slightly before catching Ebony doing the same.

My father's eyes shift to me, then to Ren. "You two, stay back for a moment."

I stifle a groan.

"Maybe we should do Karaoke or something," Zeke offers as he parts ways from the group slowly. The others follow, only a few voices agreeing as Ebony and Clint take slow steps behind the others. His lips close to her ear as his hands squeeze her shoulder. Ren steps up beside me, adjusting their jumbled suit, then squaring their shoulders to face my father. I look up at him, shoving my hands in my pockets picking at a loose string in the corner.

3

Ebony

Steam billows out of the bathroom as I emerge from the shower, a towel wrapped around my body. I shuffle around my now empty apartment pulling out a pair of baggy sweats and a tank top. My mind is a foggy mess as I continue to move.

The soft tinkle of Silver's bell tings as he peeks curiously at me around the corner. His dazzling green eyes are cautious, but filled with so much wonder. He must sense the anxiety that lingers inside of me. Slowly approaching me, he takes a moment to pause and tilt his head into the air. A glossy black nose twitches as he sniffs the space before taking another slow step towards me.

"Hey you," I greet him softly. I squat down, wiggling my fingers to beckon him closer.

His head nudges my hand after he meows softly. My hand vibrates as he purrs. His silky, black fur tickles my palm as he moves his body underneath my outstretched hand.

My phone buzzes, breaking me from my feline- filled daze. I push to my feet. I check my phone idly before tossing it back on my bed and reach for a soft hoodie. Banging from my front door starts me as Silver growls low and cautious. I hesitate, knowing that Kane has a key and that our friends would text before coming over. Another bang follows, impatient and more urgent. Silver's warnings get louder as his haunches raise, his ears pinned back as he glares at the door with his body ready to launch.

"Just a minute," I call out.

With cautious steps, I approach the door and slowly turn the door knob, but a strong force knocks me off center. The door is kicked back, hitting me in the face hard. My hands clutch my nose as I stumble back. The painful haziness leaves my eyes and I notice my father's figure, then a much larger one approaches me. Mayor Cross' lips pinch together in a snarl, his eyes dark and soulless. I shrink, dropping my hands from my throbbing nose and stumble back more, but he lunges for me.

I dodge him, bumping into the couch and falling over it before I catch a glimpse of Mrs. Cross, Vin, and my mother closing the door like this is a normal visit. My father guards the door with his bulky body, watching as Mayor Cross swipes at me.

"You incompetent little bitch," he growls, finally grabbing a fistful of my locs. He yanks me back hard and I shriek, my scalp throbbing as his grip tightens. This is nothing new, Mayor Cross' anger or my father's acceptance on how he chooses to release it. They've always been this way, haunted by demons that only come out to torture. They hang next to the skeletons in his closet, so many of them that leave me wondering if I'll be the next one.

"Please," I gasp as my hands slap at his. "Let me go."

I'm standing on tiptoes attempting to alleviate the pain in my scalp, but it's no use. He yanks hard, his grip tightening in my locs and I wince. Tears prickle the back of my eyes from the sharp pain.

"Do you know what you've done?" he growls.

"Of course she knows," my mother chuckles. There's no amusement in her laugh though. "She must have been planning this for some time. Right, Vin?"

"I-I-I don't know," Vin stammers out, then sneezes.

I'm sure he feels the way I do. Like two children caught in the crosshairs of our parents' scolding. Being punished for harmless pranks to teach us how we should behave. It was usually one of us being made an example for the other. This time, it's me.

Mayor Cross' large hand circles my wrist, gripping tightly, his short nails digging into my skin. My wrist throbs; my heart throws itself around in my chest as I panic. He yanks me forward, pulling me so close that his breath tickles my nose.

"You will retract that statement," he snarls. He pushes me back, knocking me on my ass with a hard thump. Something in my arm pops. A sharp pain shoots through my shoulder as I attempt to brace myself on the way down.

Silver hisses loud and long from the other side of the couch. His yowls grow louder as he takes in the new energy in his space. I can't see him, but I know he isn't far from me. He never is to be honest.

"Ephraim," Vin's mother gasps. One manicured hand covering her mouth as the other reaches for me. "Not here," she insists through clenched teeth, quickly locking the door that's right behind her.

She's foolishly unaware that any person that I feel safe

with has a way to get in. Kane, for instance, has a key. My gramps and Clint, too. But my current problem is none of them know that they're here crowding my living room like vultures circling prey. And I foolishly left my phone on my bed.

Mayor Cross encircles his fat fingers around my throat, slowly squeezing as I kick, slap, and scratch at his tightening grip. My eyes bulge as my vision starts fading.

"Vin," Mayor Cross grits out. He watches my face closely as he squeezes tighter. His roughness adds more strain to my aching shoulder. His eyes burn into mine, a sick pleasure dancing behind his irises as my consciousness waivers, then he releases my throat, gripping my arm instead. Violently pulling me up as I gasp for air.

"Yes, sir," Vin calls out with false confidence. I can see his eyes darting towards my feet where I'm assuming Silver is crouched, haunches up. His claws ready to go to work, leaving a few intruders wounded. Another low yowl confirms it. Normally his presence calms me, but this time it doesn't help dissipate my anxiety as Mayor Cross' thick fingers dig into my bicep.

"Talk some sense into her." He releases my arm with a shove. I stumble back, but stay on my feet. "And somebody get that fucking cat."

"Wait!" I gasp as Vin approaches. His eyes dart to Silver's alert figure, stepping around the coffee table to create space. "Don't hurt him," I plead, attempting to reach for Silver's angry body. Vin's hand grips just below my armpit, so tightly that I think I might bruise. He yanks me back, dragging me towards my bedroom as I push and stumble to reach for my cat.

Silver yowls louder as my father reaches for him with his large, thick hands. Then I can't see Silver, but I can hear him fighting, hissing and spitting as he darts and dashes away from strange hands. Breaking and knocking over various items in his frenzied scattering.

"Preferably without sticking your dick in her, Vin," his mother shouts, eliciting a few chuckles.

Vin steps in front of me, grabbing the door and inching it closed. I shove against Vin's sturdy frame, digging my shoulder into his sternum when I notice I can't get past. Silver screeches before it's dead silent on the other end. I push Vin harder, trying to edge my body around his to get to Silver. To get out of here and go anywhere but here.

He grabs my shoulders. His cloudy eyes find mine with an almost sincere and terrified glaze. "You have got to fucking chill," he whispers to me with a firm voice. He glances at the door anxiously before he releases his hold on me and paces. His red suit is rumpled at the lapels where I'm sure he got his own punishment. One of the buttons of his black shirt is dangling from a piece of black thread. It swings as he turns and continues pacing.

"Fuck you," I spit, rubbing my aching wrist. Crescent moon shapes are etched into my skin from the mayor's grip. I wipe my eyes, looking between him and the door.

"Listen," he hisses, approaching me rapidly. He grabs my shoulders again, pushing his face closer to mine. "For once just fucking listen to me. I know how you fucking get. Let this shit go. Please."

"Not this time," I shake my head and take a small step

towards my phone. Even with Vin currently being some form of an ally, there are five of them in my tiny apartment with me. And with how large his pupils are, he's been using something mind numbing. He'll let rage consume him, and the last time I saw that, someone ended up badly hurt.

"Ebony," he growls, stepping into my path. "Say that it was a joke. A music video concept for one of your music class applications or something."

"No," I say firmly, then take a step in the opposite direction heading for my phone.

"Still as disobedient as always," Mayor Cross' voice rolls out. Vin stands stock still as he stares wide eyed at the door. Taking a few steps back, I shrink away as Mayor Cross steps closer. "That young man, Kane is it? He knows that Eva person. The one you called yourself dating last year." He chuckles as he takes slow steps into my room.

His thick hand reaches for one of my locs and I step back, my dresser pressing into the small of my back as I stumble into it. A dark, predatory chuckle fills the space as he stands in the doorway. His hands shoved into his pockets as his green eyes stare into mine. Hard eyes that make my stomach clench tightly.

"Leave us, Vin."

"Dad, I—"

Vin gurgles as Mayor Cross grips his throat between his hands so tightly. Deep red conceals Vin's normal complexion, his eyes bulging and reddening as he slaps at his father's tense fingers.

"I. Said. Leave," he grits, pulling Vin close to his face. "I'll deal with you later," he finishes, tossing Vin to the side like a rag doll.

Scurrying to his feet, Vin stumbles out of the door, passing backwards glances at his father's ominous posture. He doesn't stop though, instead, he slips out the front door. The sound of it closing and his mother rushing out calling for him is my indicator. He left me here with our big bad wolf.

"I must say," he starts slowly. He unfastens one of his cufflinks, then the other. He places them on the dresser as he takes a step towards me. His hairy hands shove at the sleeves of his shirt. "That little performance was quite exquisite. Especially in the gorgeous little dress." His eyes flash beneath the light. Darkening so suddenly that bile rises in my throat.

I glance beside me for my phone, then look back at Mayor Cross as I scoot to the side. He leans into me. His nose pressing into my cheek as he breathes deeply. A shuddery breath escapes my lungs as I attempt to move.

"Always so beautiful. Like your mother," he adds softly with a smile. He steps back, eyes looking over at me. "You'll retract your statement. Accept a punishment that I decide," he says, slowly looking around my room. "And if you don't… I'll start with Gramps. Then your cousin. Maybe that little boyfriend of yours. I'll let you watch what I do to him." His hand reaches up, groping my breast and I whimper, pushing him away. He leans into my ear. "I'll leave you so utterly alone, Ebony, that you'll have no other choice but to come running back to us like a good little pet."

"Eph, we should get going," my father calls from the door. He clears his throat, an anxious kind of sound I've heard the few times he has interjected in Mayor Cross' rage. With one final squeeze of my breast, Mayor Cross drops his hand giving me a wide smile.

"Tick Tock, Ebony," he concludes, then takes long strides out of my room, muttering something to my father and mother.

I fold into myself, pulling my legs to my body as I tremble violently. My father disappears from my door and into the main room. Glass begins splintering and shattering as more stuff is knocked over before my door slams shut. Hoisting myself up, I grip the side of my dresser, my palms sweating and my knees shaking so violently that I can't do anything else but stand and breathe.

4

Kane

Han and I pull hard drives out of the system, replacing them with ones my father brought in a duffle bag. We move quickly, unplugging and replugging while my dad types ferociously. My dad's security company has a small staff, primarily for maintenance. Everything else, like recording and mirroring the system, he does himself. That's how I'm so good at it.

Han and I meet in the center of one of the server bays and slide the last drive into the bags when my father's typing abruptly stops. We exchange quick glances as we hoist the heavy bags over our shoulders and enter the computer area. My father's fingers hover over the keyboard, the backlight of the computer illuminating his face in the dark. His body is ridged, riddled with an alertness when he finds something he shouldn't.

"What did you find?" I ask, walking over towards him. Codes are littering the screen. I place the duffle at my feet as Han approaches, glancing at the screen.

"When was that chemistry class you took?"

"First year? I think," I answer, trying to decipher the codes.

"What did they have you doing?" My father asks slowly.

He turns to me now, pushing his glasses up the bridge of his nose.

"Making compounds or something," I shrug. "Why?" I finally ask, noticing the concern in his eyes.

"That was the semester they kicked you out of the class…?"

"Yeah," I laugh nervously.

I vaguely remember the incident, but I got caught mixing chemicals. That was my first run in with Dr. Sumner. He was a chemistry professor during that time. He claimed I was making a bomb and got me kicked out of chemistry. Thankfully, because his accusations didn't have "allegedly" behind them and weren't backed by evidence, I got to skirt past that class without stepping foot in the building.

"Why?"

My father studies me for a moment, "What exactly were you mixing and why?"

"Didn't ask," I answer with a shrug. "What's up?"

Sad eyes heavily regard me before my father's sigh adds to the weight filling the room. "Help Han with those and go back to Ebony's apartment. We'll talk later."

"Dad?" I ask, hearing the waver in my voice.

"We'll talk later," he says firmly. "I promise." He turns to look at me, then nods towards the door.

I contemplate pushing the topic, but let it rest. My father is just as stubborn as I am. And to be honest, with how shit went down between Ebony and Ren, I wanted to be with her. Comfort her and tell her I had nothing to do with Ren's bullshit.

Giving him a slight nod, I then follow Han towards the door as we hoist the bags over our shoulders and make our way to the car where we load our loot.

"This is crazy," Han sighs, leaning against the back of the car as I shove my duffle in the trunk and close it.

"You're telling me," I respond, shoving my hands in my pockets. The cold starts to seep into my skin as my adrenaline fades. I try to recall my first semester, but come up short.

"You said the drug found in Ebony's system had to be lab made?" Han asks. He cautiously looks at me.

"From what we've seen, yes. It was like a mix of stuff you can't get a prescription for," I answer.

"Like meth?" he asks primarily to himself. "You think that's what you helped make?"

The thought makes my stomach twist. Thinking about it now, it's possible. And I really hope that it's not what I mixed all those years ago.

"It probably isn't," Han says quickly. "Don't sweat it."

"Yeah," I say dryly, already feeling the tornado of thoughts swirl in my mind. "Look, I'm going to go talk to E. I think everyone is taking it easy tonight, but you might be able to find a party or two. Miya and E planned a bunch."

"I'm going to swing by Zeke's. Not in the mood for a party. I'll catch you later," my brother says. Then, he does something he normally wouldn't. He pulls me into his arms for a quick, tight hug. I embrace him back, clapping at his back once before ruffling his hair and sprinting off to my and E's place.

It doesn't take me long to make it to the front

door. I fumble with my keys for a moment, then step over the threshold and pause. Glass from picture frames glitter underneath the main light. Chairs are pulled from underneath the kitchen table and broken into pieces, and the coffee table's lopsided. I take a cautious step in, assessing the damage just as I hear her distraught cries.

"Silver, please," she begs between sobs.

I spot her kneeling next to the destroyed cat tower, Silver cowering behind one of the platforms that lays on its side now. She reaches for Silver and he hisses. Something he normally wouldn't do to her.

"I'm sorry," she whimpers, wiping at her eyes and trying again.

I don't bother kicking off my shoes as I rush over to her, Silver darting off into the room to find another hiding spot. Before she can rush after him, I grab her, examining her face and the new scratches and the fresh bruise around her nose.

"Ebony?" I ask, running my hand across her trembling shoulders to get her attention. She tenses beneath my touch, wincing away like it physically hurts. "What happened?"

I keep my voice even as I stamp down my anger. My eyes search her, checking her neck, then her arms. Redness peeks from beneath her wrist and as my hand grazes it, she winces.

"Baby," I whisper, dropping my head to catch her eyes.

She finally looks at me with her red, puffy eyes. Silver's bell jingles as he inches close to us, sniffing at Ebony, then me. A disapproving meow erupts from his chest as he climbs into the broken cave of his cat tower.

"We should go," she whimpers, wiping at her eyes. She

stands abruptly, slightly knocking me off balance, but I'm on my feet and stopping her.

"What happened?" I ask again, reaching my fingertips to her face.

"I upset my boogeyman," she answers with a hollow voice, dodging my hand. Her eyes are so damn terrified that my chest clenches tightly. I glance around the room, before stepping towards the bedroom. "They're not here anymore."

With a gentle nudge past me, she enters our room, grabbing a large duffle from the corner and Silver's carrying case.

"What did they do?" I ask her more firmly.

"They didn't hurt me. Or Silver," she adds looking back into his darkened area. She lets out a heavy, shaky sigh.

"Bullshit," I mutter looking pointedly at her wrist. She tucks it behind her back, then walks around me to attempt to grab Silver.

Running my hands through my hair and pulling out my hair tie, I let out a tense sigh watching her. Stress worries at the edges of her face as she attempts to calm her shaking hands. The zippers of her bags give her away.

"Take a second and talk to me," I encourage softly.

My words halt her steps as she nears the couch. She turns to look at me, then around me. She slides her hands over her face as she takes deep, shuddery breaths. A sharp exhale bursts from as she eases onto a cushion.

"I thought they—" Her voice breaks and she clears her throat before trying again. "I thought they hurt Silver."

Her shoulders shake with her sob, then another. I pull

her into my arms, rubbing my hand up and down her back as she cries. We sit like that for a moment, until she groans into my chest and gives me a firm shove to push away from me. Back and forth she moves across the floor, shaking her hands and arms rapidly. Her eyes cast up towards the ceiling as she takes deep, steady breaths.

"Silver is fine. He's okay," she says mostly to herself. "He's right over there in his cat tower, mad because I won't let him sleep."

"Are you okay?" I ask, standing and fidgeting. "Ebony?" I call out when she doesn't answer me.

"We should go," she says sharply. She rushes over to where Silver is and pulls him out. Soft growls roll from his throat as she tucks him in her arm and gently squeezes him to her chest, then places him in his carrying case, which closes with a soft zip once she secures him in. Even with her hands working, they tremor violently.

"Ebony," I call out to her softly as she shoves her emotions down.

"Everyone's waiting," she answers, shouldering both bags and trying to rush past me.

I grab one of the bags, stopping her.

"Take a moment and tell me who did this," I encourage her.

"Not right now, Kane. Please." She looks up at me. Darkness circling her eyes as she pleads with me.

I nod and usher her out the door in silence.

5

Ebony

Kane's old apartment still looks the same. Posters of swimsuit models are plastered on the walls. A large, gray leather couch, that looks like it's seen a tussle or two, dominates the common area. A tall bong is sitting in the middle of the counter like a centerpiece. Large pizza boxes now decorate the space to the left of the bong and various drinks sit on the right. Kane lurks behind me, his eyes glancing over at me periodically as I step farther inside.

"Take your stuff to Kane's old room," Zeke says with a smile. His hair wet and jostled on top of his head. He reaches for me, then falters. "The fuck did you do, Kane?" he asks before casting an accusatory glance in Kane's direction.

"Wasn't him," I mutter, giving him a small smile. Silver yowls in his carrying case as I shift the bag.

Kane's hand brushes past my shoulder grabbing my duffle and Silver. As the strap slides down into his hand, he lets Silver out, then makes his way to his old bedroom, nudging the door cracked.

"You look like shit," Zeke mutters with a playful smile, nodding towards the counter and reaching for a cup.

"Gee, thanks," I mumble with a small smile, grabbing an open bottle. "It's not everyday I get in a fight with my ex. Where's everyone at?"

"Han is getting his stuff from the hotel, Miya should be here with D and Isaac in a few minutes. Clint is taking a rain check."

"You invited Clint?" I ask, stopping mid-pour.

"Yeah?" he responds slowly. His eyebrows stitch together as he looks over at me. "Look, the more the merrier. Doesn't hurt that he mixes a damn good old fashion."

"So, what you're saying is that mine are ass?"

"Didn't say it," he states, rolling his eyes with a smile. "You did."

"I hate you."

"Love you too," he responds with a smile. "You and lover boy talked?" he asks quietly after a few minutes.

He hooks up a few wires to the TV, only giving me a quick glance before he focuses on his task.

"No," I answer with a sigh, leaning on the back of the couch. I look over towards Kane's room. "Need help?"

"No." He scratches his head, then looks over at me. With a quirked eyebrow, he nods towards the door.

"Fine," I grumble, walking into the kitchen to pour myself a stronger drink, then slipping into Kane's room.

The sound of running water takes up the space in a peaceful way. I take a moment to look around, letting my fingers touch the smooth paint on the walls and the random cologne bottles that sit on his dresser. Each bottle neatly lined up with the label pointing out. A shelf filled with trophies and books, both collecting dust, catches my attention next.

I let my fingers trace the engravings on them before examining a trophy with far less dust on it than the others. I reach for it, letting the light bounce off the gold siding before something else catches my attention— a picture. The surface is smooth and cool as I feel the edges. I take a closer look at the image. Kane's friends surround him, all smiling with their trophies raised to the sky. Eva stands beside him, curly black hair long like I remember. They smile just as wide.

"Hey," Kane's voice startles me. I drop the picture, turning towards Kane's figure and backing away on instinct. "Shit. I'm sorry. I didn't mean to—"

"It's fine," I say, sucking in a deep breath and letting it out slowly. I look at the picture on the floor before rushing to pick it up. "Sorry for snooping…"

He studies me, his towel hangs from his broad shoulders as water droplets fall from his hair. "Are you going to talk to me about what happened?"

"Why was Eva… I mean Ren there?" I ask looking up at him. Resting my hip on one of his dressers, I cross my arms waiting for a response.

"I didn't know, E. I swear I didn't," he says, tossing his towel on the bed and taking a cautious step towards me, then stopping. "They never told me they knew you. I asked. I wouldn't put you in that situation."

"But it happened," I mutter looking at him. My hand rubs at the soreness in my neck as I wince at the new tenderness that shoots through my body.

"I know," he admits, running his hands through his hair. "And had I known, had they been honest with me, I wouldn't be the reason they were there."

"How did you not know?" My voice cracks slightly as I look at him, fighting the emotions bubbling up in me. So many confusing emotions.

"I can't really answer that. Miya and I looked. There were never any indications that they were Eva. I doubt you have pictures," he offers.

I scoff, shaking my head. He's right. I burned all the images of Eva and me. Once I could look at them without my world caving in. I burned them all. Including their favorite hoodie that they never got the chance to get back. I drop my hands to my side.

"Baby," Kane starts. He sits on the bed, rubbing his palms against his shorts. "I didn't mean for any of it to go down like this."

I stare at him for a moment, mulling over the thoughts that bounce in my mind. We're at a standoff. I know he didn't intend for it to happen this way, but it did. And that triggered part of me blames him. The part of me that always wants to run is tugging me towards the nearest exit.

"Mayor Cross paid me a visit," I mumble. My fingers, still aching from the fight, pick at the frayed edges of my oversized tee.

Kane's body shifts, but he stays put. His eyes darken protectively. "I'm going to come over there and take a look at you."

"Don't," I glance at him quickly before looking down at my bare feet. "He told me to retract my statement. He said he would…" A lump forms in my throat cutting me off. I swallow around it. Squeezing my fist, my fingernails dig into my skin, helping me get the rest out. I look at him through blurry eyes. "He said he'd hurt you guys…" A tear rolls down my cheek and I quickly wipe it away with a huff. Tossing my head back, I look at the ceiling shaking my head. "I should just—"

"No," he says. His voice is firm, yet soft. He crosses the distance between us, rubbing his palms down my arms. I tense beneath them without thinking. He mutters an apology, taking a step back, but keeping his eyes on me. A chime from the bed interrupts our silence, but he lingers for a second or two before going to check his phone. His face tenses as he tosses the phone back to the bed with more force than necessary.

"It's Ren," he grumbles.

"What do they want?"

"To talk with you," he responds. His eyes are guarded as they search mine. "Tomorrow morning."

I look away this time. From him, from my thoughts. It's easy to do when my heart's trying to pry its way out of my chest. I dig my nails into the flesh of my arms and try to focus on slowing my heart.

"E?" Kane's concerned voice reaches my ears, but I'm too distracted to notice his quick movements.

His large hand rubs firm circles on my back as he guides me to his bed. I stumble over my own feet for a moment until he helps me sit.

"Focus on my hand," he states, putting pressure on my back. Cold water droplets from his hair fall on my hand, my face.

I glance up at him before grabbing his hand and

squeezing it.

Eva, my psychotic ex, wants to see me. For what reason? Only Satan knows.

I finally calm my nerves enough to suck in a lungful of air. Then another. I loosen my grip on Kane's hand.

"I'll go under one condition…" I start.

"You shouldn't—"

"Come with me. Please."

6

Ren

Kane has been my best friend since the fifth grade. I respect him more than anyone in my life, but I have my reservations. For one, once Kane grew into his chubby baby face, he led with his ego — and his dick. When he started turning heads and finally got a taste of what it's like to be with a girl, he dove in head first. The pretty boy, the ladies' man, the cocky fucker that would tell a girl he didn't want a relationship with them and she'd still be all over him.

Apparently, he's a reformed man now. Caught in the orbit of Knight University's *sweet*, party girl, Ebony Young. My fucking ex-girlfriend.

Her and I were destined for failure, but we were like ants to sugar when we met, fresh out of toxic relationships. Each dealing with grief from different traumatic life events. We ran towards each other, crashing and burning so damn hot everyone involved got burned too. Everyone around us still gets burned. I hate to admit that I love that shit, but I do.

She's the flame to my match. The gasoline I need to set everything up. And if I let her steep long enough, she leads a trail right to a massive explosion. I should feel ashamed knowing what makes her tick and using it against her, but

36

I don't. I never have. Even after finding out Vin lied about her being involved in my brother, Raeven's, death.

My brother was older than me by two years. He loved partying just as much as Ebony, but their type of partying was vastly different. She drank to feel good, then fucked whoever she wanted, whenever, and wherever. So unapologetically sexual and liberated. I stood by to watch her in her element a few times. She loved it when I did. I loved it when I did. Clearly, that wasn't enough to not want to be caught in her orbit for a short time.

However, my brother's type of partying was chaotic. He smoked whatever was offered to him, snorted coke from dirty bathroom counters, and popped as many pills as his body could handle, until it couldn't. He knew his limit though, always stopping and detoxing before his next session. Always spacing it out to make sure he stayed in his element.

Knowing this made his death so much harder to bear. It's still hard to cope with. Mainly because I didn't get the chance to fully enjoy my time at uni with him. Didn't get to experience the parties he went to or meet his friends. Users is the appropriate term since none of them reached out when he passed. Don't even think about asking if they came to the funeral. I'll save time by saying they didn't. Not even a card expressing their sorrow.

Kane did though. Even Ebony showed up on the outskirts of the cemetery in an all black dress and a bouquet of sunflowers in her arms. I remember that day because the wind whipped past her afro puff ponytail making it dance with her flowy dress.

I think she waited until everyone left to leave the flowers at his grave because they sat neatly tucked on his tombstone the next day. Every week, up until I drugged her, she left sunflowers on his tombstone.

Sunflowers were his favorite flowers. They had become mine after I realized she was the reason they were there. Those bright yellow items made me think of Rae. Made me feel like he was close to me.

To be honest, seeing her at his funeral was the reason why Vin's lie was so believable. They didn't know each other, never met beyond the conversations her and I had in class when he died. The same class we were in when the teacher awkwardly told everyone of his passing. Before my mother could reach me. Before my father.

Her and her friend, Denise, rushed me out of the class when they noticed I was panicking. Helped shield me from prying eyes. I vaguely remember rambling that he loved sunflowers.

It was hard to grasp that she genuinely wanted to support me when people I've known most of my life couldn't do the same. How dare she be supportive when I never would have done the same for her. Her kindness enraged me. I despised her for being there, for supporting me while my best fucking friend dragged me to parties to help me forget. Something about her and those fucking sunflowers made me remember. They made the pain worse. Like a butter knife cutting through my skin. Kane provided the band aid, then she'd come along, rip it off and sterilize my wound.

I confronted her at some point, the days bleed together

so I can't say exactly when, but I did. I yelled at her, screamed vile things in her face and she took it. She stood back with a blank expression on her face and fucking took it like a weak bitch, then I cried. Painful sobs racked through my body as she held me, cradling me close and telling me that I was going to be okay.

How fucking dare she tell me I was going to be okay. How did she know? How could she know when I felt like each and every day my heart was ripping out of my chest. The painful agony, the constant reminder that my brother, my first best friend, was gone and never coming back.

I screamed that at her, too. As the lump in my throat grew painfully large. I wept for my brother in her arms until I felt empty. Until my eyes were swollen and she took me to her dorm and cared for me until I could see. Until I could fucking breathe without crying.

Grief is what made me do what I did next. Grief made me kiss her. Made me run to her and cling like a desperate, touched deprived child. And not once did she seem to mind. She held onto me, caring for me in ways that I tried to be angry about. Even now, the anger for her compassion is a figment of my imagination and it only makes me more angry with myself.

I didn't love Ebony then, not that she minded when we started dating. Sure, she's a monogamous woman, but if we were honest, and I mean deeply honest, we were just passing the time. At least that's how I rationalized it. Us dating was a random, strange event that neither of us could truly explain. I admit, that's what I've been telling myself. It's easier to say that than to dive deeper and figure out whether I truly liked

Ebony for that brief time or I used her for her body, her mind.

I never told Kane the details of me and Ebony's relationship. He knew I had dated someone back then. Someone that he may have encountered a few times, but I knew they never hooked up. Ebony steered clear of him and Zeke. The heartbreak duo. She told me that much at a party we all were at respectively. I had caught Zeke checking her out from across the room and nudged her, picking fun about the instance. She didn't know I knew them beyond rumors until the gala.

My time with her was before the tattoos, the piercings in her nose, the locs that hang from her head making her look like one of Medusa's beautiful daughters. Before I knew how much fire lingered behind her eyes and how lethal it was, it is, when you cross her. Maybe that's why Vin did it. Why he lied and said it was Ebony that gave my brother the drugs.

As for Vin, I don't even remember how he and I became acquainted. Maybe the first bonfire after midterms, where the school let us burn our old assignments as a form of release while some guy wore a dull, metal knight armor that scraped and clanked as he moved. He sounded like a tin drum tumbling across pavement on an extremely windy day. Vin tried to spit game then. Did his best to convince me to sleep with him until I told him I'd prefer to be face deep in pussy. He snorted and told me his ex was the same way now. I never caught her name that night, not until he told me about his plan. That was the day he pointed her out, telling me she was the one that gave my brother the substance that killed him.

Apparently, she was a heartbreaker too. A runner. Femme fucking Fatale. I can see why, even now. And it pisses me off even more now that our paths have crossed again. I admit, they needed to; I wanted them to so she could help me. But to know she's fucking my best friend… my ex-best friend. Too close to home.

Knocking from the signs on the door catches my attention and there she is. A pair of baggy jeans and a thick, form fitting shirt adorn her body. My ex-best friend's right behind her, his clothes loose fitting and comfortable.

They look towards each other. Seeking safety in each other's eyes, movements. I notice how they move in sync. Reaching for each other in more ways than physical, much more than sexual. Quick glances pass between the two of them as he says something to her, his hand cupping her face and she leans into it, her hand brushing against his. Snow sits on their hair as they look around for me. He spots me first and only takes a millisecond to gain control over his emotions. Betrayal is the first thing I see. Anger a close second because Kane doesn't do disloyalty. He places his hand on the small of her back and leads her over to me. Both of them staring at me with controlled and tamed rage.

"'Bout fucking time," I mutter, leaning against the soft leather chair beneath me. I wince at the tenderness in my gut and lip. A painful reminder that not only did she kick the heel of her stiletto into my gut, but she also has fists of fucking steel.

"Kiss pavement," Ebony spits, glaring at me as she drops herself in the chair across from me. I pause on her neck, black blossoming under her skin. She adjusts her shirt, hiding it slightly. I glance at Kane, assessing their body language and concluding what I already know. He didn't put that there. I shake the thought from my mind and pick up my previous demeanor.

"This is getting old," I state with a sigh, looking at my fingernails, ignoring the anxiety that has me ready to bolt for the door that they're closest to. I didn't think about this sitting arrangement clearly.

"We're not doing this if either one of you are going to escalate this," Kane warns, looking at both of us as he takes a seat, then pins me with a glare.

I throw my hands up, surrendering my antagonistic antics, then cross my arms over my chest, glancing at her. Remorse making my stomach uneasy. There's a scar on her face that I'm sure she questions. It wasn't there until after that night at the party. When Vin waltzed in with his friend from one of the school's clubs. I wish I could remember his name. Garret? Henry?

"Look," I finally say with a sigh. "That night, I was told those drugs would make you lucid. You were supposed to be conscious still, not blacked out."

She looks at me uninterestedly, her jaw clenched tight as the glare she attempts to suppress steps forward anyways. She's listening, aware that I'm just handing over details freely. Kane's hand on her thigh giving her a gentle squeeze. She must have shifted because her leg stills by the time I catch the movement. I continue speaking anyway. I need her to trust me. To believe me for just this moment.

"I panicked that night when I realized the drugs didn't

do what they said. By the time you passed out, I told Vin's friend we needed to get you help."

"What friend?" Ebony asks, irritation weighing heavily on each word.

I shrug. "Can't remember. I'd know him if I saw him."

I wait for a moment, letting the silence take a seat. When I'm sure neither of them have any more questions, I continue.

"When I asked for help, he ignored me. Vin walked in shortly after and he ignored me too." I shrug, looking at her, keeping my face frozen, not allowing a single thread of emotion to make my expression twitch. Especially at this part, I could never tell her this part.

I bite my tongue as my mind remembers the way they looked over at her unconscious body. They were like vultures finding their next meal. It didn't matter that she was unconscious, possibly dying since her breathing was so shallow. They were turned on by it. They eyed her like a brand new toy. The thought makes me sick. The fact that I left her there doesn't help. Even if I left to go find help. And you would think that in a house full of people, someone would want to help. They didn't and I couldn't find Kane or Zeke.

By the time I came back, all three were gone. I can't tell her what happened in that room for sure, but I'm pretty sure I know and telling her would kill her. I may not like her, but that's not something I'd want to know. Especially if I couldn't get a definite answer.

"What do you need my help with?" Ebony asks, crossing her arms over her chest. She kicks her leg over the other, crossing them, and leans back in the chair.

She's not a threat right now, but she's on the defense. And defensive Ebony is why my fucking lip is split now. It's a little odd how much I enjoyed it. She did call me a masochist one time when she got me off during a little knife play. Don't ask.

"I need to prove the drugs found during Raeven's autopsy were the same ones found in your system."

"Why would they give him something like that?" Kane asks. His brows furrow as he leans back in the chair, his legs slightly blocking Ebony's. If she jumps up to launch at me, his leg would block her long enough for me to make a move or run. Maybe I didn't lose my friend after all. Maybe.

"Vin said something about testing a product for a shipment. He claimed he couldn't do it."

"He's an addict," Ebony says before chewing on her nail. Kane looks at her with one of his eyebrows hitched. She looks at him. "He got into his dad's coke when we were young. Then he started experimenting with oxy when he got injured on the field."

"This stuff is stronger than narcotics, Eb. I mean Ebony," I say, shaking my head. It's easy to forget that we hate each other. Especially when her brain is working and logical, putting the pieces together without too many details. But she's not giving me much. Still tense and on edge. It's easy to remember why though. I fucked up, but I had my reasons.

She looks at me, her eyes taking me in before she rubs a hand over her face. She turns, locking eyes with Kane. He reaches an arm out, placing it on her neck and rubbing circles around the side. I notice that they're always touching. Even if it's a hair of contact, when they're close, they're touching. Are they anything like her and I? Chaos? A disaster waiting to happen?

Her eyes landing on mine snap me out of my musing. She drops her hand from her mouth, leaning her neck into Kane's large hand.

"Do you have the reports?" she asks.

"What reports?

"From your brother's autopsy," she says slowly. She scrunches up her face in annoyance.

"I can't access them. That's why I need Kane's help. They're on a blocked database on campus."

"On campus?" Kane starts.

"Did you guys donate his body to the medical department?" Ebony asks.

"Yeah. It was something he mentioned a few times and my parents decided to honor his wishes for once."

"His records are going to be in the academic autopsy files," Ebony says, looking at Kane. "Which can be tricky if a student performed the autopsy and the teacher went back to examine their work."

"Why is that?" I ask leaning forward. My knees touching the glass table between Ebony, Kane, and I.

"Potential discrepancies depending on the student's level of knowledge. Files have been going missing on campus, too. Simple to leave the students' reports in the report files and not the professor's professional feedback. We would need both for validation purposes," Ebony says, then looks at me. "Right?"

I nod twice, then I look at Kane.

"For the most part, the student autopsies match the medical examiners that volunteer with them, but they wouldn't give my parents a copy."

"Wait," Ebony interjects, looking me over once more. "If your brother was doing drugs they wouldn't have accepted the body."

"My brother wasn't an addict. Sure, he'd go a little wild sometimes, but that was only at parties and he always knew his limit."

Kane sighs and shifts his weight in his chair. "What are you thinking, Ebs?" His eyes look me over too, then at Ebony.

She chews on her lip, eyes unfocused as she thinks. Her eyes shift before they focus again and she looks at me.

"You're gonna have to sign a contract or something. If we help you, you're going to have to hold up your end of the bargain. I want names, testimony, anything a lawyer needs to lock Vin and his dad up if I take this to court. And to help with a case study I've been working on with Miya."

"Fine," I say, shrugging my shoulders. "As long as my brother gets some type of justice."

"Kane'll email you everything," Ebony comments, standing up and looking over at him.

I push to my feet, looking between the two as they shrug into their jackets. They don't say another word as they walk back into the snow, his arm draped over her shoulder.

I sigh, shrugging into my thick, bubble coat. I shove a knitted cap over my head and rush out the door towards my car, snow pelting me in the process.

"They're willing to help. That's the most important factor in this equation," I say to myself as I turn on my car and blast the heat through the vents. I look at the picture hanging from my rearview mirror and touch it with red fingers. "Whoever took you away from me will pay, Rae. I promise."

I take my time pulling onto the street, heading home. Relief and excitement warms my body by the second.

7

Ebony

Denise sits on the other side of my work station in the lab. I rest my hands on the keys that I had been typing on when I told her about my meet up with Ren.

"You're fucking crazy," D finally huffs. "Out of our trio, I figured you'd be the one to know better than to make a deal with Ren, but no. Clearly, I was wrong."

She taps a pencil on the textbook open in front of her, then leans slightly back on her stool. With a head shake, she fixates on her book, but I can tell she's not focused on the words on the page.

"I know what it sounds like," I defend. "But—" I stall, not really having a real good excuse.

"Waiting to hear what you come up with to excuse this shit," D spits, placing her elbow on the table and resting her chin on her fist.

"What if it had been me, D? Back then... when we were kids?"

"I wouldn't team up with Vin to prove you're innocent. That's for damn sure. But I'd figure that shit out."

"That's what I'm doing. Someone on campus is passing out some lab- crafted drug. We've seen this shit. Vin's dad used a similar incident at our school to get elected. Every

48

election year, like clock work… another body.”

"So, you're saying…"

I nod as I chew at the skin around my thumb nail.

"Do you think Vin's dad drugged you?"

I shrug my shoulders. "Was he on campus during that time?"

"Rumor has it that he and Sumner had a meeting with some pretty big donors. I can ask around about it, but don't be upset if nothing comes of it," D offers, looking at her notebook, then back at me.

"I can ask Miya to look. Maybe even Zeke," I add, looking back down at my notes. "Can I ask you something?"

D hums her acknowledgment. Her eyes skimming her dim phone screen as she takes a moment to scroll through something.

"What if it was Kane?" I chew at the corner of my bottom lip. My belly twisting in an anxious knot as I watch D's eyes slowly look up at me. Conflicted brown eyes meet mine, her mouth a tight line as she lets the weight of my question settle in.

"First," she starts, taking a deep breath and letting it out slow and steady. "What makes you think that?"

I shrug my shoulders, tapping the eraser of my pencil against my leg. The answer to the question isn't simple.

"He brought 'Eva' on campus. Out of our group Zeke, Kane, and Miya are the only ones that know them. Ren's his best friend."

"If you accuse Kane, you have to accuse them, too," D says cautiously. "Look," she shifts to move a little closer.

Her warm brown hands grasping mine, she squeezes

them tightly.

"You know I love you. You know I'm ready to solve this shit like Foxy Brown, but you're going to start self-sabotaging this whole thing pointing fingers. Kane genuinely looked so broken when he realized that Eva and Ren were the same person. You know Eva, regardless of the name they gave you. You know how they work."

She squeezes my hands a little tighter, ducking her head down to catch my downcast eyes.

"Trust yourself. That's the only way we get through this as a group. Kane has had every opportunity to hurt you and he hasn't. Take a breather. Talk to him."

I nod with a sigh, then give her a small smile.

"So, how's the project?" D asks with her nose scrunched up as she leans closer.

"Good," I answer. "Dr. Goodwin was talking to Miya and me about digitizing the watch and data. We just didn't get enough prototypes in to sample them during Family and Friend's week."

I walk to one of the cabinets and pull out a key; I unlock the box and pull out two of the digital watches. I pass one over to her, and turn it on.

"You guys sampled a smart watch?"

"It was the easiest way to get the school to approve of it," I share. "You want to see it work?"

"Babes, I wouldn't be in here if I didn't want to see what that beautiful brain conjured up," D says with a reassuring smile that makes me smile back.

I nod, grabbing a few things then mixing chemicals. I place a clean dropper in each container, then adjust the band on D's wrist.

"To simplify what's going on, remember the basic functions of any smart watch. With that in mind," I let my voice fade as I grab a dropper and pinch some liquid on the watch band. The device beeps and lights up the screen with a message.

"Report drink to the nearest official?" D asks, looking up to me.

"We tried to mimic how blood test monitors and smart watches work. The components, and system Kane and I put together allows the watch to retrieve signals from a strip right here," I tap the side of the watch where the liquid accumulates.

"You didn't say any of this in your presentation," D says, looking at me. I shrug, then lean close to her.

"Dr. Goodwin thinks the same way Kane and I are thinking," I lean back and start cleaning the small mess I made.

"If you two are right and the school is in on this," D starts removing the watch band and taking a closer look. "Then, that's terrifying."

I look at her, my lips tight, feeling the impact of my shared hypothesis. "Let's go get some fresh air. You could use a break from studying and I can use a break from transcribing."

"Girl," D says with relief. We smile at each other, slipping into our jackets, and stepping out the door after securing everything.

8

Kane

The keys clack underneath my fingers as I attempt, for the seventh time, to find a route to get to autopsy records. With the new system intact, I notice the mazes my dad implemented that keep routing me back to the homepage. Normally, he'd do this to test me, but something about this feels different, like he's trying to keep me out.

"I need a vacation," Miya groans, sitting beside me on the couch. She looks at my computer screen, eyebrows bunching together as she attempts to decipher the codes.

"You and everyone else on campus," I mutter, looking through the codes.

"Have you and Ebony talked?" she asks quietly.

"A little. She's in her head," I respond, glancing over my shoulder, then offering a pathetic shrug.

"Did you know?" she asks.

"Know…?" I look at my sister. Rage bubbles up in my chest as realization sets in.

"No." I huff, trying to dispel my anger. "I fucking asked them. They told me they didn't know Ebony." My leg bounces in my state of agitation.

Why the fuck did Ren lie?

Miya nods her head, seemingly dropping the topic. I let

the silence settle as I mull over the green lettering on my screen. I lean back over my keyboard, trying again.

"Do you know anyone in the school's medical department?" I finally ask after getting an accessed denied screen.

"Maybe?" she says, pulling out her phone and scrolling through it for a minute. "I have a few who are graduating this year. What do you need them for?" She eyes me suspiciously as she shoves her phone back in the pocket of her sweat pants. Crossing her arm over her chest, she leans back against the back of the couch with her eyes pinning me.

With an eye roll, I look back at the computer giving another attempt, then shove my computer back with a huff.

"Fine," I grunt. "Ren's brother was taken to the school's medical department."

"He was? Even after…?"

"Yep. I need to get those records, but I need clearance."

"Just ask Isaac or Clint," Miya states like I'm a fool.

"They're not med students though," I counter.

"Isaac isn't, but he's undeclared. He might be willing to apply for a major change to get the clearance you need. Clint was pre-med last semester. He took some time off, but his clearance might still work."

"Isaac wants to do music management. He's in a music production class with Ebony." I pause for a moment. "How do you know so much about Clint?"

She shrugs a shoulder, then adjusts her position. "Maybe if you spent some time talking to him you'd know. What kind of investigator are you?" She snorts with a playful smile on her face. I nudge her with a smile of my own.

"You're kinda useful," I comment, pulling out my phone, scrolling through the contacts like Clint's would automatically be there.

"And you're a moron," Miya sighs, sending me his contact information. "You're welcome," she grumbles, getting up and slipping into her jacket.

"Where are you going?"

"To get food. I'm hungry."

"There's food here," I argue.

"Yeah, but I want a gyro from that new Greek restaurant down the street."

I sigh, standing and shoving my arms into my own jacket.

She eyes me suspiciously. "What are you doing?"

"Going to get a gyro…" I say slowly before tucking her under my arm. "Let's go, kid. Call Han too. Make it a sibling thing."

"I wanted to go alone, not with my dumbass male counterparts!" she shouts, shoving out of my arm as I lead us out the door.

"Not even if I say I'll pay?"

"You drive a hard bargain," she starts adjusting her clothes and pretending to think over the idea. "I'll allow it."

She smiles before marching through the snow towards my SUV. I roll my eyes, sliding my phone out of my pocket and dialing Han's number as my phone beeps in my ear. I glance at my screen, a message in a group message thread from Zeke.

Zeke

Karaoke round two!?

Miya

Yes!

Isaac

I'll bring pizza! Who's on liquor run?

D

Me and E will get it. We're leaving the workshop now.

9

Ebony

Han's voice is beautiful as he sings in Japanese. D, Isaac, and I clap to the beat of the song playing through the speakers around the room. A small blue bar scrolling over the lyrics on the screen as he follows along. Alcohol bottles and cups cover tables behind us in the main room. Greasy pizza boxes lay half opened and picked over. The cheese is no longer glistening from its heat, but still beckons us to dig in and grab one more slice. Smoke from a rotating blunt fills the room.

Kane eyes me suspiciously as I actively avoid being near him. My mind is still juggling the ideas that I should know aren't true. I settle for busying myself with another drink even though I'm already tripping over my feet. I take a grateful gulp before setting it down and pulling Zeke and Miya into a playful dance in the center of the room, feeling Kane's eyes track every move I make.

They laugh, stumbling slightly from the liquor that flows through their bodies. Denise moves her hips along to the beat trying to sing along with Han. He smiles at her warmly as he puts the mic between them and sings a little louder with her. Isaac pantomimes the drums from his seat. He sways, bobbing his head from left to right. A red solo cup in his right hand sloshing around the liquid inside before he takes a long drink. I bounce to the back for my drink, taking a long swig. My hips swing to the beat as it begins to fade.

Cinnamon, sugar, and spices fill my muddled senses as I feel his body heat. I glance beside me, moving my locs out of my face. Kane's reddened face and eyes come into view as he forces our eyes to meet.

"No! We should do this song!" an inebriated Miya giggles from behind us.

The song comes on, but I can't make it out. My eyes getting lost in the stormy ones of Kane. I tear them away to look him over. Creases form in nooks and crannies of his face. So many unasked questions linger in the shadows where they weren't before.

"Hey," he says shifting beside me. He guides us to the couch where we both collapse.

"Hi," I respond, leaning my head back against the cushion.

"You look like you're having fun," he offers.

I snort. I can't control the laughing fit that takes over. With a hand over my mouth, I attempt to swallow them, but fail. He joins me, soft chuckles vibrating from his body.

"I'm sorry," I say through my giggle fits, "I don't know why I'm laughing."

It's the booze. I always seemed to be the happy drunk around the right people. Always laughing at the simplest thing. The weed smoke most definitely factors into my giggle fit.

He shakes his head, bloodshot eyes looking over me before looking at everyone dancing. A ghost of a smile stays pinned to his lips as he seemingly enjoys my laughter, or is it the sight of our group falling over each other singing terribly into the mic. The melody of a Journey song playing along with their shrieks and giggles.

My own giggles subside after another minute or two and I snag two pieces of pizza from behind me. Nudging him, I offer him a slice taking a bite of my own. He looks over at me, takes it and shoves a bite in his mouth. The shadows creep back on his face as he attempts to keep his eyes from examining me too closely. He's never really been cautious, not until we started to get more serious. He never had to consider another person's feelings romantically. I wonder how new all this is for him.

I grab a napkin, setting my crust in it. Shifting in the seat, I lean over the couch to set the scraps on the table, but his hand catches me. I look at him, his brow furrowed, jaw packed with pizza. He grabs my crust, chewing and swallowing what's in his mouth, then takes a bite of what he took from me. A playful glare on his face.

"I still can't believe you don't eat pizza crust," he playfully scolds.

I roll my eyes at him, leaning back in the seat, mocking him with my expression. He smiles, finishing the remaining bite. This is our dynamic. The person that eats the food I don't like, even the foods I do. A balance that I desperately wanted when we met. A balance that I enjoy. We were fine individually, thriving, but together… There's something different about it. I still haven't decided if it's a good or bad kind of different.

My face evens out as my eyes search his again. I adjust

in the seat, turning so most of my body is facing him. "I'm so scared," I whisper to him through the thickness in my throat.

He grabs my hand, glancing at our giggling friends, and ushers me to his room where he wipes my tears. "Tell me how I can help," he urges.

"I don't know…" I finally mutter softly. "This is hard. My brain keeps overthinking this whole situation, but my gut tells me to trust you."

"You don't?"

"I don't trust myself…" I whisper honestly. "Eva came back and reminded me of all the shitty decisions I've made."

"Did you know they'd do that to you?" he asks, resting his back on the wall beside me.

"No," I answer honestly, shaking my head. "… I didn't think she'd hurt me like that."

"That just means you're not psychic, which sucks. I wanted to ask you how my future looks," he responds with a soft chuckle.

I nudge him, rolling my eyes, stifling a laugh of my own.

"Ren is very good at keeping shit to themself. They played the both of us," he says softly after a moment. "Miya warned me. She told me something was off about Ren. She had a feeling Ren and Eva worked closely together."

"Probably not this closely," I snort, looking at him.

Kane laughs with a head shake. He shoves his hand through his hair, then looks at me. His eyes scan my face, warmth bubbling to the surface as he leans close to me.

"I never apologized for hitting you," my voice is soft as

I study the slight bruise on his face. "I shouldn't have—"

He shushes me, placing his lips to my forehead.

"You were in a really bad headspace," he says scratching at his head. "Fucking mean right hook, girl."

"I'm so sorry…"

"Stop. You were having a panic attack. The look on your face… I don't know where you went, but it scared the hell out of all of us." He sighs, a pained look flashing across his eyes. "You had so many emotions come out of you in that split second that no one really knew what to do until Clint stepped in."

"Fight or flight," I mumble.

"You chose fight. Beat their ass and mine," he laughs, kissing my palm, then my temple. "What are you thinking?"

"Can I tell you later?" I ask, feeling guilty.

"Whenever you're ready. I've got your back."

"Ride or die?" I say with a laugh.

"Damn straight, mamas," he smiles at me.

10

Kane

The music is softer in the main room when Ebony and I walk back in. Our friends and my siblings sit in a circle surrounded by blankets and pillows. The pizza and liquor sit in the center of the room waiting for us to finish it off.

"You got laid to that 'Glad You Came' song. The bed was squeaking to the beat. Can never hear that song the same again," D says to Isaac as soon as we enter.

Miya gasps, looking at Isaac beside her as he stares at D. They share a couch on the left of the room, a pink blanket wrapped around her like a cocoon. My brother, Han, snorts from where he sits on the floor in front of the couch D lounges on. He covers his face, which is red from the liquor.

"You're lying!" Isaac shouts, his mouth hanging open.

"Where's E!?" D asks, looking around and seeing the both of us. She looks us over, squinting her eyes with a small smile on her face. "E, you were there that night, right?"

"What night?" Ebony asks, grabbing a cup from the center of the room. She looks up at D for a moment, then mixes herself a drink. She takes a sip, then walks to the couch we vacated. She sits down, pulling me with her. Looking at D with questioning eyes, she passes me her cup. I take a sip of her drink and grimace, the cold liquid burning my throat as it rolls down.

"Valentine's Day when you, me, and Isaac shared the suite together."

"The one right off campus?"

"Yes! With that random light that always had water in it."

Ebony cringes beside me.

"Smelled like ass most of the year," Isaac adds.

"Anyways! You remember that?"

"How could I forget? The song came on every damn radio station for weeks. I couldn't help but to hear the fucking bed springs," Ebony confirms with a gag.

I snort, watching her hand fly to her mouth as she passes me her cup. She looks at me, a playful horror in her eyes as she smiles at me.

"Oh, E, you're one to talk," Isaac says, giving her a pointed look.

"Baby, my sexcapades don't ruin lives. They save 'em. Hallelujah!"

"You goin' straight to hell, girl," D says through a drunken giggle.

"She's kind of right," Zeke says, leaning against the only vacant chair. He props his head on the side of the wall. "Before we were officially friends, I met a few people that knew her. What they described… fucking skills."

"Kane kissin' and tellin'?" D asks, fixing herself another drink then staggering back to where she sits.

"Nah. That's top secret," I respond with a laugh. Sloshing the liquid around in the cup, I take a long drink letting the bitterness swirl around in my mouth before swallowing.

"Zeke used to watch," Ebony says with a shrug. She snags the cup back and drains the rest.

"I'm sorry, he did what?" I ask, blinking between the two.

"That's right," D says mostly to herself. "Zeke's a Voyeur!"

Ebony nods her head looking over at me with a smile. She wiggles her eyebrows as Zeke chuckles from his side of the room.

"I'm so lost," Han says slowly.

He looks up at D who pats him on the shoulder with a smile on her face.

"You're so innocent," D giggles with a sympathetic look in her eyes.

"Look, it's not that big of a deal. There was this situation and she just so happened to be the center of attention. I was too fucked up, but I do know it ended with her pegging some guy. That part was what I watched," Zeke confesses.

"Come again?" I ask looking over at Ebony.

"I'm sure he did," Zeke jokes with a cackle.

Amusement bubbles at the edge of her brown eyes as she looks over my face. She smiles at me before shrugging one shoulder nonchalantly. I've never asked about her past, much like she's never asked about mine. We've heard the stories, the rumors about what we liked, but never shared the details. We leave it as is. Well, as much as we can.

"What was his name… Legacy? Larry? Big guy from the sculpting department?" Ebony asks, looking at Zeke.

She pulls a cover from the pile and throws it over herself, sharing some with me as she wiggles. I drop an arm on her shoulder.

"Lorenzo is the guy from the party. I think it was his favorite night," Zeke laughs before pausing. "Rewind, you pegged Larry, too!?" he adds shocked.

"Which one is Larry?" Miya asks.

"You remember that big ass sculpture that was on campus that looked different depending where you stood?" Isaac asks Miya.

She thinks for a moment, then nods her head vigorously.

"That Larry."

"Oh. My. God! He's like… six - six?" Miya asks.

"Thick as fuck," Denise says flexing her arms.

"And whimpered something beautiful," Ebony adds, grabbing one of the liquor bottles and refilling her cup.

"I may regret asking this," Isaac starts shifting uncomfortably, "You like getting pegged, Kane?"

Zeke's cackles pierce the air. He falls over, chest heaving and falling with each laugh. Ebony stifles her laugh, rolling her tongue around in her cheek as D laughs along with Zeke.

"Fuck no," I respond looking over at Ebony. "You see what you started?"

Miya gags, covering her mouth. Her eyes bulging out of her head as she stifles another one down. Han covers his ears, face draining of color.

"I'm not drunk enough for this shit," he grumbles, grabbing a bottle and taking long gulps out of it.

"There's nothing wrong with it," Ebony says, looking over at me. "Might like it, babe."

I glare at her as she wiggles her eyebrows at me. She takes a swig of her new drink, then looks me over. She wets her lips before turning back to everyone else.

"I didn't have the stamina for it before," D comments idly, "or the leg strength. Now, I'm pretty sure I could sling my purple strap around."

"Why do you have one?" Han asks, looking up at her shocked.

"To join the festivities. Duh," D says with a giggle.

"She calls me the freak, but she's the one that showed me where to get everything I own," Ebony laughs leaning her head back.

"What do you own?" I whisper to her.

"Getting adventurous?" she whispers back looking over at me. Her eyes are glassy from the liquor. She smiles slowly at me.

"Not that adventurous," I comment with a laugh.

"Laila Ali, are you really meeting up with Eva… I mean Ren?" Isaac asks suddenly.

The room grows quiet, somber almost, as everyone looks at Ebony. Curious eyes waiting for her to respond.

"We already met up," she answers. The cup shakes a bit in her hand and I take it from her, taking a small sip, then brushing my fingertips across her skin. I pull her closer to me and place her legs in my lap.

"What's the verdict?" Han asks.

"They want help getting Rae's autopsy report. In exchange, they'll let me use the records for my and Miya's case study."

"That's pretty big," D says softly. "Even for you."

"They're desperate," Miya says, leaning back in the chair.

"Rae was their everything," Zeke says, shaking his head. "You'd be desperate too if it was Han or Kane."

Ebony tenses beside me. Her hand finding mine as she pushes herself closer to my body. There's a light tremble in her limbs.

"I'm okay," I whisper to her, kissing her temple.

"For what it's worth," Isaac starts. "Maybe this time they won't fuck up."

"How can we help?" Han asks with the bottle resting against his bottom lip. "Ren did some fucked up things to you. So, anything to help you get them out of your hair… Name it."

"Even kill them and hide their body?" D asks, leaning closer to Han's ear. He turns and looks at her. Their noses inches apart.

"Maybe," he says softly with a smile.

"What's going on over there," Ebony asks. She sways slightly as she stands to change the song, still keeping her eye on D and Han.

They lean back, a slight blush on their faces as they shake their heads.

Watching her and D communicate via eye contact, I laugh to myself before standing. The liquor rushes through my body making me unsteady, but I manage to grab her, breaking her eye contact with D.

"Leave them alone," I mutter against her temple as she

presses play on a song and turns up the volume.

"Thank you, Kane," D says with a soft laugh.

I give D a slight nod before leaning back into Ebony.

"Ready for bed?"

She looks up at me inquisitively. A hint of mischief in her eyes before she looks back at the mass that makes up our sleeping friends. Only D and Han are awake, heads huddled together looking at his phone screen as he talks about something and points it out to her.

"I might let you show me your pleasure chest," I whisper, pulling her up and leading her to my room.

11

Ebony

Moonlight illuminates Kane's room with a white-blue film, highlighting the firm muscles in Kane's tanned back, while the rest of his body is silhouetted in darkness. His body, his heat hovers over mine. Sweat glistens on his back, forehead, and arms as soft moans fill the room. My hands slip against his slick skin as I grip him.

His rough breaths tickle my ear as he leans closer to it, placing a soft kiss on the shell as he suppresses a moan. Tremors threaten to take over as the sensation of his body on mine, his lips to my ear, and the pleasurable sounds he makes send heat through me. A sensation that goes straight down my body, straight to where ours are currently connected.

I am filled with him, stretching to the brim as he works his hips slowly into mine. Torturing me and promising an immense amount of pleasure as I feel it building up from the friction.

A thick hand covers my mouth, keeping my moans muffled, sounds reserved for only him. His free hand rubs down the left side of my body before holding the back of my knee, pinning my leg close to my chest with the crook of his arm. His hips roll effectively pushing himself deeper inside me.

A moan escapes my mouth as he grinds into me, his thrusts still slow and passionate. Moving his hand, he uses his tongue to trace my bottom lip. His teeth grab my lower lip as he gives it a gentle tug, then sucks on it. Releasing it with a soft pop, my lips tingle until I brush them across his shoulder.

His thrusts get rougher, deeper, pulling more moans from my body. My nails drag down his back as his palm covers my mouth again.

"You gotta be quiet, baby," he chuckles softly in my ear. His voice is low and rumbly. Warm breath tickling my exposed skin as he looks into my eyes.

"Kane," I gasp. I lose my thoughts when he lifts my other leg and buries himself even deeper. The sound of our wet skin connecting, mixing in with our moans. "Fuck."

"I know, baby," he whispers against my skin. His voice is soft, soothing even as he lets out a soft, pleasurable moan. "I feel it too."

He dips his head down, his lips kissing my neck before his teeth nip at my skin, then crash on to my lips until my palms pushing against his warm flesh stops him. He gives me a cautious look as he stops and adjusts his position,

"Pleasure chest?" I ask, running my hand up and the ridges of his chest.

He takes a moment to respond, then gives me a soft sigh of resignation. "You brought it here!?" He whisper-shouts.

"No," I giggle.

"Nothing crazy, E or I swear—"

I shush him with a kiss. "I promise."

We switch positions and I slip out of his large bed

and walk across the plush carpet to one of his drawers. I can feel his eyes on me as I open his drawers, finding his dirty magazines. I open it for a second before putting it on the dresser and finding two t-shirts. I hold them up before turning to catch his curious, yet simmering gaze.

"You need these?" I ask as he licks his lips.

"I need you," his voice rumbles deep in his throat.

"Then, beg," I command as I cock an eyebrow and smirk. I reach in the drawer, grabbing two of his silk ties and using my hip to close the drawer.

"You know I don't beg," he says with a chuckle.

"You will," I say, unrolling his ties and placing both over my shoulder before ripping one of his shirts. "Because you're a good fucking boy and you'll do whatever I want."

A soft rumble erupts from his chest as his dick twitches at what I say.

"One of these days," I start as I stalk over to the bed and straddle him.

His warm hands run up my thighs to the curve of my ass as he buries his face in my chest placing kisses. His brown eyes flash up at me from between my breasts. His long, curly lashes shield them slightly.

"One of these days," I repeat, cupping his face and hovering my lips over his. "You'll get on your knees and beg me." I press my lips against his, then pull back, "and you'll enjoy it."

He chuckles, pulling my lips back down to his. A heated, dominating kiss ensuing as his thick hand grips my hip. As he squeezes, I slide my hand up his chest to his neck. I slide my fingers around his thick, muscular throat.

A deep throaty groan vibrates my fingers as they slowly squeeze.

I pull away from his lips, grabbing the ties and securing them to his headboard. His fingertips raise goosebumps on my flesh as I secure the ties, then reach for his wrist.

He relaxes at my touch. His eyes fixate on my face as I wrap the smooth material around his wrist and pull it tight. I do the same with his other wrist.

"Do your hands tingle?" I ask, leaning back from his flushed face.

"My dick does," he states, pushing his hips up.

"Good," I say with a smile as I wrap a piece of torn shirt around his eyes.

"Nothing crazy, E," he warns with a hint of hesitation in his voice.

I don't say anything as I ease off of his large, muscular frame, which is stretched out across his massive bed. If I knew he didn't have an ego the size of the sun, I'd tell him how God-like he looks.

Navigating to the dresser, I grab a candle, then rummage through his knick-knack drawer retrieving a lighter. Clicking the button of the lighter, the flame ignites the wick.

"E," he calls out. "Baby... the hell are you doing?"

I walk back over to the bed, keeping a firm grip on the candle jar and climbing over him.

"Remember that candle I got you for Christmas?" I ask.

"If you burn me with a candle—"

Blue wax trickles from the jar down to his tanned skin. A hiss passes his lips until my hand rubs in the blue substance. His chest glistens.

"Fuck," he groans low in his chest as my finger grazes his nipple.

I pour more on him as he withers beneath me, distracting him just enough to slide him inside me, making his breathing hitch.

A soft groan passes his lips once I begin to slowly lift my hips. I bring them back down until soft groans rumble out of his chest. He clenches and unclenches his fist as he attempts to break free.

Cautiously, I place the still lit candle on the night stand, my hips rising with the action making Kane lift his hips until I'm sliding back down.

"You look so good beneath me like this," I moan as my hands caress. I pinch my nipples gently, then rub the pad of my thumb on the peak of my buds.

"Let me see," he groans. "I want to watch you use me."

Soft moans are pouring from my mouth as the connection between us blossoms.

"E, please," he damn near whines, making my body tense pleasurably around his. A soft whimper escapes him as I tease him with my movements.

I slowly pull the tattered fabric from his heated eyes and find myself losing control.

My hands brace his chest as I ride him hard. My body rises and falls on his rapidly.

"Fucking use me, E," he growls. "Yes, baby. Just like that. Use this dick like you fucking crave it."

A soft whimper falls past my lips as I lean closer to his body and moan as I cum.

"Such a fucking good girl," he groans, rolling his hips as my body shudders.

I remove him from my body, slip him deep in my mouth and trace the veins and lines of his dick with my tongue before taking him deep in my mouth.

He doesn't last long after that, spilling himself into my mouth as he clenches his jaw suppressing his intoxicating groan.

Satisfied, I untie him and rub his wrist before he pulls me to him, allowing my eyes to roam over his face.

"It was the pegging story wasn't it? Got you all hot and bothered?" I ask, laughing at the incredulous look he sends me.

"I swear to God, Ebony," he groans, putting his hand over his face stifling a laugh.

"It's okay to explore your kinks with me," I rub my hands down his sweaty abs, then around his back and down. He grips my wrist, glaring at me playfully. I laugh, pulling my wrist from his hand, wiggling my body under his cover, then resting one bare leg on top. His calloused hand rubs my leg, pulling it over his waist.

"What are you thinking?" he asks softly. He idly rubs my arm as his eyes search my face. Concern front and center as our eyes connect.

"How to keep you from getting kicked out of school with me," I say softly with a sigh.

"I'll probably get kicked out no matter what you do," he responds looking up at his ceiling.

"For what?" I push myself up slightly, looking down at him.

"I have to volunteer somewhere, but I haven't even looked. This season has been crazy."

I chew on my lip then nudge him. "I know the owner of the shelter I volunteer at. He's been needing an extra hand for the bigger dogs. I can talk to him for you."

"You want to work with me?"

"I won't be there as much, but I work in the front. You'll be in the back helping with vaccines and getting them checked in probably. No Koi fish involved." I smile at him playfully as he rolls his eyes and snorts.

"It was the golf cart in the pond that killed them," he says softly. He looks at me and sighs. "Couldn't hurt. And I get to check out that sexy ass girl that works at the front desk? I'm in."

"You're so lame," I laugh.

"You like it."

"Fucking love it," I confirm, burying my face into his neck.

12

Kane

Ebony sleeps curled up beside me. My eyes examine her naked body as I survey bruises that didn't come from her fight with Ren. She didn't tell me the full story of what happened in our apartment, but this past week, she's been wanting us to crash at my place with Zeke. Even after cleaning and rearranging hers.

I don't blame her. Not when she told me they showed up. Not with the condition of her apartment. Or how skittish her and Silver have been since. Neither one liking sudden movement, but looking so damn guilty when they realize it's just me or one of our friends.

Tonight is the first night she isn't so jumpy, but I think the alcohol and good company helped her compartmentalize everything better.

I look at the bruising on her neck and sigh, rubbing my hands over my face, then staring up at the ceiling.

"I'm used to it," she mutters beside me as she stretches. She pulls herself close to me afterwards, placing a kiss on my neck.

"Was it your dad?" I whisper, kissing her forehead.

She shakes her head. "Believe it or not, he's never put his hands on me. I think if he had better friends, he'd be an amazing dad.”

“Those times you didn't show up to class last year and the year before. Did this happen then?”

“You remember when I didn't show up to class?” She laughs, looking up into my face.

“Not just a pretty face,” I say with a soft laugh. “But yeah. I do.”

She laughs, rubbing her hand down my chest. “Not every time,” she whispers.

Silver's bell jingles as he scratches at the foot of my bed. His soft paw touches my foot as he shifts, then climbs onto my chest purring. I run my free hand down his back.

“Don't do anything,” Ebony says as she runs her hand down Silver's back as I scratch his ear.

“I can't make that promise,” I say, shifting my position slightly. “You're covered in bruises, E.”

“I only have a few,” she feebly argues. “I'll take everything to court eventually, but I can only do that if you stay back.”

Her fingers nudge my face towards her. I spend a few moments staring into her pleading brown eyes and huff.

“You win,” I say, kissing her. “But they come at you again, and I make no promises.”

She stares at me for a moment, then wiggles out of my grip and grabs her computer. Silver and I stare at her as she sits at the foot of the bed, body illuminated by her computer's backlight and the rising sun.

“Taking a picture would probably keep you from staring like a creep,” she mutters with a ghost of a smirk on her face.

I take her challenge, grabbing my cell phone, selecting my camera and snapping a few pictures of her.

"You're right," I say looking at my phone screen. "It's like a little masterpiece."

"You're so fucking weird," she groans, trying not to giggle.

"I was thinking," I start, putting my phone back on the nightstand.

"You think?" she jokes.

"Asshole," I mutter with a slight laugh. "We should probably look into Rae. Find his computer or something. You're going to want the full story for you and Miya's case study."

Ebony pauses, fingers hovering over the keys as she slowly turns towards me. I raise an eyebrow as I stroke Silver's fur.

"You think he kept a record?"

"From what I remember of him, guy loved to archive stuff. He was going to be an anthro-something. Was obsessed with found documents and journals."

"Okay," she says slowly, moving her computer. "That was three years ago though… we'd have to ask Ren for it."

"From what they told me, their parents didn't keep his stuff. Could be at their grandparents' storage unit or something."

"You think they'd let us check?"

"Depends on what we bring to the table," I sigh. "It's worth a shot."

"Okay, so, we get the autopsy reports and then ask for anything else that connects him to the school."

"This sounds like we're doing a lot more than getting autopsy reports. Are you sure you want to work with Ren on this?"

She stares at me, her thumbnail clicking under her gnawing teeth. I reach for her, pulling her hand gently from her mouth and she winces. My thumb gently brushes down her sensitive flesh, feeling the welts and the swelling.

"If that's what it takes," she mutters, leaning her head down to kiss my fingers.

"I'm meeting up with my dad around the same time you're meeting with Gramps." I pull her to my chest, then ghost my fingers across her chilled skin.

"You make it sound bad," she says, lifting her head to look at me.

"He was acting weird when we grabbed the servers. Something's up."

She hums, laying her head back down and traces shapes across my chest, then follows the lines of my tattoo.

"What do you think it is?" she asks after a few moments of weighted silence.

"Not entirely sure, but he asked about the time I got kicked out of chemistry," I say softly. She tenses and pushes herself up to give me a closer look.

"Why?"

Mulling over my thoughts, the lights turn out with a soft click before I gather a growling Silver. As I place him on the floor, Ebony shifts and my eyes move to hers. Tension makes her body rigid, her eyes guarded.

"I was just messing around. I can't really remember, but Dr. Sumner didn't keep anything. I watched him dispose of it," I explain.

She releases a tense breath as she looks me over. Possibly gauging whether she should trust what I'm saying or not. I can't promise her that I didn't hurt her. I didn't really know her back then to promise her I wouldn't have done something dumb, but I do know that I wouldn't drug anyone.

"I didn't think you liked chemistry," she comments as her shoulders relax a bit.

"I don't. I was told that if I helped with something, then I'd get an automatic pass in chemistry with a few extra credits," I shrug, then pull her into my lap. The need to hold her overwhelms me. She lays her head back against my shoulder, interlacing our fingers in the process.

"Say something," I whisper against her temple.

"I don't know what to say," she says softly. "Not exactly."

Her head shifts as she turns to gaze at me.

"I don't blame you for not trusting me," I offer, rubbing my thumb against the smooth skin on the back of her hand.

"I don't even trust myself, Kane. That's the issue."

"Listen," I say firmly, adjusting our position so she's looking at me better. "We made it this far because of you. You've led us here. Don't let what they made you believe back then change what you know now."

She puts her response into the kiss she initiates, then deepens by pulling me towards her. Releasing my need to control, to soothe her, I let her lead us beneath my covers where she places my hands on every part of her body that distracts her from the tornado that's brewing in her head.

13

Ebony

It takes me a few minutes getting out of Kane's apartment this morning to head out to meet my gramps, but despite the coding progress, or lack of progress I should say, I make it right on time and leave Kane to work out any kinks we managed to find.

My gramps has been a father figure for me since my maternal grandmother left me on my father's doorstep. He was the first person I met when I was almost two years old. My father couldn't handle me for even a day. So, he rushed me over to Gramps, my old Sailor Moon backpack stuffed to the brim like my maternal grandmother left it. My gramps and grams took me in with little hesitation.

I barely remember the urgency in my father's voice as he begged my gramps to take me after explaining who I was. When my grams entered the room, she took my hand, looked between my father and Gramps, then ushered me into the kitchen.

Warm, gooey chocolate chip cookies sat on the counter cooling. She offered me one with a glass of milk. Being young, I took it, then she asked if I'd liked to watch Sailor Moon. She humored me that day, and the days following until my gramps finally warmed up to showing me affection. She watched my favorite shows with me, colored vibrant pictures, taught me how to play guitar, and even tucked me in at night.

When I turned seven, I asked them where my parents were and when I would see them again. They quickly changed the subject, but as I continued to get older, and my parents' distance stretched on longer, I asked questions more frequently. By then, my father had made his bid for Governor and his inadequate parenting skills were being plastered across every screen.

I guess the ridicule was too much for him because he came to take me to live with him, which neither of my grandparents agreed with. He promised them I'd be back after a few interviews, but I wasn't. After he got his position, he told me I'd have a good life if I did as I was told and that my grandparents will come to visit on holidays.

My father and his wife detested my incessant talking, which left me with my grandparents every summer until I turned thirteen. Until they discovered how valuable I was for connections. Then, the visits with my grandparents stopped.

When my grams got sick, I begged to visit her, but my father said no. That she would be fine and I had more important things to focus on. She died a week later. He wouldn't even let me go to her funeral, only making it easier for me to spiral with Vin.

And spiral was exactly what I did. When I graduated from my boarding school, I sought out to find my gramps after receiving letters my parents told the school to destroy. My counselor, the angel that she and her team were at that time, held on to them and gave them to me on my 18th birthday.

I met with my grandfather at the park near his house and immediately broke down in his arms. The place I felt safe, loved. Then, we caught up over gelato. Later that year, I moved in with him and Clint where he'd listen to us play our guitars for hours as he rocked in his chair on the porch. His eyes closed, face tilted towards the sky until we were done. Then he'd smile up at the clouds, then down at us.

Because I was going to Knight University, which wasn't far from my gramp's bar, he helped me get my bartending licenses and let me serve drinks with Clint. We fell in sync in our own little world, the three of us. My parents had long forgotten their need for me. Clint's parents did not want to come around because they'd see me. The bastard child of their sibling. I didn't mind. Not when the two of them loved me, imperfections and all.

Slowing my hastened steps, I giddily push through the large glass doors to the coffee shop. A large smile on my face as the aroma of fresh breads, pastries, and coffee surround me. I look around the busy shop, immediately spotting my gramps at a table towards the middle. A light gray henley shirt tucked into neatly pressed khakis. A pair of restaurant style shoes on his feet. I approach him with a widening smile, wrapping my arms around his body and inhaling his familiar minty scent of aftershave.

"If it isn't my baby girl," he says through his grin. His teeth are a slight yellow from years of smoking cigars and drinking coffee.

He gives me a gentle squeeze before standing and

pulling my chair out for me. He takes a drink of his coffee, adjusting in his seat as he looks at me closely. His wrinkled hand reaches for my face and my shoulders sag as he turns to examine the bruises. He shakes his head, muttering something under his breath.

"You should talk to your father," my gramps says softly.

"Gramps," I sigh, "he had years to love me and he never did."

"I know, I know," he responds with another sigh. "But I still have hope you two can find common ground. I'm getting older, Ebony. I want to know you have someone that's going to look after you. Family that's gonna have your back."

"Denise's and Isaac's families have my back. The Yamadas and the Maríns," I point out.

"Your boyfriend and his friend will not always have your back. What happens if you two break up? They ostracize him like our family did you?"

I scratch at my head exhaling a sharp breath. Leaning back in my chair, I avoid my grandfather's gaze as I look out at the muggy, gray sky. Watching as people rush into buildings as the wind pushes and shoves at them roughly. His rough, wrinkled hand grasps mine gently, catching my attention. I look into his eyes, chewing at my cheek.

"I know he's important to you," he says softly. His thumb rubbing the back of my hand. "And you know like I know, that I'd love to say this is the end all be all for you, but I want you to think beyond the right now. He feels good for you, right now. What happens when he doesn't?"

I shrug my shoulders and sniffle. I never thought

beyond any moment with Kane. My life with anyone has never been constructed beyond immediate instances. Maybe it's the anxiety? Maybe it's the fact that I want to enjoy the 'right nows' because the 'laters' never felt good. Predicting the future is something I don't want to do, not when it comes to the people I care about. Thinking long term is what made me put up with shit I had no business in. Vin and Eva being picture perfect examples of that. They were from a time where thinking laters and forevers were important to me.

"I don't mean to discourage you. I just want you to be safe," my gramps says.

"Dad told you his theory?" I ask, looking at my gramps. Letting my eyes stare deeply into his. "His family isn't a part of the mafia."

My gramps chuckles, then leans back in his chair. His arms cross over his chest. "Ebony, does he even work?"

I shake my head slowly, then open my mouth to protest. He holds his hand up to stop me.

"What's he got planned for the future? There isn't much about him or his family online. I had Clint check." He scratches his brow, then his thick hand rubs over his mouth. "I don't want to see you in another Vin situation," he confesses.

"Kane's not like Vin, Gramps," I say looking him over. "I think that's what's driving Dad closer so you can convince me to leave him."

"I trust your decisions, even if I don't like them," Gramps says after a moment, squeezing my hand with a sigh. His face lights up with a warm smile. "I hear you broke that Vin guy's nose?"

"Just like you taught me," I say with a smile.

"That's my girl. Your Grams would be proud," he says with a soft chuckle. Sadness flashes across his eyes, then he looks at me. "You look a lot like her when she was younger."

He shuffles in his wallet, then pulls out a picture I've seen a hundred times of him and my grams. Both young and vibrant. The colors have faded some, but I can see the similarities in her and myself. Our noses, our foreheads, the way our faces shift when we smile.

I touch the picture softly, then smile. "I miss her too," I sigh.

He pulls out another picture and slides it over to me. A young woman, no more than sixteen smiles, her arms wrapped around my father's torso. The age difference is glaringly obvious. I've seen pictures of my father young, but this one is new.

"Who's that?"

"Your mother," he says softly. "Do you know how they met?"

I shake my head, grabbing the picture and looking up at him.

He taps the table, then smiles. "It's time that you hear her story," he says, grabbing one of my hands.

14

Ebony

My keys clatter in my hands as I unlock the door to my apartment, which Kane had to convince me to come back to. Shivering against the bitter cold wind, I give the painted sunset sky one last look then quickly push my way inside. Warmth envelopes me as I step inside as Silver meows at my feet, brushing his fur against one of my soggy pant legs. I reach down and scratch behind his ear before a loud clang in the kitchen scares him off.

"Kane?" I call out, peeling out of my jacket and hanging it on the coat rack and toeing off my shoes. Positioning my keys between my fingers, I slowly make my way to the kitchen watching Kane move around the space prepping something over the stove. "Hey."

He turns his head and smiles at me. "Welcome back. How'd time with Gramps go?"

Setting my keys down, I lean against the cluttered counter. "It was good. He was talking to me about my parents… and you," I answer softly, watching his face cautiously. He turns the knob for the stove then walks over to me. His warm lips pressing against my forehead before he kisses my lips.

"Good things?"

"Oh, you know. Just concerned that you're bad for me," I say with a smile.

"The worst," he jokes, wiggling his eyebrows and laughing with me.

"What are you making?" I ask, walking up behind him. I wrap my arms around his middle and place a small kiss on his back. His rough hands slide over mine, then lace our fingers.

"It's supposed to be chili," he responds with a laugh. His back vibrates with the action.

"Supposed to be?" I peek into the pot. "Looks like chili."

"Let's hope it tastes like chili," he says skeptically. "It'll be done in five minutes."

I squeeze him in my arms before letting him go and heading to our bedroom. Quickly changing, I grab my laptop and sit at the table staring at the screen in front of me.

"I was thinking," I finally say, logging into my computer. "We should set up another backdoor virus."

"I'm listening," he says, putting steaming bowls in front of me, then taking a seat beside me.

"I've heard some people can upload a virus on a flash drive," I start looking over at him as he nods his head slowly.

"I've heard of it. Never really did it though," he confirms.

"I have," I say with a grin.

"And I thought I was the computer genius," he comments, smiling back at me. "If you didn't already have my heart, you would have won it just then."

I roll my eyes, then focus on the screen. "We'll probably

need one to access files from each department. Maybe the virus itself can override some systems and get us whatever documents we need."

"And you didn't do this before because…?"

"Playing it safe," I mumble, opening up a few programs before looking at him. "I don't know what I can do with all this, but it's worth having. You showed me a few tricks I needed to make sure I did it right."

My fingers type in a few codes and I reach in my bag, retrieving the sealed flash drive package. I rip the packaging open then push the drive into one of my ports and move the code over to the device.

"When are you planting it?" he asks, taking a big bite of his chili watching me closely.

"I'm not going to," I say, smiling at him sweetly.

Pausing mid chew, he stares at me. His jaw is packed with food as he leans back in the chair, his hands brace either side of the table.

"Please?" I ask, turning to face him with my best puppy dog eyes.

He swallows his food then leans closer to me. His eyes search mine as he attempts to conceal his smile.

"You have a meeting with him tomorrow," I offer. "Plus he'd expect me to do it."

"You've done this to his computer before?"

"As a prank," I answer honestly with a shrug. "He didn't know it was me per se, but he has his suspicions."

Kane laughs, shaking his head in disbelief.

"Fine," he finally says. "My parents are going with me so I can get my dad to do it."

"Afraid Dr. Summer won't trust you?"

"Guy never trusted me," Kane laughs, eating more of his food.

A moment passes as we eat in comfortable silence. Aside from the occasional ringing from Silver's bell as he plays with one of his toys. A soft dinging sound catches my attention and I check my email.

"Damn," I groan, clicking on my keyboard and expanding an email.

"What's up?"

"They trashed the code," I mutter, spinning my computer towards him. "Even the data from the wrist bands is garbled."

Kane leans forward, looking over the lines rapidly. He sighs, scratching at the dusting of stubble at his chin then leans forward. "I can probably fix this, but it's going to take time."

"Fuck," I groan pushing myself out of my seat to pace the floor. "We worked so fucking hard on this! And Dr. Goodwin emailed about testing the bands with the data."

"Hey, Hey," he turns in his seat. "We can get this fixed. I think I saved the code somewhere."

I continue pacing, my hands on top of my head as I focus on controlling my panicked breathing.

"E?" He calls out to me before grabbing me and pulling me towards him. Large hands frame my face as he looks into my eyes. "I'll call my dad if I need to so this can be ready for any updates you and Miya need to do. Okay?"

I nod with a sigh. "Okay," I affirm with a deep breath and an idle nod. With a gentle kiss on my forehead, he stands, quickly pressing his father's contact information.

Collapsing into the chair, my fingers strum against the beaten wood beneath them. My mind is frenzied as I stare at the broken code on my screen and the to do list that glares back at me from the corner of my computer screen.

15

Kane

Howling from the wind greets me as I take long strides up from the walkway. There's a buzz in the bar when I walk in to meet my dad. I spot him at one of the small tables by a window that's normally closed at night. A dim light dangles over the center of the table. I approach quickly and smile at him.

"You weren't waiting long were you?" I ask, sliding in the seat across from him.

"Not too long," he offers, squeezing my hand. He looks me over with tired eyes before leaning back in his seat. "How's everything been?"

"Okay, I guess," I start then lean in a little closer so I can speak more discreetly. I may be in Ebony's gramps' bar, but I know he can't control which one of the mayor's lackeys steps foot in this place. There's just that many. "Mayor Cross, Ebony's dad, and their wives stopped by her apartment that night."

My dad's eyes shift towards the window. His jaw ticks as he mulls over a few thoughts, then leans towards the table. "How bad did they hurt her?"

"Scared her and Silver," I confess. I wrap my knuckles on the wooden table, then glance out the window, gnawing

91

at my inner cheek. "She's still pretty shaken up about it. Said they threatened her gramps and pretty much everyone in her life."

"Threats are threats," he says with a wave of his hand, but the seriousness still lingers on his face. "You're there with her. I know she's safe because you know how to handle any mishap."

I nod, looking at my father again. "They only show up when I'm not around."

"If you want her to have protection," he starts cautiously. "Say the word."

Miya and I may have told Ebony and our friends that our family isn't a part of the mafia, which is true, but the underground organization is just as violent. At least it was starting to get that way around the time my father separated us from them. And even with whatever he did, we still weren't completely removed. Once we're in, we're in for life.

The underground organization started out like V for Vendetta. Fighting unfair laws back in the 60's and kept out of sight until really necessary. They made strides exposing corrupt governments until those in office infiltrated some of the headquarters. Things turned violent quickly and once my dad caught wind, he worked his ass off to remove us as much as he could.

Most of the people associated with the organization are new members who have no idea about the old blood, or members like my dad. He and his comrades stayed removed, but could step in at any time. With Rae's death, and a few other suspicious ones that Miya and Ebony have documented, I'm sure my dad is ready to become an active member just to keep us safe.

"I won't need it," I say confidently. "For the most part, she's with our friends and she's been going to really public places."

"Don't do anything irrational," my father warns with stern eyes. I nod, letting him know that I understand that I'm to be on my best behavior.

He sits quietly across from me as he stares out the window, his jaw still ticks as he processes or plans. I can never really be sure in serious situations.

I catch a glimpse of Ebony's gramps behind the bar next to Clint. From what I've heard, Gramps is a man of few words, fewer than my father and, as of now, Ebony's father.

"By the way," my father says slowly, capturing my attention. "That flash drive was a great idea."

"He took it?" I ask, feeling the weight lifting from my shoulders slightly.

"Without batting an eye. Even shared with us his opinion on you and Ebony."

I roll my eyes, folding my arms over my chest. My father chuckles.

"Your mother suggested that we invite Ebony to dinner. Figure out if there's something more we can do to support her."

I sit silent for a moment, then tap the table. "She met with Ren."

My father's eyebrows raise up as he studies my face. "Doesn't look like you had to break up another fight," he says through a small smile.

I laugh, nodding. "They wanted to meet with Ebony to ask for her help with getting Rae's records."

"What would they need those for?"

"They're obsessing over his case again, don't think it's an OD and want to prove he wasn't an addict," I state with a small shrug.

"They think someone gave it to him?" my father asks. His eyebrows stitch together as his fingers tap against the table. "I wonder…" his voice trails off as he taps his finger against his lips, then scoots in his seat.

"Wonder?" I ask him after a few minutes of silence.

"Rae apparently got himself into a little trouble around the time you and Zeke did," he starts. Tension rolls over my shoulders making them tight. He glances towards the bar, catching sight of a waiter with bright blue hair and several nose piercings. Two large baskets of burgers and fries are placed in front of us.

"Courtesy of Oscar Young," the waiter's pitchy voice says as he nods towards the older man. I follow where he gestures, sending Gramps a grateful wave. My father does the same. "Let me know if you need anything else," the waiter says, then rushes back towards the kitchen.

"He's a nice man," my father says, grabbing a fry and taking a bite. "He told me that he and his late wife have been here for generations."

I sit quietly, mulling over this detail. Ebony mentioned that her family has deep roots here, but I didn't know how deep. I catch my father's eyes as he stares at me, searching closely. I see the disappointment on his face before he has a chance to vocalize it.

"He's always behind the scenes," I defend before he lectures me.

"You live with her," my father says, shaking his head disapprovingly. "I've always taught you and your brother to get to know your partner's family once you know it's serious."

"I know," I sigh. "This year has been a lot." I look down at the food in front of me. Steam rises up to greet me as I let the aroma of the food settle in my nose.

My father grunts his response, rolling up his sleeves and taking a big bite. His brow furrows before his eyelids flutter closed. "This is good," he finally says after a few more large bites.

I take a bite, reveling in the smooth, tangy taste of ketchup and mustard. I've never ordered from the menu beyond the standard wings and fries. But this, this is my new favorite. I take a few more bites of my food, trying to savor every bite, but devouring it like I'm starving.

"I did some digging," my father starts after taking a sip of his drink. "Rae was signing off on your hours in the chemistry lab when you and Zeke got kicked out."

I pause, letting the burger dangle in my hand a bit before I set it down. "I don't remember that," I mutter.

"I don't know what he had you in the lab with him for, but shortly after you were kicked from the project, Rae winds up overdosing."

"Do you think…?" I pause, not wanting to say too much in this public space.

He shrugs his shoulders, but I can tell he's thinking the same.

"I'll do what I can," my father offers. "Just be careful."

I nod, wiping my hands in my soggy napkin. My father glances out the window as he nibbles at a fry.

"Gentlemen," a gruff voice greets us.

"Mr. Young," my father says with a wide smile. He extends a hand and stands.

"Call me Oscar," Ebony's gramps says, taking my dad's hand firmly, giving him a shake. I stand quickly, doing the same and smiling at him.

"Would you like to join us?" I ask, hearing the nervousness in my voice. Normally, I wouldn't be nervous, but this is Ebony's gramps. Making a good impression, which clearly I haven't been, is important.

"Just wanted to make sure ya'll were enjoying the food," her gramps says.

"Best burger I've had in a while," my dad says.

Gramps looks over his shoulder, then back between my father and I before sitting. He glances at me for a moment.

"That drone ya'll made was impressive," he says with an affectionate smile on his face as he looks out the window.

"Thank you," I say with a smile. "All Ebony's ideas. I'm ashamed to admit I wanted to do something easier."

He snorts. "She's strong willed," he comments, casting me an apologetic look.

"That's my favorite part about her," I say idly. I catch a flicker of appreciation through Gramps' eyes as he tries to hide his smile.

"She gets it from her Grams," he offers with a nod. He sucks in a deep breath, pinning me with his steely gray eyes. "So, tell me, Kane."

I shift awkwardly in my seat.

"What makes you tick?" he finishes, leaning closer to me. I glance at my father, a smug look on his face as he laces his fingers together and rests his chin on top. He gives me a brief nod of encouragement and I clear my throat.

Better now than never right?

16

Ebony

Taking advantage of the bright sunlight, I sit in the lobby of one of the academic buildings. I examine the alert Kane and I got the night I fought Ren. My pen scratches against the paper as I write notes.

"Eb," Vin's voice drawls out slowly.

The chair across from me scrapes against the ground. He huffs as he sits down, the thick fragrance of body spray assaulting my nose. I flinch slightly, closing my notebook and pushing away from the table to get some space from his overbearing smell. I take my time, putting my things in my bookbag, but when I look up, I freeze. Bruises cover his face, his lip is swollen and split. A small knot on his forehead right above a split in his eyebrow, which is held together with butterfly style bandages. The normal antagonistic look he has is gone. His shoulders slouch slightly as he leans close to me, his eyes haunted, tortured even. He places his hands on the table in front of him. Our eyes meet before he glances around.

"Did he do that?"

"What do you think?" he grumbles, ducking his head away from prying eyes. "You gotta fall back."

"Fall back?"

"Playing that Sherlock Holmes shit. Just stop," he says evenly looking at me. "Please." His plea is softer than his initial tone.

"I'm not stopping this time, Vin," I say firmly. "But you— you can help me."

He laughs suddenly, then winces as his lip splits. With a head shake he leans back in his chair. Eyes glancing around the space before he looks back at me.

"You're still as hopeful as ever," he says mostly to himself. "I used to admire that about you. Always seeing the fucking rainbow despite the clouds."

"Vin," I say firmly. "We used to be friends."

"Used to be. Until you rebelling had me getting my ass beat."

"And your actions had my face plastered over every newspaper that your dad could think of," I snap back.

"Let me see… getting my ass beat or having my reputation ruined?"

"Physical scars heal."

"Your reputation can be rebuilt," he hisses, leaning towards me. His fingers clenched around the edge of the metal table between us.

"They hurt me too, Vin," I spit back, glaring at him. "Don't forget that."

He sucks his teeth with another head shake. He crosses his arms over his chest and stares out into the courtyard just beyond the window.

"I'm being serious," I say, trying again. "We can make them pay for the shit they did."

His eyes snap to mine. He searches my face, then my

eyes before looking around again. Popping knuckles greet my ears as he presses his thumb into each digit releasing the tension.

"What about what I did? You're just gonna forget that?"

"You know that I won't, but getting you away from your dad just means you get the help you need so no one else has to go through it."

"No one else is going through it, Eb," he shouts. "Just me. My face is his fucking punching bag because you still can't fall in line."

"Why should I!? They fucking used me!"

He stalls, his mouth opening and closing as he searches for his next words. A huff passes his lips as he leans back in the chair more. Shifting his body lower as his knee knocks into mine. I move my legs, watching his movements.

"Drop the issue," he says more firmly. "Or shit's going to get worse for the both of us."

"Threatening me?"

"Take it how you want it."

"You know, Vin," I start, shoving the remainder of my supplies in my bag. "Part of me always thought you'd find a way out of our parents' sick, twisted lives." His eyes snap up to mine as I fiercely zip my bag. "But honestly, I guess you sold your soul to the highest fucking bidder."

"You would too if you had nothing waiting for you out there. He can ruin my entire life."

"So you ruin mine? Your addiction got passed off on me! There was nothing I could say while the fucking golden child detoxed in the basement until the fucking shakes and shits stopped. Even now, you're high as fuck and you'd still try to find a way to blame me."

"Oh boo-fucking-hoo. Always the damn victim. It's getting old."

I laugh, catching him off guard.

"You actually think you're the villain?" I laugh again. "Such a sad, pathetic, little, lost boy. You're just a fucking pawn."

"Like you are for the people you call friends? They'll never fucking understand you, Ebony. They'd never give a fuck about you if they really knew you. But I do. I know who the fuck you are."

I feign shock, then laugh. "I have nothing to hide. I walk with my skeletons, Vin. Someone has to own up to being fucked up."

"You want a gold star?"

"No," I sneer, pushing the chair in. "I want their fucking heads and if you go down in the process, so be it."

He opens his mouth to say something back, but I turn on my heels and walk through the door quickly. The cold wind pricks at my skin as it rushes past me. I duck my head into my jacket and walk faster with no real destination in mind.

"Ebony?" A voice calls behind me, making me tense and turn slowly. Dr. Goodwin rushes up behind me. A small smile on her face as she greets me. "I thought that was you. Everything okay?"

"Yes," I say with a soft chuckle. "It's just cold. How are you?"

"Good," she answers with a laugh. "I looked for you after your performance. You were incredible."

"Oh," I laugh, shifting my bag, then shoving my hands deep in my jacket pockets. "Thank you."

"Honestly, the entire week was incredible. I shouldn't be surprised, but still. You worked so hard. I bet your parents are proud."

Blood rushes straight to my ears as I remember the incident in my apartment. My wrist throbs where the bruising settles, but I give Dr. Goodwin a fake laugh and a nod.

"That's one way to put it," I offer.

"I saw that you and Kane signed up for my class next semester. I'm excited to see what you both create," she says. "That drone was so beautifully built. The programming… honestly I don't know what I can teach you two that you haven't discovered on your own."

An awkward laugh bubbles out of me while I toe at the clump of snow by my boot, avoiding her eyes only for a moment.

"I have a question," I start as a beep interrupts me and startles us both. Dr. Goodwin startles slightly before laughing to herself as she pulls out her cell phone.

"Shoot. Meetings. We'll talk later?" she offers with another wide smile. I give her a quick nod before she turns heading back inside.

17

Ren

The fan of my old computer groans as I open another tab. I type in someone's credentials and I'm immediately met with an access denied screen. Slamming my hands on the desk, I push myself away and pace my room. Stepping over piles of dirty, rumpled clothes in the process.

"Reneva?" my mother peers into the room. Her eyes warm, but alert as she pushes through my door and examines my face. "What's wrong?"

"Nothing," I mutter, dropping my head from her gaze.

"Baby," she coos.

A thin hand touches my chin and gently pushes it up. I meet her eyes. Bags rest underneath them as time and grief sucks the youthful beauty from her face. I reach up, brushing my fingers across her face before pulling myself into her arms, hugging her close. My nose is consumed with her light linen fragrance as I bury my face in her chest like I did as a kid.

"I feel like I failed Rae," I mutter. Her hand rubs my back as I fight back the tears that consume me.

"Baby, there was nothing any of us could do. Rae… was sick," my mother says softly. Her voice thickens with her words as she pulls me closer.

"He wasn't sick, Mama. Someone killed him," I fuss, pulling back to look at her. Hoping that my eyes relay my conviction.

"He was. He was troubled and no one could save him but himself. His death was bound to happen."

"Please just listen. There was a girl on campus and had almost the same thing happen—"

"A girl? Reneva…"

"Mom, just listen. This girl, she has files and records and—"

"Ren, baby…" My mother sighs, scratching at her head. Frustration morphing her beautiful face. "Your brother chose to take the drugs that he did. Regardless of what some girl says to you."

"Rae and the girl from last semester—"

My mother laughs, shaking her head. "I should have known," she mutters under her breath. She looks at me, eyes low and filled with anger. "The girl you had a crush on? The one that got you kicked out of school?"

I snap my mouth shut and look down at my lap. I wasn't honest when I explained what happened to my parents. I told them that some girl lied on me, said things like I slipped her pills.

"Yes," I choke out, looking at her finally.

"Is that why you came back bruised?"

"That's not the point, Mom. The point is that Rae wasn't an addict."

"Reneva," my mother's rich Hindi accent comes out when she says my name. An exasperated sigh passes her lips as she gently runs her hands down her face. "Rae was an addict. He may have hid it well, but he was. I know you're hurting. I am too. So is your dad."

I drop the subject, keeping my lips tight as I chew on my cheek. She runs her hands through my hair and kisses my forehead.

"Look, Baba and I think you should go to your cousin's townhome for a bit. It's closer to your school and clearly being here is making you spiral. We just want what's best for you. We can't lose you like we lost—"

I admit defeat, dropping my chin to my chest to avoid my mother's haunted gaze. I give her a subtle nod. "Okay," I say softly before her arms pull me to her chest and she squeezes me tight.

"It's late. You should get some sleep," she comments, kissing my temple.

I nod, giving her a fake smile to satisfy her. It seems to work because she gives me a genuine one back and walks out of my room. Staring at my door, I grab my jacket and shove my arms into the sleeves. I grab my worn down snow boots and shove my feet into them before slipping over the threshold of my window. I brace my body as I grab an old rope anchored to the roof with my climbing equipment and scale my way down the side of the house. Snow crunches beneath my feet as I land.

Grabbing my book bag from the backseat of my car, I sling it over my shoulders and walk down the street, enjoying the cold air. I pull my cell from my pocket and press the receiver to my ear after selecting a contact. The trilling in my ear is muffled by the sound of the wind. I shove my hat down farther and throw on my hood hoping to block out the sound. Twinkling Christmas lights dance across the house across the street as an animatronic Santa lifts and drops on the roof with his brightly lit reindeer.

"This better be good, Ren," a feminine voice grumbles.

"Mel," I start. "I need your help."

"When don't you?" she grumbles. Movement from the other side of the receiver has me moving my feet. "What is it?"

"I can't stop thinking about Rae," I confess, watching as Santa lifts for the sky, then eases back down, then back up again.

Mel sighs on the other end of the phone. "Where are you?"

"End of my street. I can meet you at the rocketship?"

"Okay," she says after a moment. The jingling of keys adds to the cacophony of sounds on Mel's side of our phone call. "Be there in fifteen."

I hang up, shoving my phone and my freezing fingers in my pocket. Cutting through one of the yards towards the old city playground, I purposefully step in untouched patches of snow. My feet sink into the powdery white ice.

At some point, I count my steps and make it to 137 when I notice that I'm standing on the edge of the old, neglected playground. A rocketship with a blue tip is erected straight in the air. Rust patches decorate the red wings and yellow body. I walk closer to it, craning my neck to admire the body that brings memories from my childhood.

"I hope you didn't call me here to stare at this old hunk

of junk," Mel's voice calls out from behind me.

I laugh softly. "Nah," I say, turning and looking at her.

Thick curls cascade down from underneath her tan beanie. A multicolor pom-pom on the top. Her soft brown skin and hazel eyes are muted underneath the moonlight. The flickering streetlight only highlights a few details like her small nose, one of her round eyes, which has a slit in the eyebrow, and her full lips.

Mel, the quiet girl next door. We met on one of those dating apps during my time on "house arrest" when I got kicked out of school. We'd sneak out to meet up at the rocketship where she'd tell me about the stars and constellations. I'd sit and watch how her face lit up as she told me stories about mythical people. I can see myself falling in love with her. Maybe I already have, but with the weight of guilt for what I've done, I'm afraid I'd lose her as payment for the wrongs I've done.

"What happened?" she asks softly. She tilts her head to the side before grabbing my hand and leading me to the merry-go-round. I sit beside her, leaning my head on her shoulder.

"I saw my ex," I mutter. She stiffens beneath me.

"Are you two… going to get back together?" she asks softly.

I snort, shaking my head. "She's dating my best friend."

"Oh," she breathes. A hint of relief in her voice.

I chew at my cheek before sitting up and turning to face her. Mel's hazel eyes land on me and she smiles softly before she leans in and kisses me gently.

"I have to tell you something about my ex," I say once I

pull away from her. "And… I want you to promise me you won't leave."

Her brows scrunch together as she searches my face for a hint. "Okay," she says slowly.

"Promise me, Mel. Please."

"I promise. What's going on… did you two hook up or something?"

"Gods, no." I shake my head with a grimace. "But…"

"Wait… you guys are broken up, right?"

"Yeah, yeah. We're never getting back together."

"Listening…"

Anxiety, the pesky fucker, gets the best of me and I drop my eyes into my lap. "I'm planning on working with her to get justice for my brother." Guilt is one hell of an emotion, especially when you aren't being honest with yourself. Sure, this is something Mel should know, but again, I don't want to lose her. Not yet.

"You thought I'd leave you because she can help you get justice for your brother?" she asks with a taunting smile. She shakes her head. "You're so delusional."

"People don't like when exes linger," I confess, laughing slightly but still feeling anxious.

"She's dating your best friend. Regardless of her helping you or not, you two are bound to be in the same places. No biggie," she says, nudging me with a smile.

I nod, then interlace our fingers. The bitter cold makes my fingertips red.

"You called me at two in the morning to tell me that?"

"I also wanted to see you," I say, giving her a wide grin. I lean in, kissing each of her cheeks.

"You're a doofus," she giggles. "A cute one."

Unlocking our fingers, I place my hands on either side of her face, kissing her deeply for a few minutes. I pull away, looking at her flush lips and smile.

"So," I start leaning back on the merry-go-round. "What are the stars saying tonight?" I finish as I smile over at her.

18

Ebony

Moth balls have a unique and overwhelming smell. It reminds me of storage units, old antique stores in rundown towns. I never would have imagined Dr. Sumner's office smelling this way, but it does. Dust flutters around the rays of sunlight that peek through the blinds as the sun continues to rise. A few tickle my nose, only making the mothball smell worse.

"I didn't know you knew the Yamadas enough to come into my office to vouch for you, Ms. Young," Dr. Sumner says, folding his hands in front of him and staring at me. The sunlight from outside flashes across his glasses.

"They were interested in the project I'm working on with Miya," I say softly, shifting under his gaze.

"Look, Ebony. You know your father and I go way back," he starts, shifting in his seat. His fingers unfasten the buttons on his suit jacket. "I don't like seeing you take this path you're on."

"What path is that exactly?" I ask him cautiously.

He eyes me with disinterest. He swallows, opens his drawer and sits back.

"We've taken your project off hold," he states, sliding me a file. "I shared this with Miya and her parents, as well as

Dr. Goodwin, that your project was selected to be presented this March at Women Take Tech this year."

"We got invited to a conference in San Francisco?" I ask looking over the document. The invitation naming Miya and me specifically.

"I'm proud of you," he says shifting in his seat. "And I want what's best for you." Only a second passes before I hear him speaking again. "Drop the allegations against the Cross' and stay clear of Kane."

"You saw the documents. You saw the blood tests. You helped Miya and me mimic the compounds," I defend. "You know they weren't lies…"

"Ebony, you can ruin a lot of lives starting back up with that narrative. And Mayor Cross is not going to take it lightly this time. He's already pressuring me to expel you."

My palms sweat as I clench my fingers together in my lap. Sweaty palms are better than shaking hands though. I knew Dr. Sumner had connections to Vin's family, even if I only heard his name in passing. That was until my father introduced us when I got accepted into this school with a full ride scholarship.

"With you and Miya having clearance, I will be stopping by more frequently to check the progress of any new research. Dr. Goodwin will be monitoring you two more closely. We don't want any interference. This looks great for the school, you, and Miya. Please don't mess this up."

"Okay," I say, nodding my head slightly.

"Before I let you go, what happened at your performance at the gala?" he finally asks.

I shrug my shoulders. My eyes lock on Dr. Sumner's as he leans forward watching my facial expressions closely. With the school system back up and running with more firewalls than a normal school should have, I know their search for who "trashed" the gala would be their main goal to appease their top donors.

"I can't explain what happened. All I know is the band and I were performing, then the drone came up with all that stuff."

He hums then looks out the window. "I guess Reneva showing up was just coincidental too?"

I stall, my eyes shifting as confusion fills my brain. No one was around when they were because of the chaos the drone caused. Only reason I know this is because there was more going on around the event facilities than where we were. It was dark and we weren't close.

"They showed up?"

"Don't act surprised," he sighs. "If you know they're behind this whole cyber attack, let us know," he concludes.

"I don't speak to them. I didn't know they showed up. My friends and I left shortly after my performance," I say, adding as much conviction into my words as I can.

He nods looking away from me, then out the window.

"Very well," he finally responds. "Watch the company you keep."

His eyes look into mine. His words are more of a threat than a warning. A chill shoots through me as I watch him closely. No longer sitting in front of me is the cheerful man wanting to see his students succeed. This man in front of me is a threat, he's searching for something and that something feels more unsettling than I felt initially.

"Yes, sir," I respond softly, wanting to escape these close quarters.

"Good," he says, giving me a fake smile. "I hope we don't have to meet again under these circumstances. You really are an amazing student, Ms. Young."

"Thank you," I say, grabbing my bag and slowly walking out of his office. When the door is closed securely behind me, I run out of the building almost colliding with Kane when I reach the outer door.

"Woah, speed racer," he laughs, steadying me. His face falls when he sees mine. "What happened?"

He moves me away from the door, around the corner of the building and studies my face, then stares deep in my eyes.

"He's up to something," I say panting.

"Who? Dr. Sumner? Nah. Dude is trying to scare you."

"Well it worked," I say, shoving my hat over my ears to keep them warm. "Kane, did you or your parents mention that Ren was here?"

He shakes his head. "We just told them we had no idea how the drone got there. Thankfully my brother used a burner account for everything. They couldn't even trace that back to either of us. What did he say, Ebs?"

"He knows they were here. Was there anyone else they could have talked to?"

"Not that I know of. They didn't really text much before showing up. I just know they took the bus up here."

"Well, he knows... Something's not right with him."

Kane sighs, a small cloud puffing from his nose as he

does. He nods his head then kisses my forehead.

"What are you doing over here anyways?"

"Saw your note on the counter. Wanted to come by and snag you when you were done. Thought we could go get coffee. I needed a break from trying to figure the system out."

"Are you asking me on a date?" I ask, smiling up at him.

"Bring yo fine ass, girl," he says with a laugh, throwing his arm over my shoulder.

We trudge through the snow covered campus. Our boots crunching under murky snow heading for the coffee shop on campus. A cold wind whistles through the tree limbs making them crack and rattle against each other.

"Back to this Dr. S thing," Kane says once we arrive at the coffee shop. He holds the door open for me, then follows behind. We linger in line, keeping space from the people in front of us so we can attempt to talk privately. "What would he be involved in?"

"He knows my dad and the Mayor. He's also an admin. He has control over the documents and document requests."

"The neck that turns the head," Kane says looking at the menu.

"I feel like there's more to it than that," I say as we inch towards the counter. "You know Vin can't bring the substances here. His dad doesn't trust him."

"Relapse?" Kane asks, looking down at me.

"It's happened a few times. I think he's been micro-dosing recently. Could explain his temper, but that's not saying much. He's always had one."

"But he had it to give it to Ren," Kane defends. "So,

how'd he get it that time?"

"I need to get Vin to trust me," I say looking at Kane.

He slowly blinks at me. "No," he finally says as we get to the counter.

I roll my eyes as he orders us coffee and breakfast. He takes my hand, gently pulling me to the pick up side. We stand in a secluded corner and he looks at me.

"Vin is a loose fucking canon. All day at practice this past week he's been fucking reckless. He's spiraling. I don't want him to try to hurt you," Kane says, giving me a pointed look before I can protest.

"No," I whisper, shaking my head. "I won't let him get the chance."

"Any chance is a chance to him. He doesn't take 'no' for an answer. 'No' to him means try harder. The football field was example enough," Kane whispers back. His hands find mine and he pulls them to his chest.

"I know, but what other option do we have?"

"We don't," he starts. He looks out the window for a second then back at me. "But we'll find one."

"Kane," I say softly after mulling over what he said, my hands gripping the rough material of his leather coat. I look up at him. "I think I know what happened, but I don't know who did it. That night when I fought Eva, I remembered the *feeling*."

He places his cheek on my head, pulling me closer to him. The muscles of his jaw clenching and unclenching as he steadies his breathing. His heart thumps loudly in his chest.

He grabs my face and looks down at me. "Then let's

cause some chaos."

I snort.

"What's wrong, E? Don't want to wreak a little havoc?" he asks, wiggling his eyebrows.

He releases me to go get our stuff, leaving me to my thoughts. The hidden message in his words — *cause some chaos.* There were only a few unorthodox ways to make them listen and I'm sure he's not opposed to me destroying a few campus buildings to get their ears.

Input Wednesday Addams holding a flickering match meme. hashtag goals.

19

Kane

With Ebony at the bar early to help her Gramps set up, that leaves me time to do some digging for Raeven's autopsy report. I sit at the counter of a diner not far from the bar and place my order as I watch people mill about outside. There's a soft murmur as more people enter, muffling the tinging of the bell that rattles against the door when it slams shut.

"What do I owe the pleasure, lover boy?" Clint's thick, deep voice calls out as he sits next to me.

First step to uncovering the mysterious report was reaching out to Clint. After meeting with Dr. Sumner, I decided now was a better time to do it. He was reluctant at first, but decided that after a few days of dodging me that I was worth a smidgen of his time.

"Just wanted to ask a few questions," I say, offering him a hand. He grabs it, giving me a quick shake then shifts in the stool his large body's in.

"Shoot," he says, pointing out what he wants to a waitress. "Hope you don't mind me eating. If I don't I won't get a chance til later and you know my cousin."

He rolls his eyes to himself before giving me a look. And I do know. She'll fuss until he takes a break and eats. And lately, the bar's been busy making those breaks nonexistent. Not that it stopped her from fussing at him.

"She means well," I offer with a chuckle.

"Just like our grams," he says thoughtfully with a small smile and a nod.

I let the silence complete the semi-awkward exchange before clearing my throat and facing him. I'm not intimidated by him, I just know that I need to handle him with care for multiple reasons. Ebony being the main one. Him and Gramps are the only family that I know she'd kill for. Plus, if I plan on giving her the diamond I bought or anything of that nature, I have to make sure they know she's safe with me.

"You were a medical student right?" I finally ask as the waitress hands us our drinks and gives us a broad smile, a hint of purple from her lipstick staining her teeth.

"For a short time," he acknowledges with a nostalgic nod. "Needed to take some time off to help my gramps at the bar. Not enough bartenders he trusts beside me, Eb, and Isaac."

"What about Liam? I thought he was a bartender?"

"Liam is Liam. He's just there," Clint says, balling up the paper from his straw and rolling it between his fingers. "Gramps doesn't trust him. Says there's something dark about him."

"Why's that?"

"Liam had a crush on some girl back in the day," he says, stretching in his seat. "Got into some trouble behind it, then he set sights on E. It was short lived 'cause I wasn't havin' it. Plus she's my gramps' princess. Can't do wrong for shit."

He laughs looking over at me.

"Liam liked Ebony?"

"Liam likes every woman that smiles at him," he answers with a laugh. "He's just a guy looking for his people, like Ebs and I. The outcasts."

I hum my acknowledgment, nodding thoughtfully.

"She was in denial about it. Mainly 'cause back then, her freshman year, she was all about embracing who she was more. And not being reckless. God knows that girl could be so destructive when she wanted to be."

"She doesn't give me that vibe," I respond, shifting in my chair. "She's got that innocence about her."

"I mean yeah, she's innocent enough. Good person, *kind* person, but piss her off and she can flip. Her and Ren fighting was just playground stuff."

"What about you? You considered being a doctor because you're good and kind?"

He laughs. His gray eyes dance with amusement as he looks at me.

"I guess you can say that," he shrugs with a residual laugh. "Where Ebony is a nurturer, I'm a fixer."

"Would you go back then?" I ask, genuinely wanting to know the answer.

"To the program?" I nod and he shrugs. "I know I should, but it feels too late in the game."

"You see some of these politicians, man? The fact that you can't be president until you're at least thirty-five should be enough for you to jump back in when you're ready."

He laughs, shaking his head before taking a long drink. "You and Eb are perfect for each other," he says with a snort.

I laugh to myself, taking a drink and glancing around the diner.

"What's with the questions though? You don't strike me as a talker and I doubt you're asking solely out of curiosity."

"Ren told us that their brother's body and records are in the medical building. I wanted to see if I could get them."

"That would be around last year? Year before?"

"Maybe three years ago. He died my first year here."

"Then that's primarily on paper. They were starting to make the transition to tablets, but the system kept glitching. Might be in the basement of the medical building, but they typically have someone at the desk to keep a log of who goes in and out."

I sit quietly formulating a plan. The sound of forks scraping against glass plates, murmured conversations, and a song playing from the jukebox are the only things that penetrate the space between me and Clint.

"So, what's the plan?" he asks as he puts salt on his eggs, not even looking at me.

"You want to help?"

"She's my cousin," he says plainly. He shovels eggs in his mouth and chews before packing more into his jaw. "Murder ain't it. So, I'll help any way I can."

I nod, keeping my grateful smile to myself. His desire to help doesn't really surprise me. Especially since the two are close.

"You two aren't siblings, right?" I ask plainly, grabbing a fry from my plate and chewing on it.

He laughs, shaking his head. "Nah. My mom is her dad's

sister. She got really sick for a bit. My dad spent most of his time caring for her so Gramps took me in. When she got better, she let me visit him in the summer. Ebony's the only cousin out of a mass that I can say I grew up with."

"There's more?" I ask, marveling at the idea of a huge family. My parents didn't come from a large family. We can all fit in a handful of rooms and potentially still have space.

"Our family is huge," he chuckles, "and dysfunctional."

"She's never told me about them," I add, imagining a little Ebony playing with her cousins.

"She doesn't know them. She knows she has a lot of cousins and such, but none of them want to meet her."

"What about her mom?" I ask, looking at him. He pauses, then sighs.

"I don't know her personally. I only heard stories, but those changed rapidly. I do know she's in the area still. May have moved back after Eb graduated high school? I don't know. My gramps had an ominous card that he stashed in his drawer."

"Is she looking for E?"

He chuckles, shaking his head then turning towards me. "You ask a lot of questions for some cool guy."

"Sorry, just… curious."

"I know you care for my cousin."

He finishes his eggs and takes a swallow of his drink. "Eb's mom wants nothing to do with her. Not to be a full time parent at least. She refused to take my gramps' phone calls, resorted to sending letters in these weird, pink envelopes."

"Ebony has one in a shoe box under our bed," I say

suddenly.

He looks over at me, his eyes panning from the top of my head to my chin, then he fixes on my eyes. A slight grimace tugging at the edges of his face before he focuses back on his plate with a gentle shake. Note to self, don't mention me and Ebony's bed around Clint.

"The only time her mother ever reached out to Gramps was to tell him that her life was better without Eb in it. Gramps told Eb that as best as he could, but it didn't help with her spiraling. Honestly, I think that's why she clung to Vin so damn hard. Looking for someone to love her and here was this kid showing her an inch of attention that's connected to one of her shitty parents. He wasn't a bad kid, not for a minute."

He shakes his head and shoves a pancake in his mouth.

"You're different though," he says with his mouth full. "Like, you give her space to be herself. I see the old her peeking through." He swallows then takes a deep breath. "Everyone else pushed. They wanted her to fit one aspect of who she is, but with you and her friends… she fucking glows. Don't tell her I said that."

"Secret's safe with me, man," I say with a chuckle.

"Seriously though," he starts up again. "I may still have my reservations because you're still new in her life, but for the most part, you're cool in my book."

"Thanks," I say with a smile.

"That wasn't a compliment. She only meshes well with the weird ones," he adds, then bursts into a fit of genuine laughter. He wheezes a bit as he leans over the counter bracing himself. Despite that strained sound, it's a happy, playful laugh.

"Ha-ha," I joke back trying to keep from laughing. "You're part of the crew."

"I never said I was normal," he said, laughing a little more. "That's how I know."

This makes me laugh. I shift in my seat as more laughter bubbles out of me. I shake my head, then take a sip of my drink.

"So, while we're here. What's your story?" Clint asks, casting me a side eye glance as he takes a bite of his bacon.

We spend a few hours talking at that counter, getting to know each other like long lost friends. The nerves of meeting someone with such a rough exterior quickly dissolving as the minutes pass. I see him becoming someone I'd want in my corner, too.

Someone like family.

20

Ren

I find Miya in the chemistry department looking over records. I slip in through the cracked door and rap my knuckles against the table, capturing her attention.

"Long time no talk," I greet her. Things between Miya and I have always been tense. I chalked it up to her feeling threatened that her brother preferred spending time with me than with her, but part of me knows it's something deeper.

"Why are you here?" she responds uninterestedly. She looks back down at the records and scribbles more notes.

"Wanted to talk," I mutter, pulling up a chair and taking a seat next to her. "What are you working on?"

"Like I would tell you," she grumbles as she slides the book from my searching hand.

An awkward silence nestles between us, then the light squeaking of her pencil against paper punctuates the silence. She flips the page aggressively, then huffs. Her eyes snap up to my face as she slams the pencil down on her notebook.

"What?" she practically growls. Her tiny palms press firmly into the table like she's ready to jump over it and slap me across the face.

"Let's not pretend we can't be cordial or friendly," I

offer. I smile at her, tucking a stray strand of hair behind my ear.

"We aren't friends, Ren. You were my brother's friend."

"Ouch," I say standing from the stool and looking around the room. "I mainly came here to find out about the research you and Ebony were doing." My back is to her as I look around at the jars of various liquids labeled with compounds I barely remember, a number pad lock keeping the contents safe from the wrong hands.

"We're making a device to test for illegal substances in drinks," she says very pointedly.

I scoff. "Very fucking on par, E. Jesus."

"Why'd you do it, Ren?" Miya's voice is soft as she asks. Still just as pointed, but softer.

I turn, offering her a lame shrug as I look at her. "When you're young, you do dumb shit."

"You drugged her. Then took her to a fucking room and left her there! That's not dumb! That's intentional!" Tears roll down Miya's cheeks as she shouts at me. She wipes her face, shaking her head. "You were willing to do to her what someone did to your brother, and that's fucking sick."

"Such adult language for a kid," I state, tucking my hair behind my ear. "I don't expect you to understand. Kane and Han are perfect, yeah?"

"Pretty fucking close until you're involved."

I scoff, rolling my eyes. "Shit happens, Miya. I fucked up. I admit that, but don't act like Ebony's perfect because your brother thinks he loves her. She's a fucking phase. A moment."

She laughs, leaning against the table. "You're right,"

she mutters. "Ebony isn't perfect, but she doesn't pretend like she is. And that 'fake love' you say my brother has for her... tell me when you've ever seen him act like that with anyone."

I stare at her, lost for words. She's right. Kane's never stuck around someone for too long. Never looked at a woman with more than just lust. Not as intensely as he does with Ebony. I still remember the way they seemed to always gravitate towards each other like magnets.

"She's helping me get the autopsy report for my brother," I offer instead.

"Why do you need it?"

"To prove my brother didn't OD intentionally."

"And the autopsy is going to prove that?"

"If done correctly, yes. And apparently the documents will help with your project."

Miya looks me over with guarded eyes. Her lips pinch tightly as she keeps mum on the details of their project. It's not like I need them, those don't matter to me, but I'm still curious. Ebony asking for my brother's documents to put in a case study means she's looking into something and I want to know what. They're my brother's final documents after all.

"Miya, I didn't know you'd be in here," a woman says breathlessly. Her brown skin dull under the top lights. Her hair tamed on her head. She falters when she sees me. "Oh, I didn't know you had a chemistry student in here with you."

"I don't," Miya states. "She stopped by to ask about the project."

"Oh," the woman says, looking me over skeptically.

There's something familiar about her, but I can't place it. "Are you a chemistry student?" she asks me.

"No, I was just leaving," I mumble, glancing at Miya.

"Right," she says before glancing at Miya. "Ms. Yamada, have you heard from Ebony?"she asks, her eyes darting to me every so often.

I step out, keeping my ears strained to hear their conversation.

"She has to work tonight, so it's just you and me, Dr. Goodwin," Miya states. I catch her eyes as I slip out of the door.

Dr. Goodwin… name doesn't ring a bell, but her face does just a little.

I hop on the nearest city bus and head to the police station. Stepping onto the sidewalk, I walk into the office and tap on the counter.

"Hey. Is Officer Brown available?" I ask politely.

The older woman at the front desk nods her head, then slips in the back. I stare at the wooden door for a minute. Mel rushes out in her uniform and a wide grin on her face.

"Hey, what's up?" she asks breathlessly.

"I have a question. Can you look someone up for me?"

"Name?" Mel asks, looking down at the computer screen.

"Last name Goodwin. Don't know the first but they're an instructor at Knight U."

21

Kane

The bar is packed by the time Zeke and I head inside. Snatching off our beanies, we push our way through to the bar. I run my fingers through my hair then shake it into place. Ebony, Clint, and Isaac move around the bar mixing drinks and handing them out rapidly. Music pumps through the speakers and pool balls clatter together on the pool tables. The sharp smell of whiskey and hot wings fills the air as people eat and chug back glasses from various tables.

We find two empty stools and plop into them while Ebony zones out staring at nothing in particular. The shaker in her hand rattles as she continues to shake the drink in her fogginess. Since her meeting with Dr. Sumner and the events from the gala, she's been in a weird headspace. More introspective than she usually is and much more anxious. It would explain why she and the band haven't planned to play any gigs since the start of the new semester.

"I'm sure that drink is shaken enough," Clint says beside her, reaching for the blender.

She blinks, snapping out of her daydream. Her eyes look at the shaker, then at Clint and she chuckles apologetically.

"Sorry," she says through another anxious chuckle. She wipes her palms against the towel tied in the belt loop of her jeans.

"What's up, fellas," he nods to us as he strains the drink and simultaneously grabs two beers from the cooler below the counters. He uses the counter top to pop the caps, then hands them over.

"Thanks," Zeke says, nodding to him. He nudges me. "What you do to make her so spacy, man?"

"I didn't do anything," I say, looking her over. I take a long drink from the cold bottle.

Clint looks over his shoulder to find her spaced out again. A towel in her hand as she wipes the rim of the glass repetitively.

"You okay?" Clint asks, pouring more drinks and serving them. He grabs the tip thanking the customer, then handing her half of what he got.

"Just distracted," she says, snapping back out of her mind and getting the next drink orders started.

"You're not pregnant are you?" Clint asks with humor. His mischievous eyes vibrant under the dimmed bar light, but my brain registers what he says. I choke on my beer, coughing up some of the liquid that went down the wrong pipe. It's not that I'd mind, but we want to explore the world, live life and see what's out there before bringing little people into it.

I won't lie though, it would make sense with how she's been acting. Always sleeping, specific cravings at weird times, and irritable as fuck. I originally chalked it up to stress and tried my best to make her feel better. My efforts only last a millisecond before she's back in that head of hers.

Zeke's head snaps up. The rim of his bottle paused on the bottom of his lip.

"What now?" he asks, blinking just as rapidly at both of us respectively.

My heart pounds in my chest so hard it hurts. My stomach twists in knots. I don't even know if I'd be a good dad right now. I could barely handle getting Silver or Akemi to the vet without a mishap. Imagine me with a tiny person.

"No," she hisses, shocked. Her eyes nearly bug out of their sockets. "Definitely not," she adds, finding my eyes attempting to reassure me.

"So what's got you spaced out?" Clint asks, wiping the counter in front of Zeke and me.

More people approach the bar, taking their attention. They move quickly, mixing and serving drinks, until he looks at her wiping his palms.

"The project. Graduation stuff. The list is piling up," she says in a rush as she mixes a vodka cranberry.

She hands it to the person beside me, grabs the tip they place on the bar top, then shoves it in her pocket. She glances my way, letting her eyes assess my demeanor before exhaling deeply. She looks exhausted. Completely drained of the light that draws me to her. The only thing I hope to do is bring it back. I take another drink of my beer.

"Behind you," Isaac says, a big crate full of steaming glasses in his arms as he squeezes past. He sets them down with a grunt. They rattle and clank against each other, then still. "You are going to do great. You know that right?"

"Yeah." She idly mixes an old fashion. She charrs the

orange slice and drops it in the drink.

She passes it to an older man standing next to me. His lips curl up as he brushes his fingers over hers. She shudders, her smile turning into a slight grimace. I adjust in my seat, squaring my shoulders with the old guy.

"There's an extra tip for starin' too long," a gruff voice says from the other side of the bar.

Ebony's Gramps stands beside her. His gray eyes staring uninterestedly into the other man's. The older patron apologizes, grabbing his drink, then ducks into the crowd.

"Fellas," his gravelly voice greets all of us generally. I raise my bottle and give him a slight nod. He taps Ebony's shoulder and kisses her temple. "What ya got to be worried for?"

She shrugs her shoulders. Her eyes on him as he moves around grabbing a clean, white towel from some place under the bar.

"You're brilliant. Got it from ya grams," he says with a smile, then stalks off towards the end of the bar.

"Can we circle back to something," Zeke whispers when Isaac and Clint are busy mixing drinks.

Ebony steps forward and I lean a bit closer. Her warmth radiates off her body, sending chills down my spine. I pull my hair back out of my face with a hair tie from around my wrist, clearing the view of the fading hickey fighting against my complexion.

"You two really aren't gonna have a kid..." Zeke's question snaps me out of my musing as I glare at him.

"No," she says exasperatedly. She nudges him, grabbing another beer for him and me, then swipes the other bottles into a trash can by her feet.

"Really man?" I groan, shaking my head and taking a drink.

"Just want to know if I have to make a special room at my place for uncle duties," he says with a snarky smile.

I roll my eyes and look pointedly at Ebony. "Ignore him."

"I always do," she comments with a small laugh. "You guys want something stronger?"

"You don't have to get us drunk to have your way with us," Zeke says, earning a slap to the back of the head. He laughs hysterically. "I swear you gotta relax, man."

He rubs the back of his head before taking another drink of his beer completely unfazed.

"Stop saying wild shit," I growl, then look at E. "What's your specialty?"

"Wait and see," she says with a smile.

She wipes her hands, then tosses the towel in a gray bucket. With another secured around her belt loops. She digs in the machine and starts mixing a drink. Grabbing various bottles, she pours some of each one into the mixer, snaps the top shut, then starts mixing.

I let my eyes roam over her shaking body. My eyes stop at her chest as her tits jiggle with every shake. A slow smirk making its way to my face. My girlfriend is one of the sexiest women I've ever met. Her having an incredible body is just the icing on the cake.

"Hey, E," Zeke calls out. "Come over here and do that for him. I don't think he's getting a good enough view."

"I can just take her home to see it all," I say, slowly

looking over at him.

"I'm standing right here," she says, pulling out two glasses and dislodging the top of the mixer. She strains our drinks into cups then lights them on fire. She puts the mixer down and slides us our drinks.

"It's true," I defend, making her roll her eyes, a slight blush beneath the rich brown undertones on her cheeks. She pulls in the corner of her bottom lip to keep from smiling at me.

"Is there a special way to drink this or something?" Zeke asks, looking at the orange and blue flame.

"Blow and suck," Isaac says, placing his hands on the counter with a ghost of a smile.

"Watch," Ebony says, grabbing two more shot glasses and pouring the remainder of the mixture in those two cups.

She lights it on fire, then slides one over to Isaac and takes the other in her hand. They clink their glasses together as she starts dancing to the music. Smoke rolls from the top of the cups once they blow out their drinks and throw back the brown liquid, their lips wrapped around the rim. She swallows with a smile on her face, pulls the glass from between her lips, then wipes her mouth with the back of her hand.

"How you ended up getting someone as wild as her will always confuse me," Zeke whispers as Isaac places his glass on the counter.

I pat him on the shoulder smiling over at Ebony. "It's because I'm better looking."

"Bullshit," Zeke retorts with a soft chuckle.

"This gets better every time you make it," Isaac groans, looking at Ebony.

She makes herself and Isaac another shot. They throw it back together and she licks her lips slowly, her eyes dragging over towards mine in the process. She looks me over, the corner of her bottom lip between her teeth before she smirks. A look that has my body burning from the inside out. Blood rushing to the wrong head, or right head depending on what part of me is leading. Then again, she's been too into her head for us to drive too deep into that like we normally do. And I've been focused on easing her mind and not jumping in her pants.

I'm a reformed man and stress is a fucking cock blocker.

She braces the bar top and leans closer towards me, her eyes drinking in every inch of me. An arousing flicker of lust dances behind her eyes as she challenges me. Her pupils dilate as she scans me from head to toe. The tip of her tongue pokes out over her lip as she looks back into my eyes. I lean closer, rolling my tongue around my cheek.

"Let me see that again. I don't think I saw it well enough," I say with a smirk.

"I think someone needs to let some steam off," Zeke says cackling.

"Bathroom's down the hall to the right," Isaac says with a laugh of his own.

"Can I get a napkin," some woman asks as she squeezes past the guy beside me. Her hand rests on my biceps as she pushes her chest closer to my body. I scoot away a bit, but she doesn't get the hint as she lets her eyes trail over me. A smirk on her done up face. Hints of red in her cheeks, which only means she's drunk or nearly there.

Ebony giggles, passing the woman a few napkins.

"I thought you liked that?" she says mixing a drink for someone else.

"Much rather yours. They fit in my mouth better," I say back.

"Do they now?" she asks, quirking an eyebrow and passing the drink over and taking her tip with a smile.

"Yeah. Let me show you," I coax, nodding my head towards the back.

She lets her eyes look between both of mine, a hint of a smile on her face as she pours the drink she was mixing.

"Stop flirting," Isaac says, tapping her shoulder and rushing to the other side of the bar amused. She laughs, watching as he talks to a customer.

"Not a fan of it either," Zeke says, looking between us with a grimace on his face. "Both my wing people all mushy with each other?" He shakes his head and scrunches up his face like he tasted a bitter lemon.

"You wanted this to happen," I say, nudging him.

"I know. There's not a day that goes by that I don't regret it," he says with a frown.

Ebony laughs at him, wiping down the counter in front of us.

"Cheer up buddy," I start. "We can still be your wing people."

"When? After tickling each other's tonsils?"

"I was thinking after a good reach around," Ebony says from the register as she closes out someone's tab.

"I'm sure he gets enough of those from you," Zeke says

with a smile.

"Don't start that shit," I groan, rolling my eyes as the two of them laugh. "Keep laughing. Assholes."

"You might like it," she says, reaching for my hand and grabbing my spare rubber band. She ties half of her hair up out of her face, then looks at me with puppy dog eyes.

"No," I say firmly. "Not happening."

"She'll wear you down. Don't worry," Zeke says laughing. I shake my head, rolling my eyes again.

"Hey," she says after a moment, her eyes on me. "Help me with the code when we get home?"

"If you drop this whole reach around bullshit," I say with my eyes squinted.

She smiles, then laughs nodding her head. "We're just having a little fun."

"At my expense?" I ask.

"Hardly," she says with a smile.

"Come on, bro. I'll convince you to give it a try," Zeke says, standing up from the stool and sending Ebony a conspirative wink.

"Not happening," I groan, nudging him as I follow him to the pool table.

22

Ebony

The computer beeps as I hit another firewall trying to hack into the school system. Kane stops his typing and looks at me. His soggy hair is pinned up out of his face, but water rolls down his temple. I sigh, flopping back on the bed, my eyes staring up at the rotating ceiling fan. His hands rub my bare leg before turning my face to look at him.

"Let's take a break. We've been at this for a few hours. You just worked a full shift and probably need a decent break," he says pulling me into his lap.

"I thought your dad would make it easy for us to get back into the system," I groan.

"This doesn't look like my dad's work, but it's probably because he wanted to give us a challenge," he responds with a chuckle. "Look, we have some time to check the drone records."

He sucks on my neck, slipping his hands underneath the hem of my shirt, touching my back. I lean my head back letting my body relax into his touch, his kisses, then I sigh. All the tension rushing back into my body.

"We still have to find those autopsy reports," I sigh, leaning back and scratching my eyebrow. I pry his hands off my body and climb out of the bed, heading for the kitchen.

Silver brushes past my leg with a soft meow as I grab a cup. I scratch his head, then pick him up as Kane stalks in behind me. He sighs and kisses my forehead.

"What?" I ask running my hand down Silver's smooth fur, then put him down. I brace my hands on either side of the counter behind me watching Kane move.

"Nothing," he grumbles, grabbing a spoon and a carton of ice cream.

"Don't 'nothing' me," I mock, pushing off the counter and grabbing the ice cream carton. "Tell me."

"You're worrying about too much all at once. Killin' the mood, E." He reaches for the carton and I move it away.

"Killing what mood?"

He laughs, shaking his head.

"That doesn't answer the question," I say, frustrated. I continue staring at him as he runs a hand through his hair.

"Ebony," he says sternly before releasing a rush of air. "I'm really trying to respect that you have a lot on your mind. So, ice cream. Please."

"No. What's with you?"

Closing the distance, he grabs the back of my neck gently, pulling me towards him. A soft, involuntary gasp passes my lips as I stare up at his intense gaze. Heat bounces between his brown orbs as his lips ghost over mine. He bites at my lower lip, runs his tongue over it, then lets it go. His body is pressed flush against mine.

I moan. An inferno deep in my belly roaring to life with that simple action. His hands grasp at my thighs, squeezing and kneading them. His nose nudges my head to the side, exposing my neck to him. "What are you doing?"

I whisper.

He shushes me as his hands grab my ass and he lifts me up onto the counter. Pulling me to the edge, he stands between my legs taking the ice cream from me and putting it to the side. He grabs his spoon and drips cold ice cream on my neck. His tongue slowly licks it up, sucking on my skin when he gets it all up.

"You've been teasing me," he whispers against my skin. "Walking around in those fucking short ass shorts. Waking me up in the middle of the night grinding against me just to stop because you can't turn your brain off."

His hands slip underneath my shirt. His touch is gentle, yet firm. Soft palms grip my sides, squeezing before they roll over my breasts, taking them in his hands. I moan, arching my back, pushing them further into his grip.

"I'm not good at reading the room when I'm stressed," I whisper, wrapping my legs around his waist as his thumb brushes past my nipple. Over and over again.

He laughs into my neck, giving it a gentle kiss. His thumb and pointer finger gently pulling and tugging at my nipples, making me moan more.

"You can either keep stressing or you can be sprawled out on that bed with my head between these thick ass thighs, tasting every inch of you slowly."

His hands leave my breasts, warm fingertips grazing down my side and gripping my thighs once again. He pulls me forward roughly and smiles against my neck. His tongue trails up to my ear, then back down. Determined fingers trail to my breasts kneading them slowly. My breath catches in my throat as he nips at my neck. One of his hands slips from under my shirt, then the icy coldness of ice cream runs down my neck again followed by his warm tongue.

My body heats up more as my hands grab his waist. "I like that idea."

"Which one, baby?" he whispers in my ear. "You gotta be more specific than that."

I look at him when he leans back. Goosebumps raising up on my skin as his hands grope and caress me. "I think being sprawled out on the bed sounds much more fun than being in my head," I whisper, reaching for him.

"I was thinking the same," he says with a smile. He lifts me up, hoisting me over his shoulder and grabbing the carton of ice cream.

"Wait, why are you bringing that?" I ask bracing my hands on his back, then trailing down over the top of his ass.

"It's coming to join the party," he says, slapping my ass.

I giggle, grabbing his in the process as he carries me into the room and drops me down on the bed. He puts the ice cream on the nightstand, then crawls over me. His hands frame my face as he kisses me deeply. His tongue diving into my mouth, coaxing mine out until they dance and swirl around each other.

With the hem of my shirt firmly in his hand, he pulls the garment over my head. One of his hands grabs mine. Our fingers interlock as he pins it above my head, his lips still devouring mine in the process. He pulls his lips away, making me whimper. Heated kisses race down my neck, to my collar bone, then in-between the valley of my breasts. My nipples harden as he blows on them, then takes them into his mouth. His fingers hook into the waistband of my shorts. He yanks them off, kissing down my body, biting into my thigh. A groan rumbles in his chest as he pushes his hands up my body, touching every inch of exposed skin.

My hands dig into his hair as I move my hips and clench my thighs against him. His hand stills me as he kisses back up my body. He hovers over me, then comes back dribbling melted ice cream over my body. I tremble as it hits my skin. He straddles my legs to keep me still. A smirk on his damn face as he grabs the carton and pours more over me from my chest down to my belly button.

"What the fuck, Kane," I gasp through a shiver.

Even with the ice cream melting, it's freezing. Goosebumps pop up on my flesh as more cascades from the carton down to my body. I try to wiggle away, but his thighs effectively have me locked in place.

He shifts his weight, sucking the pool of ice cream out of my belly button, then following the line up my chest slowly. His tongue smears the stickiness across my skin, warming my body where the trail of coldness was.

The bed shifts as he moves his body back down to my belly button, then licks up the remainder of the ice cream. I tremble for a different reason. My need for him increases as his body moves again to grab the ice cream carton. He grabs the spoon, pouring a little on my nipple and sucks it in his mouth, then does the same to the other.

A shudder rushes through my body as I moan. The painstakingly slow movements allowing my mind to start whirring to life and thinking of everything all at once. I feel myself mentally leaving this moment and let out a soft whine.

"Let go," he whispers against my skin. He peeks up at me through his long lashes as he releases my nipple and kisses around my breast. "You're here with me. Focus on how good I make you feel."

I nod and he smiles.

"Good girl, now spread your legs for me."

He pulls his shirt over his head and tosses it on the bed. Then lays on his stomach, placing gentle kisses along my inner thigh before sucking on a spot near my pussy. I moan, wiggling my hips, urging him to move closer to the bundled nerves right between my thighs.

Smiling against my skin, he bites my thigh then lets it go. He grabs the spoon from the carton, a small dollop of melting ice cream on the tip of the spoon.

A mischievous glint is rushing across his face as he puts the container on the floor and hovers the spoon over my clit. He smiles at me, letting the small glob drop down, then chases behind it with his tongue.

Stars burst behind my eyelids as I arch my back, gripping his hair tightly as he sucks and licks. He moans against me, giving me long licks before grabbing another spoonful and doing the same thing over again.

"Oh my fucking God," I groan.

My eyes are rolling back as he sucks and licks at my clit. He groans again, much deeper this time, sending a vibration to my nub making me jolt.

"Right there," I groan, my hands in his hair as he devours me.

"You taste so fucking good," he groans. He flicks his

tongue before shifting, pushing his thick middle finger inside me, then a second.

I moan as he curls his fingers slowly working them inside of me right at my g spot. He continues sucking on my clit looking up at my withering body. His free hand snakes up, rubbing my nipple and tugging at it.

"Cum for me, baby," he groans, moving his fingers faster in sync with his tongue.

There's a tightness in my belly that only grows tighter, squeezing and pulsing with his movements until he gives my clit one hard suck. I cum, moaning his name loudly as my body trembles. My pussy clenching his probing fingers until he pushes himself deep inside me. I gasp at the change in sensation as he stretches me with his thickness. He pushes in deep with a moan. His mouth on my neck as he kisses and sucks on it.

"I don't think I'll get over how tight you feel," he groans into my ear.

His body slams into mine roughly. I throw my arms around his neck, his hands holding my thighs open. His hot skin brushes across mine. His name comes out of my mouth bunched together as his thrust short circuits my brain.

"That's right, baby. Let me hear how good I make this pretty pussy feel."

He shifts his hands bracing himself over my body, moving his hips harder. The sound of his skin slapping into mine joining my moans.

He groans, his breath shaky in my ear, knowing that the sounds of him struggling to stay in control turns me on more. So he doesn't hold back, not even with his pants coming in closer together as he attempts to keep himself from coming too quickly.

I roll my hips, clenching and releasing my walls with each of his thrusts. His hand grabs my hair, pulling tightly.

"That's it, baby," he groans. "Fuck me back just like that. Such a fucking slut for me."

He stops his thrusts and pulls out, his body towering over mine and his erection wobbling with his movements. He motions for me to turn over as he grabs my hips and helps me. He gives my ass a hard smack sending tingles across my skin before another slap follows. His hand caresses the spot before another slap connects, alternating pain with pleasure as I moan into the pillows.

He pushes into me, pulling my hips back into his. He groans as he sinks in further. My hand reaches underneath, rubbing my clit, then reaching to squeeze his balls.

"Greedy fucking slut," he groans, slapping my ass and lifting one of his legs.

His body pounds into mine as he grips my hips tighter. I unravel. My hands shake as I rub my clit chasing my release and screaming his name into the mattress as I cum hard. He hisses, slowing his strokes to keep from hurting us both as my intense orgasm makes my walls clench tightly around his hard dick.

"Don't slow down," I pant. "Fuck me harder, Kane."

"You'd love that huh, baby?" he groans, increasing his speed and pushing himself deep again. Fucking me through my orgasm.

"Yes," I breathe as my hands grab the sheets pulling at them, keeping myself anchored to the bed as I throw my hips back into his.

His hand reaches around, grabs my throat and pulls me back into him. His thumb traces the column of my neck as he nips at my ear. His hot breath tickles the shell of my ear in the process.

"Open your mouth and let me taste you," he growls in my ear.

I lean my head into his shoulder, opening my mouth as my body shakes with his thrust. He spits in my mouth, then dives his tongue in right after, turning my head into a better position. I moan into his kiss, reaching my arm behind me to brace myself using his neck to keep me steady. My free hand reaches for one of his. I drag it down my body and use it to rub my clit.

"That's what my baby wants, huh? You want me to play with the pretty pussy?"

I moan, my head resting on his shoulder as I let pleasure consume me. He taps my clit and I tense.

"Don't be shy," he whispers with a chuckle.

"Touch me," I moan. "Please."

His hand gives my clit gentle rubs as his thrusts get harder, rougher. His hand matches his speed. I pinch and rub against my nipples, alternating between the two adding to the pleasure Kane gives me.

"Just like that," I moan. "Fuck me like a slut."

He groans his response as one hand plays with my nipple and the other plays with my clit in sync. His breathing hitches as he attempts to hold on until I cum. I fight the urge until he gives my nipple one good pull and I shudder. My arm gripping his neck tightly as I cum, pulling him with me.

He groans my name into my neck as he shudders and erratically thrusts around the intense throbbing. He empties himself into me, then pulls me down with him as we pant. He nuzzles into my neck, kissing at my jaw and interlocking our fingers.

"I love you," I whisper with my eyes closed.

He kisses my shoulder. "After all that? You better."

I nudge him, casting a glare at him over my shoulder. He smiles at me, then gives me one final push before pulling himself out of me. He climbs out of bed with a sigh.

"I just wanted ice cream," he says with a frown.

I look over my shoulder at him as he looks in the carton of melted ice cream. Giggling, I sit up and throw a pillow at him. He catches it, tossing it back at me. Swatting it away, I stick my tongue out at him.

"Ebony flavored ice cream is better," I say getting off the bed to walk to the bathroom. I groan at the liquid warmth running down my thigh. "Why is there so much!?" I grumble looking at the mess.

He laughs, putting the carton down on the nightstand and grabs his shirt. "Just use this," he offers, following me into the bathroom.

"I need a shower," I grumble, leaning over the tub and turning on the water. "You always cum so much."

"Let me just tell my balls to tone it down. That should solve the problem," he snorts sarcastically, leaning against the door frame.

"Whatever," I scoff. I look at him trying to hide my smile. "Are you getting in or not?"

"Didn't get enough?" he asks with a smirk walking towards the shower.

"I can never get enough of you," I say, pulling him to me for a kiss.

"Good," he whispers against my lips.

23

Ren

Crazy ideas are exactly how I ended up in this mess. Or maybe it's just my lack of spotting red flags. It's probably both. Either way, it's the crazy idea that has my ass in this hard wooden booth in a pizza restaurant two blocks from Knight U's campus.

My phone buzzes in my pocket as I watch steam rise from the pizza sitting in front of me. Digging out my device, I stifle a smile as I read Mel's text wishing me a good day with the most adorable selfie of her in her uniform. Glancing around the restaurant, I send her a quick selfie.

Me

Next date. I'm bringing you here. Best pizza ever.

Mel

Careful, Ren. I might think you like me ;)

Me

You think? ;)

Any update on the name I gave you?

Not yet, but I'm sure I'll get a hit soon.

Captain's here. Gotta go. XOXO.

With another stifled smile, I shove my phone back in my pocket before grabbing a gooey slice. Dropping it on my plate, a shadow distorts the lighting making me look up.

Kane's large hands are laced in front of him as he leans forward across the table. Brown eyes harden by the second. They travel across my face before he sighs and rolls his shoulders.

I should know this is how he's going to treat me until he realizes I'm no threat to him. I'd never hurt someone that has helped me through so much, even now. I know he wants to help me, albeit reluctantly. Him dating Ebony was a misstep in my plan. I'm still surprised the two of them ended up together exclusively, but that's not important anymore.

As for Ebony, I've given up the idea that she'd open up and trust me. I don't need her trust though, not completely. I just need her to work with me. To understand that everything in our agreement is transactional. She'll help me and I'll help her. That's it. Which is why I signed that damn agreement Kane sent two days ago.

"You're not going to eat?" I ask, looking over the steamy pie at him.

"Why would I do that?" Kane asks with disdain.

"Because I drugged your girlfriend when she was my girlfriend. I've never messed with anything you consumed,"

I say, blowing on my pizza.

Grease drips from my hands to the paper plate below. The melted cheese rolls across my tongue as I chew and groan, my head rolling back as I bask in the divineness currently occupying my mouth.

"And yet you still don't give a fuck," he snarls.

I tilt my head just enough to look at him and scoff. Grabbing a napkin, I wipe my hands, then toss it back on the table. Letting the tension linger, I lick the grease off my lips and take a long gulp of water.

"I don't know why I need to," I finally say. "You were my friend before you and her became a thing."

"You know… She has night terrors some nights," he says leaning back in the chair, ignoring my comment. He stretches out one leg, unlaces his fingers, and taps the table. His hair falls over one side of his face. "Some nights she wakes up and panics. Covered in sweat and completely inconsolable. She'll talk in her sleep. Fucking begging for someone to save her from the monsters in her dreams."

"They're her own monsters," I say, taking another bite.

"Not when she's begging for you to save her," he snarls, glaring at me.

Those details make me feel bad. Just a little at least. I can hear the torment in his voice, the strain of emotions. He feels inadequate because there's nothing he can do to help her overcome the nightmares.

I had them too.

Me stuck in a wall just watching everything unfold, unable to do anything. There was a time or two where it was her revenge on me. And then I met Mel and my dreams stopped all together.

Instead of sympathizing with her, which I know he wants me to do, I say, "Don't know why she would do something as dumb as that."

I avoid his eyes, knowing the look I'll get. Kane can be scary when he's protecting the people he cares about. That look has saved me from many fucked up scenarios with my father, another man with a vicious temper. I sit here in silence knowing that Kane has to choose a side in this situation. That very fact keeps me up at night, breaking my heart in ways I hadn't anticipated. He's the only reason why I feel remorse. Hurting her hurt him and I never wanted to hurt my best friend. Kane didn't do serious relationships, he never picked anyone's side over mine. Not until now, not until her.

Lifting his bulky hand, he rubs his face and looks out the window, his head shaking slightly as he works his jaw.

"I'm going to go," he says, pushing himself up.

"Wait," I plead. "Okay, I'm being an ass. I just— there's shit that happened between her and I that just has me fucked up."

Being on the receiving end of Kane's glare reminds me of the time when I was a child. Fearful of the shadowy figures lurking in my deep, dark closet late at night during a thunderstorm. Their clawed hands reaching out to snatch me into their realm, but those shadow figures weren't real. I was ten when they vanished into articles of clothing. But the disdain, the disgust that lurks behind Kane's eyes brings up that fear again.

He swears under his breath and sits down. His leg

bounces as he looks at me. "Say something interesting or I'm gone," he finally says after a tense moment.

I notice now how much he smells like her. His own warm fragrance mixing in with hers. A hint of a hickey on his neck as he rolls his shoulders. I look away from it and sigh, clenching my napkin in my hands.

"I have a plan," I start, leaning my slim body on the table. I drop my voice to barely a whisper. "I need Ebony on board with this, but I need you to convince her."

He sucks his teeth. "I'm not promising to convince her to do anything until I know what it is."

"Get her here first. You're not going to tell her."

"She asked me to deal with you. Like it or not, you're dealing with me and me alone."

"There you go," I say with a soft laugh. I don't find the humor in the situation, but I still laugh to ease the anxiety in my chest. My heart thumps violently. My lungs are tight. "You can't make this decision for her and I know for a fact you won't let her make it. Always have to be in control."

"To keep her safe? Absolutely." He quirks an eyebrow. Unapologetic with how he decides to take charge of another's decision. His major fucking flaw, especially with me being able to get her exactly what she needs.

"She won't get them convicted with what she has. She needs something they can't say was tampered with. That's the defense they have going."

I grab my pizza slice and take another bite. My eyes never leaving his as I devour the slice and watch him think. He looks over my shoulder, then back at me.

"No deal," he starts. "You tell me, then I decide to tell

her whether it's worth going."

"How would you know?" I say with a laugh. "How would you know what she can fucking handle?"

"Nobody's saying what she can or cannot handle. It's my job to make sure she's safe from you."

"She is. Vin plans on framing me for all of this. Every last person that's ever stepped into his presence. I have the names. I'm in contact with Vin."

"She can be too. Asshole loves to fuck with her," Kane says idly shaking his head. His guard slips a bit. "It's like he wants to isolate her."

"He does," I say. "Vin has this weird obsession with her. He also has one with me. We can't go anywhere without him knowing."

"What you do to him?" he asks with his eyebrows stitched together. Contempt laced through his tone.

"Exist," I say with a sigh, wiping my hands against the soggy napkin I've been clutching in my hands. "He thinks all women that come in contact with him belong to him."

His body starts to slowly relax as he looks me over again. He runs his hand through his hair and sighs. "You fucked up, Ren," he states, shaking his head. A pained look flashing across his face as he looks down at his hands, then back out the window. "And I don't even understand why you did it the way you did."

"No one got hurt but me, remember?" I state pointing to the scab on my lip.

"You deserved that shit," he comments with a snort. "Imagine seeing someone that left you for dead."

"I didn't leave her for dead," I sigh.

It's my turn to run my hands through my hair, but it gets tangled in knots. I yank my fingers through it and drop the strands of shedded hair to the ground.

"She was allergic to whatever was in what he gave you," he shares leaning forward. "So, not only did you drug her, you almost killed her."

"Vin almost killed her," I hiss. "I may have given it to her, but how was I supposed to know that she was allergic to any of that shit?"

"The same way you expect her and me to trust you. What you did to me was minor. I didn't get hurt behind your white lie, but she did. I'm not letting it happen again."

I snort, shaking my head. "Okay, knight in rusty armor. Let me know how you feel when you realize you can't protect her from everything."

Kane rolls his eyes, leaning back in the seat. "You're not telling me anything that sounds like a plan. Let me remind you, putting Nair in his shampoo and hoping he looks like a dropped lollipop won't work."

"No," I say, putting up my own guard. I brace myself before leaning closer to the table. "We're going to set Vin up."

"How?" he responds with a furrowed brow. His interest is piqued now as he shifts in his seat and leans closer.

"This is the part that I need your help with. She trusts you, so I know she'll be okay with it if you do it."

"Spit it out."

"One of us is going to have to get drugged," I whisper.

"Repeat that?" he asks. A harrowing edge creeps into his tone.

Crimson is a color that I use to find beautiful. That was until I notice it inching its way up Kane's neck, towards his face, which is hardened. A burning glare makes me shrink away as his lips form into a tight line. I keep my mouth shut, clenching my jaw so tightly that the muscle spasms sharply. My palms stick to the table top, creating foggy marks around them now as fear consumes me.

"Ren," he articulates my name like he's a hair away from losing his sanity. "I don't think I heard you correctly."

"You did," I say softly. "It's the only way."

"No, no it's not," he growls.

"Just listen!" I hiss in a hushed voice. My eyes dart around the restaurant quickly as I lean closer. "Her and I have separately tried everything but this! It's the only fucking way. Vin is a sick man. A dangerous man, but he's fucking weak. We get either one of us, or both, in a position where he thinks he has control, then we get him before either of us gets hurt."

"You're fucking insane, Ren!"

He rubs his face harshly, then glares back at me. Disbelief sits in the center of his rage, while concern caresses his shoulders staring right back at me through his hardening eyes.

"Kane, I've thought about this. It's a controlled setting. We plan this properly, we get you to at least pretend to give her the pill and we've got him."

"I'm not pretending to drug her or actually doing it. And you may not be my favorite fucking person right now, but I'm not doing that shit to you either. Terrible fucking idea, Ren."

"What other choice do we have!? You guys have the legal documents and still can't make shit stick!"

"Yeah?" he spits, "Compared to what you've done, which is what exactly?"

"Look, you don't trust me. Fine. But I have a plan and it can work," I say softly.

He scoffs, his head shaking once again as he glares out the window. He works his jaw, clenching and unclenching it. The bulky muscle bulges against his skin as he does so.

"Get her to talk to me. She might surprise you," I urge.

"No," he stands up, grabbing his jacket and shoving his arms in it. "No deal."

He storms out of the restaurant into the blistering cold. His hands shoved deep in his pocket and his black hair whipping around in the wind as he takes long strides down the sidewalk.

I sigh, looking over at my pizza. My stomach twists and rolls as I get my server's attention. If he wasn't going to tell her, then I was. I just have to figure out how to approach her without it being catastrophic.

"I had a feeling I'd see you here," a familiar voice calls out.

I turn my head quickly, a slow smile growing on my face.

Vin stands before me, his hands shoved deep in his high school letterman jacket. His brown eyes twinkle in the light. I assume the cold weather snatched some of his rich color because he looks pale, even for a guy with some melanin. A red hat is shoved over this round head.

"Well, well, well," I say, gesturing to the seat across

from me.

"What was that about?" he nods his head towards the direction Kane walked. He grabs a slice of pizza and takes a bite.

"Trying to get you a little gift," I shrug with a smile.

"I see," Vin says slowly. His eyes fixated on the scab on my lip. "Wanting to even the score?"

"Just a little," I comment, taking a sip of my drink and leaning back in my chair. A ghost of a smile prickling at my lips.

24

Ebony

With finals done and graded, and Knight U winning the playoffs, things on campus begin quieting down. Fortunately, Kane and his dad helped me rebuild the code much stronger than it was the last time. However, the new system also means it's much harder to access the classified documents we could before.

"They don't have any autopsy records on public domain," Isaac says as he drops his keys on the counter in my kitchen. He toes off his shoes and takes a seat at the table. "And even if they did, the person I know can't even gain access without someone watching."

"They apparently beefed up security over break," Miya says from beside me. Silver lays curled up in her lap basking in her attention. "Cameras in every file room."

"So, that means whoever's behind this, doesn't want anyone finding out what's going on," I state leaning back against the chair. "I can try to override the system, get into the security footage."

I study the codes on my screen for a moment.

"Apparently, the guys on my dad's team are having problems with accessing the servers," Miya comments.

I groan and lean back, then look over at Isaac.

"I got nothing," he comments with a shrug.

"So, that means someone's actively blocking us."

"How did you get in the first time?" Isaac asks shifting in the chair. His long, muscular body looks awkward in the piece of furniture.

"The coding was easier," I answer, grabbing my computer and studying the system. "Patterns were easier to recognize, too." I peck at the keys for a moment. The screen leading me to different layers of code, then I stop.

"Holy fuck," I mutter. A smile spreads across my face.

"What?" Miya and Isaac ask, looking at me with anticipation.

"Mr. Yamada planted a thumb drive in Dr. Sumner's office for Kane and I— I just got a hit!"

Miya leans closer to me looking at the screen as I set it on the table. Isaac, climbing over the arm of the chair, looks at the screen as letters populate the screen rapidly.

"What's he doing?" Miya asks.

"Emailing the chemistry department head. Asking about shipments or something."

"This is recording live?" Isaac asks, glancing at me, then back at the screen.

"Yes!" I answer giddy. I bounce on the seat before grabbing my phone, calling Kane.

"Hey," he answers, sounding out of breath. Chatter fills the brief silence between us as he pants.

"We got in!" I gush as Miya and Isaac watch the screen closely. I slip past them, rushing into the room bouncing.

"We got in what?" he releases a lungful of air. "Hold on," he says before muffling the phone. "Sorry, had to see if

Coach would let me slip away for a second."

"That's fine. I'm sorry. I'm just excited. Kane, the thumb drive worked. My computer is logging everything right now."

"Seriously?" he chuckles, mostly to himself. "What about the system?"

"We'll have to look. We're bound to get a code or something."

"Give me an hour and I'll be home to look over everything with you. I gotta go, we're about to run more drills."

"Yeah. See you then."

"Hey, E," he calls as I start moving the receiver from my ear. "You're so fucking smart. I love you. See you tonight."

25

Kane

Large take out containers sit on the kitchen table when Zeke and I finally make it to Ebony's. Miya sits beside her, colorful sticky notes scattered around her on the floor as she writes on a large desk calendar. Isaac hovers over Ebony's shoulder, a fork haphazardly sitting between his lips. Ebony's fingers type rapidly over the keys as she works silently, her locs pinned back with one of those alligator clips.

"Hey," I call out from the door as Zeke and I drop our bags and go to the kitchen table.

"You'll never guess what this brilliant woman found," Isaac gushes. He looks over at us with a wide grin.

"The autopsy reports?" I ask, feeling hopeful for a bit.

Look, Ren and I may not be getting along, but having those reports has always been one of my goals in this whole ordeal. Giving them those reports means they can stop lying. Maybe.

"No," Isaac says, nudging Ebony.

"Huh?" she looks over at Isaac, then at me. She smiles brightly, then nods over to the screen and I move towards her.

"Is this…" I start as I read the screen.

"Raeven's journal or log or something between the two," she says with a huge smile on her face. "Why's it in the school system? I have no idea, but he mentions the school was doing something sketchy in the chemistry department before Dr. Sumner took the dean position."

"Sketchy like?"

She shrugs her shoulders and looks at me hopeful. "Kane, if Raeven's death wasn't a true OD—"

"This may contain the motive," I finish, looking at her.

She nods in response and all I can do is pull her into my arms and squeeze her.

"I have a question," Zeke says with his mouthful of food. He sets his plate down on the table and leans back in the chair he occupies. "Why are you doing this for them, E?"

"Zeke," I warn as Ebony looks over at him. Her shoulders hitched up towards her shoulders slightly. "You don't…"

"Chill, lover boy. I'm asking her as her friend. A concerned friend," Zeke says gruffly. His demeanor is more protective than angry.

"Because she wants to help. What's the issue?" I answer instead more aggressively.

E's hand grabs my arm as she looks back at me. Her eyes are telling me to cool my shit before she turns back to Zeke.

"I know this seems crazy," she starts softly. Her eyes fixed on his.

"Seems? E, that psychotic bitch drugged you. They almost killed you. This is crazy."

"Zeke, we literally have something here that can lead

Miya and me into something big for our project. It's not just about Ren."

"So just like that? All's forgiven?"

"No!" E's exasperated voice bursts out of her as she shifts. "No, all is not forgiven."

"You and Miya can do this project without them," he says softly.

"What's your deal?" I ask, walking towards him. "You come in here and start judging. The fuck is that about?"

"Don't start," he growls looking at me through squinted eyes. "You're fucking biased in this whole fucking shit show."

"The fuck you mean by that?" I growl, getting in his face.

"Stop!" E shouts at us, wiggling her body in between us. She uses most of her strength to push us apart. "Both of you… opposite sides of the apartment, now."

"Cut the shit, Zeke," I growl.

"Why don't you fucking make me, pretty boy?" Zeke growls back, taking a step forward.

"What the fuck did I say!" E shouts at us, shoving me back hard as Miya and Isaac block the distance between the room. "Bedroom, now," she grumbles, glaring at me. She nods her head towards the door before nudging me in that direction.

"Kitchen," Miya says, nudging Zeke as we continue to glare at each other.

"Hurt my fucking sister and your—"

"Shut up," E growls, closing the bedroom door hard. "What the hell was that!?"

She runs her hands through her locs and paces in front of the door. I walk towards her and she turns, pinning me with wild eyes. She points to the bed and I sit quietly. I pop my knuckles, but remain silent.

"Answers would be nice, please," she says with an exasperated sigh.

"He's stepping over the fucking line," I offer.

"So you fight him? In the middle of this amazing breakthrough?"

"I know it was bad timing, but he needed to be checked," I grumble.

"He's your best fucking friend, you don't go to blows with your best friend."

"It's a guy thing, E. I don't think you'd understand."

"Don't do that," she glares at me. "Don't fucking start that macho shit with me."

"I'm stating a fact."

"Fuck you," she spits, rolling her eyes and throwing the door open.

"Fuck," I grumble to myself and grab her by her waist pulling her back into the room and closing the door. "Hey, hey I'm sorry."

"You need a moment. I need a fucking moment and I need to check on Zeke."

I stare down at her, not letting her go just yet. I sigh, releasing my hold and sitting back on the bed.

"I'm spiraling," I confess. "My dad found something back when you fought Ren. I've been trying to figure out what."

"Any hints or something we should look for?" she asks,

sitting beside me. She keeps some space between us, but she watches me, waiting for a response.

I shake my head for a second, then look at her. "Maybe. Back during first year, Zeke, Sanjay, Zeus, and I were fucking around in chemistry. We had lab. Sumner was the reason why the four of us couldn't go into the science labs for the rest of the year."

"How'd Dr. Sumner get the Dean's position so fast," Ebony mutters. "What did you guys do to get kicked out?"

I shake my head, then shrug.

She stands, walking back to the door and opens it. "Zeke," she calls out.

"What?" he grumbles.

"First year chemistry, did Kane ever tell you why Dr. Sumner was mad at him?"

Standing behind E now, I place my hands on her shoulder and catch the panic flicker through Zeke's eyes.

"No," he breathes then looks at me. I catch the moment he recalls a million and one things it could have been before Ebony does. His eyes shift back and forth as his mind churns to pinpoint which memory from our first year that made sense. Which memory held the key to what was mixed in the chemistry that led to Dr. Sumner watching us so closely that he'd be able to tell everyone the last time we picked our noses. What was it that we mixed three years ago? Could it have been the shit that's been going around? There's a feeling in the pit of my stomach that makes me think it could be and the fact that Ebony could have been hurt because of our carelessness makes this whole thing much worse.

"I guess that goes on the list," she mutters with a

sigh, interrupting my own thoughts. She sits back at her computer scrolling through what's on her screen as Zeke and I exchange glances. The tension vanishes as we both get lost in our thoughts. What happens if we did start this whole mess? Would Ebony trust us? I may have thought bringing Ren here was the worst thing I've ever done in my life, but that's slowly changing as we dig deeper.

What the fuck did we do?

26

Ren

I have a confession to make. Ice skating is my least favorite thing to do in the world, but here I am. With a thick, army green blanket wrapped around my shoulders, I shiver and wince as my body jolts, irritating the bruises I'm sure I'll have in the morning.

An ice skater glides past me on the makeshift ice rink, spinning and twirling with a large smile on their face. I tug at my wool cap and huff. Christmas music blares from the speakers filling everyone but me with the holiday spirit. A steaming cup of hot cocoa appears in front of me before I register Mel's multicolored mittens. Tilting my head up a bit, I catch her reddened cheeks and nose as her frizzy curls whip around her face.

"They put extra marshmallows!" she squeals as I take the cup. She dances in her place before sitting next to me and taking a cautious sip of her own drink. She closes her eyes and releases a soft sigh. "It's so good," she groans into her cup. She takes another slow sip after blowing through the hole.

Swirls of white steam dance in front of me before I blow into the spout, then taking a sip of my own. Rich chocolate notes dance across my tongue as I take a small sip. "Oh,"

I mutter before taking another one, scalding my tongue. "Shit!"

Mel laughs beside me, "Take your time!" She grabs a napkin from her pocket and dabs at my lip. "Ready for another go?" she asks with a bright smile.

I groan, throwing my head back to mask the smile crawling on my face. I push up, balancing on the blades of the blue rental ice skates secured on my feet. "Ready as I'll ever be," I say with a soft laugh. I adjust my cap on my head, then step onto the ice with Mel. She glides against the smooth surface, her curls floating behind her as she twirls in front of me.

"You're so slowwwww," she whines, skating back to me as I cling to the wall. My skates slip and slide from underneath me making her giggle. She balances me by grabbing my hands, then slowly skates backwards until I have my balance.

"You should go without me," I say self-consciously as I lose my footing again. Releasing her hands, I fall. The ice biting into my ass and my wrist screaming from my failed attempt to brace myself. Thankfully still by the wall, I use it to steady myself into a standing position.

"Are you okay?" Mel asks by my side as she braces me. "We can stop."

I shake my head, looking over at her. "You're having fun. Go. I'll watch from over here."

She looks at me, her eyes studying my face before she agrees. Helping me off the ice, she waits until my snow boots are secured on my feet before flitting away gracefully.

"Reneva," a sugary sweet voice calls out to me. I glance

behind me and look up at the woman. Her hair is a blunt, layered bob with a bang. Her jet black hair is smooth and shiny under the bright overhead lights. Deep brown eyes, the color of tree bark, stand out from light brown skin. Her angular nose reminds me of the last person I'd want to remember.

She smiles when I scoot back on instinct.

"So, you do know who I am," she says smoothly. She takes a seat on the bench next to me before glancing around the ice skating rink.

I swallow, creating as much space as I possibly can from her. But with the amount of people, that's not much.

Her manicured finger reaches out and grasps the ends of my hair. The frayed edges make her frown. She drops it, then wipes her hands like she touched the most disgusting thing in the world.

"How's progress with operation 'deliver Ebony's head on a silver platter'?" she asks nonchalantly. She looks out at the skaters almost disinterested in my response. When I don't answer, her eyes pierce through me.

"I'm working on it," I sputter.

"What could possibly be taking you so long? She's a simple- minded girl."

"There's bad blood there," I defend with a furrowed brow.

"Like I care?" she laughs. "How about this," she says with a smile that unsettles me. "What would you say if I had a much better deal than what my husband and son are offering you?"

Veronica leans more into the light, sending my heart in

a haywire.

27

Kane

Howls fill the air as E escorts me around the small animal rescue. Large cages line both sides of the hall with various pairings of furry companions. Pants and whimpers mingle as we near some of the cages and she points out a few of the dogs.

"That's Lulabelle. She likes being called Lulla the most," E shares with a smile. She squats down and puts her palm up to the metal cage. Lulla, and the others, eagerly rush towards the cage licking at E's palm before rubbing their bodies against the cage's siding making it rattle.

"This one is Punkin." She points out a small black puppy that wiggles as his large tail excitedly. His pink tongue hangs out the side of his mouth as he pants. "They were found on the side of the interstate two weeks ago. No microchip, no collar."

"Are these the two that kept you out late?" I ask, squatting beside her finally and placing my palm on the cage. Lulla, as friendly as ever, immediately laps her warm, wet tongue against my palm. E gives me a bashful smile before nodding.

"They were tied to a post and it was freezing that night."

"Is that part of the job?"

"No," she answers with a laugh. "But it should be."

I nod agreeing as we push to our feet, I wipe my palm on the cage before being introduced to the other friendly pups. Each one eager for attention, primarily hers, and ready to show their best tricks for a scratch behind their ear. She beams as she greets each one with a few minutes of scratches and praises.

As we exit the room to the main hall, she grabs my wrist and pulls me towards another door. "We have the more aggressive animals and the ones we're rehabbing and quarantining in here."

The door groans as she enters the room before she softly adds, "We're in the process of re-socializing the more aggressive animals. We won't ask you to—"

"Akemi used to be labeled aggressive," I share, looking at her earnestly. "Took a lot of patience to get her where she is now."

She looks over at me with a soft smile on her face before facing a new cage. Unlike the others, plexiglass covers the front, air holes punctured at the top and bottom of the piece. A soft light glows from the perimeter of the top and bottom.

A small brown dog cowers in the corner. His fur is buzzed, fresh stitches lace up his puckered skin. A few scars linger around the space. He snarls and whimpers a bit trying to get as far from us as possible.

"This is Edgar," Ebony says softly. "Someone found him in the mall parking lot."

"What's with the scars?"

"We think he was hit by a car," she says softly. "He has

fleas and an infection so he's quarantined. Not dog friendly though."

"How is he with people?" I ask, inching closer to the glass. He cowers more, making me stop my movements.

"Like that," she sighs. "But it's understandable."

We spend a few more minutes with the animals here, a few birds, bare of feathers, huddling in a corner squawking as we get closer.

"You never told me what Ren said," E says softly as she slowly continues giving me a tour. We're back in the hall. The smell of bleach and urine sting my nose.

"It wasn't really important," I mutter running my hand through my hair. "They're more than likely playing games."

E shakes her head, disappointment evident by the way she purses her lips. She gives a nod, then shows me more of the shelter. Introducing me to various animals and pointing out the stations I'll most likely use while volunteering here. I admire her passion for the animals. Watching her interact with them, it's new, refreshing honestly. The loose cats rush to her feet, each taking turns bumping and nudging against her until she gives each of them adequate time and attention.

"I feel close to them," she says, squatting and scratching at each of the cats that trample over one another to get to her. "They just need someone to believe in them. A second chance at life."

Her big brown eyes catch mine. There's so much behind them. I can barely decipher the emotions, but they're there. Complex emotions that she wields so majestically. "Is that why you volunteer here?"

She nods before looking back down at the cats. A tiny

one meowing loudly to get her attention. She scoops it up and nuzzles it into her chest. "Just like you," she says softly, glancing back at me. "And you," she finishes, keeping her eyes on me.

She's right. I do need a second chance. A moment to rectify myself, but not in the way she thinks. Mine is more internal. Giving myself a second chance to just breathe, be a brother, a lover, a friend.

"I have to tell you something," I say, feeling what Ren said weighing heavily on me. She looks up at me, eyes curious and alert.

"Is this the mysterious Kane," a soft voice calls from behind us, interrupting any chances I have to tell her what Ren said.

Ebony peeks around my legs and smiles big. She stands, stepping over the bundle of cats that are sprawled out for her before nodding. "This is him!"

I follow her gaze towards a guy about a couple of inches shorter than me. His sandy blonde hair is slightly curly. Bright blue eyes glow from his face as he smiles at E, then gives me a more controlled one.

"I'm Jed." He reaches out his boney hand and gives me a firm shake. "I trust that Ebony gave you the tour?"

"She did. She was telling me about your plan to help the animals back there," I say, jutting my thumb over my shoulder where the animals that need more patience and love stay.

Jed nods, making his curls bounce slightly. He shoves his hands in his jeans pocket, his dingy black shirt lifting at the hem showing a sliver of pale skin.

"I can take it from here, Ebony," Jed says smiling at her. He gestures towards the front before looking down at the cats.

"Have fun," she says, mostly to me. She gives me a smile before disappearing around the corner. It's one of those smiles that makes my heart clench happily. One that makes her eyes look like stars that twinkle in the dark skies on clear nights, maybe right after a heavy rain storm in summer.

Damn, I love that woman.

"What experience do you have with shelters?" Jed asks as he ushers me towards a makeshift office. I take a seat in the chair he gestures to before he sits behind his wooden desk. One that probably came from an online boutique that has them in bulk.

"Not much," I offer, spinning the ring on my pointer finger with my thumb.

He hums his response and gives me a once over. "Ebony says you have a dog?"

"I do," I confirm with a nod. "She was kind of like the ones you have in quarantine. In bad shape and not trusting anyone. Took some time, but I got her to warm up. Big difference between when she was younger till now."

"I see," he says, sounding a little uninterested in my story, which bothers me. It's Akemi. She's incredible. Her story also shows that I know a thing or two about helping animals, even if I had a few mishaps along the way. I'm human. I make mistakes. "That's great," he says after I let the silence linger longer. "I hope you understand my reservations," Jed finally says, relaxing his shoulders and sighing.

"Reservations?"

"Yes. Your lack of experience could really get one of us, or Ebony, hurt," he says leaning back in his chair. "It's a huge risk. I need someone with hands and muscles to help me transport and move these animals. Is that something you can handle?"

"Absolutely. I'm not afraid to get my hands a little dirty. And aggressive animals don't scare me. They need a little extra love, that's all."

He laughs, a light sound that still finds a way to fill the space. "Ebony said the same damn thing when she rehabbed Silver and his littermates. That cat bonded to her after that."

"She rehabbed Silver?"

"Oh yeah," Jed says as he leans forward towards the desk nodding and smiling softly. "Him and his littermates were strays. Feral strays. Hissed and spit at any and everyone. She got swatted at and scratched a few times, but had the patience of a saint with them. Once they were okay with her gloved hand, she started getting them used to pets and head scratches." He glances at me and clears his throat. "She wasn't in the best of shapes either."

"How long has Ebony volunteered for you?"

"Since she started at Knight U. She was looking for a way to destress, I nearly offered her a job on the spot, but I was just a small establishment then. Her Gramps is actually the reason I was able to expand. He's donated so much money to us that I offered to get him his own guard dog for that rundown shack he calls a bar." Jed laughs and leans back in the chair.

"I think that little bulldog would work great in his bar,"

I say, making Jed chuckle loudly.

"He'll be bad for business!" he gasps through his chuckles. "He'll stink up the place before anyone has a chance to get one beer done."

I let a few small chuckles join his before I sit back, waiting for his to die down. When they do, he wipes at his eyes and exhales sharply. A smile still on his face.

"We get dogs in all the time," he starts after a few moments. "But at least once or twice a month is when we really get the big ones. Great Danes. Cane Corsos. We even got a wolf dog not too long ago. Such a sweet girl, but her eyes were intense."

"Really? Didn't know they had any around here." I shift in my seat.

"When you got money, you can get anything you want," he says with a head shake. He looks around his desk for a moment before sighing. "Look, I'm sure you can tell I could really use the help around here. Ebony says you're pretty reliable so we can do a week trial run. Do you have any paperwork I need to fill out or…?" his voice trails off as he looks at me.

"I can email it over with the dean copied" I confirm with a head nod.

"Okay cool." He stands, wiping his hands on the front of his jeans. "Like I said, once or twice a month is when I really need your muscles. Other than that, feeding and cleaning the cages, making sure the families get some time in the play areas with the dogs, and the dogs get out for a good walk. That's about it."

"When do you want me to start?" I ask not wanting to

sound too eager, but feeling it nonetheless.

"How soon can you start?"

I give him a smile. "I can start today if you need me."

"Then follow me," he says, returning my smile and reaching for my hand. He shakes it, then leads me to another room of the shelter to fill out paperwork and store my stuff.

28

Ren

It's been two weeks since I last saw or heard from Kane. And if I'm being honest, I wouldn't be standing outside of the quaint little animal shelter he's volunteering at with Ebony had he not ignored the first five calls I tried making to him. I guess that's the benefit of having Vin on my side still. He'll tell me exactly where to find Ebony. Creepy fucker must really have a tracking device implanted in her.

Cloudy breaths float past my body as I breathe deeply. My gloved hands are shoved deep in the pockets of my thick wool coat, my hat shoved over my ears. Mashing the green call button on my screen, I shove my phone to my ear and watch as Kane flirts shamelessly with Ebony. A cat is brushing against his leg as he leans against the counter, a cocky ass smile on his face.

He must have said something dumb because she doesn't look amused. In fact, she rolls her eyes at him and focuses on the computer screen in front of her. Her eyebrows raising as he continues talking and reaches for one of her locs.

My phone rings as I continue watching. His hand slips into his pocket, eyes never leaving her until he glances at the screen and presses the silence button for the third time since I've been out here. Make that six intentionally ignored calls

179

now. He should remember I'm not ashamed to call until he picks up, but then again, I'm standing right outside so there really is no need.

She looks up at him, seemingly asking him a question that he shrugs off. His flirtatious body language does not change even when his face turns grim. I wonder what he's saying. I wonder what he told her to begin with?

There's a brief moment where I contemplate walking inside. Intentionally putting myself in the position where Kane has to acknowledge my existence and hear me out, but the other part of me tells me not to. Either way, no matter what I choose to do, I can't force her to listen. Not until the moment happens. The moment where I can slip her exactly what I need to. From there, I can hand her over to Vin or I can set a trap to get rid of him once and for all. And even that can be in a variety of ways. Knowing that Kane likes Ebony enough to call her his "girlfriend" publicly, I could set the bait and let him ruin his entire fucking life to set me free.

He taps the counter letting his eyes drag over her body. The way men do when they see something they like. He says something to her and she smiles at him, shaking her head before focusing back on the computer screen. Then he's heading towards the back. The door closes behind him and I make my way across the street, snow crunching beneath my worn, beat up snow boots. Some of the melting matter seeps into the soles of my shoes making my thick socks soggy. Three pairs of thick socks at that.

I push through the door, the little bell over the metal frame tinkling as I step over the threshold. I wipe my feet on the black rug and step to the counter. I shove my hat back revealing my face, catching Ebony off guard. Her polite smile is frozen between the look of shock, fear, and fury. I must be a sick bitch for being turned on by the look in her eyes. I love seeing her afraid, angry even. Two emotions that are closely related, even if we don't admit it. In this situation, both emotions hold hands. They're lovers even. She's afraid of me, angry with me.

"What the fuck are you doing here?" she growls, standing from her seat, sending the cat that was curled up in her lap scrambling away somewhere deep in the office.

I may enjoy her anger, but that's not what I need right now. What I need is her fear, her cooperation to set my plan in motion. She has the means, the team to make this work for me. Once she's on board, I can figure out my next step.

"Look, I know my plan sounds crazy," I start. "But I need you for this to work. It's the only way."

Her eyes are narrowed at me, but I can still see confusion flicker across them. She places her palms flat on the counter in front of her.

"What plan?"

"He didn't tell you," I breathe out, slightly regretting outing my best friend, but also enjoying the chaos I know this would cause.

Angry Ebony is beautiful. A rapture waiting to happen. I love how her eyes darken, how her lips form into a thin line, even with their fullness out on display. I love the violence that lingers beneath her because her anger is authentic, unregulated by the confines of right or wrong. I wonder if Kane enjoys it too. Especially since he should know her finding this out from me would make her very, very angry.

One thing about Ebony, she doesn't like people making decisions for her. She doesn't like handing over control. Unless she's getting fucked, then she's pretty decent at taking orders. Still a pain in the ass, but it's manageable.

She shakes her head letting her guard drop enough. She shifts her position, her hands inching away from the letter opener I foolishly didn't see clenched in her hand.

This could have ended badly.

"I told Kane that I have a plan, but I need you to trust me for this to work."

"What plan?" she asks evenly.

If I didn't know Ebony, I'd assume she was calm, but she isn't. She's pissed and this time it's not directed at me. I'm a little disappointed. I'm a little masochist at heart, I love when she's angry at me. And I know in this situation, with where we are in this dynamic, she won't hold back. Kane fucked up — big time. And even if I feel a little bad about this, I have to shake it off. He had two weeks to tell her. Not my fault he thought he knew what was best.

"The end of year party," I start and pause when I notice she flinches.

Every year, there's an end of year party for people that stay close to campus. That was the party we were at when I did what I did, because it had also been the same party my brother OD'd at.

Look at life, coming full circle and shit.

"At the next party, you and I are going to set Vin up. We'll take something so he thinks we're vulnerable. We'll wear body cams and all that, live stream the whole thing. He's going to take the bait and with that, we'll have more than enough evidence to take him to court."

She makes a slow descent to the chair behind her. It rolls beneath her weight, but she steadies it as her eyes focus. Her leg bounces as she thinks, her thumb going to her mouth as she gnaws at the skin around the nail bed. A nasty habit she had back when we first met.

"We'll iron out all the details," I assure her. "You won't get hurt this time."

Molten brown eyes lock onto mine as she lets the weight of my plan settle in. She'd have to trust me completely. Rely on me when we get the process rolling. I see the questions rolling in her mind. If she was smart, she'd tell me to go fuck myself. If she wasn't desperate to be free, she'd say something much worse than what she surprises me with.

"Are we going to actually drug ourselves?" Her voice is soft, uncertain as she looks at me. She's hoping I'll tell her something she can stand firmly on. She'll never find that with me. It's something I've never offered her. I'm hell on Earth and God damn I'd be a fool to say this wasn't turning me on more.

She doesn't trust Kane's judgment in this, doesn't even trust herself. If I say the right things, she's under my mercy. I could cum right now with how desperate, how vulnerable, how fucking eager she is to find someone safe. I know, disturbing, but we all cope with our trauma in different ways.

I nod slowly, keeping my excitement locked deep

inside my belly. She's going to take the bait. We're both backed in corners we want to be out of and poor Kane is just an innocent bystander.

"What are you doing here?" Kane's voice startles us both.

Ebony jumps out of her seat, hands flying to her chest as she stares at his large body. Her chest rapidly rising and falling as she stares at him.

I take an unsteady step back towards the door. My hands shoot up like I'm surrendering in this battle. I'm not. I'll never give up what my plan is, but I have to make him think otherwise if he's not going to be on my side.

"You shouldn't be here," he growls, taking a step forward.

"Why didn't you tell me about their plan?" Ebony asks. Her voice is hard, authoritative. It immediately catches his attention.

His face morphs, going soft just for her as his mouth opens and closes as he searches for something to say. Her anger is palpable in the air. I can taste it. A metallic, acidic taste that bounces off my taste buds. Just like how her body used to taste after a big argument with me when I sided with Vin. Her body always creates a medley of flavors depending on her mood. Anger was my favorite.

I inhale deeply, stifling a groan as I watch her fury grow.

Get him.

"Because their plan is dangerous and fucking stupid," he finally says, throwing me a disgusted look. Look what you've done. "I tried to tell you anyway. We kept getting interrupted."

"When I asked you to talk to them instead of me," she argues, "I didn't mean for you to make decisions for me."

"What they're asking you to do is dangerous, E," his voice pleads. He throws his fingers through his messy hair, dog hair littering his black long sleeved tee shirt.

Dogs bark restlessly in the back, sensing the growing tension the same way I am. I take another step back before placing my hands on the cold metal door handle. I slip out and over the threshold as their argument escalates.

"I told you to trust me!" she shouts at him. Her voice wavering as it increases in volume.

Their voices collide violently as the bells jingle and the door closes slowly. A small smile tiptoes across my lips as I walk back to my car, hands tucked in my pocket and a spring in my step. I don't feel the violent wind that whips my hair every which way, but I do glance back as I stop at the driver side of my car.

Time to watch this fire burn.

29

Kane

"What did you do?" Miya asks, sitting beside me in the computer lab. She sighs giving me a sympathetic look, but there's frustration behind it.

The library is fairly busy as people roam and goof off through the computer area. There's a low murmur from different clusters of people at work stations around the open space. The smell of dirt and ice settles in the air as the doors open and close periodically. A few people glance our way as my sister drops her bag on the ground with her eyes still fixed on my face, a slight glare forming when I don't respond right away. My fingers stop moving over the keyboard as I turn to look at my sister. I give my head a scratch, then cross my arms over my chest as I lean back in my chair.

"All I did was try to protect Ebony. If she doesn't appreciate that, then I don't know what the fuck to say."

"Protect her how?" Miya asks, leaning closer to me. Her brow furrowed and eyes squinted a little.

I glance over my shoulder before leaning closer to my sister explaining the situation to her. I start with meeting Ren at the pizza place and end with the situation that happened last night, which unfortunately continued today with Ebony barely talking to me. I'm not getting the silent treatment exactly, but she's making it very obvious that I'm on her shit list. No matter what I say about the situation, she glares at me, tells me she doesn't want to talk about it, then storms off.

"Fucking Ren," Miya groans and leans back. "Everywhere they go, there's trouble."

"The plan is ridiculous. It's dangerous," I say, looking at my sister. I'm desperate for someone to intervene now. There's not much else I can do aside from tying her to the bed and barricading her in the apartment, but that solves nothing.

"It is, but…" Miya starts, sitting up quickly and logging into the computer beside me. "We can control certain aspects of everything. Ebony and I are still in charge of majority of these parties. Spring Break and the End of Year party being the two biggest ones."

She pulls up a calendar website that's packed with color coded tabs and highlights. She scrolls through them and clicks on one tab, closes it out, then clicks on another.

"Just as I thought," she says as a small smile forms on her face. "Several organizations contracted us to plan their play off parties, Spring Break, and the End of the Year party."

She turns and looks at me, her smile growing.

"Okay?" I question after a moment of her staring at me with that damn smile on her face.

"It means," she starts, rolling her eyes like I'm a dumbass. "That we can lure him to any of these places and have the upper hand. Most of these organizations we've worked with. I'll have to talk to Ebony, but you have to chill the fuck out. That controlling shit isn't going to help."

"I'm not being controlling," I protest, glaring at her. "I'd do the same for you, Han, and Zeke!"

"Yah. And when we need you to do that, it's great." She grabs her stuff, logs off the computer, then stands up. "But do you really want to push her closer to Ren knowing that they have a knack for lying?"

I stare at my sister's smug face as I lean back in my chair not responding. I'll have to give it to her, she's smart. And she's right about everything. Ebony wouldn't let her guard down and me trying to control everything just means I don't trust her to make the right decision. I huff in frustration shaking my head and turning away from my sister, still silent.

She pats my shoulder before ruffling my hair, then darts off giggling. I grumble, rearranging the mess on the top of my head. The door clangs against the metal frame as it closes behind her.

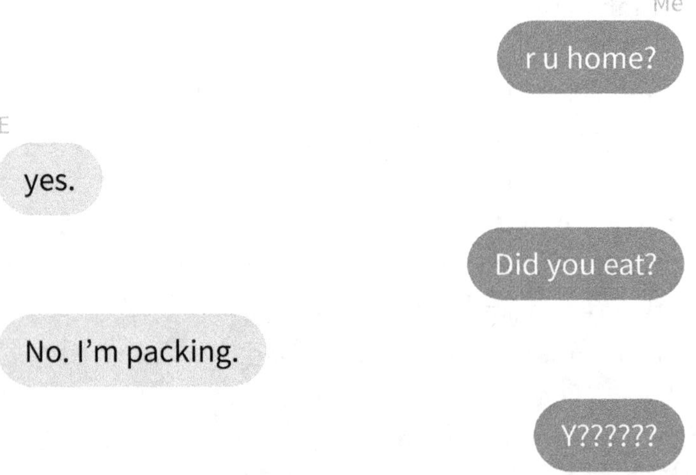

She sends me a picture instead of typing. A pink slip of

paper with big, bold, black letters demanding her to vacate the premises in 30 days. I sigh, log off the computer and sling my bag over my shoulder.

"Shit," I mutter.

I'll be there in a second.

Don't bother.

I shove my phone back in my pocket, slip my beanie over my hair and leave the library quickly. She may not want me around, but I live there too. Plus, it will be good to try and get her to fucking talk to me about the whole Ren thing.

It doesn't take me long to get to the apartment. I slide my key through the lock and twist it, pushing my way through the door. I pause, keys dangling in my hand as I take in the mess that used to be our home.

Several boxes — some open, some taped up, and some still collapsed on themself — sit in nearly every space. Music spills from our room as I hear cluttering and crashing. She swears and chucks something out of the room. It hits the wall with a loud bang. Silver hisses from his cat tower, emerald green eyes peeking out from the dark space.

Dropping my bag and kicking off my shoes, I meander through the maze of our apartment shoving my keys in my pocket.

"E?" I call out, hoping I don't get hit with whatever she might have near her. Maybe this wasn't the best idea with her being mad at me.

Greeted with nothing but destruction as I peek in the

room, I take note of the clothes thrown nearly everywhere. Our floor is covered with hangers as she fusses in the closet, a box sitting right near the entrance. There's a black contractor bag stuffed with clothes that I've never seen her wear.

With a sigh, I step in and immediately start pulling down hangers.

"I told you not to come," she grumbles, clothes thrown over her arm and her hair pulled back.

"If you're going to kick me out," I say, stepping out with an armful and placing everything on the bed to rearrange and gather them by the hanger. "You're going to have to tell me directly."

I look at her as I hang some items in a large wardrobe box I found off to the side. I run my hand down them to smooth them out, then step back towards the closet door and reach for the items in her arm.

She hesitates.

"Oh, I have your permission now?" she grumbles.

Her eyes are glaring into mine before she shoves the stuff into my arms and slips back into the closet silently. I roll my eyes, clamping my jaw tight to keep my temper in check. I'd rather patch this up and my anger would only make it worse. So, I allow the music to fill the space as I hang up the clothes and set up another wardrobe box. Hangers clang from the closet door as she struggles with something. I step in and reach over her to help.

"I got it," she growls.

"Let me help," I say, reaching again.

"I said I got it!" she snaps, turning to look at me, her

eyes blazing with rage.

"You may have it, but I'm here to help. Stop being stubborn and let me help," I counter, narrowing my eyes down into hers.

"Stop trying to control every damn thing that makes you uncomfortable!" she yells back.

"You're one to talk," I say back. Her eyes widen for a split second before she attempts to nudge past me.

My hand grabs her, pulling her back to me quickly. She yanks her arm away, pushing at my chest before attempting to walk away again. My hand laces around her arm again, allowing me to move my body to block her from the door.

The warmth of her body, the heat from her anger, rolls off of her short stature and mixes with mine as I step closer. Her chest rises and falls rapidly, then her hands are on my face, pulling herself into my arms as her lips find mine.

A soft growl escapes her as I give in, bracing her body in my hands. In one fluid movement, I lift her into my arms, feeling her legs wrap around my waist.

Greedy fingers tug at my shirt, but she gives up to pull at her own. Her body shifts as she removes the fabric off her skin. She breathes heavily as she tosses her shirt to the cluttered floor below my feet.

"Ebony wait—" she shuts me up with a kiss. Her hands pull at my shirt again.

"Shut up," she breathes against my skin. "Take this off."

I shift, bracing her against the cleared wall and pulling my shirt off, unclasping her bra in the process. Her hand grips my shoulder, then my throat. She gives it a squeeze, her tongue snaking into my mouth.

I break the kiss, pulling my face back to look at her, one of my hands on the back of her neck. Her eyes are cloudy with desire and frustration as my grip tightens. As I increase the pressure, her lids flutter closed as she swivels her hips, ripping a groan from me.

She slips one hand between us and fumbles with the button of my jeans. Her body shakes slightly in my hands as I squeeze, grip, and grope at her thighs.

My button unfastens with a pop and she's on the move, wiggling out of my hold to undress. I fall in sync with her, I shove my jeans down, then turn her to face the wall. With my head dipped down towards her neck, I enter her roughly, pushing myself all the way to the base.

She moans, her hands braced against the wall as she arches her back into me. My teeth drag across her shoulders before biting down close to her neck. Using my grip on her waist, I guide her body down to meet my hard thrusts.

I use my foot to spread her legs more, the sudden jolt from the movement forcing her face against the wall as she slips, a gasp leaving her lips as she panics a little. Her hands gripping my wrist, fingernails cutting into my skin as I fuck her hard.

"Bite me harder," she gasps. Her voice pitched and needy.

I do, leaning over and clamping down as her body shudders. I wiggle my wrist out of her hold and slap her ass hard. Her body responds animatedly as she moans, eyes pinched shut as she molds herself against the wall.

"Oh, fuck," she groans as her first orgasm hits us both hard. Her pussy clenching and squeezing me tightly as her legs shake. My hands keeping her steady she sags into the wall, her jaw clenched, staccato breathes accenting the air mixed with her strained whimpers.

I slow my pace, easing into her until the clenching slows and her breaths even out. I pull out of her to turn her body. I lift her into my arms and enter her deeply. A loud moan erupts out of her as she leans her back against the wall. Our eyes lock as my hand caresses her exposed skin, goosebumps rising in the wake of my touches. She watches me, her mouth parted and eyes glazed with pleasure.

With my hand around the back of her neck again, I angle her towards me, pulling one of her nipples in my mouth. Dragging my teeth across the balls of her nipple ring, she jolts in my grip, her pussy clenching tightly around me.

Fingernails dig into my shoulders as I pull her body down on me. Hangers snap and clatter beneath my feet as I shift my position, pinning her to the wall, my mouth and teeth still attached to her nipple.

I slow my pace feeling the tension in my body building up for my release. My hips roll agonizingly slow as I prolong it, making her groan. She rolls her hips, digging the heels of her feet into my thighs as she attempts to speed me up.

"Fuck. Me. Kane," she pants desperately.

I smile against her nipple, rubbing up her body and circling her neck with my hand. I release her nipple to look into her eyes, pushing deep inside her. A gasp passes her lips as her head rolls back as I do it again. Her hands slap against my arm as she braces herself. I roll my hips again. A raw, low groan falls from her lips as her legs shake against my waist.

"Oh baby," I taunt, looking over her body and slowing my pace more, but still pushing in just as deep. "You're so fucking close aren't you?"

She whimpers, nodding her head. Her legs tensing as her eyes find mine. The desperation makes them glassy.

"Take it," I encourage with a smile on my face. My hands grip her waist, keeping her still a moment longer. "Be a good fucking girl and take what you want."

Rolling her hips and countering my thrusts, she clenches and unclenches around me. Her eyebrow arching as she does, challenging me. Her body fights against my grip. Her devastatingly beautiful dominance rearing its head completely as she leans into my neck and bites me, rolling her tongue over the skin pinched between her teeth. I groan as her hips circle faster and faster as her breathing catches while she uses my body to chase her climax.

I thrust deeper, pushing her back against the wall, pinning her there by her neck. My body slamming into hers, chasing my own release until she shudders, her hands wrapped around my wrist as my dick pulsates inside her. Then she shudders around me, eyes rolling back as she coasts down from her high.

I pull her into me, biting and sucking at each other's lips. When our breathing steadies, she pushes away from me, unlocking her legs as she slides down my body. With her clothes tucked beneath her arm, she unsteadily walks into the bathroom. The door shuts and the lock clicks behind her.

The sound of the shower turning on greets my ears as

I pull my pants on, adjusting them. With a heavy sigh, I roll my shoulders and look around the closet. Much like our relationship, everything is out of order and piling up. I scratch my temple, leaving the room to grab some water to help clear my head.

30

Ebony

"Listen to this," I say as Zeke slides into the booth beside me. Denise sits across from me, a french fry entering her mouth as she looks at me. "'I've been working on something to send to someone in Office. He reached out saying he needs something strong, more potent. I've never done anything like this before, but for the price he put on it, I'm willing to try.'"

"Didn't take you for a creative writer, E," he says. "Jesus," he gasps.

I look at him and frown. His eyes are searching my skin as a knowing smile creeps on his face.

"You should see the other guy," Denise says, laughing.

"Kane's got one too?" Zeke asks Denise, ignoring me.

"A big ass nasty bruise on his neck," Denise confirms with a nod. "And she's been reading Rae's journey. Some real investigative shit." Denise smiles.

"Didn't take you as a biter," he mutters, nudging me with a smile.

I roll my eyes with a huff.

"What's going on?" he asks cautiously. The playfulness fleeing from his eyes as he looks me over again. "Both of you are in this weird space. What happened? Is it Ren? They're not trying to get you back are they?"

"Ew," I mutter. "Got into a fight with Kane is all."

I shrug my shoulders, taking another fry and nibbling on it. I scoot down in the seat and prop my feet up on the edges of the booth seat across from me. I look back at my screen, reading through the entry again.

"Miya mentioned you two had an issue because of Ren," he states, turning in the seat to look at me.

"It's not because of Ren. It's because of him and his dumbass ego," I protest. "He always thinks he knows best. Shit's annoying."

"I mean yeah, but we know Kane. He thinks he can take care of everyone and ends up making shit worse. Then we come along and fix it."

"I was telling her ass that," Denise says with a scoff.

"I just don't like him trying to make decisions for me," I grumble, crossing my arms over my chest then wincing. I rub my arm, then my shoulder where I have my own bruise.

There's a minute or two of silence between us, then I'm closing my computer.

"I'm meeting with a lawyer."

"Does he know?" Denise asks.

I shake my head and look down at my hands. I pick at the skin around my nails before Denise's hands grab them, forcing me to look up.

"Baby girl, you should tell him," she comments softly. Her thumb brushes my knuckles.

I accept her affection and the way the warmth from her soft fingers sink into my flesh.

"It's not really his business," I respond idly.

"So fucking stubborn," Zeke mumbles with an eye roll.

"It's just a civil case. Might get me a restraining order from Vin."

"You and I both know it's just a piece of paper." There's a sadness in his voice when he says this. A distant look in his eyes.

"And that piece of paper has never stopped him before," Denise says, giving my hand a gentle squeeze.

They're both right. No matter how many restraining orders I had against Vin, they all seemed to vanish into thin air.

I sit in my seat contemplating the decision I have to make and the many conversations I have to have.

"Ren wants to drug me again," I say softly, catching Zeke's attention. "Or themself. Maybe both of us."

"For what?"

"To trap Vin," I whisper while looking around. "They think we can get him on unaltered footage that way."

"That sounds like a terrible idea," Zeke warns. "You trust them enough to do something like that?"

I shake my head before sighing. "I can't think of any other way. What we did at the gala only has me looking over my shoulder. I feel like shit's gonna get worse."

I feel Denise give my fingers a reassuring squeeze, but she doesn't offer any words. She's been through this with me. She knows the struggle of battling Vin and his demented demons.

"Or they may not," Zeke offers with hopeful eyes. "You have Rae's journal. See what's in there. Talk to the lawyer as a safety measure, but based on what I know about Rae, which isn't much, he documented everything."

"If it isn't little miss Ebony," Vin hisses, sliding into the booth across from Zeke and I. Denise reluctantly scoots over, casting Vin a nasty side eye.

My body tenses. A prickly sensation shoots through my arms and legs as I look up slowly at Vin. Zeke squares his shoulders, his eyes staring daggers into Vin's face.

"You should know, it took a long time to get the old man calm," Vin says. His words, sickeningly sweet as he crosses his arms in front of him and leans against the table.

"Poor you," I finally sneer.

"Oh, no. Not me. Poor you." He chuckles, lifting his hands and looking at them. "Because you can't behave, I'm going to make your life here hell."

"Like hell you are," Zeke spits.

"Oh, I am." Vin cuts his eyes over to Zeke, then eyes him up and down before looking back at me. "Hope you have fun apartment hunting."

He smiles and slips out of the booth, cockily walking over to another table and draping his arm around a girl there. She smiles at him, kissing his cheek as he stares me down.

"You know what," I start, snatching my bag and hopping over the back of the booth. My legs move rapidly as they carry me out the door. I can hear Denise and Zeke following behind me.

Blinded by rage, I notice Vin's blacked out Hellcat glimmering in the sun.

Snatching a bat from a baseball player, I drop my bag to the ground, then sprint through the muddy, damp parking lot. Swinging the metal bat with all the rage bubbling up inside of me, Vin's windshield cracks from the first blow. Another strike sends shards of glass inside the car.

Ignoring the speckling of onlookers, I swing hitting the driver's side window, then the passenger. Feral growls rising out of my body with every violent swing of the bat.

"What the fuck!?" someone shouts. "Someone get Vin!"

"It'll be the last fucking thing you do," I hear Zeke growl as I stand on top of Vin's Hellcat raining fierce blows on the top of the car and the now crumbling back window.

I drop the bat and grab my keys out of my pocket. I pop the blade of my pocket knife, clear the glass with the edges of the bat, and climb into his car through the destroyed driver side window.

Piercing the authentic leather, I slice horizontally, cutting his name in half on the head rest. The stuffing seeps out as I push the knife deeper. I stab more of the leather, dragging the small, sharp blade through the rough material.

As I climb in the back, piercing the seats and raising my arm back to cut more, a strong hand grabs my arm, yanking me out of the car and pinning me to the side of the now dented body.

Soulless eyes meet mine.

"You fucking reckless cunt," Vin hisses as he reaches his hand back and slaps my face. Hard.

Red paints his face as rage takes over and he raises his hand, balling it into a fist. I swat at him, stupidly dropping my keys to the ground as his fingers wrap around the base of my throat and squeeze.

Denise's nostrils flare as she positions herself to lunge at

Vin, but Zeke steps in, yanking her back and spearing Vin to the side, successfully breaking his hold on me.

I crumple to the ground as Denise pulls me back. Zeke rears his fist back, repeatedly pounding it into Vin's face.

Getting the best of Zeke, Vin swings, hitting Zeke off of him and the two go blow for blow until their teammates break them up and separate them.

Vin's eyebrow seeps blood as he wipes the crimson fluid from his mouth, then spits.

"This ain't fucking over, bitch," Vin says, casting me a sideways glance and shoving his teammates off as he storms off.

31

Ren

The community college I attend isn't far from Knight U's campus, but of course, not nearly as large. The sun slowly descends from the sky as I work on a case study inside one of the study rooms. The vending machines hum beside me as I peck away at my keys.

"Did you really dodge a date with me to research your brother's case?" Mel complains, placing a paper bag on the table.

I smile at her, shaking my head.

"Homework," I offer. "Wanting to get this assignment done early so I can spend some quality time with you." I stand, pulling her into my arms then kissing her temple. "Missed me?"

"A little," she says with a blush. The dimple in her right cheek shows itself as she smiles at me. "Brought you dinner since you forget to eat."

Sheepishly, I laugh at her words and move my things into my bag. She busies herself arranging items like napkins and forks on the table. The white paper bag sits in the center of the table.

She sits down across from me after securing her bag to the chair. Her dainty fingers reach into the sack and pull out three styrofoam containers that she opens. Steam wafts from the two boxes holding pastas and the other box holding garlic bread. She pulls out another container that's slightly smaller than the others. With the top removed, the tiramisu taunts me.

"What's the occasion?" I ask dabbing at my mouth to keep from drooling too much.

"I can't treat you to dinner?" she quips. "Look," she starts as she piles food on a paper plate for me. "We've both been busy. I just thought I'd show up to see you for a change."

I admire her beauty as she busies herself with her task. I guess my lack of response makes her pause because she's looking at me. Delicate, guarded eyes search mine. Slowly, she sets the plate down, then gently touches her cheek, her hair, then her lips.

"What?" she asks, touching those three places again.

"You're beautiful," I offer sincerely. Reaching up, I pull her face to mine, placing a gentle kiss on her glossy lips. "I appreciate you for thinking about me."

"Always," she smiles, giving me another kiss, then fixing my plate. "So, that case with your brother," she starts and I shake my head, placing one of my hands on hers.

"Let's talk about something else."

"Oh…" she breathes, then gives an idle smile. "I went to the flower market the other day," I reach in my bag. Purple, blue, orange, and yellow carnations lay squished, decorating a white page. Fancy cursive script loops across the page. I slide the image over to her, then take a bite of my food.

Her jaw drops slowly as she takes in the pressed flower

petals. Her fingers touch each one gently.

"This is gorgeous, Ren." She looks at me with a twinkle in her eye before her smile widens. "I actually," she starts with a soft laugh as she pulls out a sketch.

Pink and red begonias sit on the edges, their petals laying over one another surrounding a large Black Dahlia. The deep red is touching the smaller flowers surrounding it in such vivid detail I find myself touching the pages to make sure it isn't pressed like my gift to her.

"As a kid, I'd study flowers and their meanings. Wanted to create a greenhouse to grow some." She laughs softly. I look at the flowers and as I open my mouth, her face lights up with a realization. "You know, there's one that grows during this time of year!"

"In the snow?" I anticipate slowly as I tilt my head to the side, my hand idly spinning pasta around on my fork. She nods as she shoots up from her seat, shoving her arms in her jacket, then grabbing me. I fumble with my jacket as she rushes towards the door. Her unruly curls bouncing feverishly as she half speed walks half jogs out the door. I zip up my thick coat, almost slipping on a patch of ice in the process. She kneels, digging through a mound of fresh snow before the off white petals peek through.

"These are called snowdrops," she says with a bright smile as she gently touches the petals. "And somewhere around here... you'll find a variant of jasmines that absolutely love the cold weather." She makes a slight gasping sound as she duck walks over to a purplish pink flower. She hovers her hand over it. "And this one... is a hellebore. My favorite, just like the begonias and black dahlias."

"What do they mean?" I ask with a hint of playfulness in my tone.

She looks up at me with bright, sparkling eyes, her smile growing wider. "They're usually sent as a warning."

I stare at her for a moment, mulling over the message. Could flowers really tell a story?

"But, some, like the hellebore, were used for medicinal purposes back in the Victorian era. And begonias' colors also have an individual meaning."

"So just pretty flowers that get a bad rep?"

She nods at me with a smile as she pushes to her feet, a dusting of snow in her hand. She leans over, gathering more up. She packs it tightly as I take a cautious step back. Before I can take off, she pelts me with the snow ball with a loud, belly laugh.

"You've got to be kidding me!" I stifle a laugh as I gather up snow between my palms. Sharp coldness biting into my skin as I pack the snow tightly.

Mel squeals as she runs from me, grabbing handfuls of snow to do the same. Launching the snowball, it explodes into tiny snowy crumbles back to the ground.

I dodge a snow attack, rolling to the ground before grabbing more snow and throwing my poorly formed masses at her. She giggles like a child as snow sits on the coils of one of her curls. Her face is reddening as the wind picks up, swirling bits of snow and moisture around us.

"Truce!" she shouts as she drops to the snow with an exhausted laugh.

Stumbling beside her, I lay in the cold snow, taking her

hand in mine. Our laughter dies down as we gasp for air. I stare up at the twinkling stars, reveling in how good it feels to not think about my brother, his death, or what I did to Ebony.

I pull Mel into my arms, placing a kiss on her forehead and squeezing her slim body tight.

"We should get inside," I offer as I stand on my feet and help her up. Her teeth chatter, concealing her response to me. I chuckle, tucking her beneath my arm and escorting her back into the building where we finish our dinner, and spend the next few hours talking about our gifts to each other and my school work.

32

Ebony

The lights dim in the bar as music begins to play the usual tunes. Glasses and bottles clank beside me, joining the soft chorus of voices. Liam slips onto the stool in front of where I'm standing. His hair has grown into the crazy cut he had months before. Golden brown eyes meet mine.

"How ya been?" he asks cautiously. The faint smell of smoke wafts from his skin as he runs his fingers through his hair and shakes out a few stray snowflakes.

"Pretty good," I offer with a small smile. "Beer?"

"Nah," he says, looking around the room. "That thing at the gala, what was that about?"

I shrug my shoulders, fixing him a glass of water. I slip a clean white towel in the belt loop of my pants. "Nothing."

"You were sending a message. I could hear it in your voice," he fusses.

"It was nothing, Liam. Drop it."

"We know the Mayor is dangerous, E," Liam states. His eyes tracking my movements. "I just want you safe. Especially after the party incident."

"And I appreciate that," I huff, scratching at my head as I watch more people enter. "I gotta go help serve."

"Before you go," he swallows, turning towards me. "You and your friends should leave the past in the past. Okay?"

"Would you say that to someone you care about?"

"I'm saying it because I care about you, E." He runs his hand through his hair. The muscle in his jaw pops for a second as he clenches his jaw. His eyes scan my face. "You've come so far with healing… keep moving forward." He finishes, then turns to talk to one of the new bartenders.

I stare at his profile for a moment, then release a tense breath and move from behind the bar.

Rounding the counter, I pop my knuckles, then pin my locs out of my face. I slip into the kitchen, grabbing a gray tub and balancing it on my hips. I direct a few of the new staff to sections to help take orders while I clean. Once they're settled, I grab dirty dishes from vacant tables, I fill the tub, then place everything on a cart so I can clean the area. I bend over, grabbing discarded straw wrappers from the floor.

"Damn, you wanna meet me in the parking lot and try that over my hood," a nasally voice says behind me.

"No," I state plainly, brushing past him.

"Come on, baby," he coos, reaching for my waist.

"Back the fuck up," I growl, grabbing a used steak knife from the tub.

"Crazy bitch," he growls, turning from me. Dropping the knife back into the tub, I adjust the tub on my hip and push through the swinging doors towards the kitchen.

Safe inside, I set the tub down and toss a towel in the sink making it hit the metal with a loud ting. With my hands braced on my thighs, I lean against the wall to steady my breathing. I fight back the thoughts that continue to roll in my head. The endless panic, worry, and planning that keeps me up at night. Pots clang as the kitchen staff works to keep up with food orders.

"You good," Clint asks as he rounds the door with a case of beer.

I clear my throat and nod rapidly. "Need help?"

"No. Spill," he commands.

"I kinda destroyed Vin's car," I mumble, knowing Clint is more stubborn than I am.

"Jesus Christ," he sighs, shaking his head. "Why?"

"He's been popping up and I got mad… so I grabbed a bat and shattered his window and damaged his pretty little Hellcat." I smile sheepishly at my cousin.

He tucks his lips, then begins to laugh. "You're fucking insane. You know that?"

"Not that insane."

"Weren't you telling everyone you pegged a guy taller and thicker than me?"

"How'd you know?"

"Isaac," he states plainly. "Like I said, insane."

He walks toward the swinging door, then stops and looks at me. His eyes search my skin for marks, then stop on my cheek.

"Hear me when I say this, Ebs. I'll fucking kill Vin if he ever thinks of putting his fucking hands on you. Kane, too."

"Kane would never…"

"I know. I actually like him. I think I need a therapist because of it. He's not all the way there either," Clint says with a shrug. He places the case on the stainless steel prep table, walks over to me, and plants a kiss on top of my head.

"Through hell and high water, kid. Fuck 'em up."

"And give 'em hell," I finish with a smile. "Love you, teddy bear."

"Love you, too, E flat," Clint responds using my old, childhood nickname. He grabs the case, then walks out towards the bar.

As I wipe my hands on my apron, steeling my nerves for more rowdy customers, a muffled argument captures my attention.

"I'm just saying," Liam's voice rises on the other side of the door. "We finally got a chance to practice and we were good. Just ask her. She might be down."

"No," Isaac answers firmly, his voice moving closer to the door signifying that he's rounding the side of the bar.

"If you don't, I will," Liam says, a hint of threat in his tone.

"I wish the fuck you would," Isaac growls.

"What's the problem?" Clint's voice rushes out.

I wipe my hands on my jeans, tug at my wrinkled shirt, and step out the kitchen door. Their heads snap in my direction, eyes locking on me.

"What's going on?" I ask, approaching them. I glance around the populated bar, then back at my bandmates.

"I want to do a practice performance," Liam starts, getting a menacing glare from Isaac.

He grumbles under his breath and shakes his head. "Only if you're up for it, E. Don't let that asshole make you do something you don't want to."

"I'm not going to force her," Liam states, turning to face Isaac.

"Let's do it," I say, cutting them off before they can start their bickering. I shrug my shoulders. "I might have some clothes in the back. Let me get ready."

I shoot them a smile, then rush off before they can say another word. I dodge drunk bodies as I walk quickly down the dark hall to the dressing room. I slip through the door, turn the lock and push my emotions down.

33

Kane

Begrudgingly, I step into Ebony's Gramp's bar with D and a patched up Zeke in tow. They demanded I go after they told me what E did to Vin's car and because she's here. Apparently, I'm supposed to stick around and take the constant side eye.

Even Zeke agreed with D. No matter what I said to defend myself, I was the bad guy. Mutiny. That's what I think that shit's called.

I guess the assholes love watching her reject me, which is still new to me.

This whole fight we're in is the exact reason why I didn't do relationships. I knew better, but for whatever fucked up reason I just wanted to tie her down. Now look, I'm barely getting any action and when I am, I'm begging her to work shit out. I don't even recognize who I am anymore.

"Isaac said they're going to perform tonight," D says to Zeke with a smile on her face. She pops his hand. "Hands, dickhead!"

"I just had to see if I could," Zeke says with a giggle.

"No," D says, rolling her eyes and leading us to a table. She sits in the seat looking towards the door, a smile growing on her face.

I hear her heels clicking on the ground before I see her. Black hair curled to make it look wavy and the highest pair of heels our mom would probably let her get. I catch Miya's smile as she wraps D in her arms for a tight hug before claiming the seat next to her.

"Thank you for inviting me," she says to D. "These two barely even respond to texts."

She glares at us, then sticks her tongue out.

"That's because I don't want to babysit," I state, shifting in my seat, already wanting a strong drink.

"Babysit who? Last time I checked, you had to carry him to bed," Miya responds. She pauses, her eyes widening. "What happened to your neck!?"

D and Zeke cover their faces as they stifle their laughter. I shake my head and look at my sister, her look of shock morphing into one of horror as she gags.

"Gross. Ew. Ew-ew-ew," she shakes her head, covering her mouth.

"You asked." I shrug.

"I will never ask about your well being again." She gags again.

"He might need some help covering it up," D says, amusement making her tone light and playful.

"Don't have sex with my friend! That's the help I'll give you."

"I need a drink," I state, standing. "Drink?" I ask glancing between my sister and D. After they tell me what they want, I place our order, then sit back in my chair.

The curtain on the stage sways as people move behind

it. I grab my glass and down the liquor quickly. I'm not drunk enough to deal with her rejection — again.

"Fighting demons?" D asks as she watches me, alarmed. Her eyebrows are raised towards her hair line as she holds her glass to her lips.

"Maybe," I say with a shrug. I get another drink and take slow sips.

The curtain opens and she walks out with the guys wearing a tight yellow top that criss- crosses across her stomach and sneaks beneath her leather skirt, which has a dangerously high slit. And of course, a pair of high top classic Converse on her feet. It wouldn't be something she'd wear without a pair of Converse.

I sigh, shifting more towards the table, focusing on the ice in my glass as I swirl it around.

"If you won't look, I will," Zeke whispers to me, tilting his head to the side. His eyes are clearly scouring every inch of Ebony out.

"I'll shove my foot so far up your ass," I growl with a glare.

He giggles, looking at me with glee bouncing behind his irises. Crazy fucker. He takes a sip of his drink.

E shifts her guitar as the light comes on and Liam starts talking. She adjusts the mic, then looks in our direction. She smiles at everyone until she spots me and looks away.

I really want to go the fuck home now.

"So, Ebony asked me to take a look into something a few weeks ago," D says, leaning towards the center of the table. "Slipped a couple USB drives to some of the cyber security guys I know. They start telling me how the system has been locking them out since the update."

"My dad wouldn't mess with the student's system," Miya says.

"Thought the same, but they told me they're not using the main system. Rumor has it that someone big wants access to the wrist band project and the drone files."

I fish my phone out of my pocket and start scrolling for a moment then select a file. "We have an IP address for anyone that's been attempting to access the drone, but they don't lead us anywhere. My dad let me examine the drives over Christmas break. E and I couldn't find anything."

"It's because you weren't meant to find it. Dr. Sumner is protecting whoever that is. His name is written all over the waivers for the cybersecurity students."

"We gotta find out who this someone is," Zeke says, leaning back in the chair.

"What if it's as simple as the Mayor," Miya offers leaning closer to the table. "No one else has a bigger investment in this school than him."

"How big of an investment?" I ask, shifting my weight.

"Are we talking like millions?" Zeke asks.

"Much more, Dr. Goodwin slipped me and Ebony a file with the budgets on it. Ebony did some digging in the system and found where she got it from. The Cross' can basically make this school anything they want without breaking a sweat."

"Money laundering," I mutter.

"Yep. It's not just this school either," D says as the mic's feedback crackles through the speaker. "Our best bet for this whole situation is to uncover the money trail and we find the culprits. The school has enough donors to not need the Cross' money."

"Their project is about more than the Cross'," Zeke says with a sigh.

"That's the thing," Miya says, tapping her manicured nail against the table. "The Cross' are the reason why the project isn't making headway."

"The problem is," I start, glancing at the stage as Liam starts talking. "Ebony wants to save Vin. If his family goes down, he's going with them and I don't think she's willing to let that happen."

D nods slightly before shaking it. Our table is quiet now as we adjust in our seats, lost in our own thoughts.

"Without further ado," Liam says with a smile on his face as Isaac counts them off and they start playing.

Can I save Ebony if she saves Vin?

The music swells as I meander through my thoughts, periodically focusing back on Ebony's performance. She stays away from her mic for the most part, letting her guitar do the work for her. A peaceful energy emanating from her as she lives in the moment. Then the lights fade more, she sets her guitar down and grabs her mic as the music transitions. She starts singing, tapping her foot before walking around the stage, clapping her hands to the beat until the song ends.

"I swear I love when she sings," D says leaning on the table.

"We're gonna take a little break," Liam says as the lights shift.

She grabs her water bottle and finishes it quickly, then

grabs a towel and wipes the sweat off her face.

"You stare any harder and you're going to look like a creep," Miya says with a grimace. "Just go up there."

"She's been giving him a mean cold shoulder."

"Not drunk enough to pretend I don't hear you," I groan, not even feeling a buzz.

"I can make it happen," Zeke says with a wide smile.

"No! Then he's going to be more of a mess," Miya protests.

"It's just a bandaid. You'll wake up hungover and even more in a funk," D says with a shrug.

"I missed the part where being deliriously drunk was a bad idea," I state, looking around the table.

"What happens if she wants to talk?" Miya asks, leaning towards the table. She tilts her ear towards me like she's waiting for me to say something profound.

"Then she'll have a conversation with drunk me. He's pretty cool actually," I stand and get two more drinks.

Two burly dudes with oversized leather jackets lean against the bar top. Some off brand lite beer clenched in their hands. One glaring at the stage while the other glances behind him, then back at his friend with a smug smirk.

"Ain't that the bitch that gave you lip earlier," he asks with a soft chuckle.

I look in the direction they're looking, then sigh. I turn back towards them, finally getting a good look at them. Their pale skin is bright even under the dim light, dark blue eyes staring towards the stage. One is covered in freckles. His reddish brown hair sticking up under his beanie. The other, the guy that's glaring, has a crooked hoop lip ring jutting out his bottom lip.

"Yeah, that's the stupid cunt," hooped lip ring answers through gritted teeth.

"I suggest you don't call her out of her name," I say clenching my drink and leaning over the bar. I shake my head before taking a slow drink. With a shoulder roll, I relax my body into my stance, my eyes looking over at hooped lip ring and his buddy.

"The fuck you gonna do about it?" he asks me stupidly.

I size him up already knowing I have him on height alone. I crack my knuckles and smirk a little.

"Let's find out," I say nodding towards the door.

"You think you scare me?" His voice waivers as he stares up at me. I'm pretty fucking sure I intimidate him. Even the way his head leans back as he stares up at me lets me know that.

"Didn't say I did. Told you we can find out what I'll do."

"Easy fellas," Vin's annoying fucking voice calls out as he taps both of the reject versions of the Jonas Brothers on the shoulder.

"That's his old lady," Vin says with a smile. His swollen bottom lip splits a little as he does. "And he isn't the sharing type, but she might let you get a taste."

I feel my face immediately react into a snarl. I fix my eyes on him, feeling my head tilt down ready to head butt him where a faint scar resides from when Ebony broke his shit. I was chill before, but now, I'm ready to cave someone's fucking head in.

The two snicker and I take a step forward. They shrink

away as Vin continues to stare with that arrogant smile.

"Want to repeat that dumb shit?" I growl, nudging past the other two.

"I'm sure you heard me," Vin says with another laugh. "I have a feeling you enjoy when she walks all over you."

I grab him by the collar, balling my other hand in a fist as I pull him up towards my face. He smiles wider. "I'll be sure to finish the fucking job Zeke and E started."

"Do it," he taunts with that smile fucking growing. "Kiss that fucking scholarship good bye, pretty boy."

"Fuck outta here, runt," a gravelly voice cuts in before I can respond. I release him, but leave little space.

Vin looks over his shoulder and immediately straightens as he stares at Gramps. He opens and closes his mouth, before nodding his head and turning. He looks at me though, his unhinged eyes attempting to intimidate me.

"Get gone or imma get you gone." The audible click of a gun sends Vin right out the door. I glance at Gramps, who's glaring at the other two. Their already pale faces grow paler.

"Dumb ass kids," Gramps grumbles, looking me over with a quick nod and disappearing into the back room.

I down my drink before sitting back in the seat, finally feeling the effects of the alcohol. My face warms up and my palms tingle as the numbness settles in across my cheeks and my nose.

'Bout fucking time.

"Last drink," Miya says, glaring at me. She worries about me too much instead of enjoying herself. Her eyes, finding mine more frequently now as the music from the speaker swells and pulses through the sound system. Despite her hovering, I enjoy my alcohol induced stupor anyways.

34

Ebony

Kane rarely drinks when something's bothering him, but I guess he ran out of options. I really didn't give him many in the first place.

He's not belligerently drunk, thankfully, just intoxicated enough to need me to drive.

I adjust the driver seat, then slide the key in the ignition after we buckle in. I chew at my cheek not knowing what to say. Not really wanting to say anything to be honest. I pull off onto the road, driving a little slower to avoid the black ice patches that hide in different nooks of the ground.

"E," Kane slurs softly, his hand grabbing my thigh making heat immediately flood my body. He gives it a tight squeeze. "We should talk."

The issue with that statement is all the topics I want to discuss, but don't have the words to. All the topics that terrify me and put more life into the fact that the silence with Vin's father, my father, and the school's admin all have a certain building block to the anxiousness that riddles my body like hooks pierced into my skin. Talking means letting my guard down. I can't do that right now, I can't afford to make another mistake or trust the wrong person because I feel drawn to them. I'm barely holding on. I'm barely present.

I take a deep breath, tightening my grip on the steering wheel. I glance at him, then decide to give him something. Try something different to let him know that I'm still here, just suffocating in bullshit.

"I'm going to see a lawyer," I offer softly. I turn the wheel slightly, pulling the car behind a few buildings not too far from our apartment. I turn the headlights off and unbuckle my seatbelt to face him. I avoid his eyes, knowing I'll give in and forgive him for not trusting me, for basically making me feel like I couldn't make my own decisions. He's supposed to be my teammate, he told me we were in this together.

"Okay," he says slowly.

He moves, his finger undoing his seatbelt and shifts. I glance up at him and watch as his hand brushes the hair back out of his red, flushed face.

"Don't ask me what they're going to say. I don't know. Your parents just set this up for me and I'm going with it," I state.

I've been tense since our fight, excluding the angry sex in the closet that picked at the frayed edges of my mind. Which had me crying in a ball on the shower floor. All the jumbled emotions in my mind had hit me harder when my second orgasm rippled through me. While he held me, looking at me like I was the most beautiful thing he'd ever seen. Him consoling me after fucking me roughly was the last thing I wanted. I knew he'd make everything feel okay, but I didn't need him to make me feel good emotionally. I wanted to do it myself. I needed to and he wasn't letting me. Toxic? Sure. I'm trying, okay?

"I can—"

"Just," I cut him off and sigh. "Don't over step."

I glance at him and meet his sad, red eyes. He blinks before nodding. His jaw works as he thinks, mulling over what's on his mind.

"And while the lawyer does their thing, I'm going along with Ren's plan," I add, feeling a little more sure in bringing this up to him. I made the decision not long after we got into that big fight at the animal shelter. Not because he thought I shouldn't, but because I knew I had tried everything but setting him up.

"Ebony," he groans, rubbing his hands over his face. "No."

"You don't get to make that decision for me."

"I know I don't! But I don't think it's a decision you should make. Ever."

"You don't know what's best for me!" I shout, slapping my palm against the steering wheel. "You'll never know what's best for me because you don't know what it's like to be me!"

"I don't have to fucking know to understand that this will only end in you getting hurt! You trusting that they won't try and leave you out to dry again is dumb as fuck, E!"

"If you think my decisions are dumb, then maybe we should—"

"Don't," he growls, looking over at me. "Don't finish that fucking statement."

I swallow but keep my glare fixed on him. I know I

didn't mean it. I know I'm a runner because I felt the push and pull inside of me. I wanted me to toss these fucking keys at him and run fast and far.

It wouldn't solve anything. Running never solves a damn thing and I hate it.

"We're not going to break up in the midst of a fucking fight."

"You make me so fucking mad," I choke out turning away from him.

"Yeah?" he chuckles.

I whip my head back to glare at him, my eyebrows bunched together. "That's fucking funny?"

"Yeah. I think it is."

"You're such a dick," I grumble.

"Am I?" he asks, lifting his brow at me. The look in his eyes is more than challenging. He's taunting me. Adjusting his position in the passenger seat before gripping himself through his pants. "Never bothered you before."

A violent shiver rolls down my spine as his fingers go to the button of his pants. He undoes it, sliding his hands beneath the waistline.

"Do you know how incredibly sexy it is that you don't put up with my shit?"

My heart beats roughly in my chest as I watch his movements. I get lost in him removing himself and taunting me with his cloudy brown eyes.

"You're fucking losing it," I choke out, tearing my eyes away from his movements.

"Maybe," he slurs, releasing a deep breath.

I look out the window trying my hardest to keep myself

from doing something irrational. Something that would make my head go cloudier than it already is. His body heat rolls over me as he leans closer, his ragged breathing right by my ear as the leather whines beneath his shifting weight.

"Tell me you don't want me," he whispers in my ear. "And I'll put my dick away."

I turn towards him, backing my face away from his. My eyes darting back to the bulge in his pants then to his challenging brown eyes.

"The way you're looking at me is telling me that you do. That you fucking crave me just as much as I crave you," he whispers huskily.

"What are you doing?" I breathe, looking at him as he leans back in the seat, adjusting himself with a huff. The button of his pants still open wide.

"Disappointed?" he asks. His hooded eyes flashing with excitement, then lazily dragging from my face, down the length of my body.

"I'm not having angry sex with you," I whisper.

"No? Then why are you leaning closer to me?"

I pause, gripping the middle console tightly. The hard leather digging into my palms as I stop my movements. He's right. I subconsciously pushed myself out of my seat to this point, invading his space. He leans closer, ghosting his lips over mine. The rich, citrus fragrance of his favorite whiskey on his breath. He licks his lips, making the smell stronger. The warmth of the car makes me sweat. I ease back, releasing an unsteady breath and watch him deflate.

"We should get going," I grumble, feeling my arousal scatter my thoughts around like marbles.

"Why? Afraid you're going to get caught?"

"Doing what?" I hiss.

"Fucking me, E, what else would we be doing?"

"Fighting?" I whisper.

"If you want to call it fighting, then we can call it fighting. Just as long as you're moaning my name and cumming on my dick."

"Kane," I whisper, looking over at him.

He lifts his eyebrow in response before sighing and shifting in his seat.

"I'm sorry," he mutters, anguish seeping from his words. He quietly scolds himself about fucking things up and not knowing what to do in this situation. Then he stops and looks at me, remorse lingering in his eyes. "I'm sorry for this... and not letting you make the decision with Ren. I just don't want you to get hurt. Not again." He covers his face, leaning towards the dashboard. "I need to sober up," he mutters to himself.

The tether I had tied to my anger snaps. I pull my shirt over my head and toss it on the seat next to him, then unlatch my bra and toss it towards the back seat.

"Kane," I call out to him. He looks over at me, his eyes haunted with lust and frayed restraint.

"Don't fuck with me," he grumbles, letting his eyes take in my breasts. The moonlight glinting off the sparkly balls of my nipple rings.

"If that's what you want to call it," I say, leaning over the middle console, shoving my greedy fingers down his waistband, and pulling out his semi- hard dick.

"What happened?" I whisper, looking up at him. A

slight pout on my lips. I slide my hand against his velvety flesh, then give him a slow, tight tug. I dip my head down, placing a kiss on the tip.

He leans his head back against the leather headrest with a groan. His eyes rolling to the back of his head as one of his hands brushes my hair out of my face and the other grabs the door handle.

"I thought you wanted me?"

I place another kiss on him, then look up through hooded eyes. His tongue drags across his lips as he studies my face. The hand in my hair brushing against my scalp sending tremors through my belly.

A slow smile forms on his face.

"It's all yours then," he murmurs, pushing my face down in his lap with a throaty groan.

35

Ren

Winter time at night has always been the worst in this little fucking town. All the cold air seems to get stuck between these tall ass buildings, freezing the slightest bit of moisture. My snow fight with Mel only adds to my discomfort.

I trudge across Knight U's campus, my jacket pulled tightly around my body. A gust of wind trying to pry it open and steal what little body heat I have left.

Snow pelts my winter coat as I pass through an alley towards the parking lot behind an old building. I curse to myself as a patch of black ice makes me slip. My legs tremble beneath me as my upper body hitches forward. I catch myself on a small, pathetic tree to prevent myself from face planting on the pavement.

"Fuck you, frosty," I grumble as I get my footing. "You and your fucking winter wonderland bullshit." The imaginary snow creature didn't do anything to me particularly, but it feels right to cuss him out. This is his type of weather. His frozen ass needs to be called out a time or two.

A strange sound interrupts my tirade, catching my attention and making me pause. Placing my hand on my taser, I look behind me. Cautious steps lead me in the direction I'm heading, then a loud, moaned "fuck," then a giggle reverberates between one of the buildings.

"Joy," I grumble, feeling like Ebenezer Scrooge as I trudge through the thick flakes of snow. I get to walk past a bunch of fucking exhibitionists who can't find a warmer place to fuck.

As I make my way through the clearing, I stop, spotting where the noise is coming from. My legs refuse to move as shock roots me to the slick path beneath my feet. Ebony's tattooed back is against the cracked driver's side window of Kane's car, his face buried in her chest as he sucks her nipples. A shaky breath leaves my body as I look around the nearly vacant lot, then up the sides of the dark buildings.

"C'mere," Kane slurs as he pulls her into his lap.

Their lips find one another for a sloppy kiss. His hands grabbing her face as if he depends on it.

"You want more?" his deep voice mutters across her lips.

A giggle is her only response as she lifts her hips. He groans as I watch her arm move between them, her muscles tensing and releasing as she watches his face. Then her body eases down. Both of their mouths open slightly before she braces the head rest and bounces slowly.

"This pussy's so damn tight," he groans, watching her move.

I look around again, tucking my body into the shadows closest to them. My breathing picks up as I watch, listening to their bodies connect as they find their rhythm.

She moans loudly as his hand races up her body, while

he licks and sucks over her breast. Then he's looking up at her like she's the most beautiful thing in the fucking world. With the tattoos, the piercings, I'd probably worship her like this too.

What the hell am I thinking?

She looks down at him, leaning her body back against the steering wheel. Her hips rolling against his as he leans his head on the head rest. Their eyes locked on each other, challenging, calling out to each other in the dark cabin of his car. The fucking moonlight doing every inch of their bodies that I can see justice.

I shift in the darkness, leaning forward amazed like I'm watching two animals in their natural habitat. I guess my movement catches her attention because her eyes immediately find mine. I freeze, my heart kicking up in speed as she stares me down, never once breaking her momentum. She plays with her nipples, pinching them between her thumb and her forefinger.

I've never seen her like this, raw, unfiltered, and completely aroused. Not even when we were together. Primarily because our sexual attraction for each other wasn't fully there. Don't get me wrong, we hooked up every now and then, but Ebony has always had a sexual appetite that I couldn't fulfill. I was always good with one orgasm, she built her endurance up to handle multiple. Which meant I would need help every now and then.

She was reluctant when I first wanted to have an open relationship. It put us in a weird spot. That was until I introduced her to someone I knew could do what she needed, encouraged her to explore her desires with them.

When she showed a little interest, I left them to explore each other. Back then, before Ebony, I wasn't fond of watching people fuck, but something changed over time. Maybe it was the trauma.

Their chemistry and attraction drew me in as they flirted harmlessly with each other like it was the usual routine. The guys got handsy, grabbing her waist to pull her towards them, rubbing her thighs, and easing past her to brush up against her ass.

All three of them were beautiful, created to be watched in moments like that. After the song and dance of foreplay, I was transfixed on the sight of two men satisfying her in ways I only saw in porn. Thankfully, that time was real. It took those two men to make Ebony sound the way she does right now with Kane.

A shiver jolts my body as I realize that her focus is back on Kane. His car rocking with her movements, her moans echoing through the pathways on campus. I look around surprised that no one can hear them. Surprised that I'm the only one that found them like this.

Kane pulls his shirt off, decorative tattoos looping and dancing up and down his arms to his chest. He flicks the garment to the back as he leans the seat back all the way back, giving her space to ride him. He groans, pulling her down towards him and slapping her ass hard.

"I'm gonna cum," she moans as Kane takes over her movement. Her body shudders as his name falls from her lips, her mouth near his ear. The sound of skin slapping skin and his hand slapping her ass taking over where her moans once were. And when she sits up, her eyes lock on mine again.

It's not just her eyes though, his eyes follow shortly after. His head turns to the side, locking on to me tucked in the shadows breathing and watching like a pervert. Ebony's hips continue to roll against Kane's. He snakes his hands up her body making me follow her curves as they watch me. His hand provides an anchor for where my eyes should go. I foolishly follow it, marveling at how fucking intoxicating it is to watch them like this. Watch her take what she wants from him.

I clench my thighs together, panting at the performance they're putting on for me. The only movement I can make is the slight rotation of my hips as my thighs rub together and I find friction on the seams of one of my clothing items.

For as long as I've known Kane, I've never pictured him to be one that wanted, or cared for, an audience when he fucked someone. He may be a cocky, arrogant asshole, but this is completely new territory for him, at least I think it is.

He pulls her face back to him and kisses her, a smile on his face as he whispers something to her. She moans, her eyes closing slightly as she moves harder.

"That's it, baby," he groans. "Show them who makes this pussy cum."

I watch as he studies her movements, one arm tucked behind his head and the other around her throat. His thick thumb brushing against the full bottom lip before slipping inside her mouth.

She sucks on it, beautiful full lips wrapped around his thick thumb. He pulls it out of her mouth with a soft suckling slurp before circling her nipple with it. His fingers gently touch the sides of her breast before gripping her neck again. His forearm muscles bulge as he squeezes her throat softly.

He dominates her in a way I've only seen her dominate me. A gentle, "I know what I'm doing so I'm teasing you" kind of domination. He matches her intensity, her energy, making her cum in ways I've never heard anyone make her cum. Those two guys from the past may have made her moan loudly, but they barely made her cum, which is exactly what she does for a second time.

"Fuck," she whimpers, her body shuddering over his as he unclenches her throat, but keeps his hand there. His free hand helps her coast her high. Her fingers digging into the headrest as Kane guides her movements.

"Good fucking girl," he growls, placing his lips beside her ear. "This dick makes you feel that good, baby?"

He practically coos as he talks to her. His thrusts are harder now, making the car shake noticeably. Making her moans louder as her tits bounce around with his movements.

I lean against the rough, brick wall behind me. My cold hand snaking down into my sweatpants as I touch myself. Dipping my ice cold fingers into my warm wetness, then swirling it around my throbbing clit. A sharp, shuddery breath leaves my mouth as I revel in the sensation. I fix my eyes back on them, immediately finding Ebony watching me.

There's a fire in her eyes as she catches me. She licks her lips before Kane captures her attention with his mouth on her nipple. He pulls back and looks back up into her fiery eyes, drinking her in.

"You're so fucking close," he taunts.

His muscles rippling as he meets her thrusts, hard. His hand between them as he rolls her clit between his fingers making her cum again.

"There it is," he praises, smiling at her shuddering body. "Eyes on me, baby. Good girl."

I release a shaky breath, plunging two fingers inside of me, using my palm to stimulate my aching, swollen clit. I cover my mouth, moaning into my hand as I watch him take control of her body.

Laying her back against the driver seat and pulling her legs over his shoulders, he pushes in deep. Her loud moans punctuate the silence in the air. He slams into her, the sound of their skin slapping together taunting me to the edge of my own orgasm.

"Kane," she whimpers as he pulls her arms up to the head rest and pins her down.

"Take this dick like my good fucking slut," he groans, sending her and me over the edge.

Her body trembles against his. My knees buckle, my back presses harder into the wall behind me, keeping me upright. My vision blurs as I hear him grunt.

I open my eyes, sliding my fingers out of my body. He kisses her slowly, tentatively before helping her get dressed in silence. I adjust my clothing, finding a napkin in my pocket and wiping my hand off.

I give them one last look before quickly walking away, feeling slightly ashamed of myself.

I have to get myself in check before I end up doing something that will blow this whole plan out of proportion.

36

Ebony

There's something about the way an acoustic guitar sings when you strum the right tune. The way the notes vibrate from the body up to the neck as it resonates in the space it occupies. Quietly commanding people to listen. It's a powerhouse that doesn't need much assistance, which is the exact opposite of how I feel right now.

I find the chords of a song that's stuck in my head, then begin humming the melody as I memorize the simple tune. After slowly moving my fingers over the strings a few more times. I stop for a moment, then piece all of it together.

"Oh my gawd," Miya gushes, sitting at the front desk of the student life office. "I love this song. It's by Pink Sweats right?"

I nod singing the first verse mostly to myself, then lead into the chorus. Miya softly sings along, slightly out of tune. I smile to myself as I continue. My foot swivels the chair slowly to the tune as I finish the last bit of the chorus. Satisfied, I put my guitar on the table and wheel over to the desk.

"Shouldn't you be getting ready to meet with the lawyer?" she asks, looking up from her pink notebook. A white pen with a fluffy pink pom pom on the top dancing as the heat turns on.

"I have two more hours," I mutter, clicking through the files on the computer. "I'm just downloading and logging results for the conference." I sigh as the loading bar moves barely a millimeter.

"Maybe focus on the case," she whispers, leaning closer to me and glancing at the door quickly.

"If I have one."

"Don't be so pessimistic. You're meeting one of THE best lawyers," Miya comments, looking at her computer screen.

I sit quietly, my pen wiggling between my fingers as my mind goes through every possible scenario. My legs alternate between anxious bounces. My teeth chew at the skin of my cheek. The tornado of thoughts dragging me down the rabbit hole of 'what if's and negativity, but I can't find my way out. Like the last time.

"Hey," she says softly, practically cooing at me. Her hand touches my shoulder and I flinch slightly. "I'm sorry, I didn't mean to…"

"You're fine," I say in a rush, looking at her with a smile that I hope is as apologetic and sincere as I can muster. "I'm just really in my head about everything."

"Do you want to talk about it?"

I shake my head. "I read some more of Rae's journals," I offer, grabbing my laptop and opening the file. I glance at her, asking her with my eyes if she wants to hear it. She gives me a slight nod.

"Mayor Cross walked into my class today. Talked about the great American dream and how he's fighting drugs and crime. He stopped me later to ask about doing a side project for him. Sort of like an internship, but nothing official. I'll get paid. Maybe get an apartment.'" I hover my finger over the trackpad as I stare at the screen.

"When was that entry," she asks as she rolls over to look at my screen.

"Six months before he died," I tell her, scrolling up to the date.

"D had shared something with us at your performance yesterday," Miya starts, looking at the door and leaning closer to me. "The cybersecurity department is doing hands- on testing and hacking. My dad has the system set to reroute any type of cyber attack. On one hand, the school thinks they're protected, but there's someone definitely covering up the drug scandal on campus. I think that's why research on our project has stalled."

I think for a moment, looking at her, then at my computer screen opening files skimming the codes. "Our codes were scrambled," I mutter, scrolling through the difference between the two. We sit, studying the screen for a moment as we look through the difference in the red and green lines on the screen.

"Ladies," Dr. Sumner's sugary sweet voice fills the room, making the hair on my arms stand up. Defensively, I close the top of my laptop and look up at him earning a glance. "How's preparation for the conference going?"

"Good," Miya pipes up. "Dr. Goodwin has set up a few meetings with us to finalize our presentation."

"That's exciting. Sounds like you guys are way ahead of schedule. With what? Two more months before the big day?"

Miya and I nod, watching him closely for any give-aways. He never shows up in this office. What's he searching for?

"Don't forget to send the budget plan and travel itinerary so the school can get it processed in time," he says with a smile. "Keep up the good work, you two. Go Knights," he cheers with a tight smile, then exits the office space. The heels of his patent leather shoes clacking against the hallway floors. He drags his left foot slightly as he walks.

"We should fabricate what he's looking for," I say. His footsteps triggering a blurry memory that I can't quite pin.

"Should we ask Dr. Goodwin, first?"

"I have a feeling she'll be on board with it," I say looking down at my computer. I lift the screen, type in Dr. Sumner in the search feature and silently read the first entry. Moments pass as I get to the third journal entry with no new information when Kane's gravelly voice calls out to me.

"Ebony?"

My eyes shoot up to him as he steps fully into the office. A black suit hugging all the right parts of his body. His handsome face slightly dark from the overhead lights, or the lack of sleep. Probably a mixture of both. He's been spending more time in the gym, especially after the other night when we left Gramp's bar. I don't blame him.

"I didn't mean to scare you," he says softly. "Zeke told me you were here."

I nod, then look at the time.

"Oh, shit." I shove my chair back and stuff my belongings in my bag, then quickly log out of the computer. "Hey, I'll be back and we can finish planning for everything."

"No worries! Knock 'em dead! Well, not dead…"

"I get it," I say with a soft laugh. I give her an awkward hug, then walk past Kane, rushing down the hall.

"Hey, E. Wait up," Kane says, walking quickly behind me.

I slow enough for him to walk beside me, but I keep a quick pace and fuss over my bag attempting to avoid the alone time with him. My stomach twisting in knots as I think about how real everything is becoming. My heart pulls, trying to force me to slow down, but I don't.

I know this will only make things worse, especially when I finally let go of my own feelings and tell him everything. But I can't do that, not with what's about to happen in my life.

Anger is the only thing I can control without crying, without feeling like I'm stealing something I haven't earned. And every moment he's sweet or kind to me, I feel like I have to earn it. Not because he said so, but because I've always had to before with others that weren't my friends, Clint, or Gramps.

Ten steps forward, thirty steps back.

37

Ebony

This place is fancy. Fancier than any office I've been in since I was a kid, which might not be saying much since I'd only come with my dad. Primarily when he needed to damage control and would soon leave me in the long corridors to fend for myself.

Hashtag character building.

Kane sits beside me, his parents flanking us, in a brightly lit office downtown just an hour from Knight U. The floor is painted an off white color and polished with dark tan swirls and a white cloud- like design. Gold outlines each panel, reflecting the bright overhead lights and the sunlight that pours through the large windows. Beautiful white gardenias and soft purple lavender sit in a glass vase on the receptionist's desk making the air sweet and peaceful. At least that's what I'd think if I didn't feel like I was about to throw up as the seconds pass.

I rub my clammy hands against my A - line skirt before standing up and excusing myself, walking briskly to the bathroom. I throw the door open and gag before finding an empty stall. My stomach recoils, twisting in sharp pain. Unable to keep whatever is on my stomach down, I brace myself using the stall walls as I retch, thankful for only having tea this morning. Kane demanded I eat, but I refused. Of course, this led to another argument right before his parents showed up to pick us up.

My skin is clammy as the sickness passes, leaving me weak and shaking. I sigh, leaning to the side and using the back of my hand to wipe the sweat from my forehead. Drained, I push the flush button on the toilet and stumble out the stall. Washing my hands and face in the sink, my skin cools beneath the icy cold water. My body instantly cooling the more water I splash on various points of my face. Finally composed enough to stand properly, I brace against the counter and give myself a good long look.

"Get it together," I mutter before rinsing my mouth out and splashing more cold water on my face.

The bathroom door swings open and the sound of confident heel clicks catches my attention. They stop abruptly. Slowly, I look up from the sink to see Mrs. Yamada looking over at me. Her eyebrows stitch together when she sees me.

"Are you okay, honey?" she asks softly, walking over to me and placing her warm palm on my back. She caresses it as I hide my face. I nod for a moment, then feel the tears spilling over my eyes.

The thing I hate most about being stressed out? My mood swings. How easy it is for me to cry at the smallest inconvenience. And oh, how I hate crying. Crying makes me feel weak, like I'm letting the world own me.

"Oh, honey," she coos. Her arms circle me as she turns me towards her, her cheek resting on the top of my head as I sob softly. "What's going on?"

"I— It's," I sputter trying to articulate my thoughts, but for once, they're silent. They hide from me like I'm the loose cannon that put them there. "I want this to be over already."

I wipe my eyes, but it doesn't help. Not while she holds me close, humming her response and rocking me like a mother. Which only makes it worse because she isn't my mother. Not the woman that left me behind that should have loved me, but showed me I wasn't enough. I cry harder at that thought, but I try to fight it and the sobs that make my throat ache. My hands are fisting into the back of Mrs. Yamada's suit jacket as I attempt to suppress each feeling that bubbles up.

I wonder how my life would have been had my mother been here instead of my father. Had she put up a fight to keep me rather than passing me over. I wonder what she looks like. My little two year old brain barely remembers beyond a faded picture at my gramps'. One I refused to go anywhere without until I turned ten and the anger set in. The anger and the rejection. Before I realized how fucked up my life truly was because of my parents' dumb decisions.

"It's going to be okay," Kane's mother coos. She leans back, framing my wet face with her hands as she stares deep into my eyes. "You know what you're doing right now?"

I nod slowly.

"You're fighting for yourself. Taking charge of your life, your trauma," she says softly. Her thumb wipes a stray tear that trickles from my eye. "I'm sorry no one else protected you."

I fight the lump growing in my throat, try to fight the hold she has on me, but it's useless. My lip trembles as I swallow back the emotions that fight to break through.

"We may not be able to erase what happened," she says with a soft sigh as she adjusts my hair. "But you're going to make them pay."

She smiles at me, wiping at my face again and placing a kiss on my forehead. I grab at her wrist gently, closing my eyes at the comfort she offers me. Then, I'm back in her arms. A tight embrace that relaxes me just enough to stop the rouge sobs that attempt to break free.

"Thank you," I say softly after a moment. I rest my cheek on her small shoulder.

"Any time, baby doll," she responds, giving me one more squeeze. "Are you going to be okay?"

I nod, forcing a tight smile on my face. She places her palm against my skin, her eyes sad as she looks over my face. Her thumb brushes my cheek one more time before she releases me and steps into a stall.

I face my reflection, release a soft sigh, then make my way out the bathroom desperately wanting a stick of gum. I avoid Kane's eyes as I sit down and dig in my purse for gum, growing a bit frustrated when I can't find one. His hand extends out to me. The untouched foil wrapped beautifully around the minty treat. I thank him softly and stick the unwrapped gum in my mouth. He gently nudges me, then leans close to my ear.

"We've got your back," he says before placing a tentative kiss on my clammy forehead.

I'm grateful for him. Still annoyed, but grateful for his constant reassurance. Especially when he could have left me to do this on my own. I glance at him finally and meet his warm, encouraging eyes. They shift as he looks over my face before his hand cups my cheek and pulls my face to his lips. He kisses my forehead in a way that I know he's trying to comfort me.

"I must look a mess," I mutter.

"No," he says with a soft chuckle. "You look stressed."

"Ms. Young?" the receptionist calls out, standing from her desk.

Her dark brown skin and long silky black hair coming into view as she steps around the desk. Her red lips pull back revealing beautiful white teeth. She adjusts her suit jacket and smoothes the wrinkles out of her perfectly pressed skirt.

"Attorney Pateki is ready for you," she announces just as Kane's mother walks over towards us.

Kane and I stand in unison, as he gives her a brief nod and I gather my jacket and purse in my arms. His hand rests on the small of my back, slightly clenching at my side, pulling me closer to his body as I wobble a bit. Nerves rendering my knees unsteady. Anxiety making me feel light headed.

"Do you want us to go in with you?" Kane's mother asks.

"I'll go," Kane says, looking over at me, then back at them.

She gives him a soft smile, then takes my hand in both of hers giving me a reassuring squeeze.

Kane and I follow behind Attorney Pateki's receptionist to the third door on the right. She gestures for us to enter inside. Large windows looking over the busy downtown streets and parks greet us. A brown oak desk to the left of it just as grand as the view. Two cushioned chairs angled toward the large desk look as inviting as they can.

"He'll be right in. He just went to grab a few things to add to your file."

I nod before thanking her, walking towards the chairs. As I sit, Kane watches over me for a second before taking his own seat once he knows I'm steady. He hesitantly takes my hand and squeezes. I hold on to him, keeping the shaking at bay. I wish he could hold my heart to keep it from violently and painfully throwing itself into my chest. The onsets of an anxiety attack creep in only making it worse.

"Deep breathes," Kane says softly, squeezing my hand. "Just like that, good girl."

It's not until this moment when I realize how comforting his dominance can be aside from the bedroom. Not that I needed it, but then again, I'm not in the mental state to protest his support.

"Ms. Young!" Attorney Pateki greets with a warm voice and a smile to match. Kane and I stand, turning to face Attorney Pateki. I shake his hand firmly, then watch as he shakes Kane's. I plaster a fake confident smile on my face as I greet him.

"Had I known you were going to bring this rascal, I would have come equipped with some funny stories about him as a kid," Attorney Pateki says with a smile.

"I think my parents beat you to it," Kane says with a laugh.

I laugh too, feeling the walls of my throat sticking together. I swallow hard and take my seat.

"So, Ms. Young. What can I help you accomplish?" He

leans back in his chair slightly, a silver pen in his hand as he looks at me thoughtfully.

"I've been searching for answers after a situation that happened almost a year ago," I start softly. I swallow, then continue. "I was drugged at a school party, I reported it, but admin threatened to kick me out."

He hums his acknowledgement, then leans forward in his seat looking over the documents I sent to his receptionist earlier this week, then looks back up at me.

"Ms. Young," he starts. Kane gives my thigh a quick, thoughtful squeeze.

"First, this is going to be a tough case, but with what we have here, I'm willing to try your case against the school."

"It's not just the school," I say softly, wringing my hands in my lap. "There's so much more than the school."

Attorney Pateki looks up at me with interested eyes. I take a deep breath and unload the events of my life. Doing my best to share every detail to help my case. When I finish, he leans back in his chair, the leather material groaning as he adjusts his position. He taps his chin with his index finger looking down at the file in front of him. His eyes unfocused as he takes a few moments to seemingly digest all the details.

"So?" I say after a few minutes of silence.

"Right now, I'll have to get some private investigators to strengthen what you have."

"Does that mean you can get subpoenas for any official documents?" I ask, grabbing Kane's hand, hopeful.

"I should be able to. I find it strange that they've given you the runaround," Attorney Pateki says with his brows furrowed. "Let me see what I can find. If it's something worth going for, then I'll give you a call."

"That's great," I gush, standing and extending my hand to shake his.

"I also saw an eviction that was submitted not long ago, but there's no reason filed. Do you know what that's about?"

I give him a short nod, "It was done to teach me a lesson."

Attorney Pateki's eyes shift between both of mine as he takes in what I said. He nods, then looks down at the file with my pictures in it. Ones with my bruises and the threatening text messages. He nods to the chair and begins typing into his computer. Hazel eyes scanning the screen as he continues to click and type around. The printer whirrs to life as he prints a few documents, but stays silent as he continues his search.

This may not be the answer I wanted, but I at least have a chance to fight whatever shit storm is brewing.

38

Kane

E seems a little lighter after talking with Attorney Pateki. After he said she might have a case and make something stick to keep her safe. He confirmed that someone from the Mayor's office did file a few claims against her, which resulted in the eviction notice. With her case strengthened by the work we put in, he encouraged her to talk to Ren, which only made us fight when we got back to our box cluttered apartment.

No matter how much I trust E, watching her attempt to put the pieces back together after Ren and her dad makes me more protective. She doesn't get to see the look on her face when the war that's her thoughts takes over. Or the way she tosses and turns at night drenched in sweat. And Ren could throw all of Ebony's hard work out the window. I told E I'd do anything to keep her safe. I mean that.

The Mayor's office did a number on Ebony's rental history, making it even more difficult to find a place. But just like they have people, I do too. I managed to set up a few tours next weekend for places I know she'll love and get the false claims knocked off her record.

She doesn't know about the record bit. I'll keep that to myself.

Heavy weights rattle on bars as my teammates rack them. I focus on deadlifting a bar with the heavy weights evenly distributed. I drop it to the ground satisfied with my progress.

"You know," Vin finally says, amusement dripping from his tone. I can hear the smile on his face as he inhales. "I didn't think you'd be this much of a threat when you started fucking Ebony. But clearly, you pose more of a problem than I give you credit for," he continues. The metal from his powerlifting belt clinks together.

"Guess you shouldn't have underestimated me, Vinny boy," I say, lifting a set of heavy dumbbells. "The fuck do you want?"

"Just cheering on my teammate in the weight room. Is that a crime?"

I quirk an eyebrow, taking him in. A healing bruise around his eye and a scab at the edges of his lip like it was busted. I'm slightly concerned, but I remember the shit he did to E and I keep my mouth shut. He probably mouthed off to the wrong person.

"You got a lot of the wrong people mad at you," he says slowly, glancing around the weight room. "I'd hate to see something happen to Ebony or worse... your sister."

"You fuck with my sister and I'll—"

His laugh cuts me off. He leans back, having the fucking nerve, the gods damned gall to wipe a tear from his eye.

"Tell me, Kane. What is it that you'll do?" he taunts me. "Your little whore already tried. And failed again."

"My little whore," I say with a soft chuckle. "So, is

this what you're here for? To pretend that E not wanting you doesn't piss you off? You're mad that all you have are memories of what she feels like, smells like, how she fucking tastes. Fantasizing that it's your tongue she cums for."

He stares at me, his jaw clenched.

Got him.

His knuckles tighten as he balls his hands up into fists. His eyes are wild with a flame that still has nothing on the rage I want to unleash on him. He threatened my girl, then had the nerve to threaten my sister. Rule number one is never fuck with my family. Ever.

"Say, Vin," I drawl. "Do you even know what she sounds like when she's screaming your name like you're her God? Like you're the prayer she needs to recite just to come back down to Earth?" I laugh and run my hands through my hair. A few people walk past as I smile and look back at him. "Your obsession isn't going to get you very far. And if you think about bringing my sister into the middle of your solo pissing contest, I'll make sure it's the last thing you fucking do. Disrespectfully."

His face turns a dark red as he continues to work his jaw. I smile at him as I continue lifting, ignoring his existence.

That little back and forth might come back and bite me in the ass. Especially since Vin has loose fucking lips and will twist words in a heart beat, but he earned it. Him bragging about something he hasn't experienced in years irritates me. Him threatening my sister enrages me. Little does he know, my campus tribe grew just a little after the gala. A few of my teammates reached out personally sharing their own disliking for Vin. Especially after they met E and realized the image he painted of her was nothing compared to who she is.

"Hey, Kane," his voice finally cuts in. I cast an uninterested glance toward him.

"I'd sure hate for that school record your mommy and daddy worked so hard to keep under lock and key to come out. What would Ebony think if she knew what you were up to freshman year or the tape from that night she's been asking about."

He steps in front of me, he sizes me up before he smirks.

"When did you find it? When you turned my phone into crap or was it after?" he asks, crossing his arms over his chest.

"What tape?" I ask, searching his arrogant face. He only smiles wider at me, finally getting the one up he wanted.

"Guess you're not so good with the system after all. I should thank you for trashing it for me. Might help me get her back under control." He takes a step back with his smile growing more than I thought it could. "You really are a great teammate to have," he concludes with a laugh. I grab him by his collar, pulling him into my face. The fabric digs into his neck as I twist the garment in my hand.

"Where the fuck is it?" I growl.

He laughs. "Someplace safe. Now, if you don't mind." He pries my fingers off his shirt and heads out the door with a bounce in his step before I can knock his ass out.

"What's up mi hermano!?" Zeke greets, clapping my back then pausing. "You good?"

"There's a tape," I say slowly.

"A tape of...? Fill me in, kinda lost."

"Vin made a fucking tape of E that night," I clarify finally looking at him. His face pales as his mind goes through everything that could possibly be on that tape, things that he never fully gave life to.

"Where is it?" he asks, his voice hard like gravel.

"Don't know," I say, putting up my weights and nodding towards the exit. "But I have a feeling it was on his phone."

"Did he delete it?"

"No, but I might have," I groan as we break into a sprint across campus.

We slip through the computer lab, rushing to a vacant computer. I type in my credentials, my bag dangling from my shoulder and the rolling chair rushing towards a work station behind me. The computer sings as the screen illuminates and I open the tab I need. I pause, a notification alerting me that I don't have clearance to access the drive I need. I scratch at my temple, then try a different way. My fingers guiding me through the code I built. The same message pops up.

Slamming my fist against the workstation table, I curse loudly staring at the screen.

"There's gotta be another way," Zeke says, standing beside me. His breathing rough as his own anger ripples from him and combines with mine.

"Only way I can get this is with my dad's help," I say, dropping my bag and running my hands through my hair. "And knowing Vin… my dad can't find that video."

"So what? Do nothing!?" Zeke shouts at me. His eyes glaring into my own. "You don't want to find this and help her?"

"That's not the case!" I shout back. "Imagine the shit we thought actually being in a video! He can't see it. We'll find another way, but my dad doesn't need to know."

"Do you fucking hear yourself right now!?"

"It wasn't just that video that he had, Z," I groan, rubbing my hands over my face. "There were others she sent. He won't know what to look for."

"Even those videos should be taken into consideration," Zeke grumbles.

"Yeah? Well, first I have to be able to get to the file that has them before they delete permanently… if they haven't already."

"Tell, E," Zeke says, looking at me. "You need to tell her. She needs this video."

"If it's real. It's Vin we're talking about."

"But you believed him. We wouldn't be here if you didn't. So, either tell her or I will."

"With nothing to back you up?"

"Yes! Because she's my friend and I love her. I'm going to tell her shit even if it's not true because hiding shit like this from her is not a good look. You should know that by now."

"I'd rather have it and give it to her. Vin is just talking."

"Bro," Zeke growls. "Tell her whether you have that shit or not."

"You don't know how hard she fucking cried after confessing what happened to her!" I shout glaring at him. I take a step towards him, toeing the line of starting a physical fight with my best friend. "You weren't there watching her grasp at vices that didn't fucking hurt her and watch how she fell apart when nothing, and I mean nothing, fucking helped."

"Look at you. The entitled dick that thinks he knows everyone more than they know themselves. In this case, my friend, you get to witness the aftermath, but you weren't there when it happened. When she had so many questions and only got the run around and no one was willing to help her. She was hollow then, man. Her eyes had no life in them. One step away from ending it all and you think you know best?"

I suck in a ragged breath and step back. He has me there. I wasn't around when it all happened. When her entire life got turned upside down and nothing made sense initially.

"You think this wouldn't make her go right back to that place?" I finally ask. I stare at him, my eyes searching his as he sucks in a gust of air.

"You're being fucking ridiculous," he grumbles. "When you find it, tell her or I will."

"Yeah," I confirm weakly, nodding. I scratch at my head then pick up my bag and log out of the computer. I shove my chair underneath.

"Look, man," Zeke says with a weighted sigh. "You don't always know what's best. Drop that shit before you set more fires than you can put out."

"I didn't set this one," I defend, looking at him.

"No, but you're fueling it. Don't let Vin win," Zeke advises.

I nod, my mind buzzes as the wind pushes past us. I chew on my inner cheek making a plan of attack.

I can feel the threads that I use to put myself together unraveling the more we uncover. No real answers, only questions exist in this mystery, even on my end. With Vin's threat, I can only feel myself spiraling more.

Even with wanting to protect her, Zeke's right. I can't keep this from her, but I want her to hold on to her happiness… I want to provide answers this time, not more questions.

39

Ren

Mounds of snow sparkle up at Mel and me as we walk across the crunchy surface towards the faded yellow door to my two story townhome. The afternoon sun hangs in the sky melting icicles into puddles on freshly salted pavement.

"So she lawyered up?" I ask as we carry bags of groceries up the crumbling front steps.

The latch on the door clicks as I unlock it, then we enter. Papers lay scattered on top of the center table and a jumble of blankets lay on the long couch from where I crashed last night reading news articles.

"According to the database, yeah. There's no case pending yet, but there are papers being filed," Mel responds.

"Wow," I manage to mutter as we set the bags on the dirty countertops. "What does the record say?"

A frustrated sigh escapes Mel's mouth as she looks at me. Her mouth is a tight line as she shrugs. "I didn't ask because I quite frankly don't give a shit about your psycho ex and neither should you."

Mel storms off toward the living room where she aggressively grabs papers, then stops.

"You know," she says, turning. "I may seem cool and

256

understanding to the whole you reconnecting with your ex thing because it's not my place, but it's fucking weird Ren."

"Not that weird," I respond, opting to put away the groceries and tidy up the mess around me in the process.

"It is weird!" she shouts. "Every time I see you, if you're not talking about your brother, or your fucked up best friend, I have to hear about that bitch."

"Mel!" I shout back. "She's not that bad. Neither is my best friend. Things are just crazy right now."

"Here you go again." She laughs incredulously. "You always defend them. Never fails."

"Because you don't need to go so hard." I huff, then walk over to Mel and grab her hands. I notice the slight height difference. "I'm just trying to build a case for my brother and my parents to submit to my mentors. If I can convince them that there's a case, then imagine the justice my family will get."

"With you front and center?" Mel asks softly, then she smiles. "I don't know why you don't use your pre-law skills to help your brother without them."

"There's more going on," I respond, releasing her hands and grabbing the jumbled pile of blankets. Walking down the sun soaked hallway, I open the door to the living room where mounds of clothes lay.

"Why are you so… obsessed with Ebony Young?" Mel asks softly. She flips on the light switch, then leans against the door frame.

"She almost died," I mumble, then begin sorting the clothes. "At first, I thought she was lying to make me feel bad, but she wouldn't lie about something as serious as that."

"Are you sure?" Mel asks as she steps in to help. She tosses a few items in the old, white washing machine. The one where you can leave the top open as it fills with water.

Mel turns the nozzle letting the machine click on as water pours into the tub of the machine. We work in tandem, putting dirty items into the washer before I fill the containers with soap, close the machine, and start putting the small stack we manage to sort into laundry bags.

"I'm sure," I finally respond to Mel.

My phone buzzes in my pocket as the machine clicks and whines as it begins to rotate.

"I think you two need space," Mel finally says as I check my phone.

I glance up at her, mulling over what she said, then nod in consideration. She lets the conversation end there as we spend the next few hours taking care of the messes I've left lingering.

I stop as she busies herself in the kitchen, and check my phone again.

Vin

> Fucking bitch destroyed my car a few weeks ago.

He sends a picture of the damaged Hellcat and I do my best to suppress my gasp. Ebony did a number on it. All the windows are shattered or spider webbed. The leather of his seat spills and puckers out from large angry gashes.

> Bitch is going to pay. Do your part. My dad will compensate you and you'll be able to go to any law school you choose.

I stare at the message, realizing the weight of what he's saying. If I hand deliver Ebony, I have a chance to go to any school I choose, giving me limitless access to resources to take him down myself.

Me

Working on it. Her and Kane are fighting. It'll be easier.

So there is trouble in paradise…

Her and Miya are planning some end of year parties. I have to connect with my person.

A person that doesn't exist yet, but I may have a few in mind.

No need. I already have someone in place. You just focus on getting Ebony where I need her.

"Ren?" Mel's voice breaks me from my trance and I look up. My eyebrows raise as I give her my full attention.

"Dishes?" she asks as she nods to the now clean stack that submerges the dish holder. I nod, rushing over to help her finish cleaning my disgusting kitchen. Mel's a fucking cleaning machine.

"Thanks for your help," I say as we maneuver around each other starting a late lunch.

"Depression has a way of stealing things away from us," she says, pulling me to her and smiling at me. She kisses my nose. "You miss your brother and you may try to hide it in research, but your body knows that it misses him. So does your mind."

I nod, giving her a sad smile. "I'm sorry."

"For what?" she asks with a small laugh. "It's life."

She pulls my face towards hers, kissing me deeply. Soft, warm lips make moans involuntarily seep into our kiss as my hands grab her hips pulling her to me.

Blood rushes through every vein in my body as her tongue slips into my mouth. Our bodies smush together as we wobble somewhere. We manage to make our way to the couch, where we collapse onto the bouncy surface.

Mel's hands touch my hot skin as she breaks our kiss to place kisses on my jaw, then down to the column of my neck.

My hands slip beneath her shirt, lingering on her warm sides until her slim fingers drag my fingertips up her skin to the silk cloth of her bra. She moans as I allow my hands to have a mind of their own.

I knead her breast before pulling the fabric down and placing my other hand on the back of her head. I lean up, kissing her so fucking deep that I convince myself that I can do this with her. Go all the way. Deepen the intimacy in our relationship.

I pull the cup of her bra down, slipping her budding nipple in between my fingertips and pinching them. A soft, erotic moan vibrates her mouth, still molding into mine.

We fight her shirt and bra off before her nipple is in my mouth and her panted "yeses" and moans fill the room. She reaches for my shirt, pushing me back. A heat in her eyes that I fall into, but this doesn't feel right...

"Wait. Wait..." I say, stopping Mel as her fingers fidget

with the button of my soggy jeans. "I can't do this… I'm sorry. I'm not ready."

"Oh," Mel says, sounding defeated. "Was it something I did? Said?" she says quickly, flashing me a small smile.

"I just— I," I look at Mel apologetically. "Vin's planning something to hurt her and I have no idea if I should tell her. Would she even believe me?"

"I swear to the fucking Gods, Ren. What the fuck!?"

She jumps up, quickly dressing as she collects her things.

"Mel, I'm sorry. Wait."

"I need some space, Ren. I— I have a lot to think about," Mel sighs as her eyes get watery. "Have a good night."

She rushes out my door and I rush to follow her, but I'm too late. She slams the door shut and damn near peels out of my driveway, ice be damned. The red lights of her car illuminate the darkening sky, then she speeds off down the road.

I pull my phone out to text her, but another one catches my attention.

My breathing catches as I read it. Bile rises up in my throat as I digest what it says.

Kane

Vin says there's a video.

this true?

I think back to that night, letting my mind tear apart the fabrication of the room in my mind. Phantom fingers ripping and tossing a mirage of furniture. And just as faulty as my memory, I come up with nothing.

I've learned early on, that if Vin threatens to expose you, chances are he will. His locker room talk is for annoyance purposes, but the fact that he hasn't mentioned anything like this to me puts a heavy weight on my chest.

I suck in a rough breath of air, regret slamming into me with every deep lungful of air I take. There's potentially a video. And only Vin knows what's on it, and it's powerful enough for him to say something to Kane.

So, I do what I do best.

I lie.

40

Ebony

One of the things I hate most about this awkward phase with Kane is the fact that I don't know how to act. I want to trust his judgment, but I can't let go of being angry with him. Maybe because I'm struggling to trust myself and my judgment.

Even as we tour apartments off campus, I avoid being close to him unless it's necessary. We haven't talked, and I mean really talked. And that situation with Ren last week didn't help at all. I can tell by the way his eyes cloud over every so often he's got a lot on his mind, but I'm too in my own head to ask. We dance around that subject, just as much as I dance around the subject of us really making up. Only giving him snippets of my thoughts, placing verbal landmines around our dialogue to push him away. I can use stress as an excuse, especially with one week left to find a place within my price range, but I know I'm projecting.

"This is our two-two. We'll have one available next month," a woman from the management office says. Her high heels clack against the dark brown wood. Bright red hair cascading over her shoulder. Her freckled face pale in the light reflected from the snow. Her green eyes look at Kane, taking in his large frame and smiling flirtatiously.

She sways her hips a little more as she moves around the open space. He looks around, eyes scanning each corner, his hands tucked in his jeans pocket, barely noticing her. I laugh to myself as he walks past her towards the rooms.

"Will the one you have available look like this?" he asks, finally looking at her.

"More or less," she says with a wide, toothy smile. "This is the perfect roommate layout since the rooms are across from each other."

She gestures to the rooms on either side of the apartment. The living room and kitchen being the space between them. I look into the room closest to me. A bathroom connected to it and the living space. It's slightly smaller than the one across the way.

"We won't have a roommate," he says flatly. His footsteps bounce off the naked walls as he looks out the floor to ceiling windows. I move near him, crossing my arms over my chest as I watch the river bubbling a few feet away from the property. I imagine the flowers and vibrant green grass that might sprout in the field. The skyline of downtown is a perfect contrast to the secluded place.

I walk into the kitchen, admiring the stainless steel appliances and rub my hand across the cold marble countertops. I open the cabinets, looking in them before leaning against the counter. My eyes glaze over everything around me.

"This is beautiful," I say softly. "Breath taking really."

This apartment is one of my dreams. The space, the seclusion, the layout. Just the apartment for me, but too fucking expensive for my pockets. I don't know how I managed to be born with such expensive taste with the wallet size of an acorn top. The universe is cruel in that aspect, but my tastes did make me fight harder to be able to achieve it. Even if that means slumming it for a bit.

"So, what are you thinking?" she asks, stepping near Kane and looking up at him. She flutters her lashes and tucks some hair behind her ear.

He looks over his shoulder at me and quirks his eyebrow, then turns. Approaching me with slow steps, his eyes drag across my body making me feel warm and tingly. I hide my blush by looking out the window. He's been trying subtly and I feel guilty for shutting him out. His warm hands take mine and he pulls me towards the window. His breath tickles my ear as he leans into my ear.

"Help."

I snort, covering my mouth trying not to laugh. Kane's never been one flustered by attention. He could literally have a woman every hour if he wanted. Why he's sticking around while I'm acting like a raging bitch? Maybe because I learned a trick or two that he likes.

He pulls me closer to the window and I watch the view. It's breathtaking even with mounds of snow covering every surface. Even as the sky opens up, pelting the soft mounds with sleet.

"Can you give us a moment to discuss?" he asks, looking over my face.

"Uh yeah. Sure," she says with a guarded smile.

She steps towards the front door, pulling out her cell phone. She pretends to be busy writing something, but I can tell by the way her fingers don't quite touch the screen that it's just an act. This is only confirmed by the way her eyes dart towards us every so often, and by the way she tucks her hair and cranes her neck a little closer to us.

"It's too expensive," I whisper with a sigh.

"No, it's not," he whispers back, shoving his hands back into his pocket.

"Of course not for you," I quip with an eye roll.

"Don't do that," he protests softly. He looks at me, eyes hard and guarded. "You can be mad about the Ren situation, but that takes a back seat to this. Do you like this place or not?"

"I love it, but I can't…"

He holds his hand up, silencing me with a playful smile on his face. He backs away from the window and strolls over to the agent. His charm turned up as he leans against the wall near her. She blushes, looking up at him as she tucks her phone in her pocket. Kane is clearly not afraid to use what he has to get what he wants. At least charm wise. And he has a lot of that.

I shake my head, backing away from the window to hide my amused smile, walking around the space again slowly this time. I visualize all my things in various arrangements, then mentally convince myself that no matter how good Kane is, he's not good enough to make this apartment a reality. Even if he were to help.

"Eb," Kane's voice calls over to me.

I look over my shoulder at him and he nods his head towards where he and the agent are standing, her eyes sparkling as she stares at him. Her slender fingers fidget in her hair as I approach. Her eyes never leave Kane's face. I catch his flirty glance towards me and I shake my head.

"Head out the gutter," he says lowly to me. "She was telling me she might be able to get us in sooner than the date she gave us."

"Oh? Really?" I ask with a smile on my face.

"Yeah," she says, smiling at me, then beaming up at Kane. "We can start the process right now. You guys explore some more and I'll be done in a second."

We thank her as she walks to the kitchen. She pulls out her laptop from the bag she stashed in one of the cabinets and starts typing. Her fingers flying over the keyboard as Kane nods me towards the balcony. We step out onto the large space, pulling our jackets tighter around our bodies. I take in everything outside once again, looking up at the sky as I pull my hood over my head avoiding the sleet.

Kane's boots crunch against the snow as he steps closer to me. He pulls me towards him and the rail, then positions himself behind me. Leaning close to my ear again as he takes in a deep breath.

"Imagine me making you cum against this rail. Then pulling you into that big ass bedroom and making you cum against the window. I don't think you can stay mad at me with the city lights praising your perfect fucking body," his deep voice rumbles in my ear.

I nudge him with my hips, rolling my eyes. A smile forms on my lips as my brain paints a very detailed picture of it. Him bracing me on the railing, balancing between crashing to the ground and cumming so hard that the stars' brightness increases, making me concerned I've gone to some form of heaven. Or hell.

I can tell by the way he pushes himself closer to me that he's thinking something similar, which doesn't help the ache that's happening right between my thighs. I may feel awkward about our fight, but my body doesn't. Especially with the way he knows how to make every inch of me sing so damn beautifully it puts my own singing to shame. We're tethered together by something powerful, something deep in both of our souls because we always gravitate towards each other. My body always hums when he gets closer, when he brushes past my hand, when his eyes are on me, much like they are now, in the most loving way.

"Is this really going to be our apartment?" I finally ask softly, trying to break the sexual tension. It doesn't help. There will always be some sort of sexual tension between Kane and I. A pull that brings us right back together. All of it so damn intoxicating when our relationship is in sync.

"Is there another one you want," he asks, turning me around to face him. His hands gripping the rail as he cages me in. "Say it and it's yours."

"I don't want you spending money on me," I sigh, leaning my back against the rail to put some space between us. Does this help? Hell no. Not while he's staring at me like he wants to worship me like it's his only salvation. And I know he would—will. Every inch.

"This place is yours," he says. "I'm not going to hold this over your head, baby."

"How'd you know?" I say a bit sarcastically. He knows most of my story. Enough for him to be able to fill in the blanks.

"I'm not them," he says with a scoff. His brown eyes are

hard as he leans back and sighs. He releases the rail and runs his hands through his hair.

"You're going to make me go bald," he grumbles.

I grab his hand and pull myself towards him, circling my arms around his waist as I lay my head against his thumping heart.

"I don't like this," I start, "but I appreciate you." I look up at him, placing my chin into the center of his chest breathing in his aroma.

"What was that? You're not telling me to shut up and fuck you? Let me make sure the world isn't ending."

I roll my eyes, slapping my hand against his chest as I shove away from him playfully. He laughs, pulling me back into his arms. He kisses my forehead and sighs.

"I want us to be okay…" he mutters looking down at me.

"You're all set," our agent says, interrupting us. She falters when she spots us. Disappointment present in her vibrant green eyes as she looks between the two of us.

"Thank you," Kane says with a soft smile on his face.

We step inside, sign the paperwork, then watch as she scans and uploads all the necessary documents. Her eyes stay focused on the computer screen or the floor. She submits the paperwork and gives us a tense smile as she escorts us out of the apartment. I turn to thank her, but she bolts towards the office not acknowledging either one of us.

"So, roommate," he says as we head towards his car. "Are you going to finally talk to me about the Ren situation?" he asks as we slide into the car. His hands grip the steering wheel as he stares at me, while I secure my seatbelt and shift in the seat. I shake my head and look out the window. "I don't want to talk about it right now."

"I'm not talking about them watching us," he mutters, turning on the car. "I don't even think I can talk about that."

I scoff, crossing my arms over my chest as we head back to my old apartment to finish packing. Music filling the space that I could be filling with an apology or a thank you. He deserves both, honestly. I just struggle with finding the right way to say it. This type of relationship is new and I'd be a liar if I said I'm not afraid to mess it up.

"Hey, E?" he calls out as he slows the car to stop at a red light. My eyes focus on his anxious one. "Are we okay?"

Agony. Immediate and present in his voice as he asks such a simple question. Kane Yamada. The man that doesn't do love… loving me. A man that can have anyone he wants, begging me to accept what he has to offer. And here I am, clamming up when I should be screaming to the heavens how much I love him.

A car from behind us honks, saving me yet again from baring my soul, but I don't miss the flicker of disappointment as he pulls off.

I should have answered, but for some reason I don't.

41

Kane

Sitting at the library across town, I turn on my VPN and a few other programs to block my tracks as I log in to the software I pushed to Vin's phone a while back. My fingers are scrolling through the programs and the files I used to erase his phone to check for anything remotely close to an incriminating video. Sure, he has a bunch of questionable nudes from women on campus, including E, but that isn't what I'm looking for. And based on the text threads, all pictures I come across were sent willingly.

Ren may have told me that there isn't a video, but something in my gut tells me to search. Especially with how shady they moved a month ago. I'd rather know for sure that there is nothing, than be blind sided again. And when E's involved, Vin's threats aren't idle.

"Any luck?" Zeke asks, plopping down in the leather chair beside me. The legs scrape against the cement floor. The intense smell of frozen earth wafting off of him as he peels off his jacket and gloves.

"No," I grumble. He sighs, leaning back in his chair. "I asked Ren. They said no, but…"

"You don't believe them," he finishes with a nod. "Good. I wouldn't either."

"We're finally in a decent space," I say, laying my head on the back of the chair. I shift my body lower using my legs. "I know keeping this from her isn't good, but I want to give her this with answers."

"What if you checked the security system?" Zeke asks, looking over at me with his eyebrows stitched together.

"Those don't work," I sigh, bouncing my leg restlessly.

Freshman year, I attempted to rush a fraternity wanting to outrun the few bad apples that trickled in my life. I learned how to disable cameras and keep them disabled with a simple command from a program I no longer have access to thanks to the upgrades.

"Even the security system outside?"

I shake my head looking over at him.

I should have gotten into the fraternity with that task completed because no one else could do what I did, but they wouldn't let me in. They claimed to be an "elite" brotherhood. I ended up rushing another one and getting them back. I covered my tracks well enough to get a slap on the wrist, but my dad did have to come in and clean up the loose ends. It doesn't help that Vin and a few of his lackeys are actually a part of that frat now too. That's a house full of people that will do whatever he wants, just to get back at anyone Vin wants. Money talks and unfortunately Vin has a lot.

42

Ren

I magine my surprise when Ebony's number pops up on my phone with a message from her asking me if I have a moment to talk. It takes me several minutes to write the three letters that I send her.

I squeeze into a pair of jeans and one of my oversized sweatshirts, then cram my toes into my snowshoes.

I rush out to my car to meet at the address she sent me. Twenty minutes later, I'm pulling into the parking lot of a large internet café. I see Ebony's little black car parked not far from the front door. Grabbing my bag, I slip inside immediately searching for her. My phone chimes in my pocket as I step towards one of the wooden bookshelves and glance around. I pull my phone out of my pocket and check the message.

Tucking my phone back into my pocket, I trudge towards the records and find her. Head bowed as her fingers flick through the old record binders. A storm of emotions floods me as I approach her. My teeth worry at my bottom lip remembering seeing her bare body vibrating at the hands of my best friend. Former best friend.

I stick the wool of my gloves between my teeth and yank my hands out in an attempt to focus on something more present. Once I remove both gloves, I shove them in the pocket of my thick jacket and walk around the record table, placing it between her and me.

"Didn't take you as a record collector," I mutter, looking at the old, cracking cases. The painted papery material chipped, exposing the brown cardboard beneath a few. I pull out one, Michael Jackson lounges stoically on his side. His brown eyes stare back at me, almost like he's disappointed in me. "Billie Jean" is scrawled just beneath his name in red font, which is slightly rubbed off with age.

"I'm not," Ebony responds with a rumbly voice as she tucks another record beneath her arm. There's a total of three in her possession. She glances up at me before looking back down and using her finger to flick the ones she deems less worthy out of her way. "Say we go with your plan," she says after a few minutes softly. "What's the escape route?"

She stops what she's doing and finally looks at me. Faint dark circles sit beneath her eyes. She looks tired, worn down by the uncertainty of everything going on in that brain of hers. It's a look I've seen before.

"I know some of the chem kids—"

"I do too, what about it?" she counters, cutting me off, her face telling me to cut the shit and get to the point — quickly.

"They can make a formula of something that reacts in a similar fashion. Wears off quickly."

"No," Ebony says, shaking her head, her locs falling

over her shoulder with the simple action. "Too much of a risk."

"How do you know?"

"Miya and I created digital bracelets that test drinks for drugs. We're going to a conference in Cali, which means that Miya and I won't be at the mercy of the school. I can't jeopardize this opportunity."

"Then let it be me," I say as she starts moving down the records looking over the labels, her fingers touching the edges softly. Rings decorate nearly every finger. Dainty little things that spiral up her digits. I can tell the bands are adjustable by the way they swivel and open at the top where the embellishment is. Her ring finger is the only one without anything on it.

"No," she says a little more firmly, looking up at me. "That's even worse and you know it."

"I can refuse the band," I counter.

She shakes her head and sighs. "Then people will think you have something to hide. Imagine you even showing up to any of these parties. Doesn't look good Eva — I mean Ren."

I pause and look her over. "You can call me Eva…"

"Eva is a pastime. I'd rather use Ren," she spits back without giving me a second look. She pulls out another record, looks it over, then tucks it under her arm.

"What do you propose?" I finally ask as she continues to slowly peruse the next stack. "What bright idea does the brilliant Ebony have in that pretty little head of hers."

"I have to prove that Vin and his father are bringing the drugs on campus. Or someone on campus is helping them manufacture it."

"Doesn't really get us to the point where we have undeniable proof," I grumble, placing my hand over the record she's fussing over. "This can't be a half- assed plan, Ebs."

For a brief second, the warmth of her hand sinks into my palm before she pulls it back and looks at me, her eyes hard and angry.

"I'm being serious," I say again with a shrug. I bristle under her penetrating gaze. This new Ebony is kind of intense.

"If the school is covering for them, how would we even manage to get any type of proof? I'm being watched like a hawk. So is Kane. You can't step foot on campus."

"That's where you're wrong. I can, I just have to keep it low key."

"This plan isn't low key," she fusses with an eye roll and a head shake.

"I figured it was worth a shot," I protest, feeling deflated.

"For what it's worth," she says looking at me, her eyes much softer than they were a few seconds ago. "It was a nice idea."

I nod as I let my eyes look into hers. I sigh, realizing that I genuinely want her to trust me. And I don't care whether she does or doesn't, she never would because of what I've done. I don't blame her, but the guilt that I kept at bay keeps creeping up.

"That project," I start, then clear my throat because I immediately feel awkward. I shove my hair out of my face, then pick the peeling blue polish from my nails. "When did you start it?"

"Last year," she offers idly as she focuses primarily on the records. She huffs again, more so to herself, then nods towards the back where the computers are. I follow mindlessly to one of the old desktops. The computer drive groans and hums loudly as she wakes up the system. She sets the records on the table, then pulls up a chair beside her.

I take it, slowly easing my body into the seat watching as the screen illuminates her face and sings a little tune. She digs in her bag for a second, pulls out a thumb drive, and then sticks it into the computer. Her fingers fly across the keys before the school's insignia takes over the screen.

"Did you just hack into the school system?"

"Yes and no," she answers, her fingers still clacking against the keys that reverberate their own unique sound right back to her. "I have to use off-loaded software to reroute how I access certain files."

I nod like I understand. Truth is, I'm more intrigued with the numbers and unintelligible codes that she works with. She turns to me, a small, amused smile on her face.

"It means that I shut down any obstacles they have on the system."

"On a flash drive?" I ask, raising my eyebrows and stifling my own smile. I think I'm failing because there's this sparkle in her eyes as they scan my face and her own smile grows.

"Technology is pretty dope," she offers before turning back to the screen and scrolling through a few things.

I study her profile. The way her relaxed face gives away

little that's going on in her mind. How her eyes focus on the screen moving line by line as she moves through one file to the next.

"I thought you were a music major," I mumble.

"Double majoring now," she answers, then pauses on a file.

I hum my answer and give a slight nod as I focus on the screen. "What's this?"

"The data from the bracelets," she states, then glances at me. "Chem department helped us mimic a bunch of different drugs. LSD, Meth, Cocaine, you name it."

"Why? Those aren't really date rape drugs."

"They're not, but with cases like your brother... It might be lab made. Same as the drug you gave me."

"I don't think Vin is your guy then. Isn't he like sports management? Or personal training?"

"Something like that. His minor is in one of the chemistry departments. Not pharmaceutical, but pretty damn close, but I don't think he made whatever was in Rae's or my ... cocktail." She scrunches her face up as she hunts for the right word in her mind, then gives up by slapping a placeholder word in there.

"Couldn't we say we're doing a test run with the chemistry department? Trying to mimic real world situations?"

"School isn't allowing it. Miya and I tried when we had test bands. The most they allowed us to do was let everyone wear the bands."

I release my lungful of air and lean back in my seat feeling dejected. She pats my leg idly before focusing back on the screen. Now entering a different file.

"Anything on my brother?" I finally ask her.

She looks at me with a grim expression before pinching her lips tightly and shaking her head. "We were able to access some documents, but it's not a smoking gun. Maybe Kane knows something, but I haven't been able to find anything other than the fact that since the night of the gala, the records room has been under lock and key. No one gets in or out without the school system knowing."

"Then trick the system," I say, leaning forward with my brow furrowed.

"We're working on it. The key cards are more complicated than this. They work with a completely different company than Kane's dad's."

I nod, feeling my mood souring as she looks me over. Her eyebrows raise as she gives me a sad, sympathetic look. I struggle to find the lies in her words, but it doesn't stop me from forcing the idea. Anything to create distance.

"I," she starts, then stops, turning away from the computer and fishing a binder out of her bag. She runs her hand over the smooth surface and extends it to me. "Kane and I found Raeven's digital journal. I've been reading it, looking for clues or anything to indicate what may have happened."

I grab the book and quickly flip through the pages. So many pages. My heart clenches as I read an entry to myself, my fingers running over the font. "How'd you find it?" I ask softly.

She's silent for a moment, which makes me look into her sad eyes. "It was on Sumner's hard drive."

It's my turn to let silence settle between us. I stare at her. Watching the emotion flow between her eyes as I consider all the possibilities. Dr. Sumner has a copy of my brother's journal. So much of my brother's stuff was missing, but this wasn't something I expected or knew about.

"That scar on your face," I finally say, looking at her then down at the records on the table. My fingers pick at the sharp edges of the binder. I look back up and catch her touching her cheek where the skin dips. I'm sure she needed stitches. "That night, you fought the drugs so hard that you ended up falling off the bed."

I lower my voice and focus on keeping the emotions that bubble up at bay. It's hard when her eyes seem to glisten with unshed tears.

"The night stand in one of the frat houses was busted. The wood ended up cutting you so damn deep. There was a lot of blood." I swallow back the lump in my throat. "I was able to get the bleeding to stop a bit… but you were already passed out."

She releases a shaky breath, her head nodding as she digests the information I just gave her. Trembling fingers trace the line in her cheek as her eyes fade out into a distant memory.

"Do you… do you know anything else about that night?"

"I should get going," I say instead. Gathering my things, I rush out the door already regretting opening up about that night. I don't look back as I head into the cold and slip into the driver's side of my car. Tears spilling out of my eyes as I grow angry. Dropping the heavy binder in my lap, I slam my fist into the steering wheel.

I scream at myself, at the images, at my cowardice. I scream for her, the pain, and the fact that I have little to nothing to offer her for all that she's doing for me.

Why can't I just tell her?

43

Kane

T hank God for friends and family.

With E in class today, that leaves me moving our stuff into our new apartment. One that's much nicer than the one we were originally shown. Sure, I sold myself a little bit, but E needed a place to stay. And the way her eyes lit up when we toured the apartment told me everything I needed to know about this place.

Zeke and a few guys from the football team, and student life —thanks to Miya—help me carry in large boxes from the parking lot. Our feet crunching and squelching in the melting snow as we move quickly up the stairs to the fourth fucking floor. Damn elevator is in service mode for some repair apparently.

Miya points us in the direction of where each box goes based on a list E sent over to her this morning, both of them being very particular about organization. My mother busies herself in the kitchen, placing mismatched plates in the cabinets.

My parents were completely against the whole "me moving in with E" thing for a bit. Imagine their surprise when I told them it was too late and we already had the place. Their disappointment was short lived when they arrived and had breakfast with us, which probably wasn't the best idea since my mother noticed we weren't our usual "couple in love" selves.

Cue my mother asking questions and pointing out the two instances she noticed we weren't staring at each other like love sick puppies. I played it coy and distracted her a bit, but it's short lived. I know she'll ask again. I'll also credit being able to talk to her about Han's enrollment this semester. With him on campus and now living in my old apartment with Zeke, my parents have been stressed with making sure everyone is settled.

"We should have dinner here," my mother states as I slide a box on the counter and take a breather. I use the hem of my shirt to wipe the sweat from my face and look at her. She examines a pot, giving a satisfied nod before storing it in a cabinet and emptying the box.

"Yes!" Miya says with a large smile. "I bet she'd love it."

"I don't get a say?" I ask.

"No," my sister and mother say in unison. They look at each other laughing as they continue emptying boxes.

I shake my head and help grab the last few boxes. Zeke passes me covered in sweat and possibly regretting being friends with the both of us. I'll have to get him something special for this shit.

Just left class. Be there in 15.

Take your time. B safe.

The response bubbles pop up, then disappear a few

times before they ultimately disappear. We still hadn't really talked about anything, but it helps that she's been coming around more, doing little things to show me that the little ice wall she put around herself is melting. At least I hope it is.

I push my phone in my pocket and grab what's left from the truck and wave my teammates off.

E shows up in less than fifteen minutes and immediately starts unpacking the boxes. Music swelling around the space as Zeke, Miya, D, Han, my parents, E, and I all work quickly to get the place set up.

She asked if Isaac could help, but apparently he just got his nails done and preferred to come to the housewarming party instead. Smart decision.

My mother wipes everything down in the kitchen as my father binds the boxes up and sets them outside the door.

"Kane," my mother calls from the kitchen while Zeke and I rearrange the furniture for the fifth fucking time. Miya standing and watching our efforts, a hand on her hip and one on her chin as she studies the space when we set the heavy piece down.

"It doesn't look right," she says. "Move it back."

"Miya, I swear to God," I growl as Zeke and I lift the couch and turn it.

"It stays right here," Zeke says, sitting on the floor, then falling to his back panting. "I need air."

"Kane," my mother calls again and I look at her.

"Don't forget you and Ebony should hand out rice cakes to your neighbors."

She taps the big box on the counter before wiping her

hands on an apron I didn't know she had.

"Where'd you get the apron from?" I ask, wiping the sweat from my face.

"She brought it with her. Don't be surprised if Ebony finds one in the drawer," Han mutters beside me.

I know he intends to scare me with the idea that my mother is trying to make this much more domesticated than it is, but something about Ebony in an apron does things to me. Mental things I shouldn't be thinking about while others are in the room.

"Rice cakes," she nods towards the box. "Before the day is over."

E walks out of the room, in sweatpants. Boxes tucked beneath her small arm as she leans them against the wall.

"E," I call out, walking over to her. "My mother gave us very clear instructions to hand out rice cakes."

She looks up at me surprised, then glances at the box on the counter, then back at me.

"That's a big box," she marvels. "I can't carry that."

"E," I sigh, shaking my head. "I'm carrying it. You just have to pass out the rice cakes and be all… cute."

"I can't do cute," she says, crossing her arms over her chest.

"You absolutely can do cute," I smile at her before slipping into the room to change my clothes. "I'll be ready in a minute."

She nods glancing over her shoulder at me as I take my clothes off. I send her a wink before unbuttoning my pants. She panics, in that "if I see you naked this is going to turn X rated" kind of way and quickly pulls the door closed before

I drop my pants chuckling.

44

Kane

After discarding the box, we head back up to our apartment in silence. I rub my shoulders, feeling the muscles cramping up already. While my fingers knead at my shoulders, I roll my neck around hearing it pop. I groan.

"You okay?" E asks softly.

She looks over at me before moving to replace my hand with hers. She pushes her thumb into my muscles and I clench my jaw, suppressing a groan. Girls got the fucking magic touch when it comes to working out muscles. I'd never gone for massages after practice, girls offered but it was primarily for other activities. E surprised me by actually giving me a massage that always puts my ass to sleep in fifteen minutes or less. No sexy time necessary.

She shifts my position, angling herself behind my body and standing on her toes to get closer to the knot in my muscles for the short elevator ride. Once the ding sounds in the metal box, we step out and head towards our apartment.

Reaching out, I grab her hand and pull her back to me. Wrapping my arms around her body, she gives me a gentle nudge, then relaxes in my chest.

"You're thinking too much," I whisper into her locs. I rest my lips on her forehead.

"Can't turn my brain off, Kane," she mutters against my chest.

"No. You can't, but you can share your thoughts with me."

She sighs and looks up at me. "I'm still upset about the whole 'you not trusting me' thing."

Her voice sounds small, vulnerable in the narrow hallway just outside our door. Like the little girl she locked away to keep safe is peeking out reaching for my hand. And I want to take it. I want to protect every form of her.

"I do trust you," I say, brushing my thumb across her soft cheek.

"If you're not giving me space to navigate this situation, then you're not trusting me. Protecting me also means letting me figure shit out without you interfering."

"After the way you looked at Ren… I don't think—"

"What you think doesn't matter. Is it important to me? Yes, but what you think will not make this situation any better or easier for me." She takes a deep breath and looks down the hall before continuing. "You said you're my teammate right?"

"Yeah and—"

She shushes me with a look. "Do you make calls for your teammates on the field? Do you tell them how to play the game when they're all in motion and they're assessing the situation they're in?"

"It's impossible to," I say with a sigh already knowing that she has me beat.

"Let me figure this out." She grabs my hand as she stares up into my eyes. "And I'm insulted that you think I'd let my guard down and trust Ren freely."

I respond with a slow, thoughtful nod, then guide her back into our apartment. Only a few boxes remain unpacked and pushed off to the side now. I push the door closed as E drops to the couch near Miya and D. My father checks a pot in the kitchen.

I make my way to the bedroom after dropping my keys on the counter. I walk in and pause. My mother stands in the middle of the room. A black velvet box in her hand, open. She stares down at the small shiny artifact that glitters beneath the overhead light.

"Whoa," I breathe out startled. I crack the door and reach my hand for the box. My mother looks up at me. Her eyes shining, brimming with questions and a series of emotions. She grips the box and turns it towards me, quirking her eyebrow.

"Kane," she says softly. "Is this what I think it is?"

"Maybe?" I offer lamely, running my hand through my hair. My heart pounding in my chest as I search my mother's face for the emotion she's settled on.

"This is a big step you know?" she says, placing the box on the dresser, open. The diamond ring winks back at me in the bright light.

"Yeah," I answer, swallowing hard. "I haven't asked yet. It's still pretty early."

She nods her head. "Is there something we should be concerned about?"

"No. No. I got it after Thanksgiving. Being impulsive," I ramble rubbing my palms against my soft sweatpants.

"How long have you two been dating?"

She looks around the room, then nods towards the private balcony attached to the primary bedroom. I grab two of my jackets, offering my mother the thickest one. We slip into them and step out into the cold. Clouds form as we breathe into the air, blowing warm air on our hands as the cold immediately attacks.

"So?" she finally asks, looking at the cars speed past on the freeway.

"Oh, um, almost two months officially, but we've been in that unofficial dating stage since late August? September-ish."

My mother sighs, examining my face as creases alter her normally smooth skin. She reaches for my face, placing her soft palm against my cheek. I'm sure she can feel the slight stubble forming.

"I want you to make sure this is a decision you want to make. And with this, you're talking about your future. The rest of your lives, baby," she finally offers with another sigh.

"You seemed to really enjoy her..." I mutter.

"Your father and I do," she defends quickly. "We would absolutely love for you two to go through life together. I just think it's too early. You have your entire life ahead of you. So does she."

I let the cold settle in the air as I shove my hands in my pockets. I stare at the scene around me, which honestly is beautiful, peaceful after a long day of moving.

"I haven't asked. She doesn't know I have it," I finally offer.

My mother laughs a little, then looks up at me. "If I can find it, she probably has too."

"That's not why we were fighting."

My mother hums her response and thinks for a moment, then looks up at me. "Why were you two fighting?"

"I met up with Ren. They have a crazy idea that could get the both of them hurt and I decided not to take it to Ebony. Ren showed up out of nowhere, telling Ebony and we started arguing."

"I see," my mother acknowledges before rubbing my arms. "I'm sure you'll figure out what's best for you and what's best for your relationship. Your father and I argued a lot when we started dating."

"Really?" I ask leaning against the railing of the balcony. "You two barely do now."

"That's because we took the time to figure out better ways to be together and communicate. It's not easy. It takes a lot of work. A lot of forgiveness and patience."

There's a knock on the door interrupting our conversation. We turn, walking into the room. I scoop up the box, shoving it in my pocket just as Miya peeks in.

"Dad says dinner's done," she says with a smile before slipping back out.

"Kane," my mother calls, capturing my attention again. "Make sure this is something you both want. You are a lot like your father, when you guys get set on how something should be or how you want them to be. Let her come to you, okay?"

I nod with a small smile. She hooks her arm with mine and we leave the room to join everyone else at the table.

45

Kane

I find myself at E's Gramps' bar with a beer bottle in my hand practically begging Clint to break a few rules. I never would have guessed this guy would be the rule follower out of him and Ebony.

"That's a bad look," he offers, passing a beer over to someone and looking back at me. His face firm as he shakes his head.

"It's for, E. She won't let this go until she gets those records," I offer again. "If it wasn't for her, we'd be having a different conversation."

"She's still trying to help Ren?"

I nod, taking a swig of my beer. He rolls his eyes as he wipes his hand on a white cloth looped in his belt loop. "My sentiment exactly."

"What brings ya here?" Gramps grumbles, which is as friendly as he gets.

"I'm just having a—" he casts me a look that has me quiet in seconds and immediately confessing a few of my sins. "Trying to convince Clint to help me break into one of the school buildings."

Gramps nods his head thoughtfully. His lanky, wrinkled fingers scratching at his chin as he looks between me and Clint. He shrugs his shoulders, then nods as he has a silent conversation with himself.

"Where's Ebony?" he asks.

"Working on a music project. Stress relief after the move and everything."

"I'm not going to do it," Clint says, sounding more innocent and childlike than I could imagine. Trust me. His voice is Barry White deep, childlike is not something that comes easy with that type of baritone.

"Why not? You could use a little trouble," Gramps said with a slight smile on his face. "It's slow. Go. Add it to the stories you can tell ya kids."

Before Clint can protest, Gramps walks over to a few tables, passing out beers and cleaning up the place. A few new bartenders are moving around the bar, filling in the space Gramps can't.

"Fuck," Clint curses under his breath before looking at me. "I hang out with you just a few times and I'm already about to catch a charge."

I smile widely at him before shrugging my shoulders.

"And I used to think E was a bad influence. Match made in hell the two of you," he finishes in an amused grumble, stifling a laugh. "Give me five."

My motorcycle rumbles to life as I adjust my position and lift the kick stand.

"You fit every stereotypical cliché known to man," Clint says with a laugh as he swings his keys around his finger.

"Nah. I'm shit," I say, making us both laugh.

"Alright pretty boy, let's get this over with," Clint says

heading around the building. He lingers back there for a moment before I hear the rumbling. A sleek bike rounds the corner. The plum color vibrant in the light, which oddly fits him.

"Can't have you showing me up," he shouts over the rumble of our motors.

He closes the flap of his helmet after flashing me a smile and we speed off across campus to the medical department, a large building with oversized windows that looks sterile and pristine compared to the older buildings surrounding it. I pass him a fake badge as we make it to the building, earning a skeptical glance from my companion.

I ignore it and follow behind Clint as he makes his way to the door and swipes the badge against the keypad. The lock clicks and he throws the door open for us to enter.

We walk in silence as he approaches the records door and holds the badge up to the sensor. The light flashes red and he tries again.

"Let me help," someone offers from behind us.

We step to the side, allowing him to slip his badge. "The department has been going around re-coding doors and keycards. Accessing any of these rooms has become a nightmare," the guy says as the door clicks and he holds it for us to get through.

"Thanks, man," Clint calls out as we part ways and head to the next floor. "We're going to have to find another way into the file room," he says over his shoulder, heading to the door and trying his badge anyways. The lock beeps and flashes red.

He nods towards the front desk and makes his way over.

He leans against the counter top, then smiles a smile I've never seen before when a student dressed in blue scrubs walks from the back. He glances at me, shooting me a look that tells me to keep this between us. Hiding my amused smirk, I slide my phone out of my pocket and mess around with system remotely to ensure Clint's documents, which were flagged, are replaced with dummy information.

"Clint!" a young woman gushes as she stands. "I was wondering when we were going to see you again!"

She leans towards the counter, her bright blue scrubs pressed and almost stiff. Her hair's pinned back tightly and her chestnut brown skin is lightly decorated with dark spots. There's an occasional pale spot. Vitiligo I think is what the skin condition is called.

"Wanted to check out some of my old work, but my card isn't working on the doors," he says. "You look really good today." She blushes, deep dimples appearing in her brown cheeks. She ducks her head from Clint's eyes. She looks back up. "Think you can help me out?" He slides the badge over towards her and she takes it. Giving him another wide grin before she scans his badge and looks through her system.

"I can get you a day pass, but because you aren't enrolled in classes, that's it," she says. She scans the ID again and slides it over to him. "By the way, the mayor's wife, she might be able to help you with access. She's been coming around more," she offers. Clint and I exchange a cautious glance, then file it away for later.

"Thanks," he says, winking at her as he puts the badge in his pocket. He approaches me. "Don't say shit," he mutters as he goes to the door to the labs and swipes his card.

I stifle my laugh and wait for the system to register his actions. The light flashes green and the latch clicks as the door unlocks. He smirks at me, then waves at the young woman at the desk before ushering me in.

We walk around the pristine halls of the building, peeking into classrooms and mock surgical rooms. A chill settles through my body as we take the stairs down to a lower level with plain cement floors.

"Files would be in that room right there," Clint points to the metal door. A simple silver door that gives little to nothing away.

Clint walks up, swings his badge and we watch as the light turns green. He looks at me with a triumphant smile.

"I knew you'd cross over to the dark side," I say with a chuckle. We dap each other up before walking the opposite direction and heading up the stairs.

"That's not all I need your help with," I say with a sigh. I stop at the top of the stairs where the humidity hangs like a heavy sack. "Vin mentioned he has a video of E."

Clint tucks his hands in his pockets, hooking the thumb of each hand outside the pocket. I see the rage burning beneath his eyes. "He has a what?"

"A tape. I can't bring myself to tell her," I confess. I lean against the wall and sigh.

He looks around for a moment and I get the hint. Digital eyes are everywhere on campus now.

I nod towards the stairs, taking them two at a time until we make it up the last set of stairs and quickly exit out the building.

The sun begins to set as we start our bikes.

"Café?" he calls out and I tip my chin at him.

Our motorcycles rumble to life and we peel out down the street. The roads are clear for the most part making the ride easy. We pull up to a light, slowing our bikes near each other and we lift our visors.

"I don't know when to tell you to tell her. If he has a video, she'll have questions," Clint says as he adjusts his footing and shifts on his bike. "I think you're doing right by not telling her now, though."

I look over at him, surprised. "Really?"

"Yeah… Vin makes a big deal out of little things. He's just a fucking immature bitch," he mutters. He scratches his arm.

I nod, feeling the weight fall from my shoulders as the light turns green. We ride off, staying together as we take the winding back roads leading towards the café.

46

Ebony

Plucking at the strings on my guitar, I record the melody of a song, then layer it using the keys on my computer. I tap the spacebar roughly, then play a few more chords before listening to it playback. Grabbing other instruments from the room, I add a few other sounds to the track before walking into the studio booth and pressing the record button.

Adjusting the headphones, I lean into the mic and sing softly into the mic. Layering my voice the way I did with the guitar. I channel my emotions into every note, getting lost in the sounds. After the music fades, I hit the spacebar, stopping the recording and listening to the playback in my headset.

"Your voice sounds different since the first time I heard you sing," Ren says, clapping their hands as I exit the booth.

"Did you need something?" I asked uninterestedly as I close my laptop.

"An update?"

I continue working on the computer for a moment, then give them a smidgen of my attention. "Haven't had the chance to read his journal today." I wait a breath before adding, "My lawyer wants you to be a witness for me."

"I'm no snitch, Ebony," Ren responds, shaking their faded pink hair. "You could have just said you didn't want to help."

"How is getting a lawyer not helping you!?" I grumble, breaking internally as something deep inside me reaches out for them, begging for them to take the olive branch I'm extending and save themself.

"Because they never helped before. Why help now?"

"Don't be so pessimistic," I huff, leaning back in the cloth seat behind me. I pick at the strings of the faded red material. It's probably seen better days, like me. I laugh to myself shaking my head.

"Stop being so damn stubborn," I mutter, looking up at them.

"I'm not being stubborn," they hiss, adjusting uncomfortably in the seat.

"Then what is it? Shame? Feeling guilty still?"

"Never," they glare at me.

A soft hum passes my lips as I cross my arms over my chest. My leg bounces anxiously as we stare at each other. Both angry people, waiting to strike. The tension in the room is suffocating and only gets worse when Kane walks into the room.

"E," he starts, then looks at Ren. His eyes guarded as he glances between the two of us. "What are you doing here, Ren?"

"Hello to you too," they spit, shaking their head and breaking eye contact with me. "I'm gonna go."

"No," Kane says suddenly. A panic flickers through his eyes. "I was with Clint earlier, he's actually out in the lobby."

"Cut to the chase, Kane," Ren grumbles.

He shoots Ren a glare that makes them shrink an inch.

"Clint can get us into the medical lab with the autopsy records," he says with a hint of pride in his tone. He looks between the two of us, lifting his eyebrows. "Are you two coming or no?"

I grab my bag without a second thought, turning off the system, then nudging past Ren and giving Kane a peck on the lips before going to greet my cousin. His large arms engulf me as he gives me a squeeze.

"Working on something new?" he asks, throwing an arm over my shoulder as we wait for Ren to come along.

"Just another cover," I say softly, nudging him.

"Isn't the autopsy lab on the other side of the campus?" Ren asks beside Kane.

"It is," he states, pulling his phone out of his pocket. His thumbs fly over the screen as he smiles. "I got a ride waiting for us."

I look out the window, the small headlights of a golf cart shining into the window. "I thought you were banned from using one."

"I am," he gives me a cheeky grin. "Got some help this time."

"How do you get banned from driving a golf cart?" Clint mutters to me.

"Killing Koi fish," I say with a shrug and hint of a smile.

"It wasn't intentional," he grumbles defensively as he holds the door open.

"I didn't take you as a cold blooded killer, Kane," Ren says playfully. He looks at them and shrugs as he tries to conceal his playful smile. The warmth in his eyes flickering for a moment before it dies down.

Once outside in the cold, Zeke's brown hair blows in the breeze before he pops his head around the windshield. "Your chariot awaits!"

"Aren't you a sight for sore eyes," I gush, smiling and giving him a tight hug. His hand slides down my back, dipping dangerously low before I pop his hand. He yelps, then giggles.

"I know, I know," he mutters, rolling his eyes. "Hands, asshole."

"I'll kick your ass," Kane grumbles, glaring at him.

"Oooh, so scary," Zeke taunts, dodging a hit with a laugh.

We pile into the golf cart and hold on tightly as Zeke speeds down the sidewalk. The wind cutting through the warmth of our clothes as we go up the hill and hang a right towards the old chemistry building a mile and a half away from the music department.

Zeke whips the cart into the back of the building and turns it off. He pockets the keys as Kane presses something on his phone. A soft beep echoes around the building and he nods towards the door.

"Disabled the cameras. We got a few minutes before they come back on or someone notices they're out," he says, slipping out of the golf cart and walking up to the door. He rustles in a black bag I just now notice he has. Pulling out his hoodie, he pulls it over my head, then steps back so I can slip my arms through. He adjusts my locs as my body trembles from the nerves.

"In and out," he mutters, kissing my forehead. "I'm with you every step of the way." I nod, grabbing his sides as he tosses Ren a beanie, then adjusts his sleeves to conceal his tattoos.

Clint pulls out a badge and swipes it. The door light flashes green and we enter one by one. I give one last look behind us before rushing in behind them. We make it to the basement level quickly, each of us spread out, looking through the old record cabinets. I look through the files, feeling sadness in my gut as I look over the countless names. I stop at one, pulling out the file.

"I think I found it," I say using the flashlight on my phone to illuminate the file name. Everyone rushes over. The lights brighten the contents in the drawer as I pull out the folder and sit on the floor opening it. I look over the printed documents, hand written notes on the margin and lines, then the diagrams marked and labeled.

"This is it," I breathe, looking at the official records and then pause.

"What?" Ren asks, their phone light bright on my face.

"Dr. Sumner signed off on an amended document last week…"

"Around the time you went to the lawyer's office?" Zeke asks looking over my shoulder.

I nod before digging through the file some more. "Not all of the documents are here."

"Check the binders. We can find out who taught the class in those records. We might be able to see if it was uploaded," Clint suggests, gesturing for everyone to spread out.

Everyone disperses but Ren. They stare down at me and the file, their flashlight's beam wavering as they shake. I take pictures of each document, then reorganize them before shoving them back into the drawer. I glance behind my shoulder at them, catching their hand wiping their eyes roughly.

"What did it say," they mutter in a broken voice. "In his file, what did it say? Did he suffer?"

"No," I say softly. "It was almost like he went to sleep."

They nod, sniffling. "That's what the reports said?"

Instead of telling them, I find the images of the documents and show them, keeping the autopsy photos away from their grieving eyes. They read through each file. A broken sob bubbles out of them and on instinct, I grab them, pulling them to me. They drop their head on my shoulder, throwing their arms lazily around me as their shoulders shudder. Keeping their back to the group, I rub awkward circles on their back.

The guys are preoccupied with looking through the binders for a moment before Zeke waves the others over and begins snapping images of what he found. Clint, still holding a binder, takes pictures of the one in his hands.

High heels clicking rapidly catch my attention. Ren's head pops up, as they mouth 'hide' and rushes in the room turning off the flashlight.

Kane swears softly, locking eyes with me from across the room before ducking into a dark corner like everyone else.

Ren's small frame squeezes in front of me between one of the walls and the filing cabinet, their hand slapping over my mouth as their eyes grow.

We jump, squeezing closer together as the door swings open and bangs into the wall. Light floods the room as Ren and I slowly shuffle deeper into the dark nook we're in. I place my hand over their mouth to mask their shuddery breaths.

"I checked, Epharim," Veronica Cross' annoyed voice reaches our ears. "The camera's are working— what do you mean they're looping?"

She steps farther into the room, the door slamming shut as she huffs. Metal clangs as she throws open the file drawers and slams them shut.

Slowly, Ren and I peer around the corner of our hiding spot. Veronica, dressed in her best gray pant suit and stilettos, stands with one hand on her hip and the other clutching her phone. I shuffle with my phone, sliding it between Ren, who protests violently, and myself to muffle the sound of me pressing the record button.

"I'm telling you right now— I hear you, but no one is here!" She huffs again as she slides a key in one of the filing cabinets. A soft pop greets our ears and she pulls open the drawer. She removes a folder, flips through it, then grabs another. She presses the speaker button, placing the phone on top of the filing cabinet and rifles through the drawer.

"I swear if that little bitch snuck into that filing room––"

"Epharim! Everything is still here! Untouched. I'm looking at them right now!" she slams the door shut.

"Anything fucking happens with any of those records and they get released, it's your ass, Veronica!" Epharim shouts through the phone.

Veronica slams the cabinet door shut and snatches her phone off the top of the filing cabinet. She grumbles under her breath as she tucks the files she removed from the cabinet under her arm and slips out the door. Her muffled instructions to set the sensor alarms reach mine and Ren's ears. We wait several tense minutes before shoving out of our tight space.

"We gotta go," Clint urges, double checking the drawers.

A siren blares in the building as the room lights up with red flashing lights.

Kane tucks the papers he took beneath his arm, sprints over towards the door, grabs my hand, and rushes out the room.

I drag Ren behind me as our little group sprints back to the golf cart and peels off into the night, leaving the sirens blaring into the darkness.

47

Ebony

"Good morning, ladies," Dr. Goodwin beams as she walks into the chemistry lab. Her heels click against the floor. Beakers clatter on the table as one of the chemistry students looks over one of the medical records I showed her. Chemicals pour and combine in the beaker creating chemical reactions for only a moment before she starts over.

"I didn't expect to see you in here today," Miya says as she walks in. Her designer bag hangs from one of her shoulders as her heels click clack across the linoleum floor.

"Yeah," I say, looking at her with a message in my eyes.

We need to talk. Confidential information.

She studies me before nodding and taking a quick glance around. "I'm going to put my stuff down in the office," she states cheerfully.

I excuse myself and make my way to the office. Closing the door part of the way, her mask slips. Excitement physically present on her face.

"What did you find?" she whisper-shouts, bouncing on her toes.

I hold up a flash drive and give her a small smile. "Smoking gun," I respond finally. Her eyes grow wider before she struggles to pull out her laptop. It boots up quickly and then we're diving into the file.

"We have numbers and statistics that were never in the records they gave us," she states as she skims each document and clicks to the next.

"These are Raeven's?"

I nod. "We got them last night. Kane disabled the cameras once Clint was able to get access to the lab. We got his file with everything in it. Official reports and then some."

"I'm surprised they kept this," Miya says, clicking through the documents again. Her eyes are bright. "Is the chem student mixing what's found in these reports?"

"She's trying. She doesn't know it's from the school. I've also been reading Raeven's journal. He partnered with someone in the school to make a chemical compound for a project."

"Wait." She taps her lip with her finger then looks at me. "I think Kane or Zeke helped him with a chemistry project the year Rae died."

"That's something to ask, but this will help our project. We can get accurate readings on the bands," I state before letting the realization hit me. Kane and Zeke helped Rae. They could be the people I'm looking for.

"Ebony," Miya starts softly. She points to one of the journal posts I have up on the screen. Her soft voice reads it aloud.

"'I spoke with K the other day to help me with my project. He's a good kid, smart as fuck. The teacher agreed to give him credit for helping me. He doesn't know what

I'm doing though. He can never know what Mayor Cross has me making. The mayor's contact, some rookie cop, told me she would help me get the product moved under the radar. He wants me to mimic a few different variations of street drugs, just enough to spike the rates so he can use it for his campaign. I saved the recordings of the calls and meetings. I may like the money I'm making, but there's something off about him. Especially now that his son is coming to school here.'"

"What did they make?" I ask, looking over what she read.

Miya places her hand on my shoulder, horror laced eyes are what meet mine when I look up.

"Miya?"

"What if what killed Rae is what he had my brother help him mix together?"

"Kane wouldn't though…" My voice breaks as disbelief frays at my edges. Pieces of the puzzle slowly fall into place. I sit in the seat focusing on my breathing. "What if it's what Vin gave me?"

"A year later? A new batch maybe—"

"Veronica Cross walked into the file room… She mentioned something about 'her file.'" Miya's eyes clash with mine as we try to conclude whose file. A light tap on the door pulls us out of our prying.

"You ladies okay? One of the chemistry professors is here to go over storing the compounds for the demo."

"We'll be right there," I say looking at Dr. Goodwin. Her eyes linger on Miya's face, then mine before she slips through the door.

"You two look like you've seen a ghost. What's going on? "

We cast glances at each other for a moment, then at Dr. Goodwin.

"Do you think it's possible for a student to mimic a reaction to a certain drug?"

Dr. Goodwin pinches her eyes shut as her brow furrows. She scratches at her temple and sighs. "Here? Anything's possible," she offers. She leans towards Miya and me. "Be careful with the questions you two start asking," she warns. "Not every place is secure," she warns, glancing around before heading out the door.

Taking heed to her warning, we gather our stuff and make our way silently out of the office.

48

Kane

My bag sits securely on my bike as it rumbles while I wait for Clint on the street beside Gramps' bar. I scroll through my computer, searching through files before I hear his bike's engine roar to life.

Shifting my bag, I slide my laptop inside the hard shell case, then secure it on my back. I balance my bike, lifting the kickstand as Clint rolls to a stop beside me.

"Aren't you a sight for sore eyes," he says with a smile. He pounds his fist into mine.

"I'd say the same for you," I comment with a chuckle. "Ready?"

"Let's get it," he pushes off, leading us out of the parking lot and on to the road.

We dart past trees as we speed down the road. The chilly air biting the flesh beneath my leather jacket. I lean closer to my bike, revving my engine and flying past Clint goading him into a race.

My ear piece rings and I answer, "You're gonna get yourself killed, pretty boy," Clint says in a chuckle.

I laugh. "Scared to see how fast these things can go?"

"Never. Try and keep up, Yamada," Clint says before the line goes dead and he flies past me.

I smile to myself, leaning as close as I can and opening up my bike down the road. I maneuver around the corners feeling my heart pound in my chest as I watch Clint's speeding bike draw closer.

My phone beeps in my ear again, and I answer it.

"You need to get to the warehouse with the information," my father's voice says. "Are you speeding?"

"Uh… no?" I respond slowly. I signal to Clint as I pass him and slow my bike. "I have Clint with me."

"That's fine. Bring him and the documents you found. Someone should be there to get everything secure. I'll be up next weekend."

"Got it," I respond.

"And Kane?" his voice calls to me before I end the call.

"Yeah, Dad?"

"Stop racing on that death trap," he fusses. "And your mom wants to have dinner when we get there. Love you," he adds before hanging up.

I laugh to myself as I lead Clint to the warehouse. I notice the setting sun on the horizon as I round a corner. I ring Clint, telling him to keep up and I'll explain everything when we get there. Not saying another word, we listen to the roaring of our bikes' engines.

As we round the corner, headlights of a car come straight at us. I swerve, narrowly missing the front bumper but feeling it graze past my leg.

"Fuck!" I grumble as I attempt to navigate my fishtailing bike back on the road. Gravel makes my wheels spin and slide before I manage to get my balance. I immediately seek out Clint, finding him directing his bike and gearing up to take off.

We speed up, meeting in the middle of the road as we look behind us. The sleek, cherry apple red car turns, gravel crunching beneath its wheels until it screeches. The car flies in our direction. Unruly curly hair reflects in the sunset before I focus on retreating.

"Gramps' bar!" I hear Clint shout as he leans closer to the body of his bike and darts off. I follow him. Praying that I make it back home to Ebony.

The car lights flicker behind us as we turn the deep corners, leaning our bikes dangerously close to the ground, but that doesn't stop the person behind us. Their engine roars over the sound of our rumbling bikes as she speeds up. The bumper clips my wheel, making me spin out. I lose control of my bike, losing sight of Clint as a large cloud of dirt rises in the tree line, sliding off my bike.

A hiss erupts from my chest as my bike lands on my leg and the gravel bites into my skin as it removes layers of my flesh. Despite the searing pain, I manage to push my bike off and roll my damaged body to the side of the road.

"Clint!" I rasp, looking in the direction I saw him go down as my sides throb and the edges of my vision blur. Smoke billows from both of our bikes, but I can't see him. I can barely stay conscious.

I look to where the car stopped, the headlights bright on my weakened body. The engine revs as the car turns again. The screeching of the tires and rapidly approaching front bumper speed right for me and I'm too weak to move.

This is it… my last moment.

Fuck, I just got a taste of happiness was like.

And I never got to tell her I wanted to spend the rest of my life with her.

The roaring of the engine getting closer pulls me out of my thoughts of Ebony, our friends, our life together. And the last thing I see are the tires as I embrace the darkness that swallows me up.

49

Ren

The internet café is less busy today compared to the first time I met Ebony here. The slight hint of mildew, old books, and dampness lingers in the air as I trudge into the building.

Parents with small children sit on battered and patch worked bean bag chairs. Their heads lean towards their miniature selves as they smile and read softly. It makes me think of Rae. Always soft and mild mannered with me when he scooped me up in his arms to tote me on some big adventure.

I look at my mush covered boots to gain my composure. So much has happened in the past 48 hours and crying isn't going to top that list. Not yet anyways.

I see Ebony looking through books in the library bays before she sees me. Her head tilts to the side as she skims the spines of computer books. Her arms are crossed over her chest while her legs shift her weight between black biker boot covered feet.

"Hey," I offer, not getting too close.

She glances at me and nods her head before looking back on the shelf. She must have found what she was looking for because she grabs a book, which looks fairly new, and stuffs it under her arm.

"Follow me," she orders, leading me towards the computer area.

She grabs a seat, then nudges one in my direction as she sits down. I zone out as I take a seat. The café becomes a blur as my memories and visions of happy times with my brother are reduced to documents locked tight in the university's medical basement.

I didn't sleep much. And when I did, I was haunted by Rae's body splayed out on a table fresh after an autopsy. I've never seen him or his body like that, but just the fact that one of the people that brought me to this point may have doesn't make my imagination move any slower.

"Are you okay?" Ebony asks softly, snapping me out of my trance. I look at her after blinking a few times. Warm tears roll down my cheek and before I realize it Ebony's index finger is brushing them away. Her brown eyes soften as she gazes into mine with so much concern I almost forget that we aren't friends. I drop my head, leaning back from her touch and roughly wiping the rest of my tears.

"Why'd you want me to come down here?" I ask a bit harshly.

"Here," Ebony offers, a small, blue thumb drive in the palm of her hand. Before I can reach for it, she places it on the table top in front of me. "Everything we found is on this."

"Do you have a copy?" I ask softly.

"Yeah," her voice reaches my ears void of all emotion. I can feel her watching me. Probing, searching eyes that seek my rebuttal about her keeping a copy of my brother's records.

"Okay," I offer, not willing to fight with her on this. Maybe it's the gravity of it all weighing down on me. Maybe it's the fact that even if she omitted the most triggering things, I'll come out of this still broken and torn. "Would you…" I swallow hard before finishing. "Look at everything with me?"

I finally glance at her blank face. Her eyes do this shifting thing as she does more searching before giving me a slight nod, then moving so I can squeeze my chair in beside hers. She opens her laptop screen, types in a few things, then begins to scroll through the documents slowly.

"On this document," she starts, "it mentions how his body was handled. They took pictures of him clothed and unclothed for any markings or bruising."

"That indicates foul play, right?"

"Yes," she answers, then clicks to the next document. "The original mortician has notes of how the autopsy is performed and notated the students in charge."

My phone buzzes in my pocket as Ebony continues breaking down the documents they retrieved for me. Half listening, I glance at the screen and ignore a call from Mel.

"Do you have the autopsy photos?" I ask, looking at her.

"I do," she says softly. "But I left them out of what I gave you."

"I want everything," I demand.

"You shouldn't look at those."

"Show me, Ebony." I'm defensive now. Anger lingering beneath the surface of my words.

She sighs and looks back at the screen. "They're

graphic, Ren."

"I don't care. They're of my brother. I want to see them. I deserve to see them."

Her head snaps over to me as my voice escalates. "You're going to spiral."

"You don't know me!" I shout, jumping out of my chair and knocking it back. More eyes look in our direction as Ebony looks at me with her eyebrows raised. She nods her head, then packs up her stuff.

"Where do you think you're going?" I ask, more frantic than angry.

"You're acting like a child," she states, pushing her laptop in her backpack. "And I have a project to work on." Her bag rustles as she throws it over her shoulder. She turns to look at me. Her shoulders square with mine, "And before you say I owe you, this was our deal. I helped you get your brother's records. That's it."

"Wait," I shout desperately. Echoing the chaotic feeling that bubbles up in my chest. "Please… I —"

"You what, Ren? You can handle it? You'll be fine?" The look in her eyes silences me as I watch her grapple with something deeper than my emotions. Haunted eyes darkening with so many unspoken thoughts. They're there though, fighting their way forward to tear her apart. "Let me make this clear." I take a step away from her as she approaches me. "You won't be fine. All those happy memories you thought of to keep you sane? They're gone. They're replaced with images that will haunt you every step of the way. Is that what you want? Can you handle that?"

I swallow, then shake my head knowing that she's

right. If I were to see those images… They'll ruin my last memories of Rae. I don't speak. Instead, I wipe at my threatening tears and sniff violently as we stare at each other. With a brief head shake, mainly to herself, she adjusts her bag and takes a step around me.

"I don't get it," my voice cracks. "Ruining my image of Rae would be the perfect get back for what I did." I glance over my shoulder at her. She stares down at her toes though. Listening to what I'm saying, grappling with the fact that her heart is so damn big. Foolishly so. "You could have hurt me back."

"I could have," she states before yanking her phone out of her pocket and placing it to her ear. The vibrant brown fades rapidly as her eyes fill with tears. And before I can ask, she sprints out the door. The book she pulled from the shelf abandoned at the table.

My phone buzzes in my pocket and I pick it up in my fogginess.

"I have been trying to reach you all day!" Mel complains with a huff. "Are you okay?" she pivots suddenly.

"I got it," I mumble into my phone. "She came through."

"Holy shit," Mel breathes. "Where are you?"

"I— I need a moment. I'm sorry. I'll call you when I can. I'm sorry," I mutter before hanging up my phone, snagging the book from the table, and rushing after Ebony.

50

Kane

My vision's blurry once I open my eyes. I hear E sniff, then the keys on her keyboard clicking.

"What did you find?" Miya's thick voice whispers.

"This is from January 3rd, 2015. 'Kane and Zeke move fast. We've been working on some variations for a while, but Mayor Cross wants us to move faster. I don't think I can if I want this compound stable. His son had to be rushed to rehab, same with a girl who I've seen him with a few times, I don't think she made it. I think they sampled what I was mixing… and if they did, then it's much different than the first batch.

"'There's a rookie helping me compile evidence. I have a meeting with her so I can pick her brain to see what she knows. I don't know how long she's known them, but she looks scared when they're around,'" Ebony reads aloud, then sighs.

"And after that, the OD's on campus increased?"

"Yeah," Ebony says softly. "He makes a few more references of Zeke and Kane helping him mix some chemicals, but he never specifies what."

I hate how her voice breaks as she explains it. The uncertainty mixed with the strain of emotions starting with worry and ending with betrayal. Then her warm hand caresses my hand before she slides her fingers into mine.

A soft groan slips past my lips, slightly startling Ebony and my sister. I blink as I hear them rushing to my side as they look down at me.

The ointment and gauze stick to my face creating an itching sensation. The pain begins to ripple in, dull at first, but intensifying to a throb that matches my heartbeat.

"Water," I rasp as I realize my throat is sticking together.

"I got it," Miya says, grabbing a large, gray plastic cup and speed walking out the door.

I manage to sit myself upright, then swing my legs over the side of the hospital bed, which makes E panic.

"You need to lay back down," she fusses.

"I just want to see," my voice crackles out as I hobble over to the mirror. I peek beneath my gauze covered leg and see the angry road rash that replaces my skin.

"I'm going to get your doctor," she whispers, giving me another look then rushing out the door.

I sigh, checking out the cuts and bruises on my body before slipping into fresh sweats and a t-shirt I'm sure someone grabbed for me. I want nothing more than to go home.

Ebony's screen lights up and I glance. A rapid procession of messages from Ren pop up on the screen.

Ren

I'm sorry.

> Ebony, please! Pick up.

> I need you…

> I'm spiraling. I didn't mean any of it. I'm so sorry. Ebs, please pick up.

The screen lights up again with Ren's number popping up. I take a step back, digesting the messages and trying to convince myself I'm thinking too much about it.

"Have you heard from Ren," I tentatively ask, as she walks back in. She pauses, looking up at me for a moment.

"Briefly," she offers. She pushes me towards the bed and I wince.

"E, can we talk? Things still feel.. weird."

This captures her attention. Her eyes find mine, then begin their searching. Head to toe gazing that accesses the total weight of the situation. Her phone buzzes again sending my head in a tailspin because I know it's Ren. And my mind hasn't let go of the solitary idea that Ren's trying to get her back. That maybe… just maybe, her and Ren have been communicating more frequently than I thought.

"What were you helping Rae make in the chemistry lab?" she asks softly. Concern laced in each word as she pulls up a chair to sit in front of me. She places a hand on the edge of my knee, but I all I want is for her to take my hand.

"I don't remember," I mutter, looking down at my lap, then back at her.

She sighs, nodding her head as she processes my response.

"I wouldn't do anything like that, E." It's my only defense. It's a weak one, I know, but it's all I have.

She stares at me as she stands up and looks out the window. My lack of answers has me wanting to provide her with something else, anything else.

"What do I have to do to show you that you can trust me?" I finally ask.

I begin to loathe the way she makes me feel so vulnerable, but I stare at her. My eyes pleading with her to let me back in, showing her how much I miss her being herself around me. I want to reach out my hand to pull her to me, but I don't. I can't. The voice in the back of my head, the person I used to be, tells me to leave. To pack all my shit and storm out the door and never look back.

"I do trust you," she finally says. Her shoulders drop slightly as she bows her head. Her locs shielding her face from my eyes.

"You don't and I need you to trust me on this."

"I'm trying, Kane," she snaps, looking up at me. Her eyes are watery as they lock with mine. "I'm trying so fucking hard."

"Is that why you didn't mention meeting up with Ren?"

Her jaw opens a bit, then she closes it tightly. The muscles clenching as she squeezes her teeth closer together.

"Look," I start with a sigh as I stand and wander around the room looking for my things. "I found something," I say, then look around. "Have you seen my bag?"

"They said there was nothing in it. So they tossed it," she responds.

"My computer was in there. In that unbreakable case,"

I say looking around. I ignore the screaming in my limbs as I look in and under everything I can reach. "Fuck… how am I gonna find that video Vin has?" I mutter, feeling the panic rising up higher in my chest.

"What video?" she asks, making me look at her. I noticed my slip up and I swear. "Kane. What. Video."

"Vin said he has a video of you," I offer. "I can't tell you much other than that because I can't find it."

She looks at her phone, avoiding me actively. It lights up, more messages from Ren stacked together on her screen.

"I can't do this," she mutters, moving away from me.

I rush to her, getting in front of her before she can find a place to hide. "Don't run from me," I demand. "Fucking talk to me, E."

"I can't!" she shouts as her tears skitter down her cheek. "I don't have the words to say how I feel about this situation. I can't tell you something I can't articulate."

"I hate this shit," I start softly. "I love you so fucking much, E. So much that I don't even know who the fuck I am anymore. I hate that I don't remember what the fuck Rae had me doing in the chemistry lab, but I was in there with him. I hate that I think that Rae made the shit that Vin gave you and I helped him." There's a strange sound that comes from me. A mix between a pathetic sob and a growl. I run my hands through my hair. "So, I need you to tell me right now, and be so fucking real with me, E. Are we gonna be okay? Are we gonna be good because I'm spiraling and I need to know that me and you are going to make it through this."

Her eyes move from mine so rapidly that my heart starts

to shatter. Piece by fucking piece falling at her feet. I don't move though. I don't beg even if I want to. And believe me, I fucking want to.

"I don't know," her voice is so soft and broken that I barely hear her. When her eyes land on me, I see her own regret. "I'm sorry—" she starts.

I stare at her and shake my head as she pushes to find something to hold me over. "Fuck it then," I say grabbing my coat from the closet and shoving my feet into my boots so quickly that she flinches.

"Kane," she pleads. "You're hurt and it's going to storm soon. It's not safe."

Her shaky hands are on my arm, pulling at me to turn towards her. My jacket shifts as she pulls at it to remove it from my body. I pull away, not letting her see my emotions, my own fucking tears.

"Kane, please," she pulls at me with more force. Desperation takes hold of her voice as she begins to pry at my clothes, my waist band. She's attempting to offer her body to me like a bargaining chip, but I don't accept her offer. I'm not her past. I can't take from her. Not while she's like this, while we're like this.

I gently remove her fingers from me and storm down the hall with my keys in my hand.

"Kane!" she screams frantically as I take long strides toward the exit, even passing my sister with my cup of water. They both call out to me, but I'm through the doors and in the parking lot.

I'd rather be anywhere but here.

51

Ren

A loud pounding on the door startles me from my stare off with the wall. My phone is still clutched in my hands from the last few messages I've sent off to Ebony. I straighten my clothes and peek out of the window before unlocking the door.

"To what do I owe the pleasure?" I greet Kane's semi- soggy frame. His head is slightly bowed and his hair hangs in his face creating shadows. He doesn't budge or open his mouth to speak, but I catch his eyes. They're dark, tormented with something he's not saying. "What happened? Is Ebony okay?"

I dip my head to get a closer look at him to figure out what's going on as the anxiety prickles my skin. I search for answers in the depths of his eyes, but only find pain.

"Why are you texting her?" he finally grumbles, wiping the water from his face. He angles his head, standing more upright. I notice the angry scratches and bruises on his face and stumble back.

"I— I just," I don't know what to say. I felt bad for our exchange that pushed her away when all she did was help. She was just trying to protect me from things that would destroy me.

"Did you fuck my girlfriend? Are you still in love with her?" he asks with such a dark voice that I hesitate. His face is tight, tense with anger. He isn't hiding any of his feelings. Not like the Kane I know… knew. My eyes widen as I stumble back more, urging him to come in out of the rain that's picking up and pelting his back. I shake my head adamantly as I pull him in.

"No! No, Kane I'd never fuck her. I promise!"

He yanks his arm from my hands.

"Then why the fuck are you texting her!?" he shouts.

"Because… She gave me the file and I said some things," I look at him. His eyes track my movements closely. "I promise Kane, I wouldn't fuck Ebony."

"But you're still in love with her?"

I look at my toes, then back up at him. My head shake is slow and I can already tell that he knows I'm unsure of my own answer.

He growls. A dark, feral sound that rumbles low in his chest. He pivots on his feet and I grab him.

"I'm sorry! It's all fucking complicated, Kane!"

"It's not fucking complicated!" He spins getting in my face. "Stay the fuck away from her."

"I wouldn't… I wouldn't hurt you…"

"But you did, Ren! You fucking did!" Kane doesn't show much emotion besides arrogance and anger, but here… I can see the pain in his eyes as a tear rolls down his cheek.

"I'm sorry," I whisper.

"Are you!? I asked you if you knew her! I asked and you told me you fucking didn't, just to come in and fuck up my relationship."

"She's mad at you for not telling her about my plan, Kane. Don't blame me."

"That you told her about… why?"

"Because you weren't going to!" I shout.

"I was," he mutters with a bitter laugh. "But you had to have it your fucking way. I wouldn't be surprised if you and Vin planned this shit."

He turns away from me, allowing me time to gain my composure. I wouldn't hurt my best friend. Getting Ebony away from him would save him from the torture Vin has planned.

"I was mad at her for not showing me images of Rae," I mumble, hanging my head. "And even now, she was trying to protect me."

"Yeah," Kane's broken voice rumbles. "She's like that." I see him hesitate as he glances over his shoulder at me, then he huffs. "Look, you should know this… Rae was mixing some shit in the chemistry lab before he died. He had me helping. I don't know what it was, but I don't think his death was an accident. Not anymore… and I think…" he stops, his eyes going distant. Pain flashing through his eyes before he looks up at the rumbling sky.

I open my mouth to ask, but he shakes his head. His eyes turn glassy as he fights whatever thoughts come forward in his mind.

"Ren? Everything okay?" Mel's voice calls from behind me.

Kane glances at her, then at me. His eyes scan my frame before he shakes his head again and stalks off into the darkness.

"Kane, wait!" I shout after him. I curse as I look for my boots.

"Let him go," Mel says softly, grabbing me. "Please, it's about to be a mess."

"There's a storm coming, Mel. I have to make sure he's okay. I'll convince him to go home and come right back."

"You leave," she starts, her tone, threatening. "And you will never see me again."

"He's my best friend. I can't leave him like this," I damn near plea. "I'm sorry."

I kiss her softly before yanking my rain coat from the coat rack and rush off into the heavy rain behind Kane.

52

Ren

"I can't reach Kane," Ebony says frantically. She lets me into their massive apartment. She called me after I searched the streets for him for about an hour. Apparently he walked out of the hospital in a fit of rage. The panic in her voice echoing the panic I was feeling about not being able to find him and the shit I said to her.

I look around their place as I kick off my shoes and move them to the side. Only a few lights on, giving the room a yellowish-gold glow. Pictures hang neatly on the wall. Random images of them, their friends, and the Yamadas. I examine the life they started building together and revel in the peace that may have once lingered here. She rushes past me, breaking my thoughts.

"I've called everyone. No one can find him. So, don't get the wrong idea. I thought he went to meet you."

"He left an hour before you called," I confess.

Rain pounds on the windows and lightning brightens the darkened rooms before a loud boom startles us and her cat. The black fluff ball hisses at the window before sliding underneath the couch, ears pinned back to his head.

She curses, kneeling down and clicking her tongue to get the cat's attention. "Come on, Silver. It's okay," she

329

says soothingly as another clap of thunder startles her. She grabs her chest, laughing to herself before leaning against the couch. She looks over at me, her giggles subsiding and her smile fades.

The wind violently whips outside the window. Tree limbs sway violently, waving and bending as the wind plows through them. The rain obscures any view a few feet in front of it. It was honestly a miracle I made it here safely.

"Why'd he leave?" I ask, stepping into the apartment.

She pushes to her feet and walks into the kitchen. She grabs a bottle of wine and two glasses. She nods toward her filling both glasses and pushes one to the edge before sitting on a stool. She checks her phone before sending a text.

"I'm being dumb," she confesses. Her eyes still locked on her phone as she writes another message. I peek over, catching a glimpse of her endless blue bubbles. She sighs, locking her phone before looking up at me.

"Dumb how?" I ask, taking a sip of my wine and swishing it in my mouth. I sigh as I swallow, grateful that she bought dessert wines. At least she still likes the sweet wines like I do.

"He wanted me to reassure him about our relationship and I didn't. He's mad that I've been giving him the cold shoulder."

"I would be too. My girlfriend talking to her ex that almost killed her. Yep. I'm storming off."

"Not helping," she groans, putting her hands on her head.

"Not trying to," I inform her, picking up my phone and calling Kane. "He may not answer."

The receiver rings in my ear for a minute or so before going to his voicemail. I hang up and type a message asking him if he made it in safe. Awkwardness settles between Ebony and me. I look up and notice her writing a message on her phone, then zoning out facing the window.

"He's going to be fine," I say softly.

She looks over at me startled before nodding slowly. The silence continues as the rain and thunder continue to grow more intense.

"Hey, Ren," she calls to me softly. I look at her and meet her warm, brown eyes. "I don't think we should go through with your plan," she finishes softly.

"Why?"

"Because I think you should talk with my lawyer," she concludes, getting up and grabbing something from a drawer. She slides a business card over to me. Gold writing against a black background. I rub my fingers over the lettering, feeling the lumps and lines of each letter. "He plans on helping."

"You want to help me after all I did to you?"

"I'd foolishly help Vin too. We didn't ask for what happened to us in our past," she says with a sigh, looking out the window.

"You're stupid for that," I tell her, putting the card in my pocket. "For wanting to help people that hurt you."

"Well, I can't help Vin. Not anymore."

"Good," I say, pouring myself more wine. "Because he wouldn't help you."

"But you're helping me," she says softly. She grabs her wine glass and downs the rest, then refills her cup. She looks at me. "I still don't understand why."

"You trust me enough to drink around you," I comment, ignoring her statement.

She pulls the bottle and her glass closer to herself. No humor in her eyes as she realizes that she may have put herself in harm's way. "What happened that night, Ren?"

I hesitate, focusing on the grooves of the wooden floor. I don't know exactly what happened, but Vin was there when I left and his friend who I'm still searching for.

"I can't tell you that, Eb," I whisper, looking up at her finally. "I left to get help and when I came back you were gone."

She chugs her wine before wiping her hands over her face and pressing the call button. She gets up, pacing the floor before remembering her cat is under the couch. She grabs a toy and finally coaxes him out as she hits the end call button, then redials.

"Fucking pick up," she shouts, putting her hands on her face. "Please," she begs, her voice strained and distant as she lays her head on the back of the couch. Her knees touching the ground like she's praying.

"Give him time," I say, finishing my wine and slowly approaching her. "Look, it's picking up out there. I should go."

"Oh," she says, leaving her phone on the couch and standing. "Yeah, sorry."

We both look out at the balcony, the rain only coming down harder as the trees nearly snap in the increasing wind.

The front door opens, capturing our attention and she visibly deflates, but then gets tense again.

"Where were you?" she growls, putting her hands on her hips.

Looking at the two of them this close again is interesting. His body towering over hers. She's tiny compared to him. And with the disinterested glance that he casts over her, I picture a Cane Corso with a yapping Yorkie trying to dominate him.

He looks at me, then back at Ebony.

"They were here trying to help me find you," she huffs, pushing her locs out of her face.

"Yeah? Well there's no round two for a show," he grumbles, kicking off his soggy shoes and putting them up. He limps past Ebony, keeping his distance.

I roll my eyes, crossing my arms over my chest. I open my mouth to say something, but Ebony beats me to it.

"So you're going to ignore me?"

"Not exactly," he comments, pulling out a whiskey bottle and a glass. He pours himself some and downs it quickly, then refills his glass.

"What the fuck, Kane? I've been worried sick about you!"

"Oh, you do care," he responds, sarcastically.

"The fact that you questioned that shit. That's fucked up."

"No, no. What's fucked up is me asking you if we were okay and you not giving me a straight answer. That's fucked up."

"So, you punish me by not picking up?"

"I thought I'd take a page from your book and give you the fucking cold shoulder."

"Oh fuck you," she spits. "Do you not see how crazy it is out there?"

"I'm going to go," I say, inching towards the door. A loud crack of thunder responds as a storm siren cries in the distance. Our phones blare and I check mine as the two lovebirds glare at each other.

"Shit," I groan.

Ebony grabs her phone and looks at it, then sighs. "Just stay here," she says over her shoulder.

"Guest room is right there," Kane offers, nodding towards the open door.

Quickly walking into the room, I close the door behind me as they continue to bicker. The soft light from outside casts a low glow in the room from the large windows to the left of the bed. White curtains hang beautiful and still.

Walking over towards the bed, I slip out of my clothes, stripping down into my underwear. I ease into the bed and sigh.

"This is so fucking weird," I mumble laying back on the soft, plush bed.

53

Kane

Ebony chugs her large glass of wine as she glares at me. A scoff passes her lips, then she grabs the first aid kit from the cabinet.

"Sit," she commands.

I don't. I move around her, grabbing the whiskey and hoping that will dull the growing pain that I physically feel, not just from my argument with E, but the bike accident from earlier today.

"Dammit, Kane," she growls, grabbing my injured arm. I wince and she jumps back apologizing profusely as she attempts to look over my arm.

"I'm fine," I mutter, attempting to escape her prying eyes.

"I almost lost you!" her broken voice shouts at me. Thick and heavy with emotions. "I almost fucking lost you and then you… you leave the only place that can keep you safe. So sit the fuck down."

I look down at her small figure, contemplating whether or not I should listen to her. This time, I do.

The cushion sinks beneath me as she sighs and rolls up her sleeves. She grabs her phone, pressing it to her ear.

"Yeah," she says, sounding exhausted. "He's here. Yes.

Okay. I will. Thank you." She hangs up her phone and drops it on the counter as she turns on the electric tea kettle.

"I'm scared," she says softly, but loud enough for me to hear. The tea kettle pops and she pours the water in a basin from the hospital. She walks over to me and slowly cleans my wounds. "I want us to be okay."

"You have a hell of a way of showing it," I mutter, then hiss when the hot towel touches one of my road rash spots. I feel my muscles tremble beneath the pain.

"I know," she mutters. "And I'm sorry…"

I look down, finding her big brown eyes looking at me. We stare at each other for a moment. Long enough for me to see the tears pooling in them.

"Does Vin have a tape of me…?" she asks softly.

I pull her to me, despite the screaming in my limbs, placing her forehead to my lips, then cradle her in my arms.

"I don't know," I mutter. "But if he does, I'm killing him slowly."

She scoffs slightly, letting herself finally relax into me. "He's not worth it," she mumbles.

"Doesn't matter." I let a moment pass. "I think he had someone run me and Clint off the road."

"That's what Clint was telling me," she offers, getting up and cleaning my wounds again.

"How's he doing?"

"To be expected. Gramps is up there with him. Told me to get my stubborn ass home and make things right." She laughs.

"Did you not want to?" I ask cautiously.

"Of course I did," she responds. "I just… everything

else was happening and we never had a moment until the hospital."

"And I told you there was a video," I complete. "I'm sorry for not telling you sooner—"

"Clint told me he advised you not to. That you should find it and then tell me," she answers.

"I was already doing that," I confess.

She sighs, sitting back on the floor as she stares at my legs. "Who ever did this to you," she starts eerily calm, then she stops. A dark look passing her eyes before she stands to dump the bloody water in our bathroom, then returning to fill the bowl with more water.

The threat lingers beneath the surface and the way she moves around the room taking care of me.

"Stop hiding stuff from me," she says, recleaning the spots on my leg before putting ointment on it. "We've been through this."

She walks into the kitchen, grabbing two orange prescription bottles, then hands them to me with an ibuprofen.

"Yeah, I get it," I respond, taking the ibuprofen and drinking the water she hands me.

"We'll be okay," she finally mutters, looking at me. She leans into me, kissing me deeply.

On instinct, I wrap my arms around her, pouring everything I have into this kiss with her.

"Can I ask you something," I ask her as we pull away. She keeps her eyes glued to me and quirks an eyebrow.

"Ren didn't try to fuck you, right?" I ask with a hint of playfulness.

"Ew. Gross," E responds, rolling her eyes, then she presses her lips back to mine.

54

Ren

I must have dozed off at some point because the deceptively soft rain is the only remnant sound of the storm that passed. I roll over, snuggling deeper beneath the covers before kicking my legs over the edge of the bed. Shoving my head in my shirt, I walk out of the room into the large living room. A soft, rhythmic thump from the room across the way greets me. Their door hangs slightly ajar. I hesitate glancing between their door and the kitchen. I know what I'll find if I step closer to their room. I'm just fighting myself to not confirm.

Taking a cautious step towards the kitchen, I huff, ignoring the peekaboo sliver that opens their room up to me. I grab a glass from the cabinet and fill it with water.

The cold liquid eases down my throat as I take long grateful gulps before I notice the nearly empty whiskey bottle on the counter. The one that was practically full when Kane walked in. Another bottle of wine sits open and empty on the counter. I grab the bottle of whiskey, twisting the top off and sniffing at it. I glance at their door, then down the rest of the contents. The bitter liquid burning down my throat as Ebony moans softly.

I fix myself more water and take a cautious step towards

their door, peeking in slightly before cautiously pushing the door open further. My mind runs on autopilot as I watch the muscles of Kane's sculpted back flex against his slow, steady movements.

Their sheets cling to his hips slightly as he moves, pushing into Ebony and being rewarded with an erotic whine. He drops his head down, his body following as the sound of them kissing and muffled moans take residence in the darkness of their room.

"I love you," she mutters into a moan. Her tone is a slight whimper as hushed apologies and love confessions fall from her lips.

"Tell me again," he groans, his shoulder shifting as he pushes inside her so slowly she gasps. "Say it again, baby."

She does, softly at first until he picks up speed. Their sweaty bodies slapping together as she grips his back, dragging her nails down his glistening skin.

I blame the alcohol for the tingles that scatter through my body as I watch them closely. Heat rises throughout as my hand grips the cold, glass cup tightly. I'm stuck watching them again, marveling at the beauty of their bodies, their sounds. I'm much closer than I was last time, with a much better view. They're beautiful, almost like marble sculptures tricking our mind into seeing sheer fabric over delicate body parts.

So caught up in my private musing, I almost miss Kane's eyes on me.

I blink, taking a cautious step back as he moves his body off of Ebony's, then leans down towards her ear.

His deep voice rumbles from his chest as he whispers

to her. Then her brown eyes find me, glazed over and filled with dark desires locking me in place. I'm stuck again, caught up in her allure.

She kisses him deeply, her hands caressing his muscles before she looks over at me again as she pushes herself off the bed.

Her beautiful, naked body heads towards me. Even as she stumbles slightly the closer she gets. Before I know it, she's grabbing my glass, placing it to her lips, and taking a slow drink. Her eyes still watch me over the rim.

The warmth of her hands makes me melt as she grips the back of my neck, pulling my body close to hers. Those full lips that Kane devoured hover a centimeter from mine.

Her body—these lips—ask me to take what I want and I do. Like a fucking fool, I do.

My lips crash onto hers as my cold hands grip her slick body, keeping her flush to me. My fingertips trace her curves as her tongue inches into my mouth, beckoning me to play.

A medley of whiskey and wine dances across my tongue with every swipe of hers. Sweet intermingled with bitter. The perfect representation of our relationship.

Her teeth tug at my bottom lip, then she sucks so softly my knees nearly give. She shifts in my hands, her body moving us as her tongue traces the outline of my lower lip, before sliding back into my mouth to taste my tongue.

My mind swims, not taking in the direction until she's helping me on to the bed and Kane's hair brushes past my hand as he kisses her shoulder, then sucks on her neck. His hands rolling over her hips, chasing behind mine until I'm palming her breasts, coaxing a moan from her.

"You should be naked," she slurs, tugging my shirt off and leaning back into Kane's kisses.

My eyes are fixed on them until Kane's drag up to mine. "You heard her," he says against her skin. His hands rubbing up her body as I lean back watching her shudder against his touch.

I remove my shirt, letting the material fall to the bed, before shoving it to the floor.

Her fingertips trace the fading scars on my chest like a work of art.

Circling my hand behind her neck, I pull her back to my lips, kissing her fiercely. Her skin slick beneath my grip as we grope at each other.

"Taste them," Kane whispers into her ear as he nips at her ear lobe.

"I don't like dick, Kane," I glare at him, setting my lips free from hers. She looks at me, her eyes drinking in my naked body.

"I'm not touching you," he says flatly before he looks Ebony in her eyes. He kisses her deeply, his hand turning her head towards him as his tongue tastes hers. "You're not touching me," he adds, glancing at me, then places a soft kiss on her lips. "She's touching you."

"What?" she and I ask in unison as we stare at him. I mean yeah, I'm naked in their bed. Her hands are still pulling me towards her, but that is the last thing I expected to hear.

She looks at me, catching my attention. Her eyes sparkle in the dull moonlight as he kisses her skin again.

She moans as his tongue traces up her neck right behind her ear, then his eyes are on mine. An invitation to join him in pleasuring her and using her to pleasure myself.

It doesn't take much to convince me. Again, blaming the alcohol even though I'm not drunk.

I kiss her tentatively, then intensify as she relaxes more. I take what I want from her kisses, rolling my tongue over hers as she moans into my mouth.

This feels weird. Not the threesome aspect. I've been in plenty of those, especially with couples, but never with them.

I admit, the idea did cross my mind when I saw them in the car, but I never imagined it happening. Told myself that I couldn't let it happen.

My lips are torn away from hers as Kane helps lay her back, then lays on his stomach and buries his face between her thighs. She moans, digging her hands in his hair. Her eyes close as he sucks on her clit, his eyes watching her with so much pleasure that I shiver.

She reaches for me, pulling me over to her, then guiding one of my thighs over her face. I hesitate again, my brain split between giving in and running. But then, I feel her tongue. A slow, agonizingly long lick against my clit down my pussy has my resolve shattering.

She moans into her actions sending vibrations through my pussy and I moan with her. My thighs tremble as I watch Kane. Her actions mimic his.

Her tongue flicks lightly against my clit and I shudder, my fingers squeeze my pebbled nipples before grabbing her breasts. I bend awkwardly, taking her nipple into my mouth and rolling my tongue over it slowly. I suck hard before pulling my mouth back, stifling another moan.

I barely feel the bed move as Kane shifts between Ebony's thighs. But I feel his body heat, smell the sweet, sticky sweat from his skin as he sinks into her and she moans, gripping my thighs so tightly it should hurt, but it doesn't. Not when her lips are wrapped around my tiny bud, sucking despite her moans.

Kane's movements are slow for a moment until one of Ebony's hands grips his side as she rolls her hips attempting to get him to move faster. He chuckles, pulling himself out slowly, then pushing in so deep she gasps. He does it over and over until her tongue and mouth stop moving on me.

"You stop, I stop," he commands, halting his movements.

I look up at him, his eyes trained on to her chin, which he can see just between my legs. She taps my thigh slightly and swings my leg from over her.

"On your back," she huffs. Her face flustered as she pushes Kane back and rolls towards her stomach.

"Even better," he mutters, kissing her neck, then her back.

I lay against their pillows, spreading my legs just enough for her to fit. But she grabs my thighs, looks me in my eyes with a devilish look, and pulls me towards her roughly. I yip, but immediately moan as she dives back in.

Slow, lazy licks that make my thighs tremor uncontrollably. She drinks me up as Kane sinks into her and a muttered "fuck" is breathed into my pussy.

"Look at that," he groans, rubbing his large hand up her

back as his other hand holds her steady.

Her tongue is moving again. Flat and steady against every part of my pussy. I throw my head back, moaning up towards the ceiling as her body rocks into mine pushing her face deeper between my legs.

She slides in two of her fingers, curling them right where she knows my G-spot is and pushes them slowly. Her tongue rolls as she watches my face. Our eyes lock as pleasure passes between the three of us in varied ways.

I roll my hips for her.

"Faster, Ebs," I moan and she smiles against me. Her fingers push at such an agonizing pace. She's prolonging my pleasure, keeping me just at the edge of lust and frustration that I know my orgasm will be catastrophic for me in the best ways possible. Even knowing that, it doesn't help my frustration.

A loud pop sounds from behind her and she yelps.

"You heard them," his voice is low, dominating. "Tell her what you want, Ren."

I move her fingers out of me, then lean towards her, kissing her as Kane pushes deeply into her. She moans against my lips. I hold my face back to watch her half lidded eyes morph with pleasure.

"I hate to admit this, but you look so fucking pretty being fucked like this," I whisper against her neck. I kiss it gently, then suck the salty skin into my mouth. I lean back to look at her, running my hands down her body.

"Like a perfect little slut," Kane agrees with a groan as his hand lands another smack on her ass. She pinches her eyes shut.

"Taste me," I whisper to her, laying back and rubbing my hands over my body.

"You heard them, baby," Kane says, kissing her shoulder blade. "Face down. Show me how good you eat pussy."

She pulls me towards her again, kissing down my inner thigh before she kisses right on my pussy again, then she's working her tongue. Adding her fingers shortly after.

Her moans sending unexplainable pleasure through me as Kane fucks her from behind. She adds a third finger and I damn near cum. She moves slowly, allowing me to adjust to the sensation of her fingers filling me. Then she's moving again. Her tongue drawing circles around my clit.

"That's right, baby," Kane groans. "Fuck them with your fingers."

I'm lost in a dizzying world of pleasure as I cum hard with her lips wrapped around my clit, sucking me softly.

I dig my heels into their mattress. My head pressed back against their pillows and my hands anchoring her face to my pulsating pussy. My thighs shake as she helps me ride out my orgasm.

Then she's watching me pant. Her lips kissing and sucking at my inner thigh until Kane pulls her up towards him. Her body stretched out and on display so damn beautifully.

His large, tattooed hand circles around her throat as he kisses her. His tongue diving into her mouth before he pulls back and spits in her mouth, just to kiss her deeply again. She moans taking it all.

I'm lost in the smoke of desire as I adjust my position

and lick her clit. They both moan.

"Make her cum on my dick, Ren," he groans, thrusting harder. "She's so fucking close."

I flick my tongue to his rhythm and she moans his name loudly. Her cum drips down his dick to his balls. I sit back and watch as he cums in her. His groans muffled in a sloppy kiss they share.

He eases out of her and staggers off the bed as I continue to stare at her body. The way her chest rises and falls. Her eyes tracking Kane's movements and her fingers brush down her body to her clit. She's not fucking done and I hear him chuckle from the other side of the room.

"Always so fucking ready to be filled," he taunts her.

I don't even look for him as she dips her fingers inside of herself, then slides the cum coated digits into her mouth. She's teasing him, teasing me. And I take the bait first. My mind is still in a frenzy making me do irrational things. I taste her. My tongue cleans up the mess between her thighs like a sex starved maniac.

She shudders against my mouth, whimpering as she pulls at my nipples. Her body shifts over mine. One hand sinking into the mattress below us, the other caressing my curves.

Then, she cums again with muffled moans deep in her throat. I sit back, finding Kane's dick in her mouth as he thrusts. I move out of their way as he pushes deep inside her again.

I watch them lounged back on their bed like I fucking belong in it. I don't know what's gotten into me, but I don't move until I'm sure I want another taste of Ebony. And even when she's damn near satiated, Kane and I take turns making sure she's completely satisfied.

55

Ren

I sit at the counter as Kane shuffles groggily around the kitchen. He slides a coffee cup in front of me and pours the dark liquid in the glass. Then, with his cup to his lips, he leans a hip against the counter as he sips.

The silence, awkward and weighted, intrudes on our time together.

Ebony left earlier to get to the shelter early, which leaves me and Kane to figure out our dynamic.

"So," I start. "Have you read Rae's journal too?"

Kane shakes his head. "Ebony's got it covered."

"You don't want to know what he was getting into? He was kind of your friend."

"Don't want to relive it," he says bluntly, taking another drink. He places his mug down and grabs the prescription bottles, dumping a pill from each in his palm and taking them.

"How are you handling everything?" he asks, bracing the counter with both hands as he looks at me. And I mean finally looks at me.

"Not good," I confess. "I miss him so much."

He nods his head before grabbing a tissue box and sliding it over to me. "What are you going to do with the reports and journal?"

"I didn't think that far ahead. I thought it would make me feel better, but I'm spiraling. I said some harsh things to Ebony when she gave them to me."

"And that's why you were texting her…" he concludes mostly to himself with a sigh. He takes another drink from his coffee.

"Yes. I — I didn't want you to think it was something. I didn't want her to feel like I was going to use her and I getting along as leverage to destroy her relationship with you."

"Ren," he calls over to me, shifting his weight on his feet. "I feel like you're not being honest with me, or Ebony."

"That's because— it's because I haven't been."

"Explain," he demands, getting guarded again.

"Vin contacted me. He's been in contact with me for a while and he … he's been using again, so I don't think anyone is safe."

"Don't bullshit me, Ren," he sighs, shaking his head.

"He's not right in the head, Kane. You and I both know this."

"What are his plans?"

"I think he's going to try to kill her… he's mentioned it a time or two. That or someone close to her. He's out of it." I watch as Kane limps around the kitchen now.

"Is there a video?" he asks as he halts his anxious movements.

"I don't know," I mutter. "I haven't seen one. I might be able to get him to come to my place and check his phone."

"You know his passwords?"

"No, but can't you just hack it?"

"Not without an app or physically having it." His eyes unfocus for a moment before he looks at me. "Give me a second, I have an idea."

He walks away, but returns with his computer and a phone. He hooks up a small device and starts typing, then plugs in the phone.

"We're going to clone his phone," Kane offers, still working. "I want you to send him a link. Once he clicks it, the program I'm running now will download everything and I can access his phone."

"What happens if I can't get his phone?" I ask quietly.

"You shouldn't need it, but if he refuses to click the link. Take this phone, there's a program on it that will pull his data . Should be quick, but it works through Bluetooth." He shows me where the app is located and briefly explains the steps I need to take. "If the program becomes faulty, use this phone as a decoy so you can attempt to get two things for me. One being his serial number and the other being the EIN number. Those are in the settings. Whichever route you have to take, you have to move quickly. Got it?"

I pause, stalling as Kane's eyes drag up from the screen to my eyes. I swallow hard, looking down at my hands. Tracking what Vin does means that Kane will know that I was working with Vin to help him get revenge. Whatever progress we've made will be ruined.

"Will that be a problem?" he asks. There's an edge to his voice.

I shake my head vigorously, willing to do anything to make my best friend my best friend again. "Are you busy today?" I finally ask shyly.

"I have a shift at the shelter with E," he looks at me for a moment. "I want to say all is forgiven, but you fucked up, Ren. It's going to take time."

"Okay, yeah. I get it," I say, running my fingers through my hair. "I should go."

He nods his head. Without another word, he walks me to the door. Feeling like a child as I wring my fingers together, then I turn. My feet on the other side of the door frame as I suck in a huge breath.

"I just want to let you know, it's not your fault. Rae… he protected you and Zeke. So, what happened to Rae… Ebony, everyone else… It isn't on you."

His eyes get glassy as he swallows hard, then nods, digesting what I just told him.

"We'll talk more later," he mutters with another nod.

With that, I give him a small smile, then a wave, and start my trek down the hallway towards the elevator.

56

Ebony

The metal door in the back slams shut as Kane and Jed finish cleaning the kennel for a sweet, gray doberman that sits up front with me.

Her bright blue eyes looking around the space as her tongue hangs out of her mouth. I bounce a tennis ball towards her and she darts off, her feet slipping on the slick concrete floor for a moment before she gets her footing and grabs the ball. Her long tail wags as she lays on her belly, gnawing at the bright yellow toy.

"You're supposed to bring it back, princess," I say to her with a soft laugh. She nudges the ball with her nose before pouncing. A soft growl erupts from her chest as she nudges the ball again. I snap a picture with a smile, then check my messages.

Ren

So... last night...

My fingers hover over the screen as I attempt to figure out the words to write. Last night was an event that I don't want to think about. It complicates things and makes my thoughts go haywire.

Ren

...

Okay. Too soon.

I'll talk to your lawyer.

Really?

Yea

Do you need his info again?

No. I still have it. I'll let you kno tho

A low growl emanates from the puppy again, making me look up. I push my phone in my pocket, watching as her haunches rise as she bares her teeth towards the door.

"Beautiful dog," Mayor Ephraim's voice calls out from the desk, making me jump. It's a soft, mid baritone that could be calming if he wasn't who he is. The hairs on my arm stand up as I push the chair between me, the desk, and him. A thick, metal mail opener gripped in my hand tightly.

A slow smile forms on his face as he watches me fumble. Probably watching the way my chest rises and falls as I stare at him and the exits he managed to block. I don't know when he waltzed in, I didn't hear the bell, but from the time I watched the puppy play till now, he managed to slip in like the untouchable ghoul he is. I am cornered and terrified.

I open my mouth, sucking in air prepared to yell for

help when he closes the distance. Slamming my head into the wall, his thick, callous -covered hands over my mouth.

"Don't fucking touch her," my strained voice demands. I wipe my eyes quickly as I push the point deeper into his skin, my lip tingling as it begins to swell. The throbbing in my face distracts me for a split second. He slaps at my hand sending the mail opener flying and throws me into the puppy. She yelps as she rushes away from my body.

"You think you're so fucking tough," he growls, picking me up and dragging me. "I'll fucking show you."

I kick my legs, digging my nails deeply into his skin as he drags me into the back office. He hoists up my body, slamming it, face first, into the wooden desk. The oxygen rushes out of my lungs from the sheer force of his action. My hands brace either side of my body as I thrash.

His hand grabs the back of my neck, forcing my face farther against the cold desktop. His knuckles brush past my hip as he unfastens his belt.

"You know what bitches that think they're tough get," he hisses in my ear as he huffs.

I whimper, tears spilling out of my eyes as I push against the desk and try to use my hips to get him off.

"Please stop," I beg through a whimper. The painted white cement wall blurs as the tears pour from my eyes.

"Shut the fuck up," he snarls as his grip on my throat tightens.

"Get the fuck off my granddaughter," my gramps barks as he cocks his gun.

Mayor Cross releases me quickly, scrambling back, his hands going up, his belt clanking loudly.

"Ebony, you, oh—" Jed's voice stops short as he and Kane pause at the door.

The puppy rushes to the Mayor as he attempts to adjust his pants. He chuckles awkwardly as the puppy growls and snaps at him. I muffle my sobs as I rush away from him to a corner, fighting with my pants the entire way. Kane pushes past everyone, pulling me to him and looking over my battered face, he shifts me behind him, glaring at Mayor Cross. He pops his knuckles, rolling his shoulders.

"Oscar," Mayor Cross says with a panicked laugh. "Long time no see, old man."

"What's going on?" Jed asks, but only my sobs answer him. "Look, I'm going to need you to put the gun down."

"Not until he explains to me why he had my granddaughter face down on your desk," my gramps says, keeping his gun steady and pointed at Mayor Cross.

I grip at Kane's shirt as he moves, a low snarl in his chest as he takes a step forward. He falters, looking between the gun and Mayor Cross. There's nothing anyone can do with my gramps' gun trained on him. No man, no matter how fast, can out run the bullet I know my gramps has loaded in that chamber. And the fear of losing Kane because he stepped in the way is more terrifying than the beating I took just seconds ago.

As Kane takes in Mayor Cross' full appearance his body goes ridge, the anger that radiated off of him moments before fades as his hand pulls me flush to his back.

"Mayor Cross," Jed starts cautiously. His hands raised to his small chest as his lanky body moves towards the center of these two men. "What exactly happened?"

Jed's soft eyes look me over, studying the bruises and gashes in my face, then at Mayor Cross, and back at the gun.

"A misunderstanding," Mayor Cross states with a soft chuckle. "It's not what it looks like."

"Then why are your pants undone?" Kane growls, keeping his grip steady on me.

"Keep your mouth shut, *boy*," he hisses at Kane.

"Watch your fucking mouth, Cross," my gramps growls, leaning the gun closer. "Now, answer his question."

Mayor Cross laughs softly. "They take everything out of context."

"Kane," Jed starts. "Call the police."

Kane hesitates, then casts a glance back at me. His eyes search my face.

"I'll be okay. Go," I weakly reassure as I walk over to my gramps. Kane slips into the back, his ear pressed to the phone.

It's my gramps' turn to look me over for a second before glancing back at Mayor Cross. "I got you my girl," he mutters, positioning his body in front of mine.

"You don't need to call the cops," Mayor Cross says, shifting.

"Don't. Move," my gramps threatens as his finger adds more pressure to the trigger.

"He's still here," Kane says, stepping into the front glaring at Mayor Cross. "I'm sure she wants to press charges."

A chill races through me as Mayor Cross sets his cold glare on me. His eyes are hard and cold like ice on the asphalt. A look that sends me spiraling back to my childhood, cowered in a corner. The time before Vin embraced his likeness and added to my torment.

It doesn't take long for the police, Mayor Cross' lawyer, and my lawyer to show up. Pictures are taken, but he's released with a warning, despite the footage Jed freely shows them.

Ren

Thank God for the warmer weather. There's still a chill in the air, but I can manage a sweatshirt and a pair of jeans without an additional layer finally. The birds have finally returned and sing loudly to each other. The smell of wild flowers mingles in the air as I walk past them heading to the coffee shop by my parents' house.

I order a coffee, one of the specialty drinks with cinnamon and caramel drizzle on top, then slide into a booth. My laptop fan hums on the table as I open a program and begin typing. I study a book that lays open in front of me for a moment. I jot notes in my notebook before a shadow covers a portion of my table. Glancing up, Ebony's battered, but healing face, decorated with an oversized pair of sunglasses, greets me. I gasp, dropping my pen to cover my mouth.

"Jesus Christ, Ebs!" She sits before I can stand to examine her face. She drops her head slightly. "Who the fuck did that to you?" I whisper to her.

"Mayor Cross," she confesses. "Showed up at the shelter."

Kane slides into the booth silently, his face tight as he glances around. He gives me a brief nod, but doesn't offer much.

"What is his problem with you?"

She uses her eyes to assess me for a moment. "I think it has to deal with that file Veronica took."

"That wasn't your file?" I ask.

"In the morgue?" she asks with her eyebrows raised and an incredulous look on her battered face. "No. There was someone your brother was working with. Maybe it's hers? We need to figure that out."

"We think," Kane finally says, tense and tight. "He came and attacked Ebony because of what's locked away in one of those files. Your brother's may just be the key to it."

"Any idea what?" I ask, looking between the two. They shake their heads slowly and I look out the window.

"Hey…" she starts in a small voice. "That thing that happened at our apartment…" I turn and look back at her. She swallows before glancing over at Kane, then back at me. "I hope that didn't give you the wrong idea or anything."

I nod, mulling over the thoughts that spring forth before I deflate. "I'm okay with that," I offer with a slight nod.

"I'm sorry. I just… I'm not functioning properly and—" I grab her hand, cutting her off. "It's fine. One and done. I don't think we'd work long term."

Kane snorts beside her. A small smirk on his face as he shakes his head, but I can see the tension leaving his body. He reaches over, rubbing her thigh for a moment, finally looking over her face, which I'm sure he's done several times before I've seen it.

"Everything is complicated," she sighs, leaning back.

"And I slipped back into Pandora's box of shit that doesn't help fix anything. Dragging you both in this, now that I'm not so… jaded… I'm so, so sorry," she offers, looking from me to Kane. Her eyes linger on his as I take in the whirlwind of thoughts that pass between them.

I clear my throat after a moment. "Look, I would love to sit here and chit chat a little bit more about our failed harem status, but I'm meeting Vin in a few minutes."

They look at me before nodding and scooting out of the booth. Ebony slings her bag over her shoulder as Kane wraps his arm around her. "Be careful," she whispers to me before pulling me into a hug. "Please."

"I got this," I say to her. "Promise."

"Fuck 'em up kid," she says, pulling away from me.

"And give 'em hell," I retort with a smile. A phrase that her, D, and I used from a life that felt so far away months ago. I look at Kane and nod towards the door. He fist bumps me, then ushers Ebony out the door and into the mix of people.

Finally alone, I think back to what Ebony said, her confession of confusion. I let out another slow breath, relieved I don't feel anything other than peace. Something had shifted in me during my time spent bickering with the two of them. Maybe it was Mel, and the affection and kindness she poured into me. Maybe it was them, being unfiltered and angry in a way that ripped the rose colored glasses off my face.

"Thanks for meeting me," Vin greets me, ripping me from my musing. He sits in the spot that Ebony and Kane vacated. Dark circles decorate the undersides of his eyes.

"You've seen better days," I comment, looking him over.

He shrugs. "Blame Ebony," he grumbles, rubbing his hands together under the table.

"What happened?"

"My pops showed up at the shelter she's working at. Her crazy ass gramps pulled a gun on him."

"What!?" I feel my eyes widen as I gawk at Vin. "When!?"

"Couple weeks ago? A month? I don't remember, but it's been a shit show," he says, scratching at his head and shrugging. "Her lawyer has some pull," Vin finally states, rubbing the back of his neck. I realize this is the first time I've ever seen him look anxious.

"Can't be more pull than you and your dad."

"He got the case moved from this district. My pops doesn't know the people in the court system she filed her case in."

"But you said she doesn't have evidence."

"Not credible stuff, but the shit with my dad… it's all bad, man."

"Tell me why it's bad, Vin."

He grabs a small metal device from his pocket and swipes it under his nose, sniffing deeply. A grateful sigh passes his lips as he wipes at his nose and leans his head back, almost like a lizard basking in the sunlight.

"I want a coffee," he grumbles as he pulls his phone out of his pocket and trudges up to the counter.

With a quick glance, I pull the decoy phone out of my bag, power it on, then slide it on the seat beside me. If Vin is taking bumps, he won't remember having his phone. Risky, I know, but it's worth a shot.

As Vin approaches with his coffee and a few pastries, he slides into his seat.

"Vin," I call out to him, getting his attention. His pupils large now as he focuses on me. "You know the details of what happened with your dad and E?"

"No, but I need to know whether you can get her quiet or not."

"Like I said, it's going to take time. She's slowly starting to let me in."

"We don't have time. They're trying to push the court date and if my dad makes another mistake, I have a feeling it will be much sooner."

"You know Ebony, it takes her a while to forgive someone."

"Then make her depend on you. Take the people she cares about. Kill them if you have to," he stares at me, unmoving and dead serious.

"I'm not hurting anyone else. No one is dying because of me," I state, staring back at him.

"She might," he says thoughtfully. "If you don't get her in line, I will kill her to save my family."

"That only makes things worse," I counter, calming my nerves with a sip of my coffee.

"I have a much better idea," Vin says with a deranged look on his face. His eyes wide and wild as the coke takes hold of his senses making him feral. He smiles at me. A smile that doesn't reach his eyes and is laced with so much malice that I shrink back.

"Don't do anything crazy, Vin," I warn as he laughs to himself.

He rocks in the seat. Something he does when the drugs have completely taken effect. He nods his head like his internal monologue is giving him the best sermon it has to offer.

"Vin," I call out to him again. My palms burn as the blood rushes through my body. Fear etches into my movements as I wave my hand in his face.

He swats it away and glares at me.

"I have a solution to the problem. Just do your part. Don't fuck it up," he finally says.

"Is this what you did back then?" I ask. My fingers grasping the phone beside me as he sees a flicker of something pass between his eyes.

He drops them, those dark orbs tormented by a memory. "With my dad?" he starts. His voice is so broken that I freeze. "He was more mad that he was stopped. Back then, when she and I were kids…" He stops, looking up at me. "No one would stop him when he'd beat us. He owns us…"

Vin shoves half a bear claw in his mouth and chews as he stares out the window distracted by memories. I've never seen him like this. Remorseful, broken. But before I get to ask another question, he stands, sliding out of the booth rapidly. He makes haste toward the door, leaving his phone on the table along with his sugary treats.

I take my chance, quickly going to his phone and trying to unlock it as I glance at his quickly retreating figure. He stops, pivots, then runs towards the door, sending my heart in a tailspin. Panicked, I try a date Vin mentioned one time in passing and the phone unlocks. I don't have time to connect the dots for those numbers to make sense.

Instead, I look at the side of his phone and the duplicate, I study the sim card slot and fish a paper clip out of my bag. Quickly popping the small tray, I retrieve the card and wait for the program to start pulling Vin's data. I glance out the window as the loading box taunts me, Vin stands in the center of the sidewalk, patting his pockets before he turns and stomps back towards the café.

Ping ponging my attention, I watch as he pushes through clusters of people as the phone buffers, white blocks popping up on the screen to animate the process. He pushes through the door roughly, the small bell tinkling as he does. My eyes dart back to the phone as I bounce my leg. Vin navigates through the crowd only a few feet away from me. A beep captures my attention. I fumble with the devices to put everything back in place and leave the phone where he left it as he gets to the table. I shove the clone in my bag.

"My phone?" he asks as he gets to the table. "Have you seen it? I think I left it."

I nod to the spot where his phone sits, lighting up with a new notification. He laughs softly, tapping his head before swiping the device. He shoves it in his pocket, then makes his way back outside.

A tense breath expels out of me as I grab an uneaten pastry and shove it in my mouth, then slide my phone out to type a message.

I lean my head against the back of the booth. My stomach twists in knots still. I pull out the decoy and begin scrolling through his messages. The contacts are still populating as I read the incoming messages between him and a few people. There's a plan happening, but with everything uploading slowly, it may take longer than we have to decipher what their plan is.

58

Ebony

Dr. Goodwin leans close to the computer screen evaluating the codes and new designs of mine and Kane's prototype. Her eyes move quickly as she checks each line as thoroughly as she can. Her soft breaths waft a sweet scent of honeysuckle in the air, reminding me of a summer day. There's a hint of something else, but I don't let my mind wander enough to make a connection.

"This looks great," she says with a smile on her face. "Even better than the last one."

"Thanks," I say as I smile at the screen. I avoid her eyes, which always seem to be studying me closely lately. Something that she's actually doing right now as she leans back. She steps away and I finally breathe.

"Did you do something?" Kane asks, looking between me and Dr. Goodwin. I hike my shoulders up to my ears, then glance at her. Thankfully, she's busy helping other students. But her eyes are back on me, catching me staring, and she offers me a soft, tentative smile.

"If I didn't know any better," Kane whispers, leaning back. "I'd think she might admire you."

"Jealous?" I taunt, sticking my tongue out at him. He laughs, shaking his head.

"Teachers aren't really my thing."

"I'd say," Denise says, rolling her chair up behind ours. "That she's trying to figure you out."

"You think?" I ask, scrunching my nose up in confusion.

"Maybe. Don't get me wrong, it's weird as fuck, but it's almost like she's memorizing your face. Kane gets a look similar to it, but his is much more…"

She furrows her brow as she thinks for a moment.

"Much more… " he probes. His eyebrow quirks as he leans his head forward urging her to continue.

"There's no word for it. Kane looks at you like his entire world revolves around you. And like he's picturing you naked."

"Accurate," he admits, laughing.

"Who wouldn't?" I tease, coaxing laughs out of them.

"I see you're back to your good ole cheerful self. Good news?"

"Sort of. Attorney Pateki was able to grant me a restraining order and an emergency hearing for my case," I whisper. "He called this morning as soon as he saw the email."

"That's incredible! How'd he manage that?" she asks.

"Attorney Pateki suggested we file our lawsuit with one of the judges that transferred in from a completely different state. Because he doesn't know Mayor Cross, I'll have somewhat of a fair trial."

"They're doing jury selection now," Kane adds. "Anyone that knows Mayor Cross or his family is out. That even means extended connections."

"Sounds like it'll be difficult to get a jury," Denise says with a sigh.

"Difficult, but worth it."

"Alright guys," Dr. Goodwin calls out from the middle of her room. "Off to a good start with this assignment. Make sure you post the finished product before midnight on Sunday!"

The room erupts in noise when she's done talking. We join in, packing our bags and pushing our chairs under our table.

"Ebony," Dr. Goodwin calls out. She fiddles with her fingers as she moves out the way as people pass by. "Can you come with me to my office?"

"Uhh… yeah. Sure," I answer looking back at Kane and Denise. "I'll catch up with you guys after this. Meet in the courtyard?"

They nod their heads glancing between me and Dr. Goodwin once more. Tension and confusion rising slightly as they do.

"Text us when you're out," Kane says, kissing my forehead, then placing a gentle kiss on my lips. He smiles at me before heading out behind Denise.

Dr. Goodwin doesn't say anything as she grabs her belongings and ushers me into her office a few doors down. She flips on the light switch and the small room fills with artificial light. A small L- shaped desk sits against the wall with the light switch. Books and papers lay scattered across the desk's surface.

Family photos decorate the top shelf of a bookcase. Black and gold frames holding precious memories, freezing life changing moments beautifully. Several of the pictures are family photos with Dr. Goodwin, her three young kids and her husband. A former professor that I've seen a few times in the music building.

I wonder what it would be like to be a part of a family like hers. Surrounded by talented, loving parents that smile at you like you are their entire world. Sometimes, when shit got bad in my mind, I pictured being a part of her family. Christmas dinners around a fire as we watch a plethora of Christmas movies until it repeats again. She really is the only teacher that makes her students feel like people, like family. Even Denise told me she wouldn't mind Dr. Goodwin being her mom.

Light cascades in, breaking me out of my thoughts as she opens the blinds. They rattle against the window as she releases the strings. With my focus casted out the window, I notice the pond just beyond the hedges that kiss the window sill.

"Some one killed all the Koi Fish last semester," she comments, shaking her head. "Gotta wait for those to mature before I can appreciate their beauty again."

I drop my head, stifling a laugh by tucking my lips between my teeth. When I think I can handle looking at her without giggling, I roll my tongue around my cheek to smooth the lingering smile. Knowing that Kane was the one that killed *and* replaced the Koi Fish makes the situation a little humorous.

"You okay?" she asks as she places the straps of her bag on a hook located on the side of her desk.

"Oh, yeah. All good." I look up and smile. "Should I…"

I point towards the door and she nods. I push the door closed, then take a seat across from her. Her fingers laced under her chin as she studies me from head to toe again.

"I heard about the case," she finally says, scratching at her head. She shifts uncomfortably in her seat. Almost like she's nervous.

"Oh," I nod slightly. "Yeah…"

"That's a pretty big decision," she offers awkwardly. She adjusts in her seat again. Her eyes tense as she looks at me, then away from me. Her lips twisting as if she's contemplating something.

"Some scars don't heal with an 'I'm sorry,'" I respond softly.

I subconsciously touch my face where a large gash distorted my face for a few months after the incident. A long scar is now resting in that same place. I'm still growing accustomed to it.

She flinches slightly. Her hands clench tightly as she looks at my scar sympathetically. Her eyes tracing the jagged edge of the lighter spot that feels glaringly obvious. She slowly nods her head, seemingly digesting the weight on my shoulders and sighs.

Then, she hesitates. Her eyes drift up to a golden picture frame that's angled more towards her. She slowly reaches to it. Her hands shake slightly as she does. With the frame in her hand, she touches the glass thoughtfully as a smile graces her face, lighting up her expression. Her brown eyes crinkle on the edges. She really is a beautiful woman.

She sets the frame down. Her smile is gone. A thousand painful memories must pass because she swallows hard and grimaces as she ducks her head for a moment. I notice the mistiness in her eyes.

"I was sixteen," she starts as she looks at me. "Sixteen when I met him."

"Met who?" I ask, immediately perplexed by her seriousness.

She hands me the picture frame, then digs in her drawer for a moment, producing another one. She passes it over to me after looking at it for a moment. The edges are bent. I look closer and notice the picture was torn and taped back together. The edges jagged and angry even as they lay in the proper spots.

Then I freeze, looking between each image again. Studying the people frozen in time before looking at her with my eyebrows stitched together. I recognize these two pictures. One being so accustomed to my gazing that I even memorized the pattern of the baby blanket.

"My gramps has this at home," I say softly.

"I know," she says softly. "He told me that he would do his best to keep something of me to show you."

"That's odd," I say with a soft chuckle.

"How so?"

"You're my teacher," I say looking up at her, then back down at the picture. The exact one that my mother's mother left with me when I was dropped off at my dad's. Instead, this one the face wasn't rubbed off.

A teenage girl, who looks no older than seventeen, cradles a baby. Her small face glowing as she looks in the bundle of blankets. Gramps told me there were only two copies of the image in the frame. My mother has one and my father gave his copy to my gramps. He claimed it was for me, but I noticed the guilt on his face whenever he looked at it in my hands.

"My parents decided that they were going to take care of you so I could live my life," Dr. Goodwin states slowly.

I flip the picture over and notice her name on the back. Slowly, the puzzle pieces line up and snap into place as I read 'Elaine "Elle" Young' in pretty cursive handwriting. My grams' handwriting.

And what do I do when things don't make sense? Deny.

"I'm sorry for your loss," I say, placing the pictures down. "But I'm not your daughter. I'm sure you would have recognized my name."

"I never got to name you. Never knew your name," she says sighing. "Trust me, Ebony. This is the last thing I wanted in my life. I felt… relieved when my parents said that your father took you in."

"Look," my voice is firm as I feel the anger bubbling up in me. I always thought Dr. Goodwin was nice, but this is beyond that. This is cruel. "You aren't my mother."

She slides a document with a diagnostic label on it towards me. She nods to it and I take it between my shaking fingers. I look over it and notice my name on one paper and her name on the other. I pause, then read the document again.

Then I finally take in the second picture. Letting all the details register. I've seen a few pictures of my father young, but I know enough details to know that this is him. I wheeze on an exhale as I put that picture down. The paper wrinkles and crackles as it shakes in my clenching hand.

"Your gramps is a very persistent man. When he saw me at the gala, he told me you were there. That was my first panic attack in years. I had no idea we were that close. I should have known, but I didn't think you'd be in my class."

I put the paper on the desk and run my fingers through my locs. My chest rises and falls rapidly as everything comes rushing in at me. The realization, the understanding, the magnitude of what's being revealed to me.

"This isn't possible. You would have known. *Should* have known." My voice is shaky, uncertain in the space that seems to fill with so much tension that I gasp as I suck in a lungful of air to try to steady my breaths.

"My parents took you away when I was very damaged. Your father paid them to not press charges."

"Just—just give me a second," I say, holding a hand out to her, trying to steady my breathing. My stomach twists and turns as the queasiness in my stomach increases. "You can't be my mom."

"Trust me, kid. I don't want to be," she says softly, leaning back in her chair. "Don't get me wrong. You're amazing despite it all, but I don't have room in my life to be your mother."

I sit silently, my eyes fixed on my lap. The rejection prying open the wounds I thought finding her would heal. Pain shoots through my chest as I look up at her frustrated face. Looking around again, my eyes finally realizing the subtle similarities in her and myself. Even in her children and me… my siblings. All of the thoughts I had in my mind rushing back, laughing at my stupidity for thinking them, for not knowing. She's living this perfect life. With a beautiful, full family. Enjoying milestones and doing it all without me. Without even a hint of grief.

Then it hits me. They both started a life intentionally leaving me out of it. I have half siblings that were wanted while I was discarded, passed around like a meaningless sack of nothing.

"I can't be your mother," she affirms coldly. "I love my life the way that it is, Ebony." I flinch involuntarily and a tear skitters down my cheek. "But my God do you look so much like my mother when she was young," she finishes.

"Fuck you," I mutter through a sob. "Fuck you, fuck your mother, and fuck anybody that let you leave me behind."

"And a temper just like your father," she spits with a laugh. She shakes her head as her eyes look me over. Amusement in her eyes. She didn't even look happy at this revelation, that she found the baby that started her entire life.

"We all can't be fucking perfect now, can we? Not like you and the fucking lie of a life that you've been living. How long have you known? Did you know when I told you that I was drugged? Was it before then?"

"I wish I never knew," she says softly, looking down. "I wish I could take it all back. Let you choose someone else to be your mother, because I— I wish I never had you…"

"Yeah? That makes two of us." I push to my feet quickly, grabbing my bag.

"Ebony, wait. I—" she huffs as she rubs her hands over her face.

I stop. My hand ghosts over the door knob, but I don't look at her. I try my hardest to move, but that pesky little shit called hope keeps me right at her fucking door hoping for her to tell me she wants me. That she missed me.

"You just look like my mother. So much like her," she says in a strained voice. She exhales sharply. "I know it's hard to hear and grasp all this. He hurt me so bad, Ebony…"

I shoot her a side glance and watch as she takes me in with disgust.

"You were a mistake," she mutters more to herself.

"Go. Fuck. Yourself," I spit, throwing the door open and rushing out.

"Ebony, wait. Please!" She swears under her breath as I retreat. Her heels clack rapidly behind me down the hall as I speed walk out of the building, then break into a sprint once engulfed by the bright sun and the cool weather. I run, my lungs and legs screaming as I keep going. The wind whooshing past my ears as my legs and arms pump, carrying me down the sidewalk.

I fight a sob, fight the pain where my heart shatters from the callous words she said. They repeat in my mind, shattering the images of a happy reunion. Thoughts and ideas that I made up in my mind to keep me going. Her words shatter and tear away at the fabric of some semblance of having a loving parent. Just one. The fact that I know that she meant every word of regretting me causes me to stumble. Mentally, physically, emotionally.

I have more siblings, more family and none of them want me. The walking image of trauma for my mother, guilt for my father and those attached to him. And here I am, a person that fights the darkness that tries to swallow me as I run from the demons that chase me.

"Ebony!" Isaac's voice shouts behind me. "Wait up!"

My feet slow and I brace my thighs as I pant. A ragged sob falling past my lips as my knees give slightly. I right myself before collapsing, willing myself to shove everything deep down inside of me. I'll deal with them later. The thoughts, the feelings. I'll probably let the water scotch my skin until it's so tender that laying down hurts. Maybe I'll ask Kane to pin me down and fuck me like he hates me, but then he'll just tell me I'm beautiful, that he loves me, and I'll be a fucking sobbing mess underneath him. I can't hide from him.

Pushing up to my feet, I watch as Isaac and Zeke approach me with wide happy grins that further tear at my composure. How could anyone be this happy to see me when my own parents weren't? Their smiles fade as they get closer. Concern flooding their expressions as they run the last few steps towards me. They surround me, looking over my face, then scanning the area searching for something or someone.

"What's up? What's going on?" Zeke asks, his hands gripping my shoulders.

"Dr. Good— Dr. Goodw — Dr. Goodwin says she's my mother," my voice croaks out. A painful lump lodged in my throat as I confess this much to them. "And she… and she never wanted me."

I manage to move out of Zeke's grasp and stumble onto the bench behind me as I sob. Not wanting the affection and barely able to stand as my muscles lock up and ache.

My hands viciously wiping at the tears that betray me.

"She's what?" Isaac says stunned. He squats in front of me catching my eyes. He places his hand on my knee. "I don't think I understood you."

Zeke appears beside him, his hand reaching out and wiping a tear. His eyebrows are stitched together as he stares at me waiting for me to respond.

"The gang's here!" Denise yells in the distance. Kane, Miya, and Han walk with her as they smile. Kane's and Han's arms are thrown lazily over Miya's shoulders as they approach. I shrink away from their happiness feeling like a heavy gray cloud. I bow my head willing the tears away, then look up plastering a fake smile on my face. They don't buy it though.

"The hell happened?" Denise asks before Kane can get the words out. Miya slides in beside me, her tiny arms pulling me into her so tightly. A hug that reminds me of the one her mother gave me. One that wills me to fall apart and promises me that I can rebuild myself into someone more whole. A hug that makes it that much harder to hold myself together.

"We're trying to make sure we heard her right," Zeke says over his shoulder to Denise and Kane. "Because I don't think we did."

I take a deep breath, nudging out of Miya's grasp. I lean my back against the bench and look at each of them. My teeth gnaw on the inside of my cheek. My eyes lock on Denise's, then Kane's.

"Dr. Goodwin took me to her office and told me that she's my mother."

"Bitch, shut the hell up right now," Denise gasps. "How long has she known?"

Kane's head tilts to the side, attempting to rationalize the information like everyone else. His eyes squint in confusion as he battles the thoughts in his head. The composure of his face changes with every rapid thought.

"She's known since the gala apparently," I answer, taking another deep breath, feeling the sadness tug at my heart, hanging on to it like it belongs there.

"That's a good thing then, right?" Han asks innocently. "It should be good. You found your mom."

I shake my head, swearing under my breath as I feel tears drift down my cheek. I wipe at them roughly.

"She didn't want to be found," I say, bouncing my leg. "She didn't want to know me. Didn't want me."

"You gotta be fuckin' kidding me," Isaac mumbles shaking his head.

"I'm so sorry," Miya mutters, pulling me back into her arms.

"How did she not know?" Kane asks as he nudges me to the side and sits next to me. His hand rubbing up my back, then gripping my neck in an oddly grounding way. He gives my neck a gentle squeeze and my body relaxes into Miya's embrace.

"Right, what parent wouldn't even recognize their child's name?" Dense adds, shaking her head.

"Apparently she didn't name me. Her mother did. I don't really want to know the details. She kept saying she was sixteen and I get that. I do. But she never looked for me. *Never.*" My voice breaks and I groan, sucking in a deep breath.

"That explains why she was looking at you like she was memorizing your face."

"It's because I look like her mother. I don't even know what that lady looks like, but I'm apparently walking around with her whole face and physical features from everyone else." I release a bitter laugh, shaking my head trying to align my thoughts. Not much makes sense beyond what I was told.

"You think she's going to tell Dr. Sumner that we did the gala de coup?" Han asks, looking around the courtyard.

"I won't let you guys go down. I may snitch on select people, but not *my* select people," I say, giving him a soft smile as Kane releases my neck and puts a hand on my shoulder.

Silence settles around me as everyone digests the news. The wind whispers past us, howling softly like a song for a few seconds. I inhale deeply, closing my eyes and pushing away my thoughts.

"Now that that's done," I start as the silence becomes almost too awkward for me. I grab my bag and step away from the group throwing my bag over my shoulder. "I'm hungry. What are we eating?"

Everyone stares at me, all varying looks from amused to concerned. My whiplash reaction clearly familiar to some. I raise my eyebrows looking around at each pair of eyes that watch me closely.

"Earth to the cool kids," I call out. "I'll leave without all of you." I use my index finger signaling to all of them for emphasis. I challenge them with my eyes forcing all the negative thoughts back in the box of bullshit for me to never sort through later.

"Wait," Isaac whines then pulls me into his arms. "Are you okay?"

"There is this gnawing pain in my stomach that can only be cured by food," I say with a smile. "Now someone feed me!" I add with a laugh and push away from him. His affection cracking at the surface of my shield.

If I was being honest, I'd tell him I'm numbing. So used to disappointment that I'd rather crawl in a secluded hole and not exist with others. But that's not fair to them. Not when they show up. Not when they genuinely care.

"Let's go!" Zeke bellows, throwing his arm over my shoulder as we run towards the parking lot. The others following us, the mood lightening as Zeke and I play fight along the way.

"Hands, Asshole," I grumble, popping his hand as Kane hits him on the back of the head with a soft thwack. Zeke rubs his head with a pout and a hint of a smile as Kane drops his arm over my shoulder. We fall in line laughing towards the parking lot.

59

Ebony

I sit on the balcony connected to my and Kane's bedroom. My foot rests on the rail as I stare up at the stars that twinkle above me. A warm fleece blanket wrapped around my body as the cold settles in. The stream just below bubbling and rushing peacefully in the darkness. Somewhere in the woods a little ways away from the stream, a twig cracks beneath the weight of some wild animal.

I slip into the room, grabbing my acoustic then slip back into the cold. I stabilize my guitar on my lap and start plucking the strings, playing a few chords and humming a tune as I go.

"Running away from the party?" Kane asks, kissing the top of my head, then sitting beside me. Our friends laugh loudly inside as the TV blares the dialogue of a comedy movie.

"Not really. I needed to clear my head," I say, looking over at him. My hands rest on the smooth edges of my guitar. "It's not everyday you meet someone that says they regret your existence."

He looks over at me. His face twisting with each passing thought. Then, he reaches his hand over, touching my face softly. His thumb brushes softly against my cheek and I lean away slightly.

"I hope you know I love your existence," he offers, dropping his hand down.

Reaching into the pocket of the sweatpants I'm wearing, I hand him the picture that I had tucked deep in a box in the back of our closet. The sepia colors fading and the face of the young woman slightly rubbed out. For as long as I could remember, the woman's face has always been a mystery to me. Then I see it in Dr. Goodwin's office. Out on display with the sepia colors vibrant and beautiful.

Hope starts to emerge in my heart, pushing past the resentment, the pain, the anger and taking hold of my delusional thoughts making me think that she lied. That there is a chance. That same hope creating scenarios where hurting me was an option she had to choose to keep me safe, but I know better.

"This picture is very well loved," he comments, offering it back. I nod slowly, then take a deep breath. I place the picture in my pocket and I lean back in my chair.

"Her words changed what this picture means to me," I sniff, gripping the neck of my guitar tighter as I pull it to my body. The strings resonate as I do. "And I'm not even completely angry with her."

"Why?" he asks, leaning back in the chair, angling his head near mine. He looks up at the sky towards the bright stars.

"Because she was a victim, too. My father has ruined so many lives and Dr. Goodwin was one of them."

"You can be angry with what she said. She went too far," he states.

"I know," I mumble defeatedly.

"How'd she not even look for you?" he marvels, shaking his head slightly. My arms squeeze my guitar tighter as I feel that ache growing in my chest.

"She was a minor. And my dad… he'd face jail time as he should. Gramps and Grams had no idea he stayed with her after they found out how old she was. He cut ties when they demanded he end things."

"You never researched your grandparents? Not even once?"

"I tried, but their last name, my last name, is so common that I wasn't sure how to verify. Their names aren't on my birth certificate. I don't even have pictures I can cross reference."

"You know," he starts, turning his head to look at me. His warm eyes tracing my face. "I can always change your last name if you want." A hint of a smile on his lips before he smiles proudly. I roll my eyes laughing at his suggestion.

"Right," I sarcastically respond with a laugh. My eyes lock on his and I notice the seriousness in his playful remark. "You'll change your mind," I tease, setting my guitar on the stand then getting more comfortable in my chair.

"Let me tell you something," he says softly, gently gripping my chin to turn my face to his. "Me and the people in that room," he gestures behind himself, "we're not changing our minds about you."

I don't respond, but I look over at him acknowledging that I heard him. Then I focus back on the stars that illuminate the vast darkness.

"Things are finally starting to feel… less questionable.

I mean, they're still fucked up, but… I don't have as many unanswered questions," I confess as I chew at my thumbnail.

He reaches over, taking my hand and rubbing his thumb over my battered digit. Our fingers interlock and he gives my hand a reassuring squeeze.

"After all this time, I'm finally going to tell my story," I say with a sigh. "He's saying around the time for midterms or something," I add.

"Fuck midterms," Kane grumbles, then laughs. "Such a damn goody two shoes."

"Oh, fuck you," I fire back, yanking my hand from his, laughing. "Such an asshole."

"I'm a what?" he asks, turning his head towards me, eyebrows raised and a challenging smile on his face.

"You heard me. You. Are. An. Asshole."

He yanks me up, tossing me over his shoulder before dropping me on the bed. I kick at him playfully as we wrestle, rolling across the comforters, jumbling them up. He grabs me as I giggle and tosses me back on the bed as I try to scurry off. I slip from beneath him, rolling to the other side of the bed. As he reaches for me again, I roll over the edge of the bed to my feet.

I dodge his reach again and run to the opposite side of the room panting. Until I realize that I put myself in a worse situation. With my back in one of the corners, I watch as his large body stands at full length. Broad shoulders squaring towards me. The playful glint in his eyes as pride flashes across them.

"Oh no," he taunts me with a predatory voice as he

stalks towards me. "You have nowhere else to go."

A slow smile creeps on his face as he edges closer like a hunter. His broad body blocking any way of escape as he approaches me slowly. I fake left, then right, but he's faster. As he steps closer, I manage to slide between his legs, then crawl under him quickly.

He spins, grabs my leg making me stumble to my hands and knees. Then I'm up in the air laughing as his fingers tickle my sides. My legs kick as I wiggle. My laughing labored as I beg him to stop. His chest vibrating against my back as he laughs with me. Then his lips are on the back of my neck as he plants a sweet kiss on it and sets me on my feet.

I brace my hands on my knees as I attempt to catch my breath, immediately regretting not even trying to work on my endurance. I groan as I drop to the bed, my breathing coming out in labored huffs. He shifts, catching my attention. His eyebrow quirked and an amused smirk on his face. His breathing even like he wasn't just tossing and chasing me around the room.

"Don't start," I pant as I push myself up to my elbows. He barely broke a sweat.

"I didn't say anything," he defends, laughing.

"It's written all over your face!" I retort back with a laugh. "Your face is so expressive."

"You say it like you don't love it," he says, crossing his arms and leaning against the dresser beside the bed. He rolls his tongue around his cheek in that sexily suggestive way to challenge me to deny it.

"Nah," I admit, rolling to my side. "Who wouldn't?"

"I'm not worried about anyone else," he says, climbing onto the bed kissing me. "Just you."

He lays on his side, pulling me closer to him as he nudges his tongue in my mouth. His large hand presses into the small of my back, then slowly glides up sending a shiver down my spine. He smiles against my lips.

I rake my nails across his scalp, grabbing his hair and giving a light tug as I shift my body so I can kiss him better, deeper. His chest vibrates as he groans into my mouth, chasing my lips to seal mine with his. I tease him with my tongue, tracing his bottom lip, then moving back as he leans closer.

"Uh uh," he grunts, placing his strong hand at the back of my neck and pulling my mouth back to his. "Don't tease me," he mutters against my lips.

"Now look who's pretending not to love something," I taunt. He chuckles, pressing his lips to mine, putting his hand on my thigh, giving it a tight squeeze.

We move in tandem as he pulls me on top of him. Our bodies press flush together as he slides his hands down my sides, then back up. Goosebumps popping up on every inch of my skin from his delicate touches.

He presses his hips up, letting his fingertips slip beneath the fabric of my shirt as our simple make out session gets more intense, more heated. My moans are captured by his mouth as I move my hips with his.

"You're gonna get us started," he mumbles against my lips as one of his hands grips my throat. His eyes darken with lust as he admires me. He pulls me down and kisses me. "You don't know how fucking sexy you look like this."

"Like what?" I whisper. My eyes go from his eyes to his swelling lips.

"Like this is the most euphoric thing you've ever experienced," he mutters, pulling me back for a deep kiss. His hand sliding to my ass as he grips it tightly and removes his other hand from my throat.

"It's pretty close," I whisper against his lips, letting my fingers ghost up his thick arms, then over his shoulders. He smiles against my lips as he continues to grind against me. His tongue snakes into my mouth, coaxing mine into his. He sucks on my tongue, then my lower lip before doing it over again. Sneaky fingers slide up the back of my shirt, unhooking my bra effortlessly. Then, slowly lift the hem of my shirt.

"Hey! You two!" Denise yells on the other side of the door banging on it. "Get dressed!"

"Shit," I gasp, stopping his movements. My shoulders sagging slightly as he releases my shirt with a soft frustrated groan from somewhere deep in his throat.

"We are dressed!" I shout back, sitting all the way up on him. My hands on his chest as he shakes his head, laughing.

The door swings open as Denise waltzes in and sits beside us. "Tell them I'll beat all they asses in that Ghoul Hunter game."

"Oh my God!" Miya shrieks, then gags loudly from the door. Kane shifts below me, looking towards the door rolling his eyes.

"Don't be so dramatic," he calls towards her.

"She's on top of you!" Miya gags again. "Denise! How can you sit in there with them like that?"

A wrinkle forms between Denise's brows as she pinches her lips together, then looks between the two of us. "Me being here bothering you two?"

I shake my head with a shrug. Kane laughs below me as he runs one hand through his hair, then places both on my thighs.

"I'll probably be in the room when she has our niece or nephew. Maybe one of each… oooh!"

"Woah," I say, grabbing her attention. "What's with everyone and the damn baby talk."

"Well," Denise starts as she shifts beside us to give us her undivided attention. "When two people come together and have unprotected sex, a baby can be made."

Han and Miya groan from the living room.

"No more, please," Han begs. "I will do whatever you want, just don't…"

"Anything I want!?" she shouts with a mischievous glint in her eyes.

"I think you fucked up, Han," Kane says laughing.

Denise rubs her hands together as she smiles imaginatively.

"He definitely did," Isaac shouts back cackling.

"Should I be worried?" Han asks a little more quietly. Uncertainty evidently hangs in his tone as he repeats the question a little louder.

"Yes," we say in unison as Zeke breaks into a fit of laughter.

"You're in for it, kid," Zeke says, still chucking.

"I'll pray for you," Miya says playfully. The sound of her hand slapping gently at his back carries to our room as Isaac laughs.

"You look like you're going to throw up," Isaac cackles.

"I'm not *that* bad," Denise says with a shrug.

She slaps my ass and skips to the room, then pops her head back in as she grabs the door knob.

"Pull out method only works for so long," she whispers, giving us a wink and closing the door.

He glances up at me before laughing. "That's your friend."

"Like Zeke is any better," I shoot back, climbing off of him.

"What I do?" Zeke asks, startling the both of us.

"When the hell did you get in here?"

He shrugs his shoulders with a smile, then slips out of the room leaving the door open. We exchange glances, then look back towards the open door before breaking into more laughter.

Fucking weirdos.

My fucking weirdos.

60

Kane

E's moans fill the air as she rides me. My hands on her waist as she rolls her hips over mine. Her hands on my shoulders as she braces herself. Rays of sunlight spill in from the window casting a glow behind her, illuminating her like the goddess she is. Fuck she's so damn beautiful.

"Slow down," I groan, pulling her down to me and holding her hips a little tighter. "We got all day, baby," I mutter against her ear, rolling my hips slowly. A moan from deep in her throat falls from her mouth as she buries her face in my neck. My hands immobilize her from moving against me as she slides her arms under my neck, pulling herself flush to my body.

"Faster, Kane," she gasps into my neck. She wiggles her body trying to loosen my grip.

I stop, then move her underneath me, my hands pinning hers down as I look her over. Her eyes hooded and dark, but haunted with the emotions she's trying to hide from. I kiss her, slow and deep as I release my grip on her. She melts into my kiss, letting me lead us through the maze of her emotions with just my lips, but she reaches desperately for me.

I push back from her hands and she whimpers. A soft,

disappointed sound that breaks free in my mouth. I pull my face back from her, my eyes gauging how close to the surface those emotions are, but she's quick, pushing them right back down before I can find them. She pulls me back to her and kisses me hard. I give in, wanting to be whatever it is she needs in the moment. I'm okay with not being her savior. With that thought, I'm pushing back inside her warm, wet entrance, fucking her the way she likes, the way she needs.

She gasps into my mouth as I kiss her, my hand giving her clit a slow rub as I coax an orgasm out of her.

"This what you want?" I groan into her mouth.

"Yes," she moans, pinching her eyes shut as she falls into the sensation. Her hands on my forearms as her body shakes from my thrusts.

"Fuck me back, baby."

She opens her eyes, rolling her hips, catching my rhythm after a few moments. Heat passes between us as we stare at each other like this. Bodies rocking in sync as she grabs my hips urging me to push into her harder.

I drop my head down to her neck, kissing and sucking on the soft, warm skin where her pulse beats beneath my lips. Our skin slapping together as I push into her. Her breathing comes out in jolts as I bottom out into her repeatedly.

"Do you know how fucking pretty you sound when I fuck you like this?" I whisper in her ear. Her body clenching around me as she moans from my words. "Let me show you." I lift her up, carrying her to the bathroom with me. I flip on the switch, setting her feet on the floor.

I put space between us as I turn her towards the mirror. Watching her reflection, I kiss her neck as our eyes lock in the mirror. My hands roam over her curves, grasping at every bit of flesh on her body before palming her tits. She exhales slowly, leaning her head into my chest as I trail one of my hands down between her thighs. Circling my middle finger around her clit, I watch as her chest shakes as she exhales a shuddery breath.

"Watch yourself," I demand. Her eyes refocus on her face, then trace over her body using my hands as the stopping point. "Good girl."

I push her over, letting her hot skin touch the cold countertop. She tenses at the piercing cold, then relaxes, lifting her hips and pushing to the balls of her feet, then arches her back.

"So fucking eager for me," I praise leaning over and placing kisses down her back. My hand sliding up to grip her locs as I force her face towards the mirror. A moan slipping past her lips as her head snaps up.

She steadies her body, her hands gripping the edges of the counter as I position myself behind her and slowly push my way through. Hot, wet, and eager, her body accepts me. She curses as she struggles to keep her eyes open and on her reflection.

"You fit me so perfectly," she moans softly as her eyes drift up my reflected frame to my eyes. I ease out and back in slowly. "So, so perfectly," she moans more, her eyes getting hazy as I pick up my pace.

"I feel it," I groan. "Hold on tight," I warn her.

I grip her hips to steady her on her toes, then pull

her back, meeting my hips halfway. Her eyes close for a moment before they're locked on to mine in the mirror, then back on herself as she moans my name.

"That's it. You're doing so fucking good," I commend, feeling her getting lost in the sight she lays out for herself.

She pushes her upper body up a little more, keeping her back as arched as she can. Using the counter's edge, she pushes back into me. Our bodies collide roughly in the cool bathroom. Our moans fill the space as we get lost in the rhythm. Her hips bumping into the counter as she pulls away from me, then slamming into my hips as she pushes back.

"Oh my God," she groans so loudly as her second orgasm hits so hard she can barely hold her position. Her legs tremble as I keep her steady, riding her through her orgasm so intensely that she barely makes a sound.

One of her hands slips, and she catches herself by pressing her sweaty palm into the mirror. Her body stretching out, her ass pushing up letting me push deeper. She curses under her breath as I take advantage of this position. Slapping her ass hard as I groan, watching her face contort in such a beautiful array of emotions.

"One more," I pant as her body slightly sags. "Give me one more. I know you can."

She whimpers, but continues pushing back into me once her legs stop shaking. I watch as her pupils dilate as she watches her face morph with pleasure. Brown eyes taking in every inch of her slick skin. She grips my wrist in one hand, then slips the other between her thighs as she rubs her clit.

"Not yet," I whisper in her ear as I feel her clench around me. I bite at her ear, then her shoulder.

"Kane, please, I'm right there," she gasps, frustrated. Her hand slaps at the counter as she moans and glares at me in the mirror. I slap her ass hard, then grab her throat, pulling her back against my chest. I turn her chin towards me and kiss her hard before biting at her lip.

Her glazed eyes look into mine as her body bounces against mine. I move my hips faster, harder against her.

"I'm such a filthy slut," she moans against my lips.

"Fucking disgusting," I tease with a smile on my face. "Now, cum for me."

My fingers slip between her legs as one of my arms grabs her body, holding her to me. I rub quick, light circles around her clit until she cums loudly on me. Her body tenses until I release inside her. A few muttered curses falling from my lips as I lean us towards the counter for support. She eases herself out of my arms and lays against the counter. This time enjoying the cold against her hot, sweaty skin.

I place kisses across her back, my hands rubbing against her smooth skin, then I smile against it.

"What?" she breathes, glancing over her shoulder at me.

I use her sweat to write my name along her back. Then find another spot to write it again. She swats at my hand weakly as she wiggles away from me.

"Stop writing your name on me," she groans, stumbling into the room and collapsing on the bed.

"Tired?"

"You're not?"

"I could run a whole marathon," I tease, then flex.

She flips me off laughing before sitting up to look at me.

"You should read Rae's journal," she says suddenly as I lean against the door frame.

"I don't think I can," I confess.

She watches me. I can tell she wants to push me, but she's respecting that I'm not there yet. Not like Ren. I'm tempted to read it, but what happens when I can recall the moments, the details so vividly that I start to miss what used to be? Rae and I weren't extremely close, especially since he was older than me, but he was still someone I did look up to.

"You know, I'm here whenever you want to talk about… everything," she offers.

"I know," I say with a small smile.

She pushes to her feet, moving around the room in silence, then stops to pick up the picture she showed me last night. Sadness muddles her expression before she throws the picture in a drawer and slams it shut with more force than necessary. I don't interject, just watch as she moves around her emotions, around the room. One more graceful than the other.

"Are you coming with me?" I ask, crossing my arms over my chest.

"Oh, yeah. Start without me and I'll be in in a second," she responds.

"I wasn't talking about the shower," I laugh. "I'm talking about watching me practice for that charity scrimmage."

She laughs at herself, a small blush on her face as she covers her mouth. "I would love to, but I gotta work the bar tonight. Stop by with Zeke. Should be a slow night."

"Bet," I say looking behind me as the steam fills the bathroom. "Feel free to join me in the shower too."

She walks over to me, placing a kiss on my lips. "Don't be an asshole," she mutters against my lips and I laugh.

"To you? Never."

An hour after leaving, I'm heading into a warehouse. Various colors of graffiti decorating the wall as I head past the entrance. My head ducked as I avoid the cameras that are undoubtedly watching me. As I step into the darkness, the odor of stale, sitting water surrounds me. The undeniable smell of cigar smoke greeting me.

"Kane," a dark, pitchy voice calls out from the darkness. The cherry end of the cigar lights up, but not enough to reveal who I'm meeting. "I thought you weren't going to show."

I don't offer a response. I can't with the way my heart beats in my chest. I know I'd disappoint everyone if they found out I was here. And I know that if I didn't show, Ebony would be targeted.

"Tell me, Kane," the voice starts again. The sizzling sound follows shortly after. "Have you heard from my favorite friend Ren lately?"

Acknowledgements

Book two was the problem child of the series, but the necessary problem child.

Thank you so much, Eve Miller (@evemiller_author), author of *The Astrian Trials*, for the countless hours spent helping me stay motivated to get this book ironed out. Your unwavering support has been everything I didn't know I needed. Thank you for helping promote this series and these characters the way that you do.

Sydney Wiswell (@sydneyrwiswell), author of *The Starlight Assassin*, thank you for taking the time to read book two and attempt to help make sense of the chaos that exist. Your support, feedback, and hours writing together helped put this series on track. Thank you.

Haley Hamilton, author of *The Elflaine Chronicles: Ballad of Dawn*, and Pretty Good writers, thank you for the support and encouragement. I swear you've pulled me out of ruts I didn't realize I was in!

To my editor, Ambria (@my.chemical.romantasy), thank you so much for your guidance and making sure these sentences made sense! I love the feedback you provide and the way you love these characters just as much as I do.

Reyna Rochin (@reynarochinart) you did such a

phenomenal job with the character art cover. Thank you so much for bringing my characters to life yet again. It means the world to me!

Nero (@neroreads): Thank you so much for reading through this book and helping point out how to make Ren a better character. Your insight is so valued and I honestly can't thank you enough.

To my family and friends, thank you for supporting me by sharing a post or gushing about this book to someone. You have helped make this dream a reality. Thank you! I love you.

And to you my readers, thank you for sticking with me. Thank you for loving these characters and their crazy story. I hope you're ready for book three.

Until next time!

About the author

Aneka Bailey lives in Duluth, Georgia with her daughter. As a lover of fiction of all kinds, you can find her mostly reading dark romance, dark romantasy, romantasy, thriller/suspense, or horror books in her free time. Her interest in writing piqued when she discovered indie authors in social media groups and finally decided to start, and finish, one featuring a Black female main character. Thus, the Pretty Something Series was born.

You can connect with Aneka on her social media pages.

Instagram and Threads: @anibwriting
TikTok: @anigoeswhoa and @anibwriting

To access the books playlist and stay updated, scan the QR code below.

PRETTY PETTY